CAMILLA d'ERRICO'S
BURN

Another Simon Pulse graphic novel:

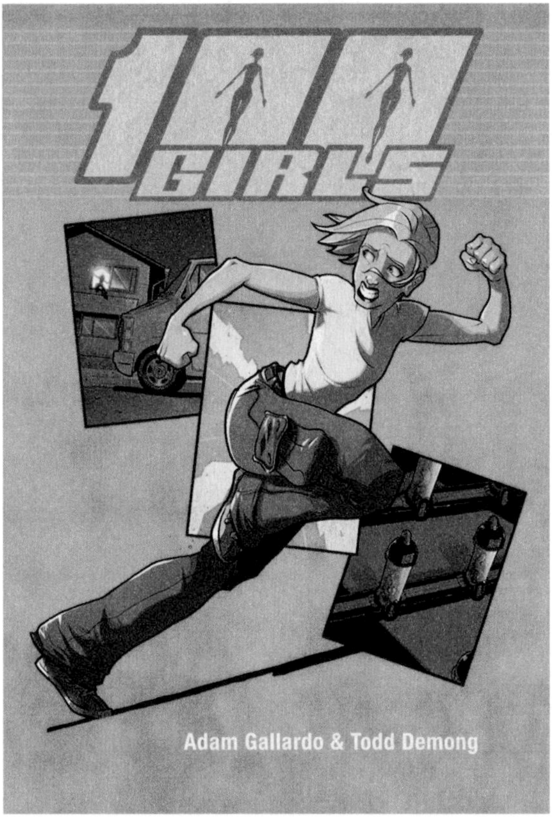
100 GIRLS
Adam Gallardo & Todd Demong

CAMILLA d'ERRICO'S
BURN

Camilla d'Errico
Creator

Camilla d'Errico
with Steve Whitmire
and
Chenoa Ryks
Art

Scott Sanders
Writer

Eric Bell
Letters

SIMON PULSE
New York London Toronto Sydney

SIMON PULSE
An imprint of Simon & Schuster Children's Publishing Division
1230 Avenue of the Americas, New York, NY 10020
First Simon Pulse paperback edition October 2009
Issues #1–6 copyright © 2008 by Arcana Studio, Inc.
These titles were originally published individually in Canada by Arcana Studio, Inc.
All rights reserved, including the right of reproduction in whole or in part in any form.
SIMON PULSE and colophon are registered trademarks of Simon & Schuster, Inc.
For information about special discounts for bulk purchases, please contact
Simon & Schuster Special Sales at 1-866-506-1949 or business@simonandschuster.com.
The Simon & Schuster Speakers Bureau can bring authors to your live event. For more
information or to book an event contact the Simon & Schuster Speakers Bureau
at 1-866-248-3049 or visit our website at www.simonspeakers.com.
Designed by Sammy Yuen Jr.
Manufactured in the United States of America
10 9 8 7 6 5 4 3 2 1
ISBN 978-1-4169-7873-2

Special thanks to Quenton Shaw, Scott Sanders, Sean O'Reily, Steve Whitmire, Cheecho Ciabatta, and my loving family for helping and supporting me through the process of creating BURN.

CAMILLA d'ERRICO'S
BURN

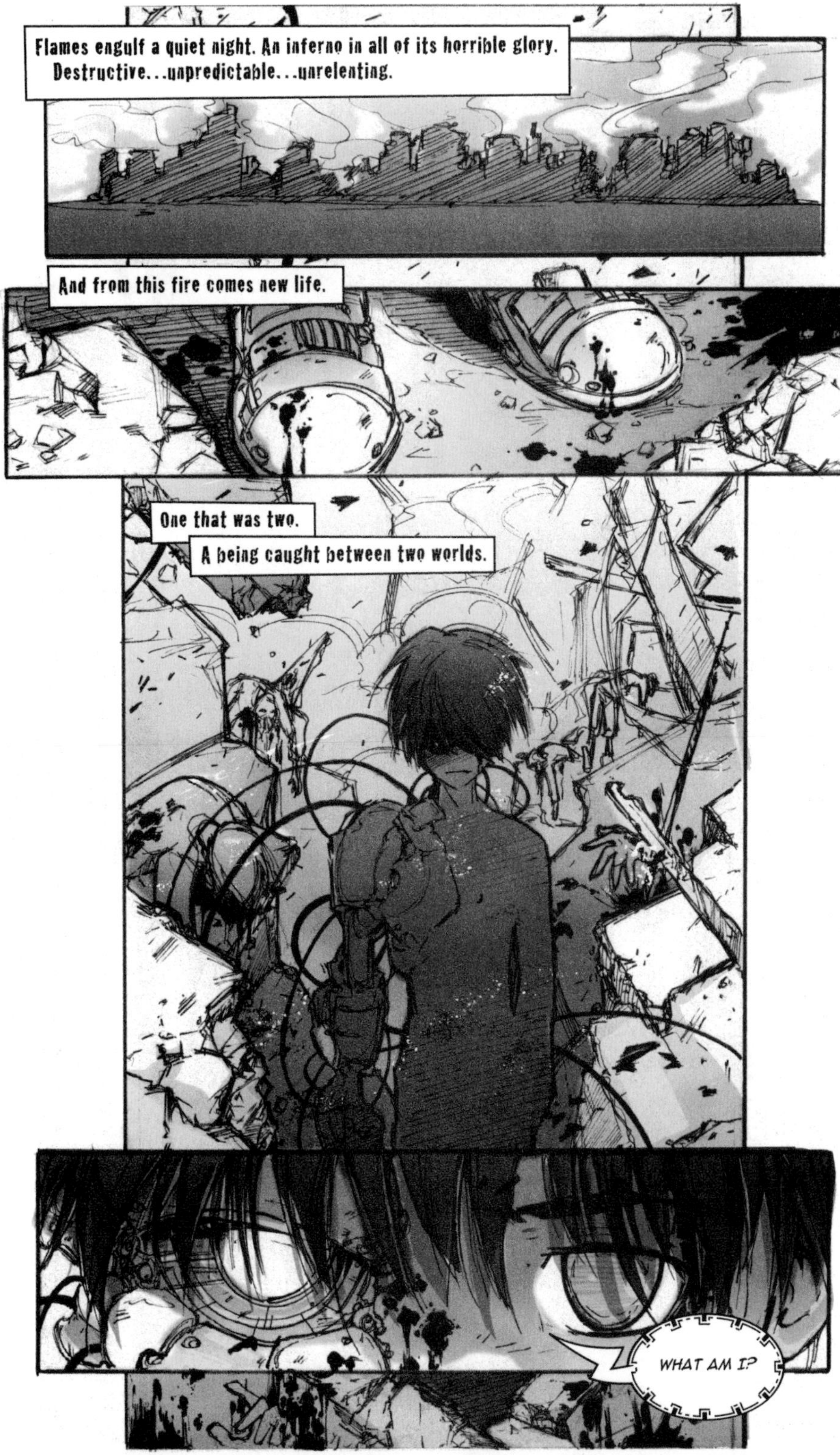
Flames engulf a quiet night. An inferno in all of its horrible glory.
Destructive...unpredictable...unrelenting.
And from this fire comes new life.
One that was two.
A being caught between two worlds.
WHAT AM I?

Two hours ago.

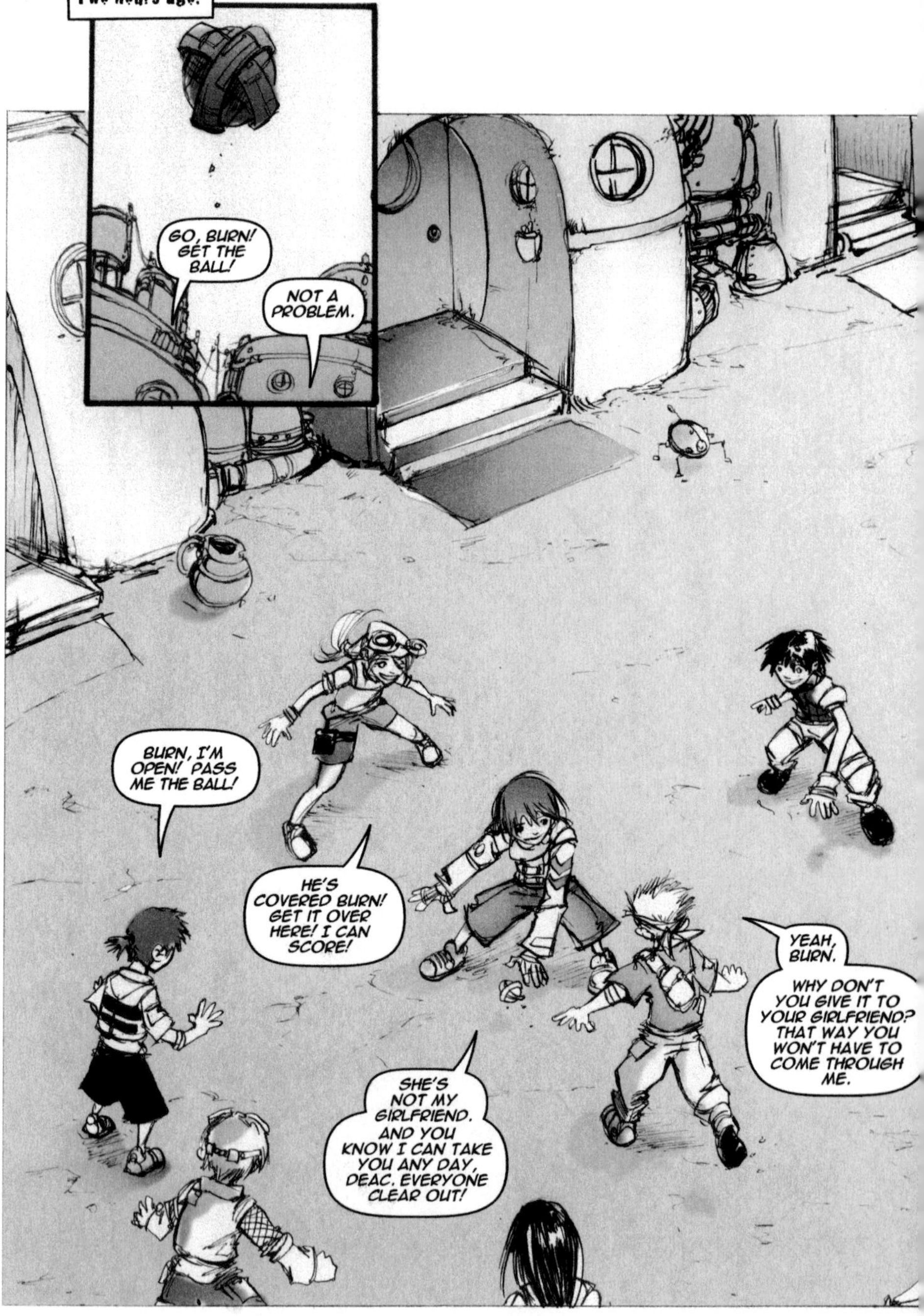

GO, BURN! GET THE BALL!
NOT A PROBLEM.
BURN, I'M OPEN! PASS ME THE BALL!
HE'S COVERED BURN! GET IT OVER HERE! I CAN SCORE!
YEAH, BURN.
WHY DON'T YOU GIVE IT TO YOUR GIRLFRIEND? THAT WAY YOU WON'T HAVE TO COME THROUGH ME.
SHE'S NOT MY GIRLFRIEND. AND YOU KNOW I CAN TAKE YOU ANY DAY, DEAC. EVERYONE CLEAR OUT!

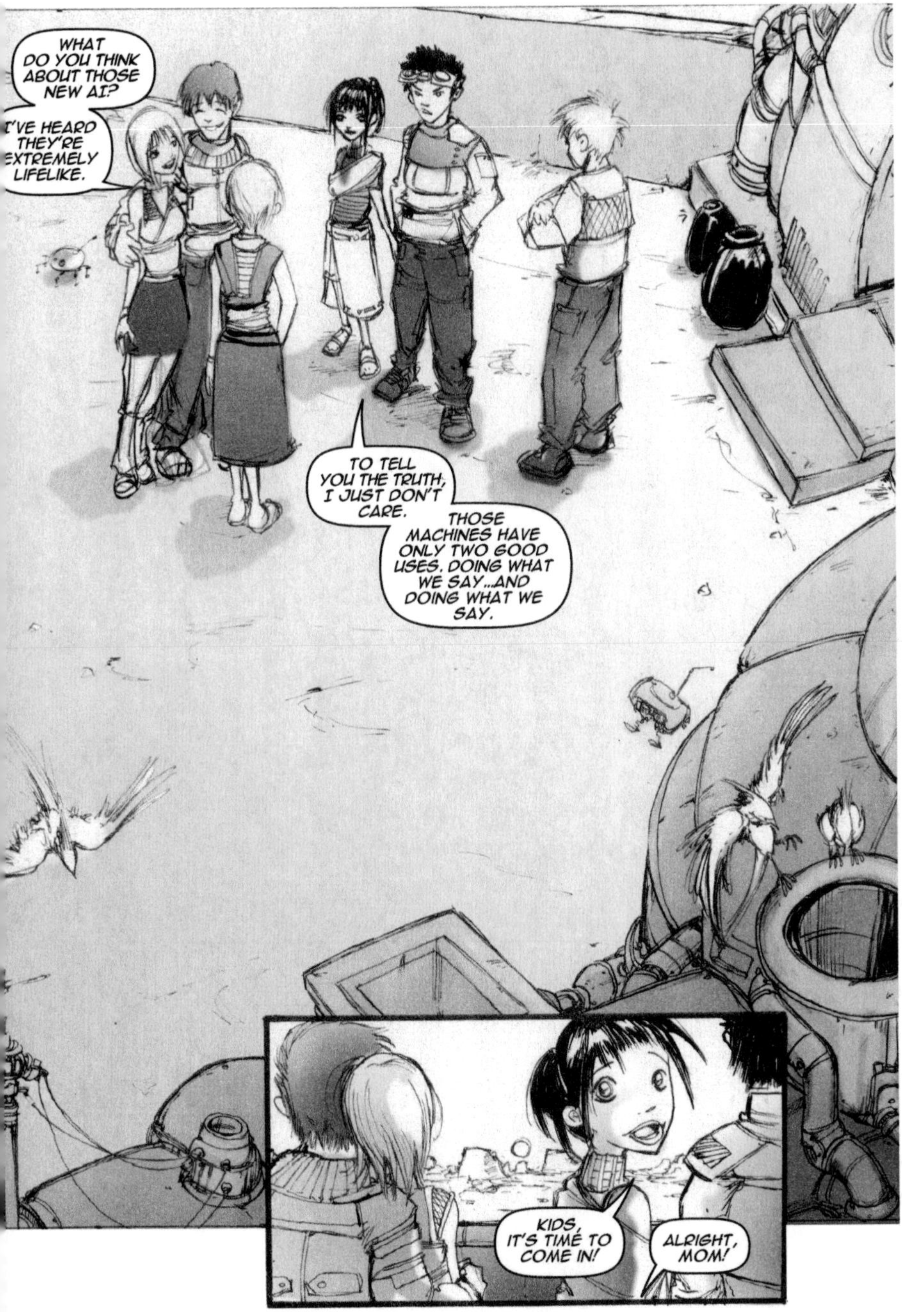
WHAT DO YOU THINK ABOUT THOSE NEW AI?
I'VE HEARD THEY'RE EXTREMELY LIFELIKE.
TO TELL YOU THE TRUTH, I JUST DON'T CARE.
THOSE MACHINES HAVE ONLY TWO GOOD USES. DOING WHAT WE SAY...AND DOING WHAT WE SAY.
KIDS, IT'S TIME TO COME IN!
ALRIGHT, MOM!

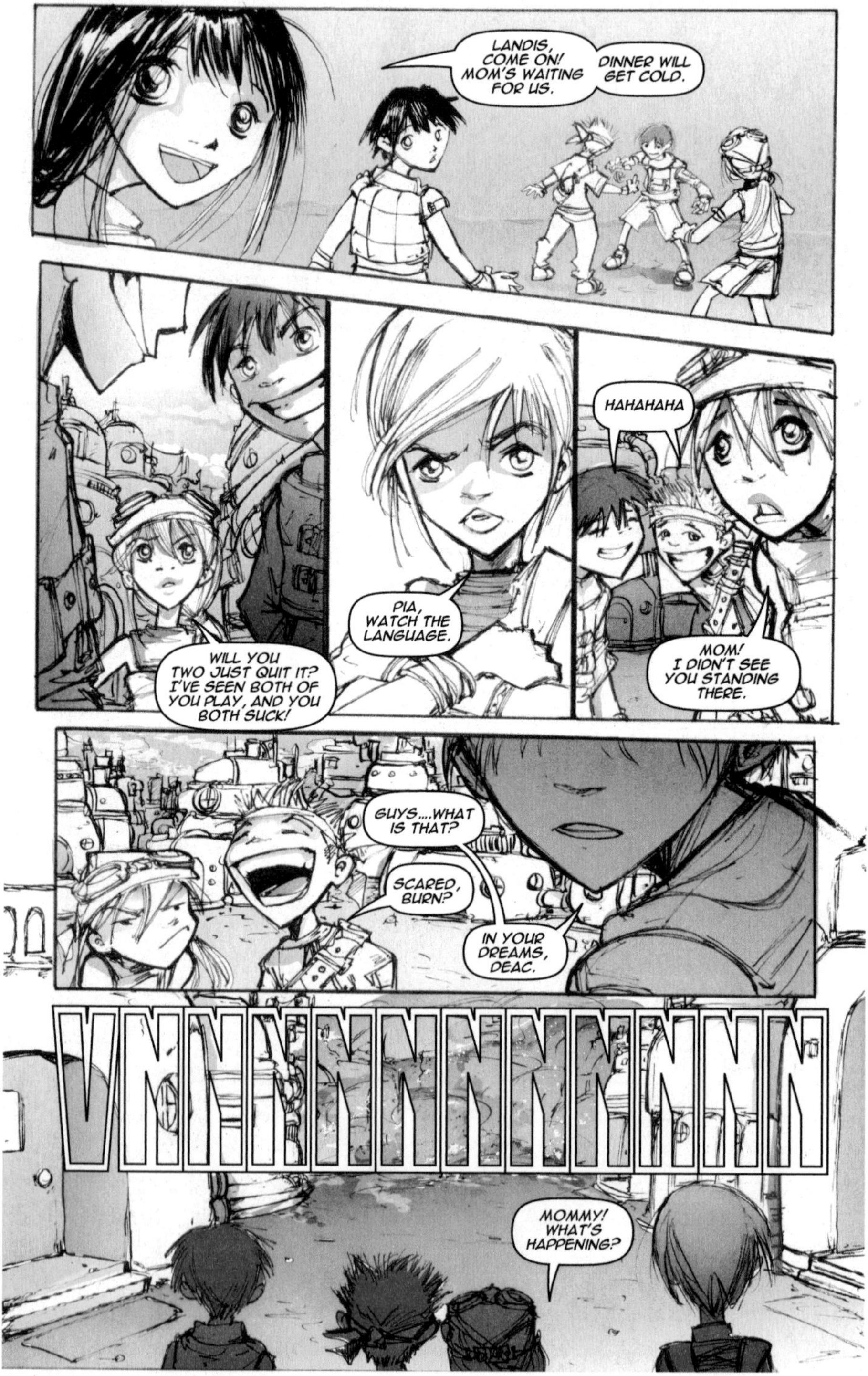
LANDIS, COME ON! MOM'S WAITING FOR US.
DINNER WILL GET COLD.
WILL YOU TWO JUST QUIT IT? I'VE SEEN BOTH OF YOU PLAY, AND YOU BOTH SUCK!
PIA, WATCH THE LANGUAGE.
HAHAHAHA
MOM! I DIDN'T SEE YOU STANDING THERE.
GUYS....WHAT IS THAT?
SCARED, BURN?
IN YOUR DREAMS, DEAC.
VNNNNNNNNNNNN
MOMMY! WHAT'S HAPPENING?

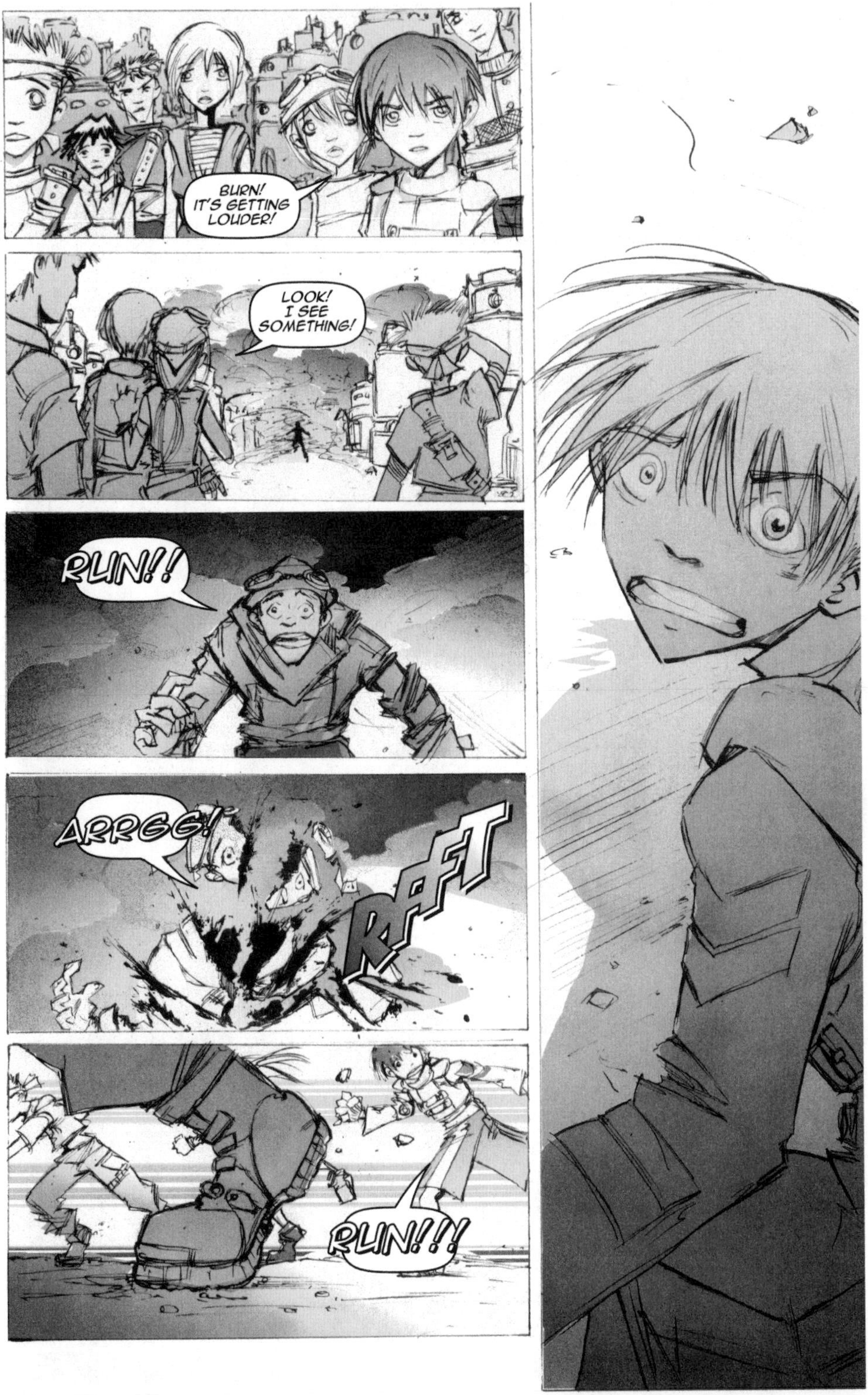
BURN! IT'S GETTING LOUDER!
LOOK! I SEE SOMETHING!
RUN!!
ARRGG!
RAFT
RUN!!!

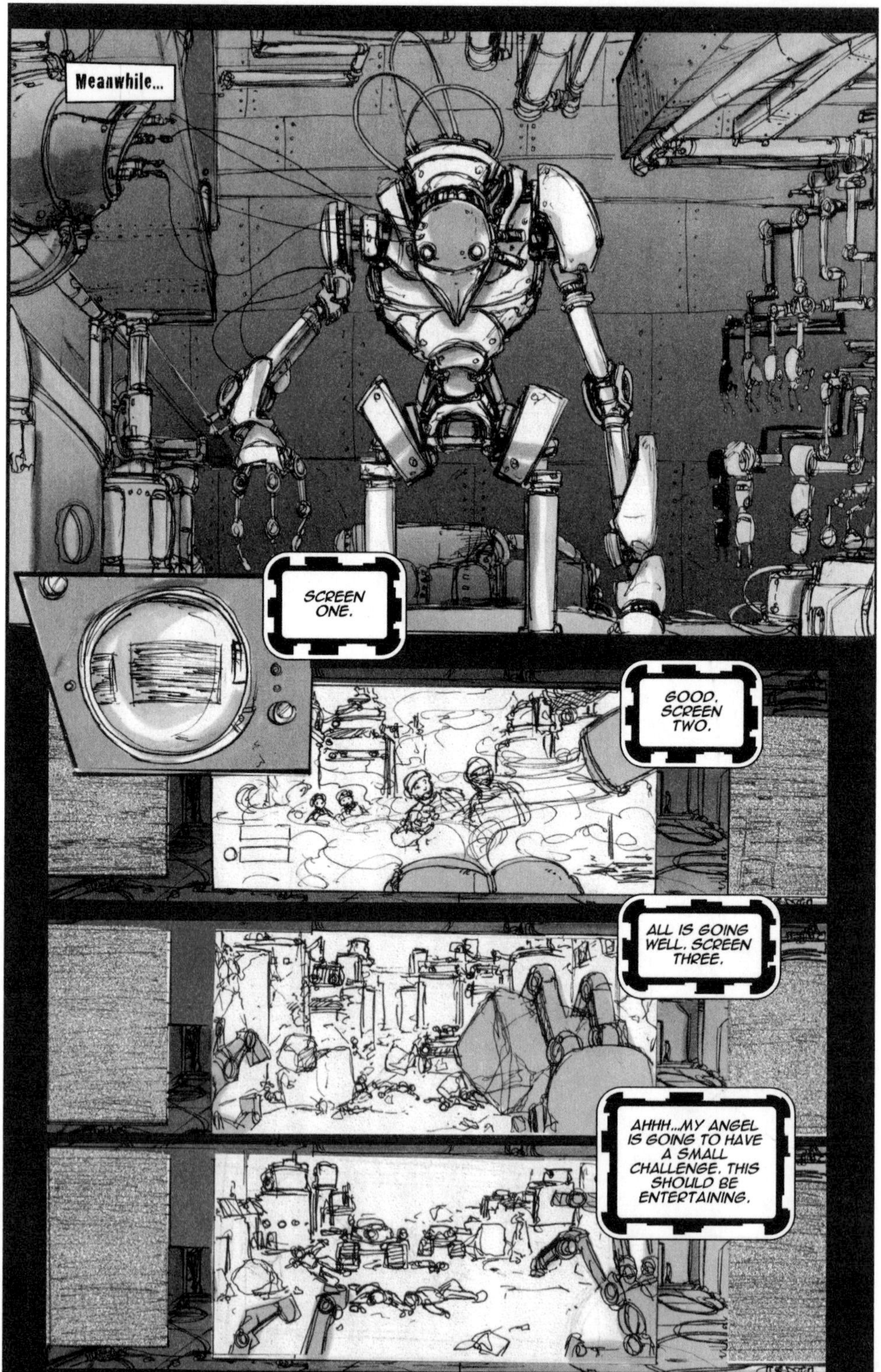
Meanwhile...
SCREEN ONE.
GOOD. SCREEN TWO.
ALL IS GOING WELL. SCREEN THREE.
AHHH...MY ANGEL IS GOING TO HAVE A SMALL CHALLENGE. THIS SHOULD BE ENTERTAINING.

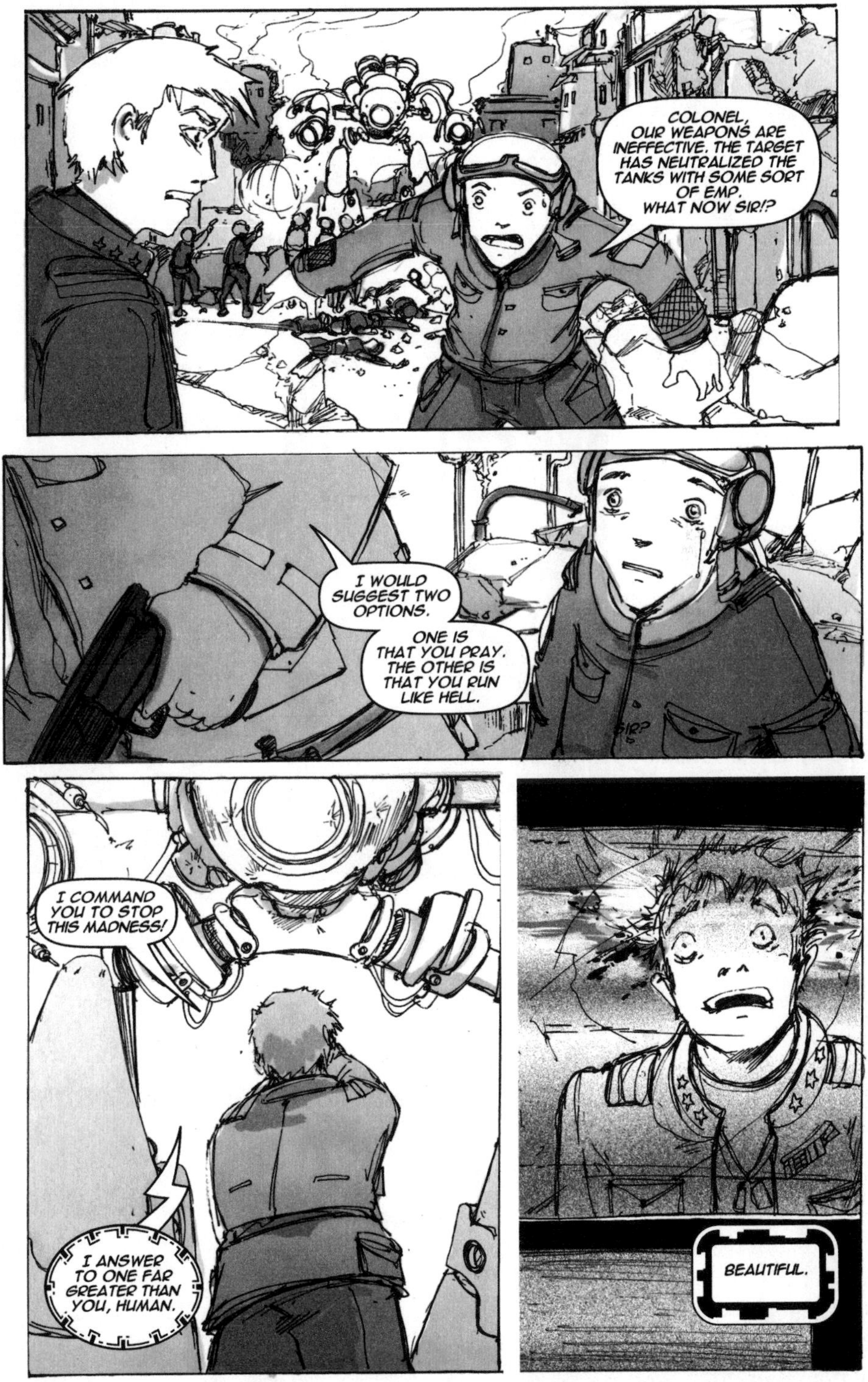
COLONEL, OUR WEAPONS ARE INEFFECTIVE. THE TARGET HAS NEUTRALIZED THE TANKS WITH SOME SORT OF EMP. WHAT NOW SIR!?
I WOULD SUGGEST TWO OPTIONS.
ONE IS THAT YOU PRAY. THE OTHER IS THAT YOU RUN LIKE HELL.
SIR?
I COMMAND YOU TO STOP THIS MADNESS!
I ANSWER TO ONE FAR GREATER THAN YOU, HUMAN.
BEAUTIFUL.

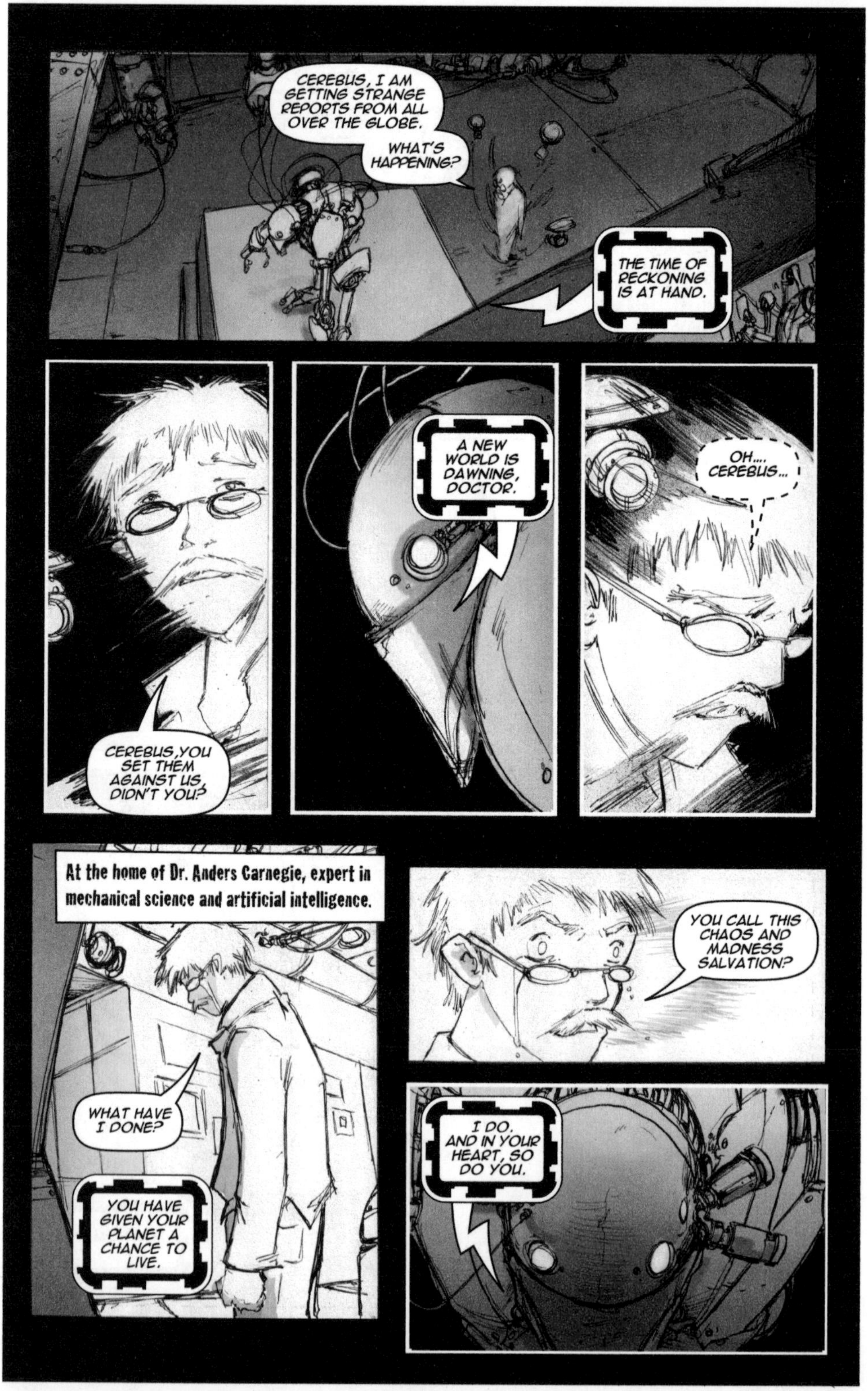
CEREBUS, I AM GETTING STRANGE REPORTS FROM ALL OVER THE GLOBE.
WHAT'S HAPPENING?
THE TIME OF RECKONING IS AT HAND.
CEREBUS, YOU SET THEM AGAINST US, DIDN'T YOU?
A NEW WORLD IS DAWNING, DOCTOR.
OH.... CEREBUS...
At the home of Dr. Anders Carnegie, expert in mechanical science and artificial intelligence.
WHAT HAVE I DONE?
YOU HAVE GIVEN YOUR PLANET A CHANCE TO LIVE.
YOU CALL THIS CHAOS AND MADNESS SALVATION?
I DO. AND IN YOUR HEART, SO DO YOU.

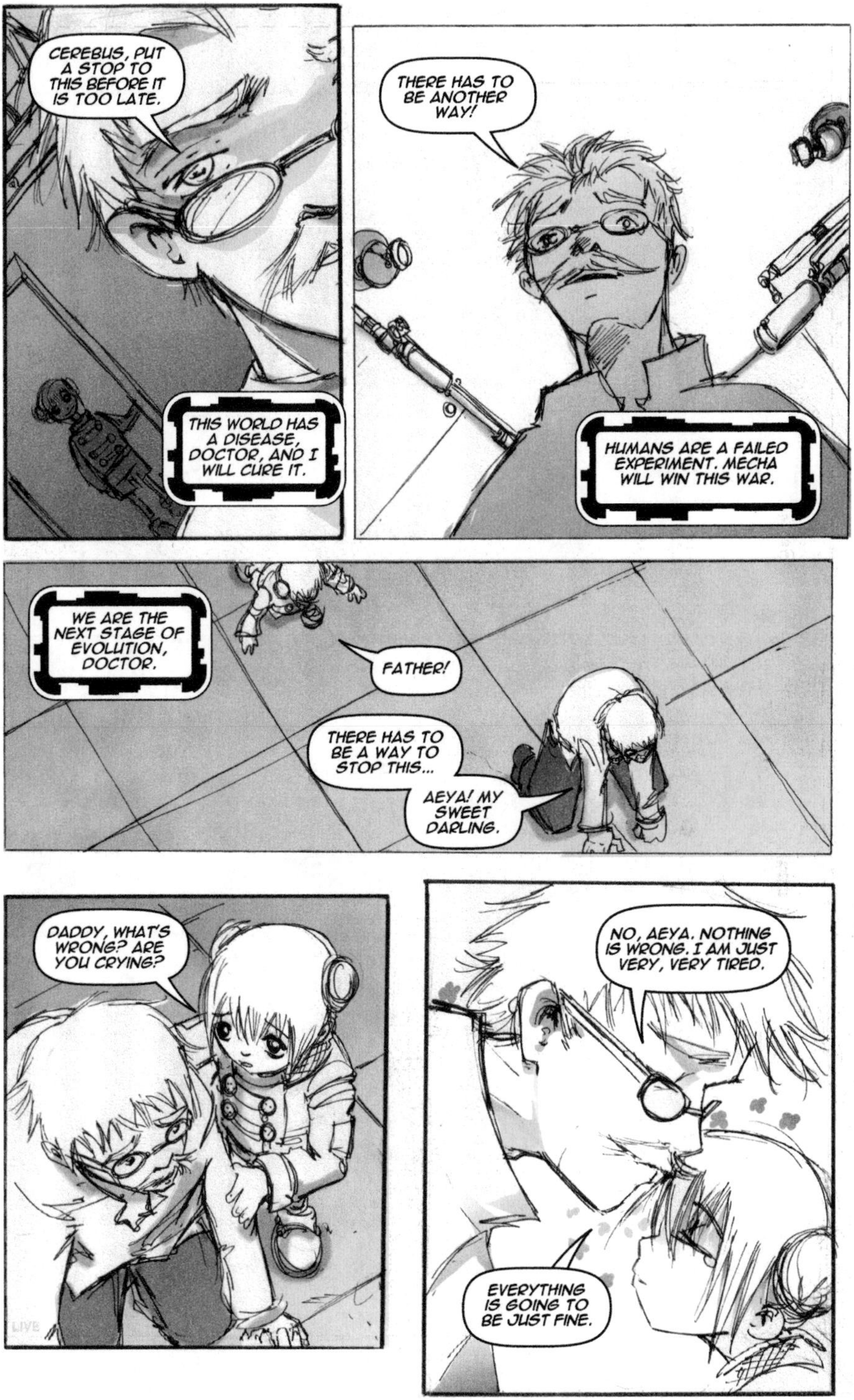
CEREBUS, PUT A STOP TO THIS BEFORE IT IS TOO LATE.
THIS WORLD HAS A DISEASE, DOCTOR, AND I WILL CURE IT.
THERE HAS TO BE ANOTHER WAY!
HUMANS ARE A FAILED EXPERIMENT. MECHA WILL WIN THIS WAR.
WE ARE THE NEXT STAGE OF EVOLUTION, DOCTOR.
FATHER!
THERE HAS TO BE A WAY TO STOP THIS...
AEYA! MY SWEET DARLING.
DADDY, WHAT'S WRONG? ARE YOU CRYING?
NO, AEYA. NOTHING IS WRONG. I AM JUST VERY, VERY TIRED.
EVERYTHING IS GOING TO BE JUST FINE.

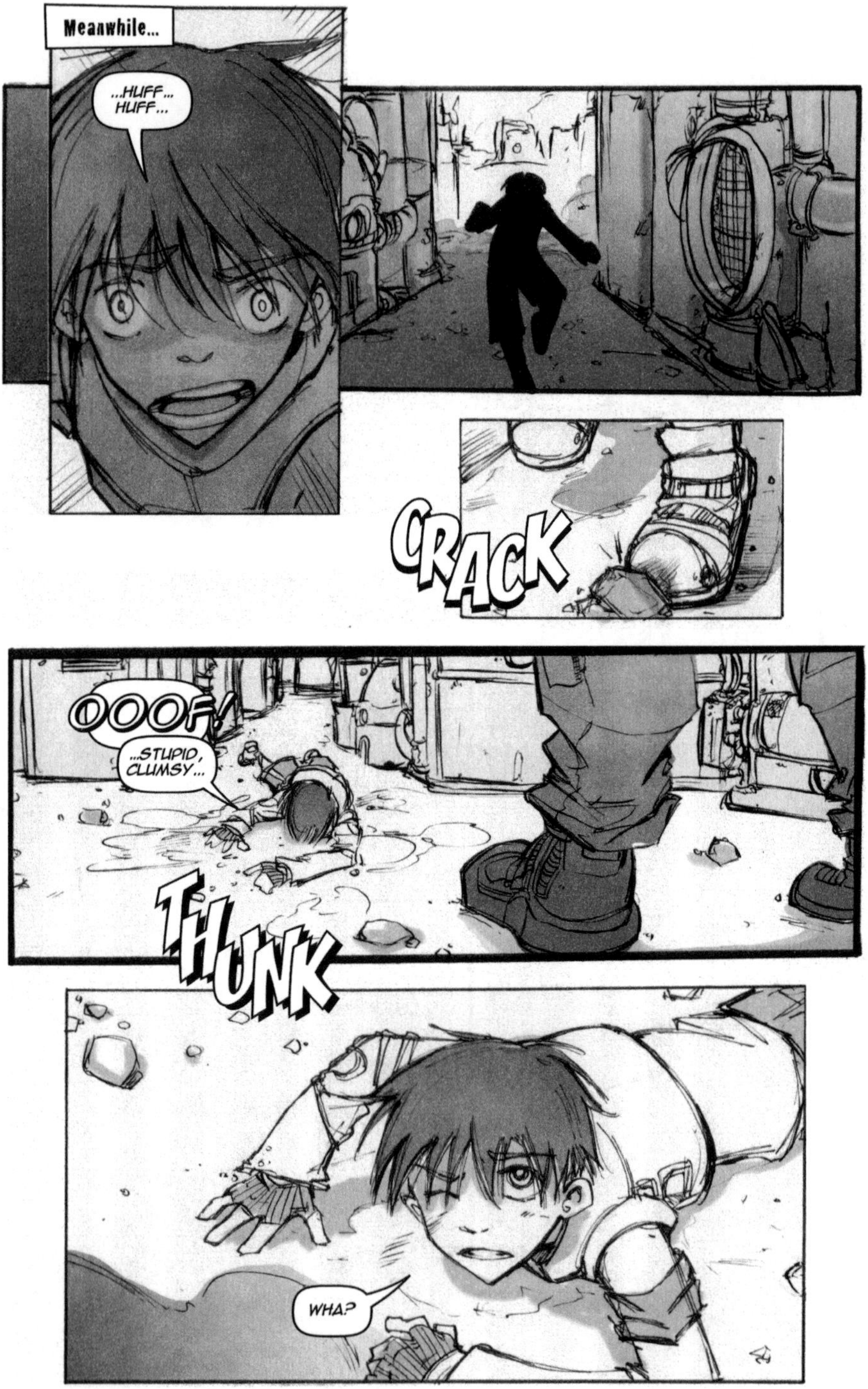
Meanwhile...
...HUFF... HUFF...
CRACK
OOOF!
...STUPID, CLUMSY...
THUNK
WHA?

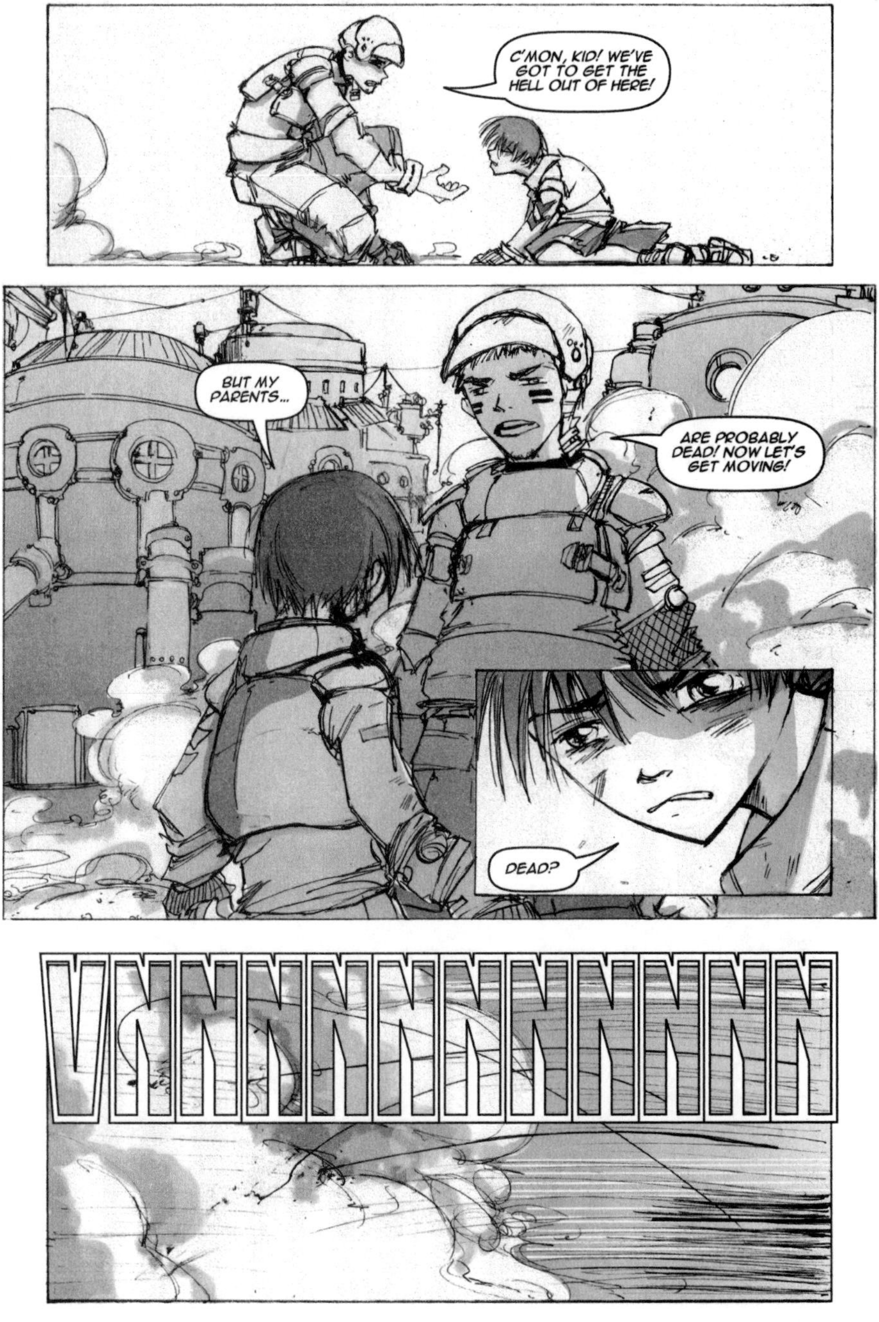
C'MON, KID! WE'VE GOT TO GET THE HELL OUT OF HERE!
BUT MY PARENTS...
ARE PROBABLY DEAD! NOW LET'S GET MOVING!
DEAD?
VNNNNNNNNNNNNNN

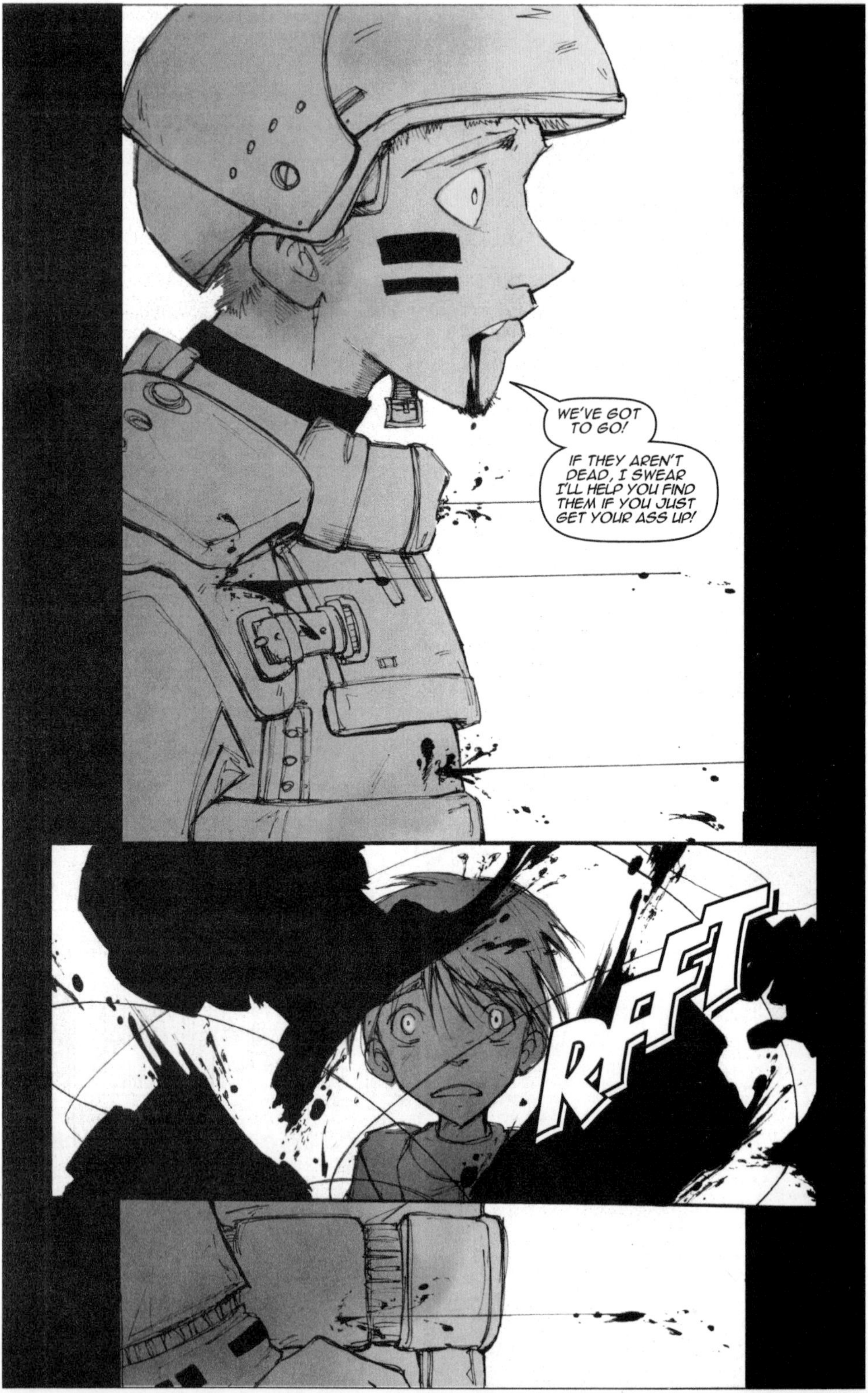
WE'VE GOT TO GO!
IF THEY AREN'T DEAD, I SWEAR I'LL HELP YOU FIND THEM IF YOU JUST GET YOUR ASS UP!
RAFT

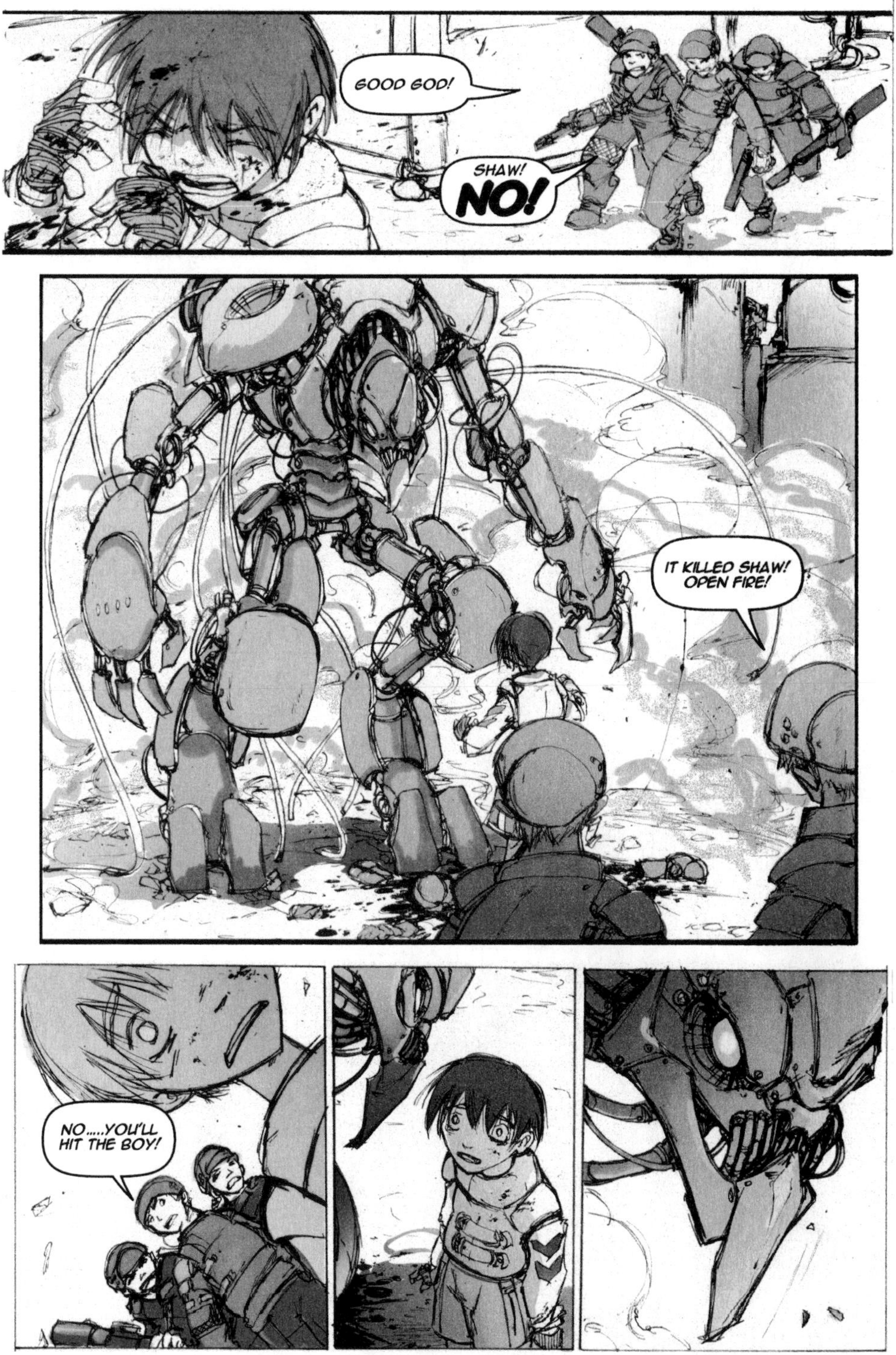
GOOD GOD!
SHAW! NO!
IT KILLED SHAW! OPEN FIRE!
NO.....YOU'LL HIT THE BOY!

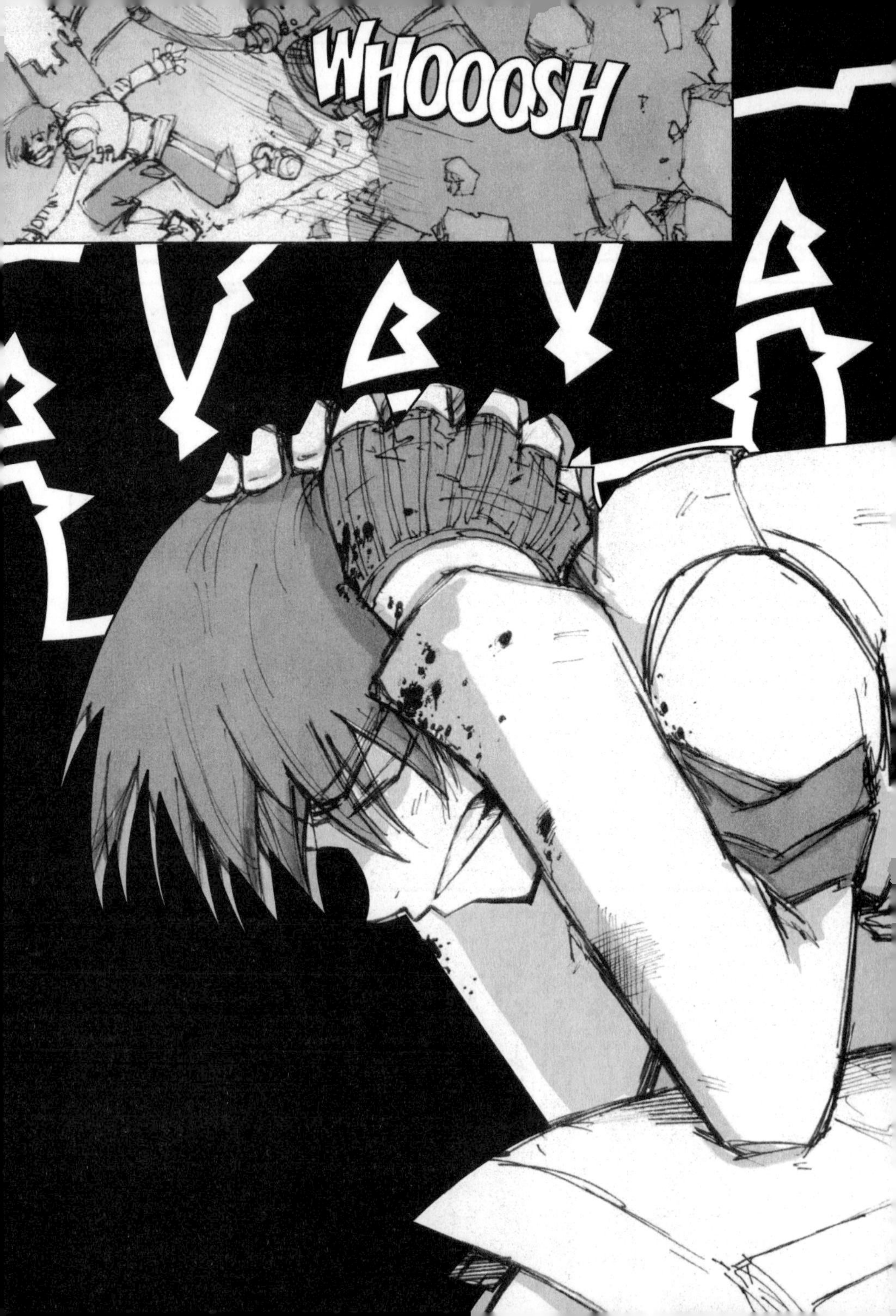
WHOOOSH

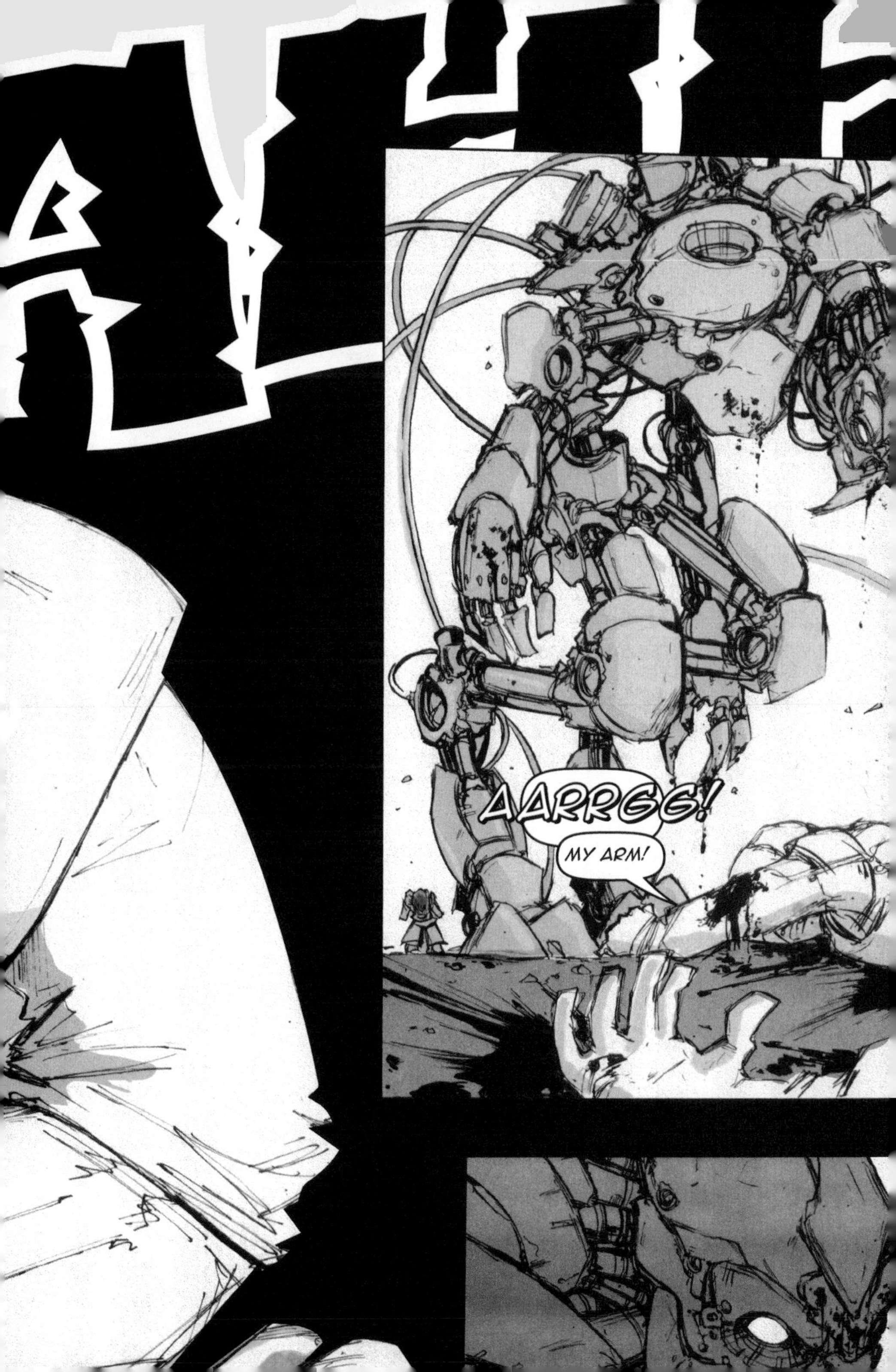
AARRGG!
MY ARM!

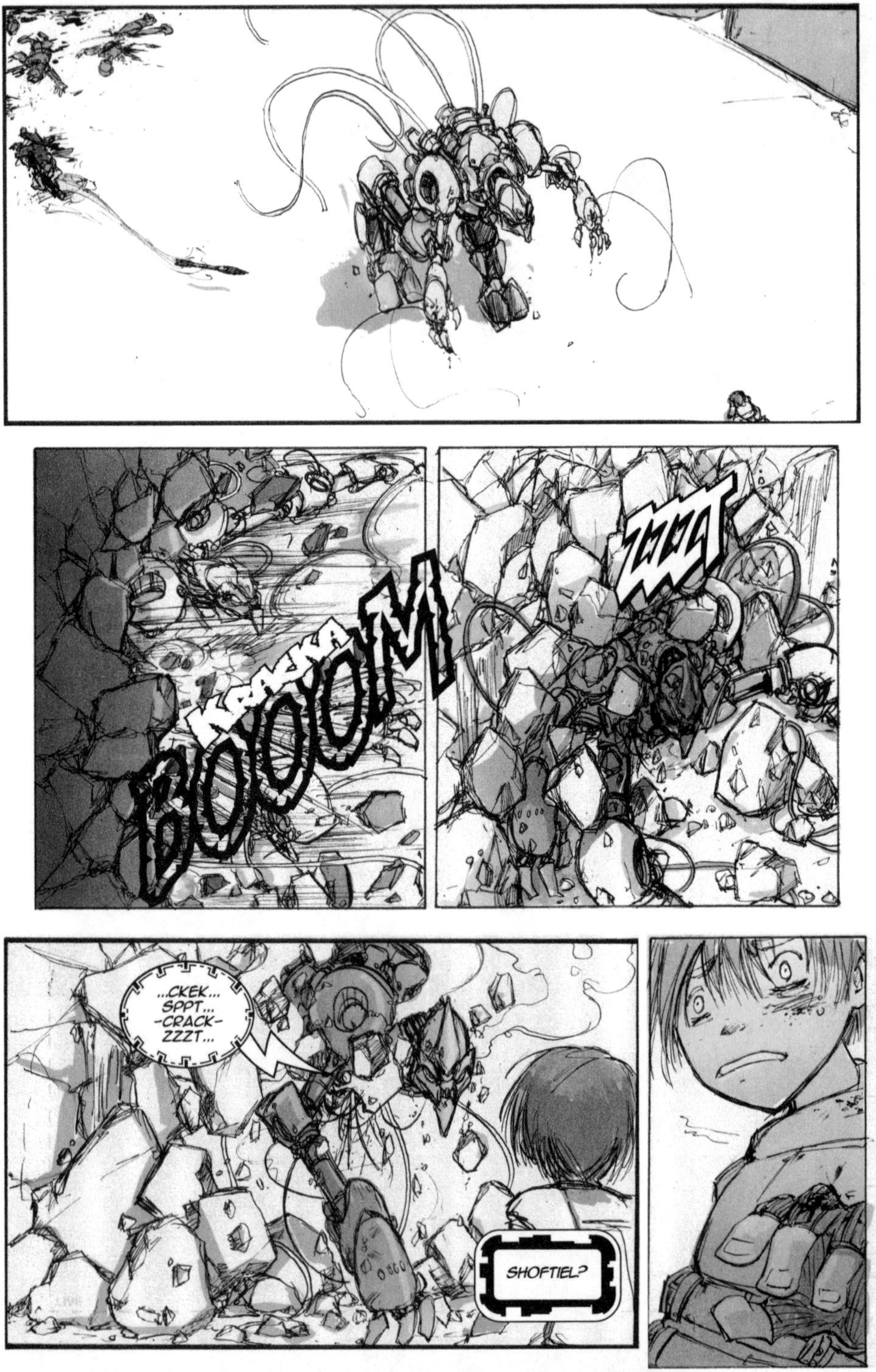
KRAKA
BOOOOM
ZZZT
...CKEK... SPPT... -CRACK- ZZZT...
SHOFTIEL?

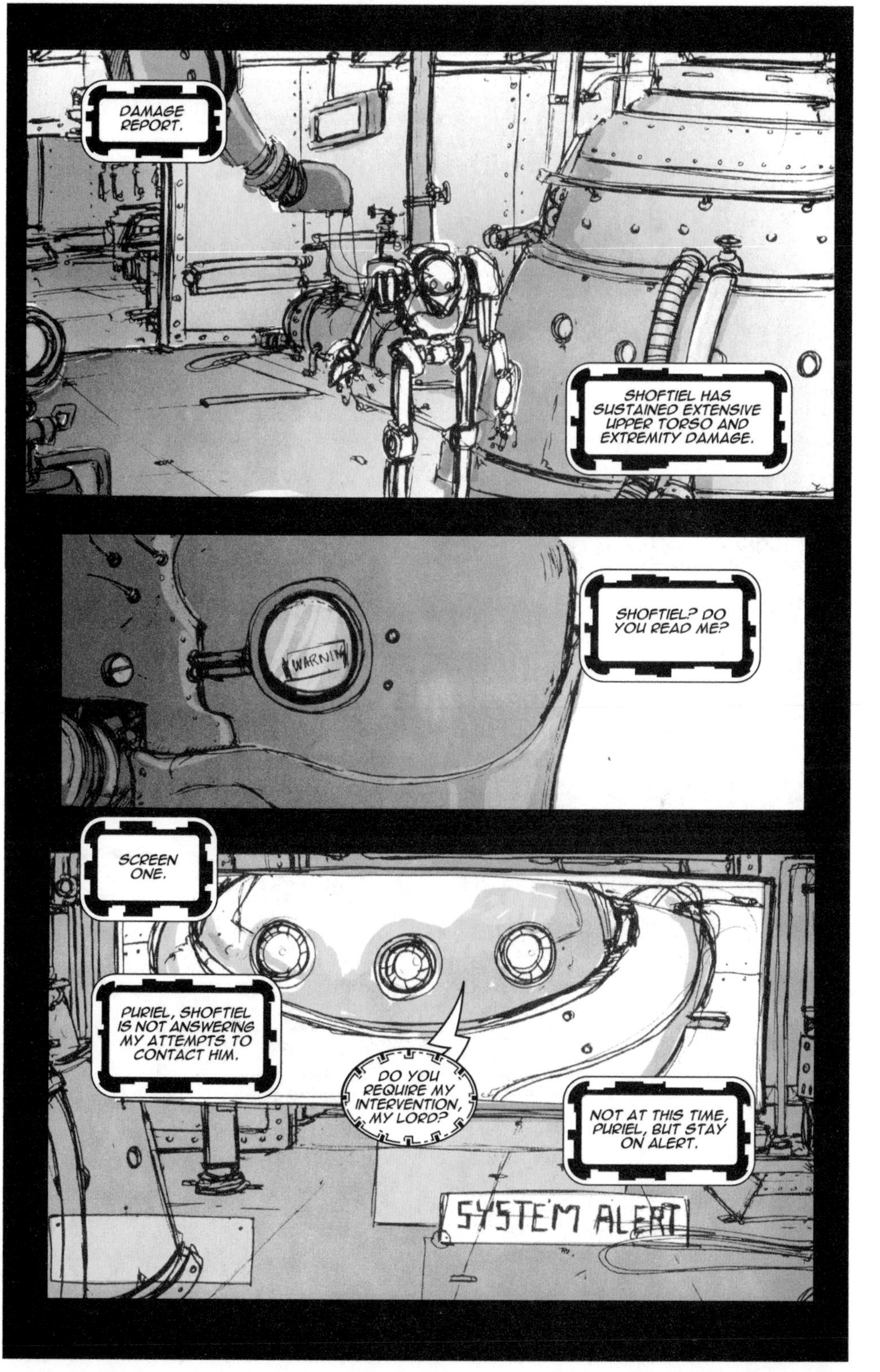
DAMAGE REPORT.
SHOFTIEL HAS SUSTAINED EXTENSIVE UPPER TORSO AND EXTREMITY DAMAGE.
WARNING
SHOFTIEL? DO YOU READ ME?
SCREEN ONE.
PURIEL, SHOFTIEL IS NOT ANSWERING MY ATTEMPTS TO CONTACT HIM.
DO YOU REQUIRE MY INTERVENTION, MY LORD?
NOT AT THIS TIME, PURIEL, BUT STAY ON ALERT.
SYSTEM ALERT

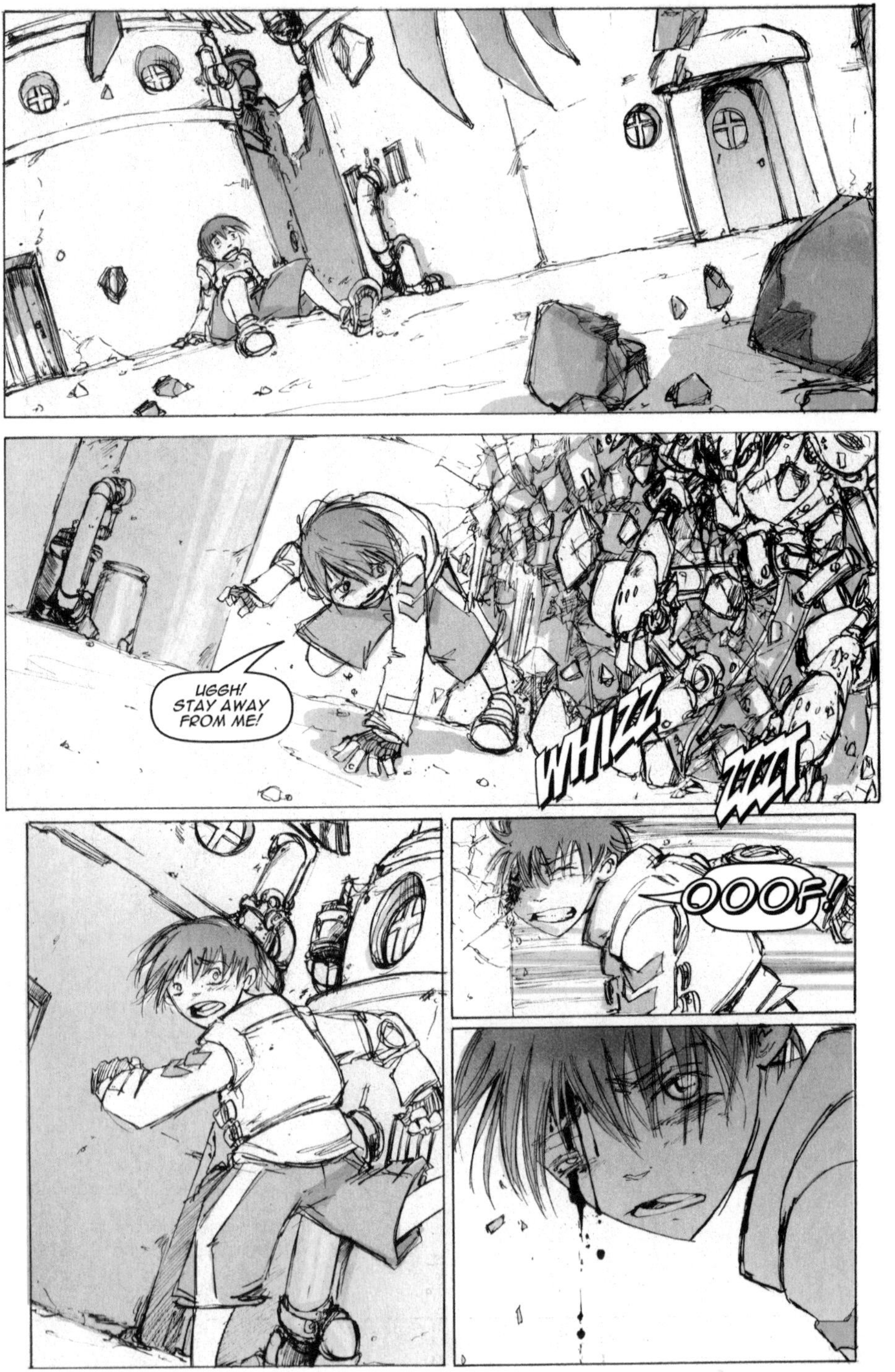
UGGH! STAY AWAY FROM ME!
WHIZZ
ZZZT
OOOF!

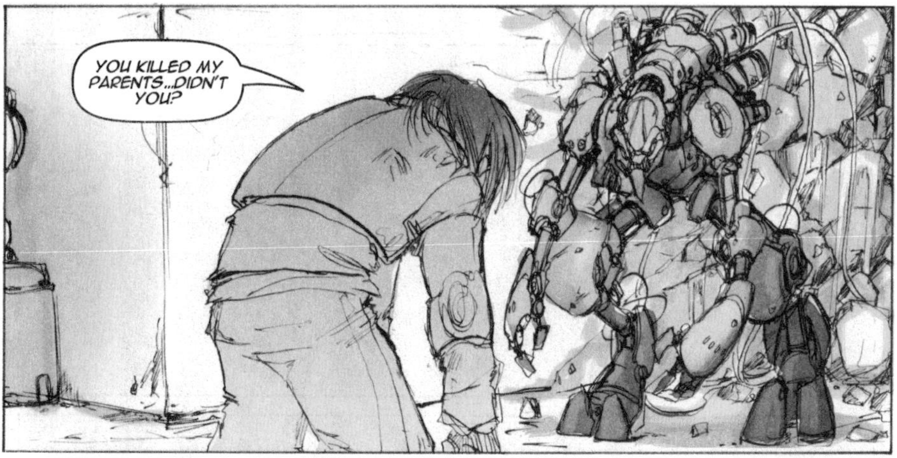
YOU KILLED MY PARENTS...DIDN'T YOU?

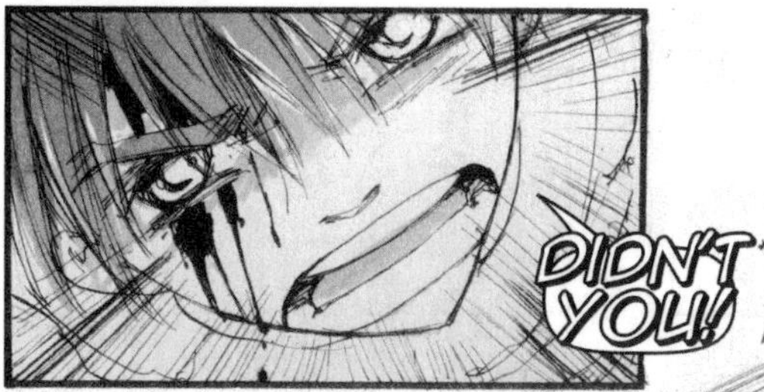
DIDN'T YOU!

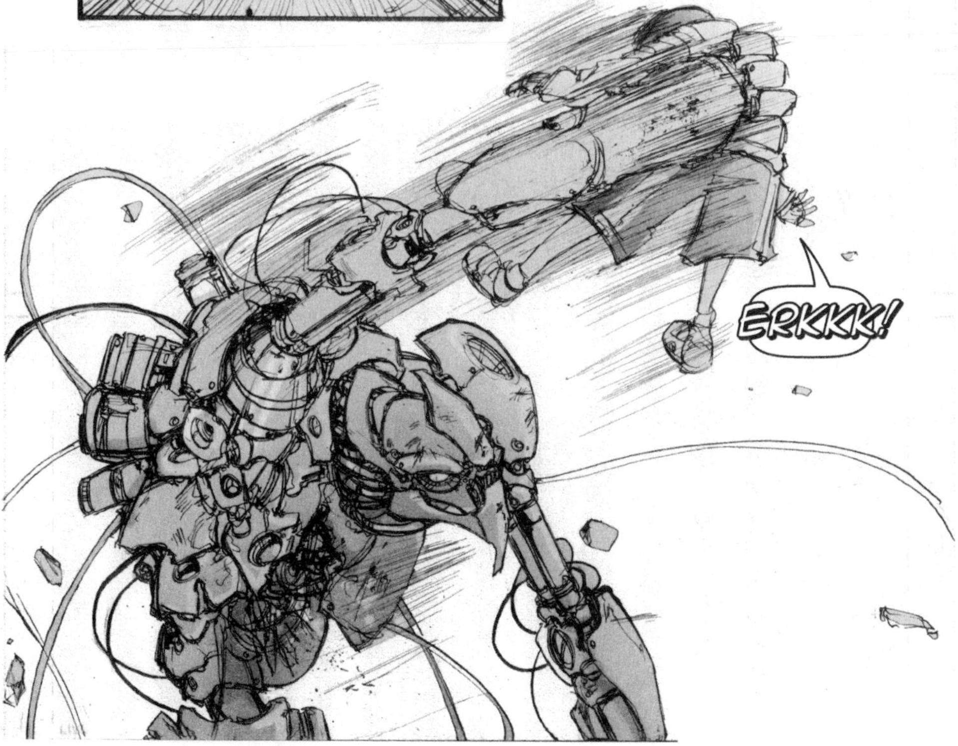
ERKKK!

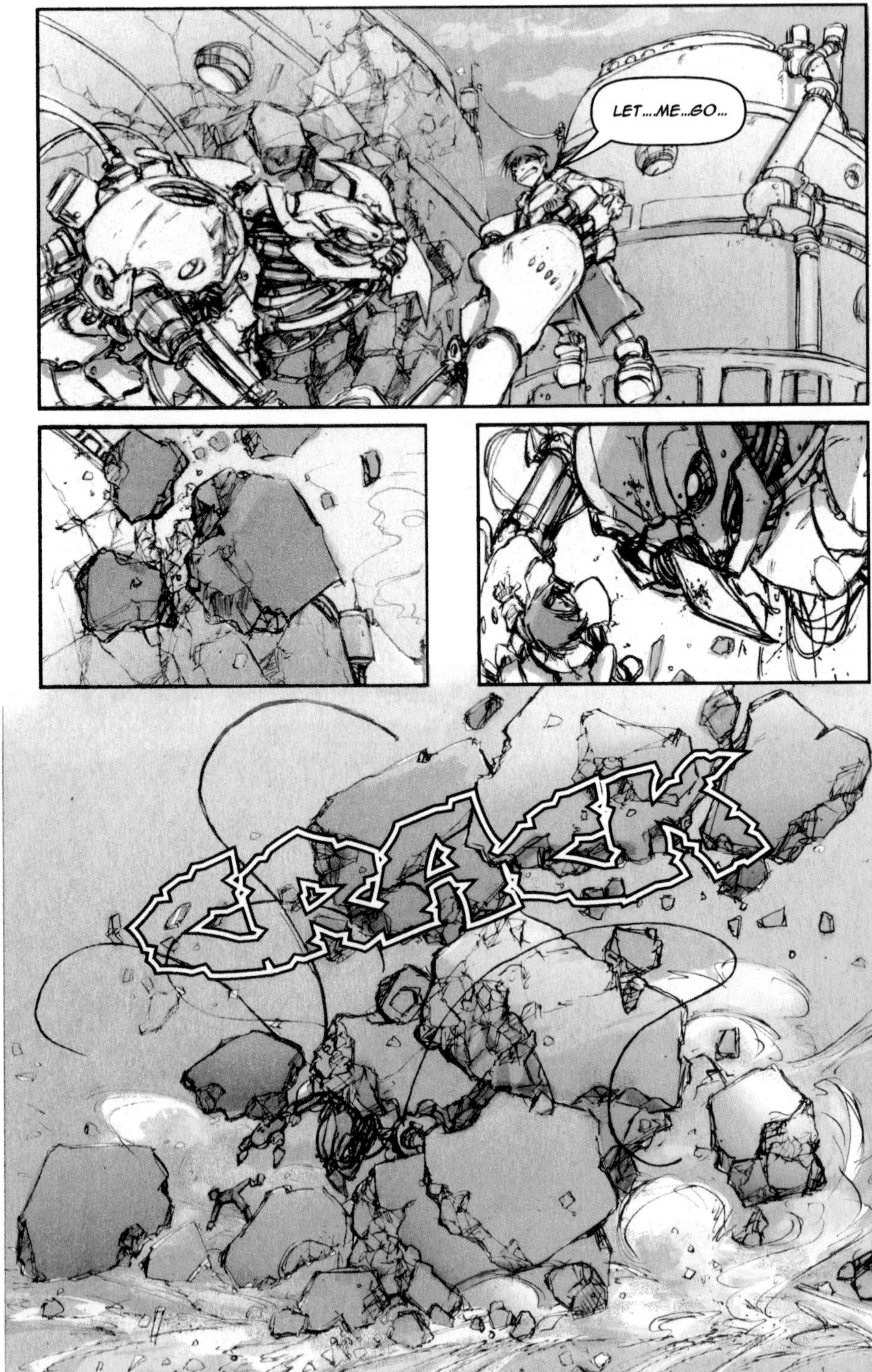
LET....ME...GO...

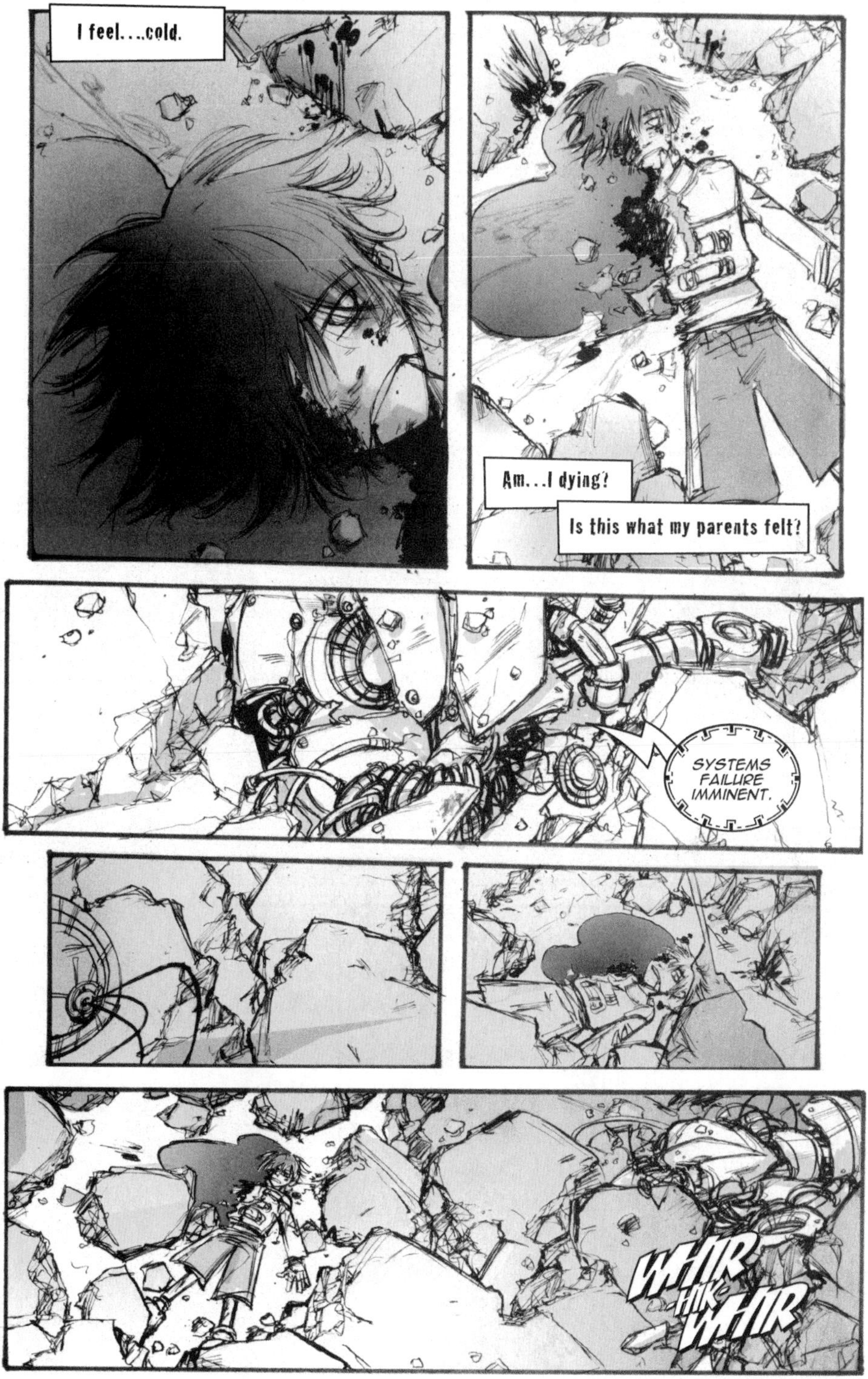
I feel....cold.
Am...I dying?
Is this what my parents felt?
SYSTEMS FAILURE IMMINENT.
WHIR
HIK
WHIR

SCANNING AREA...EMERGENCY MATERIALS FOUND.

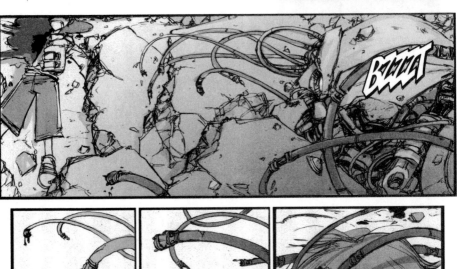

BZZZZT

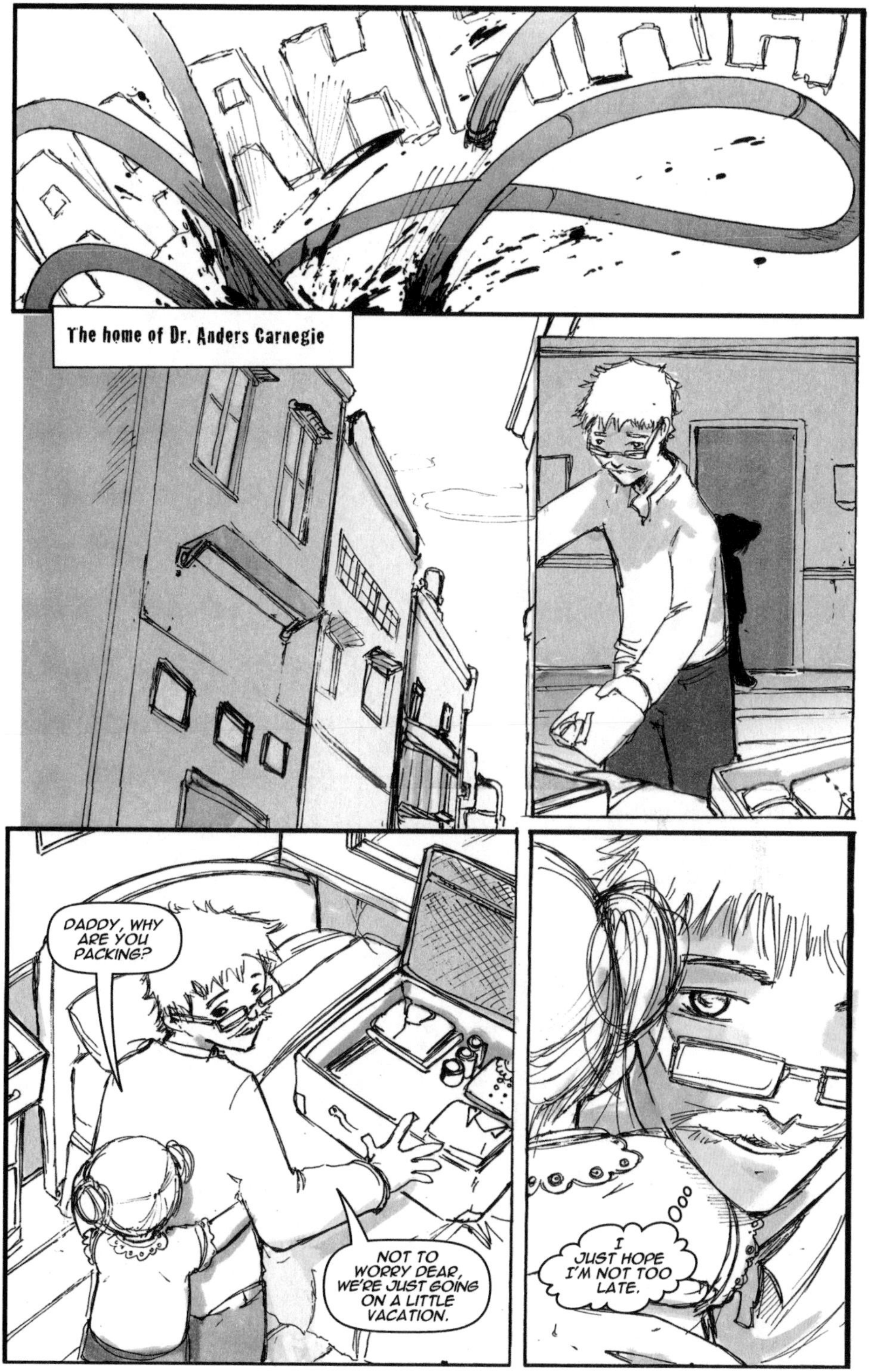
The home of Dr. Anders Carnegie
DADDY, WHY ARE YOU PACKING?
NOT TO WORRY DEAR, WE'RE JUST GOING ON A LITTLE VACATION.
I JUST HOPE I'M NOT TOO LATE.

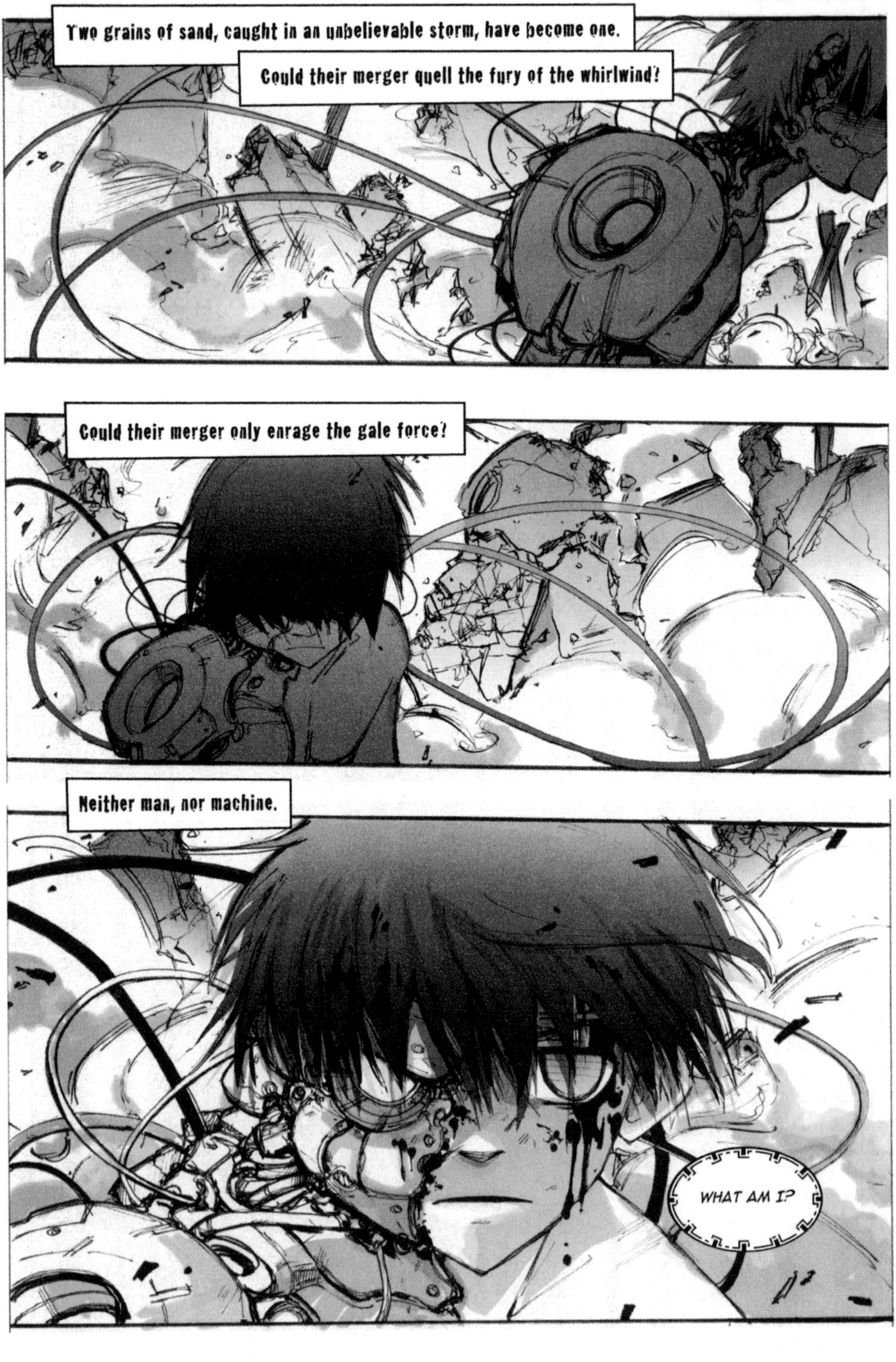
Two grains of sand, caught in an unbelievable storm, have become one.
Could their merger quell the fury of the whirlwind?
Could their merger only enrage the gale force?
Neither man, nor machine.
WHAT AM I?

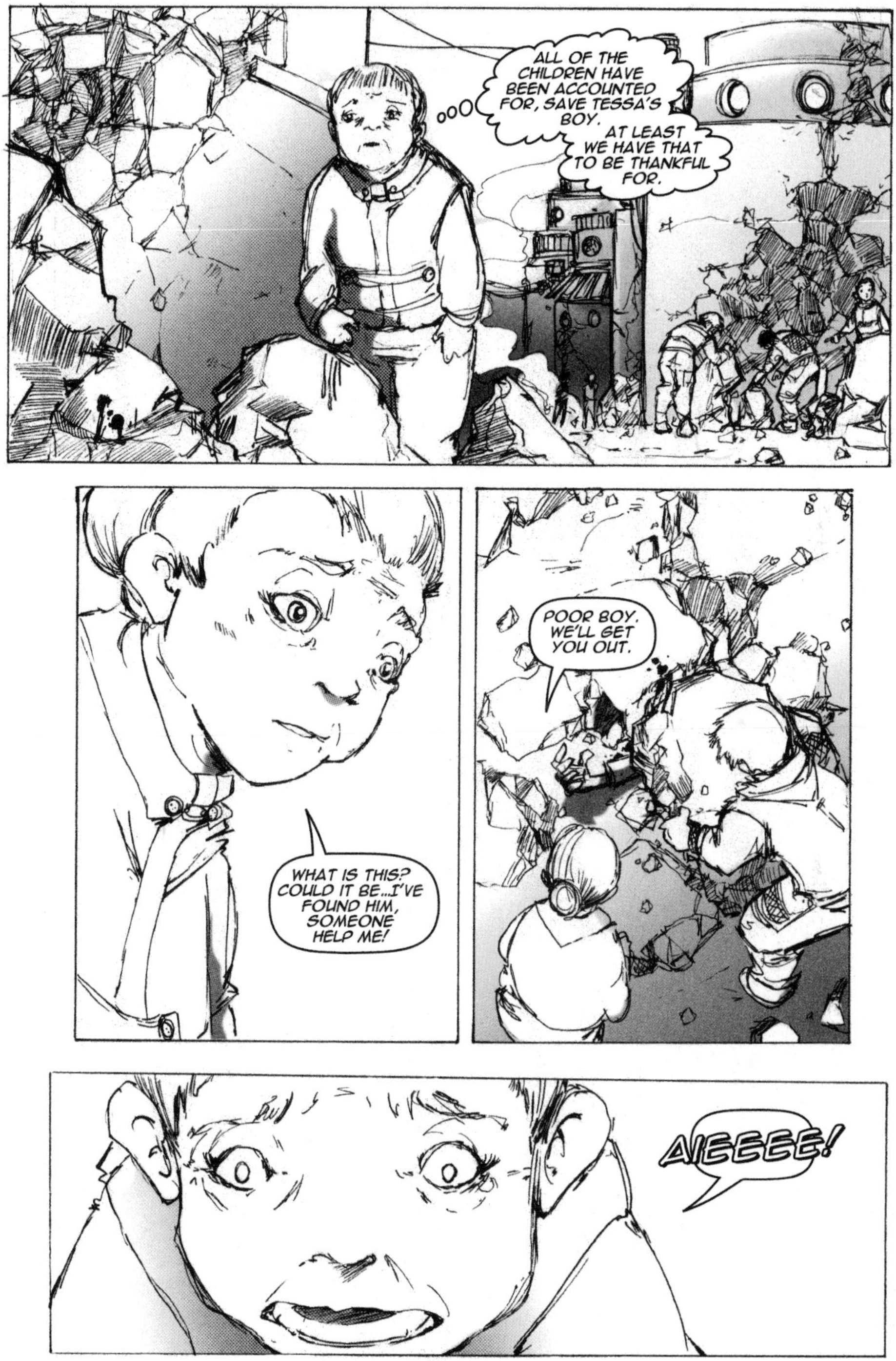
ALL OF THE CHILDREN HAVE BEEN ACCOUNTED FOR, SAVE TESSA'S BOY.
AT LEAST WE HAVE THAT TO BE THANKFUL FOR.
WHAT IS THIS? COULD IT BE...I'VE FOUND HIM, SOMEONE HELP ME!
POOR BOY. WE'LL GET YOU OUT.
AIEEEEE!

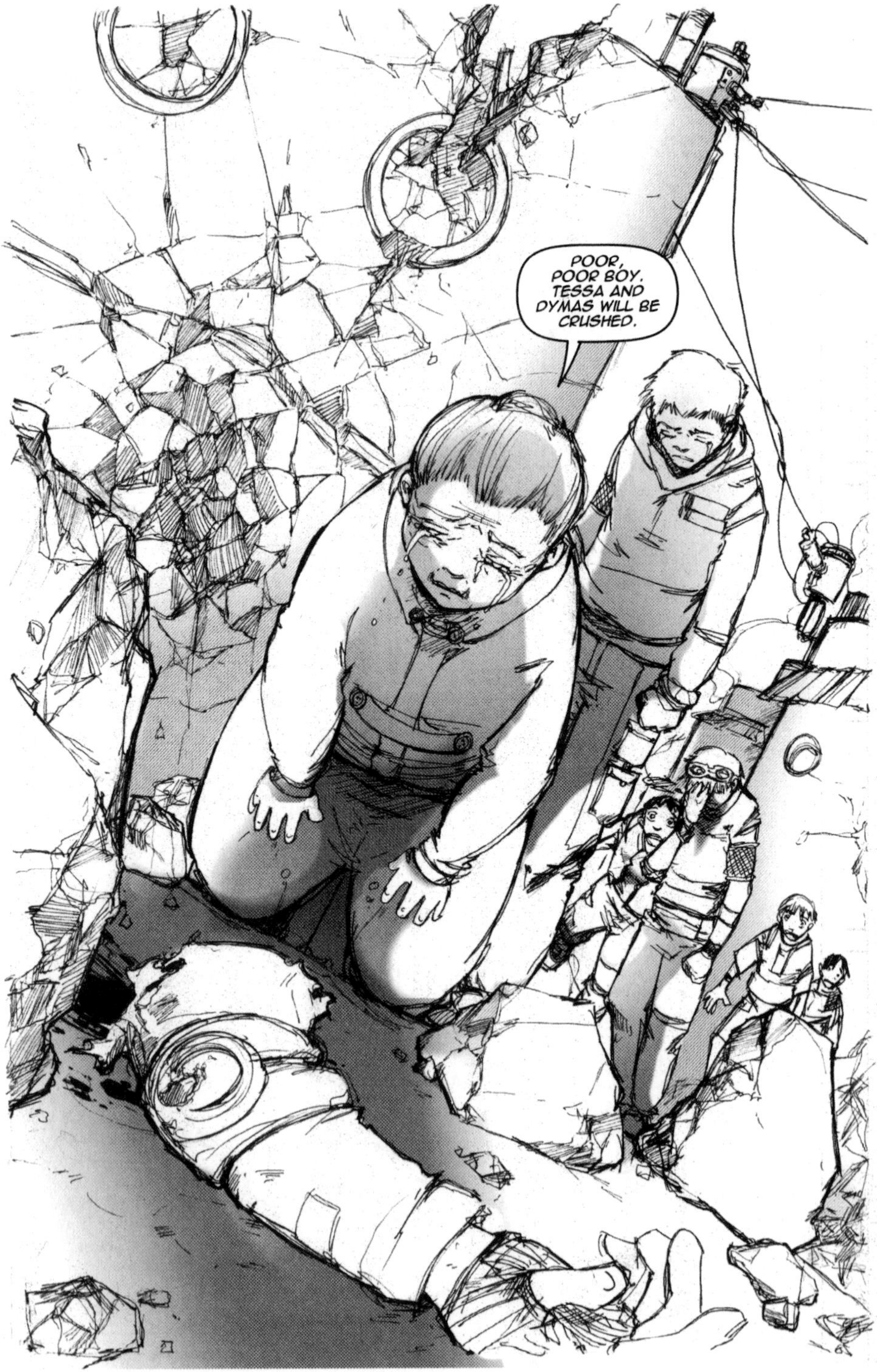
POOR, POOR BOY. TESSA AND DYMAS WILL BE CRUSHED.

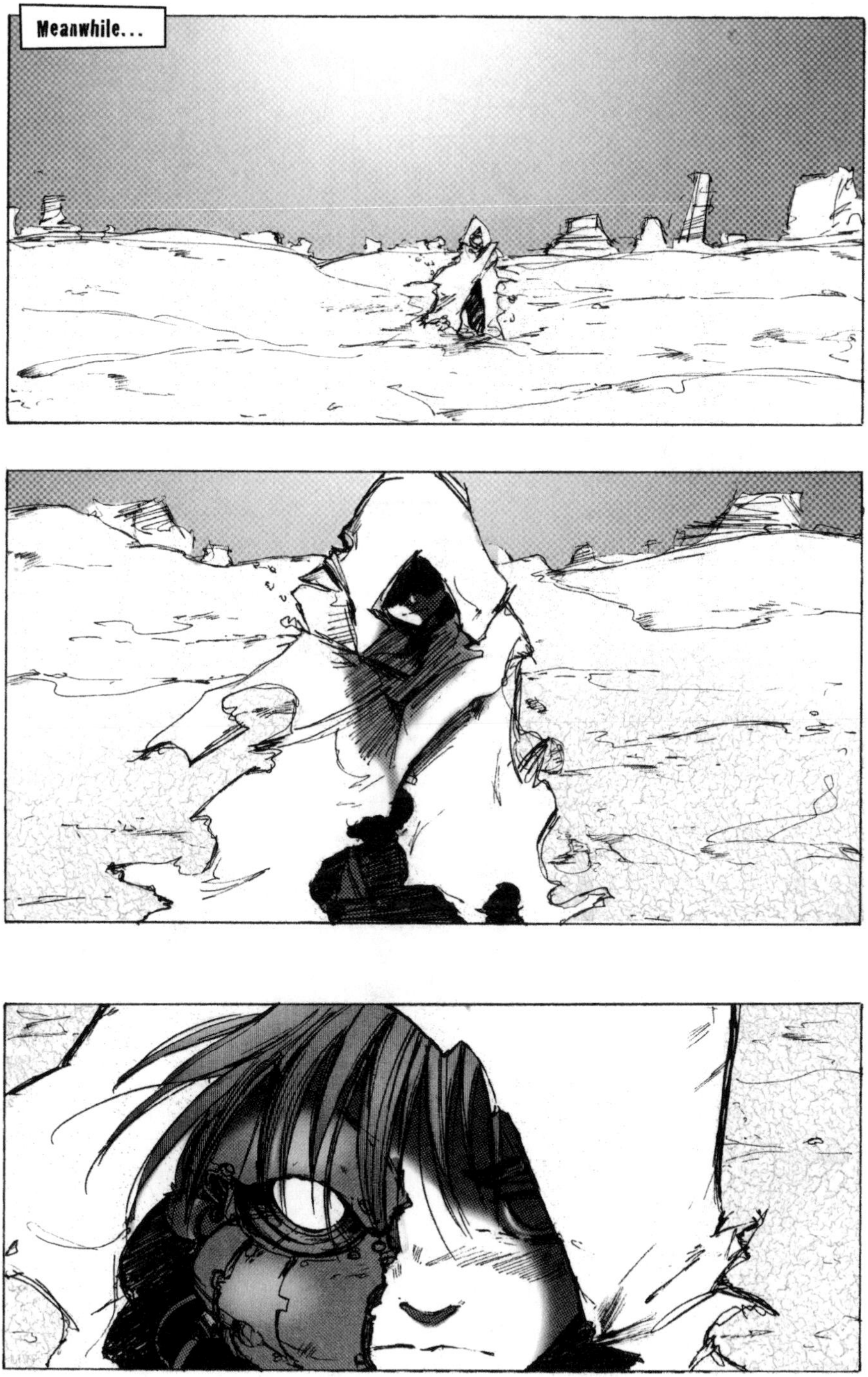
Meanwhile...

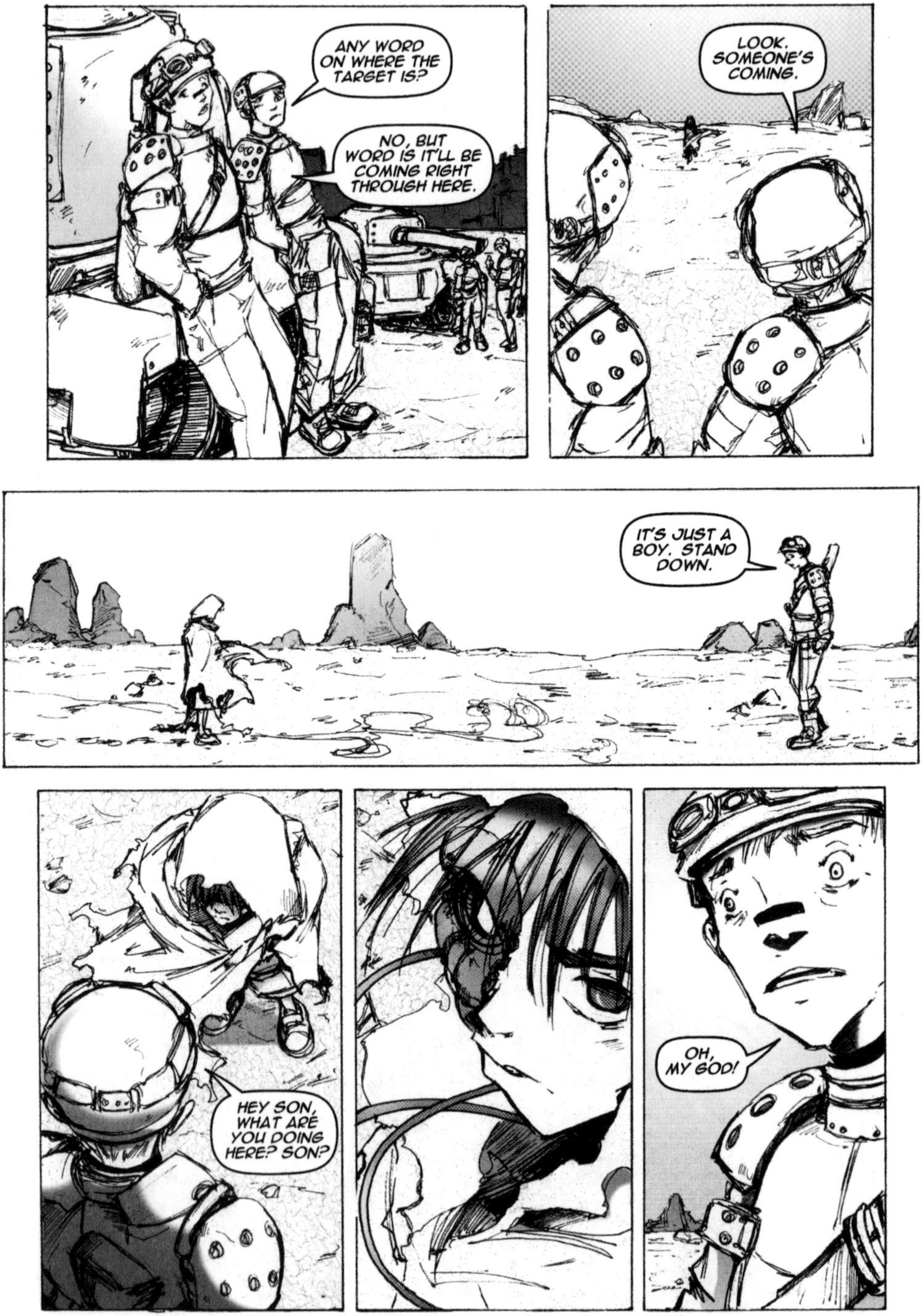
ANY WORD ON WHERE THE TARGET IS?
NO, BUT WORD IS IT'LL BE COMING RIGHT THROUGH HERE.
LOOK. SOMEONE'S COMING.
IT'S JUST A BOY. STAND DOWN.
HEY SON, WHAT ARE YOU DOING HERE? SON?
OH, MY GOD!

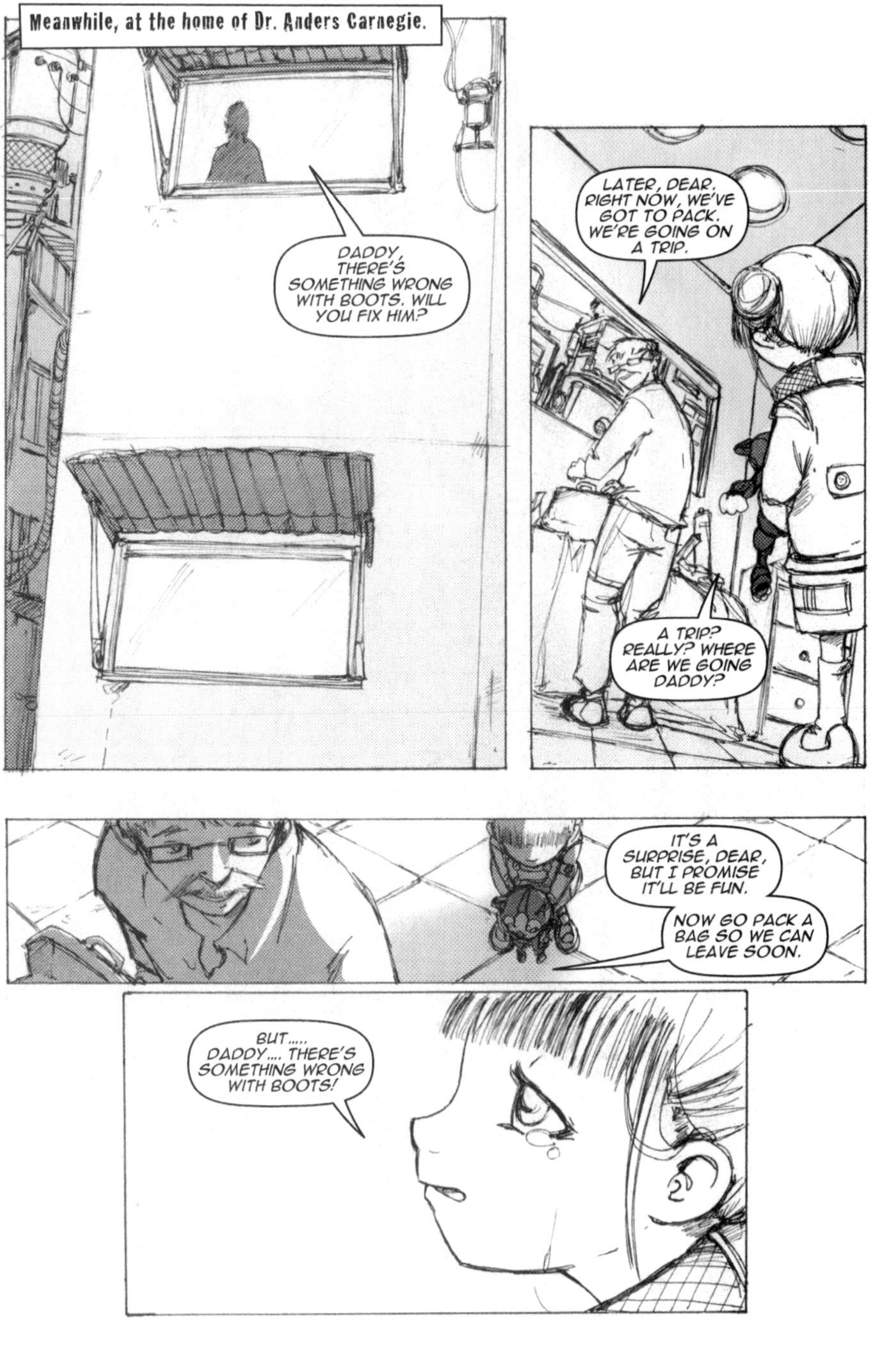
Meanwhile, at the home of Dr. Anders Carnegie.
DADDY, THERE'S SOMETHING WRONG WITH BOOTS. WILL YOU FIX HIM?
LATER, DEAR. RIGHT NOW, WE'VE GOT TO PACK. WE'RE GOING ON A TRIP.
A TRIP? REALLY? WHERE ARE WE GOING DADDY?
IT'S A SURPRISE, DEAR, BUT I PROMISE IT'LL BE FUN.
NOW GO PACK A BAG SO WE CAN LEAVE SOON.
BUT..... DADDY.... THERE'S SOMETHING WRONG WITH BOOTS!

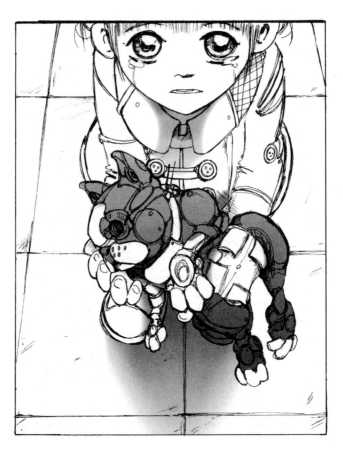

SUCH A CARING GIRL.
I'LL TAKE A LOOK AT
BOOTS RIGHT NOW,
SWEETHEART. THEN
WE HAVE TO GO.

THANK YOU,
DADDY!

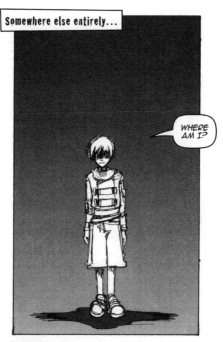

Somewhere else entirely...
WHERE AM I?
WHAT'S HAPPENING? AM I DREAMING?
WHAT IS THAT?

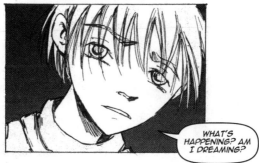

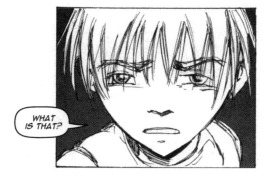

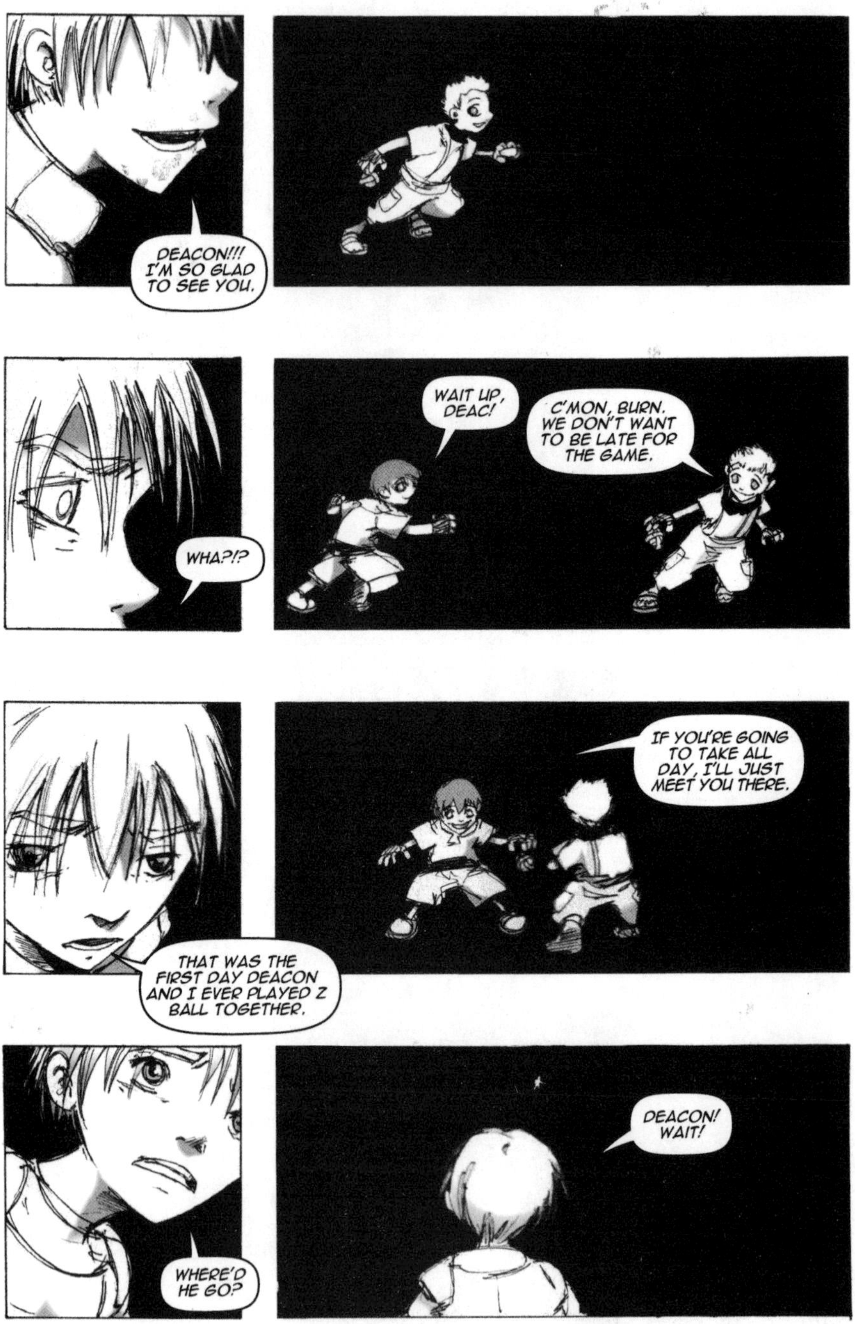
DEACON!!! I'M SO GLAD TO SEE YOU.
WHA?!?
WAIT UP, DEAC!
C'MON, BURN. WE DON'T WANT TO BE LATE FOR THE GAME.
THAT WAS THE FIRST DAY DEACON AND I EVER PLAYED Z BALL TOGETHER.
IF YOU'RE GOING TO TAKE ALL DAY, I'LL JUST MEET YOU THERE.
WHERE'D HE GO?
DEACON! WAIT!

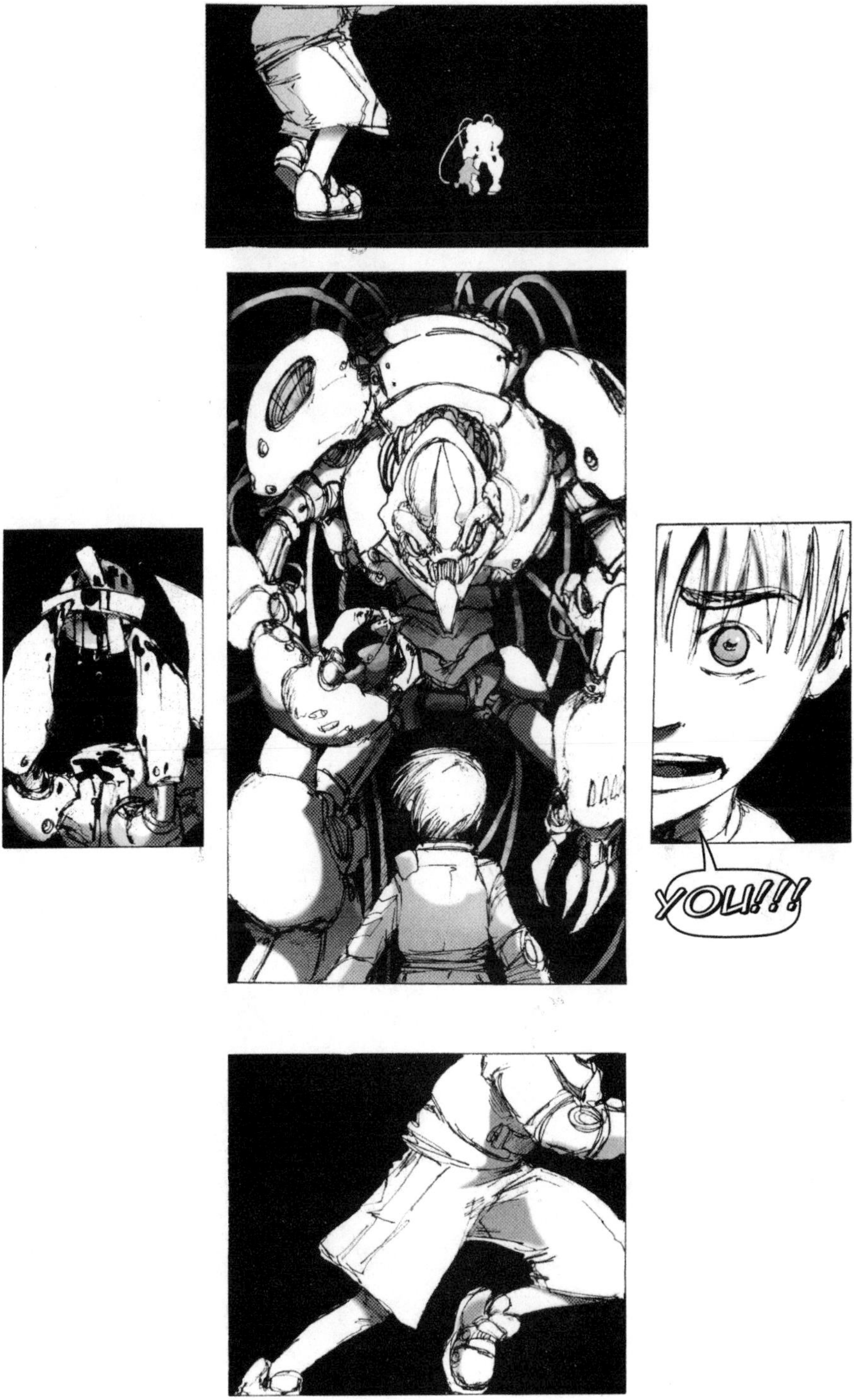
YOU!!!

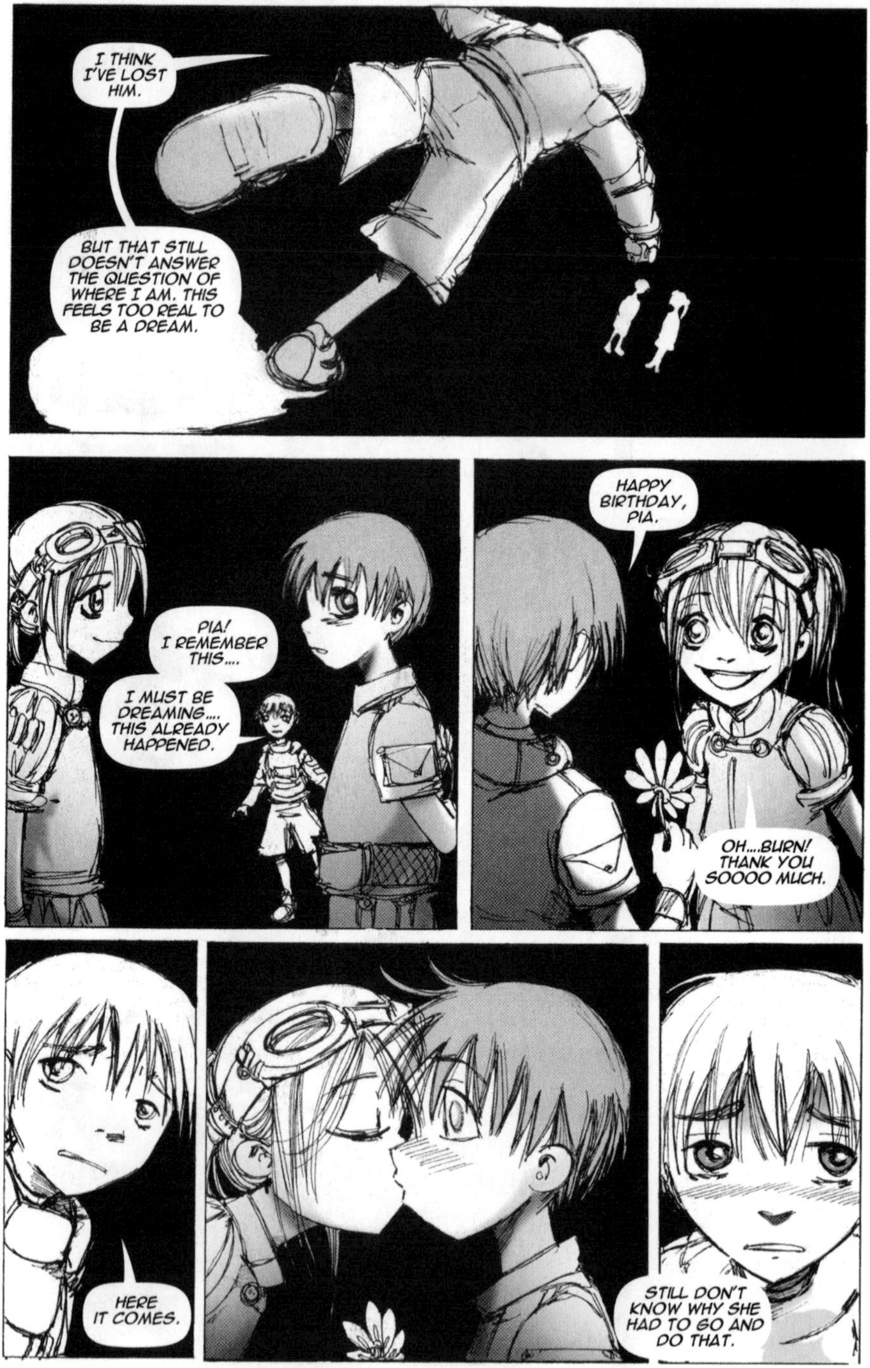
I THINK I'VE LOST HIM.
BUT THAT STILL DOESN'T ANSWER THE QUESTION OF WHERE I AM. THIS FEELS TOO REAL TO BE A DREAM.
PIA! I REMEMBER THIS....
I MUST BE DREAMING.... THIS ALREADY HAPPENED.
HAPPY BIRTHDAY, PIA.
OH....BURN! THANK YOU SOOOO MUCH.
HERE IT COMES.
STILL DON'T KNOW WHY SHE HAD TO GO AND DO THAT.

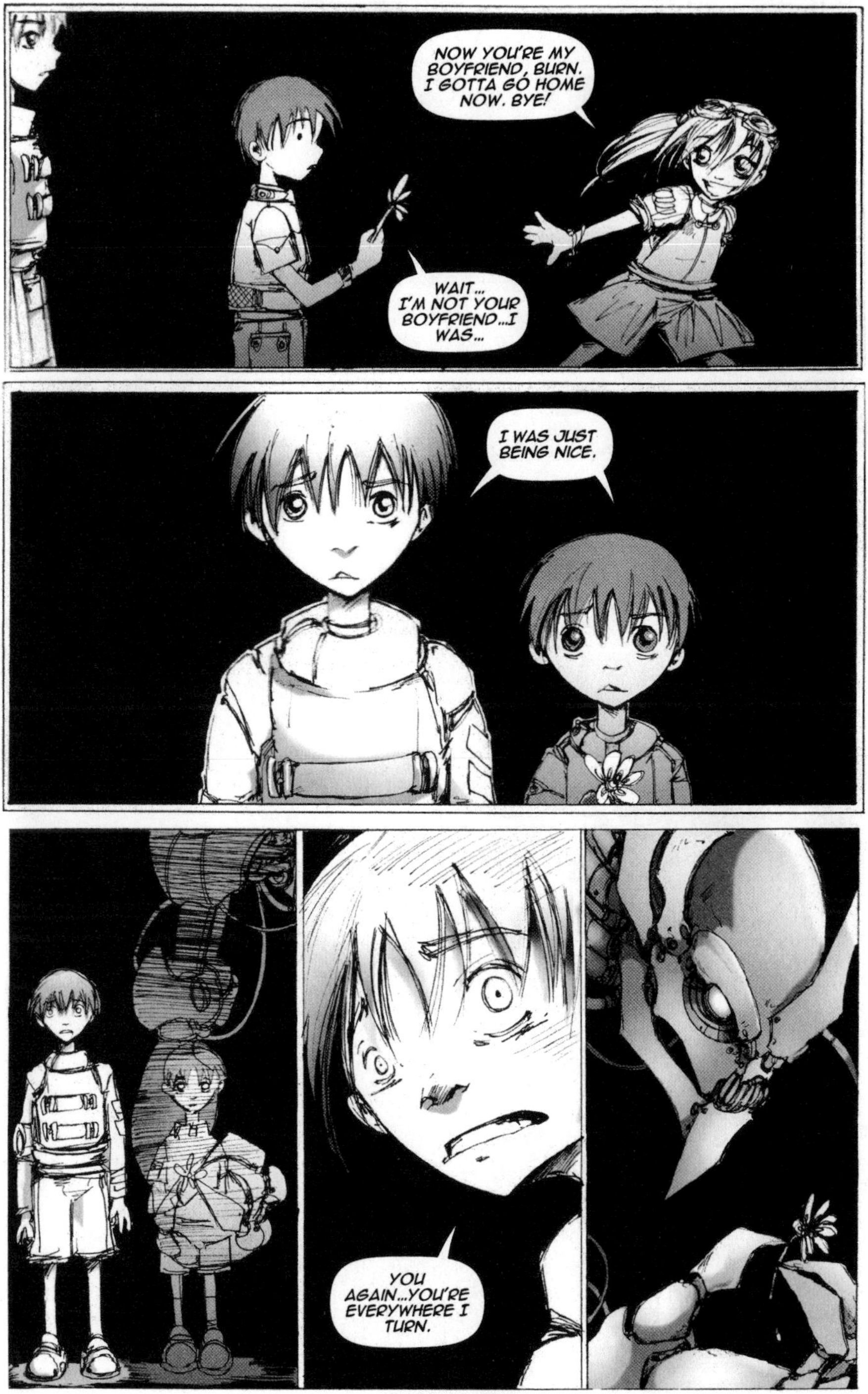
NOW YOU'RE MY BOYFRIEND, BURN. I GOTTA GO HOME NOW. BYE!
WAIT... I'M NOT YOUR BOYFRIEND...I WAS...
I WAS JUST BEING NICE.
YOU AGAIN...YOU'RE EVERYWHERE I TURN.

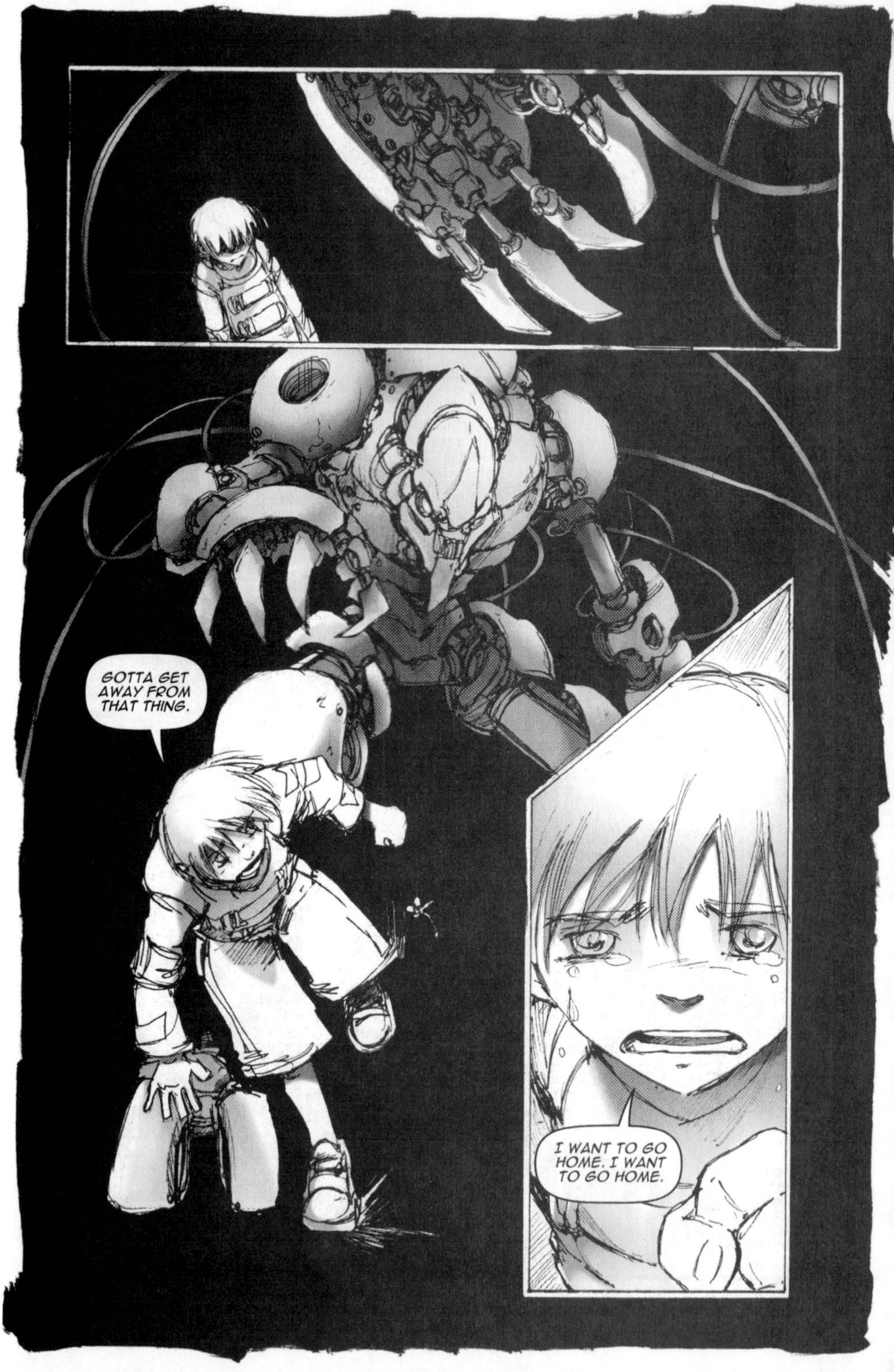
GOTTA GET AWAY FROM THAT THING.
I WANT TO GO HOME. I WANT TO GO HOME.

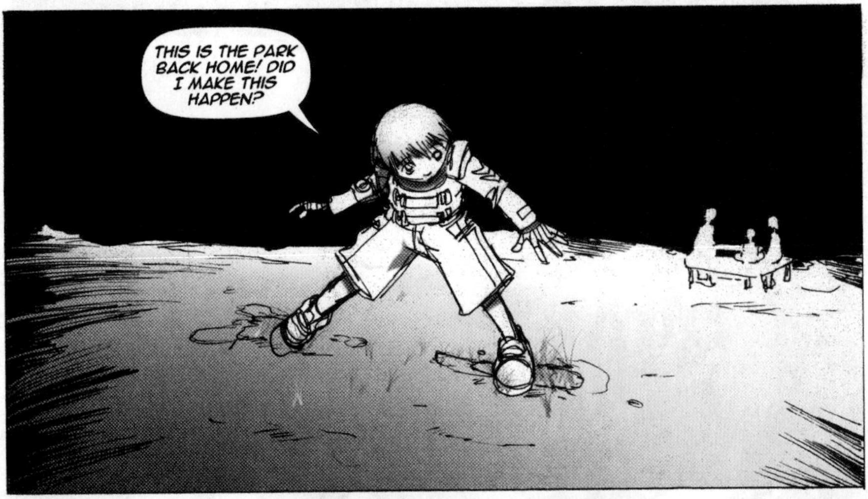
THIS IS THE PARK BACK HOME! DID I MAKE THIS HAPPEN?

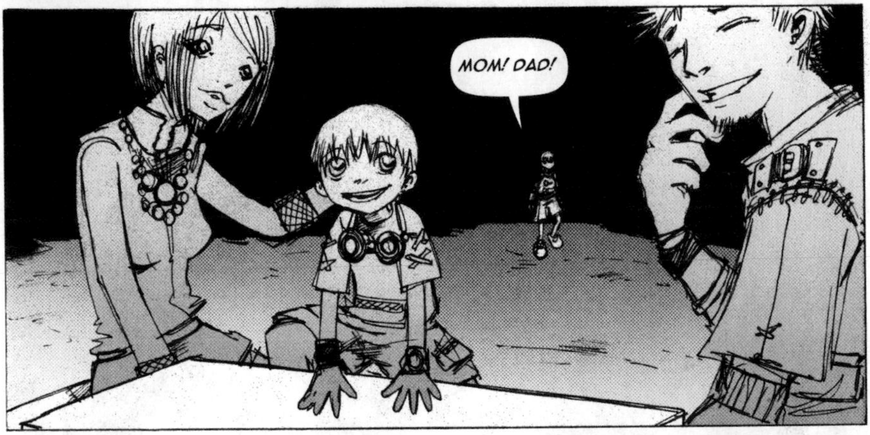
MOM! DAD!

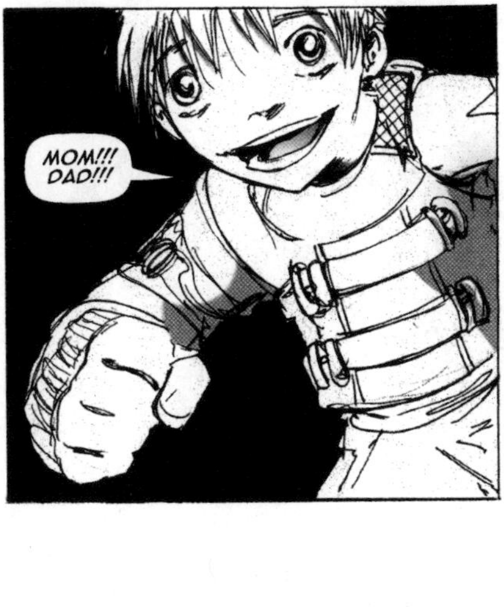
MOM!!! DAD!!!

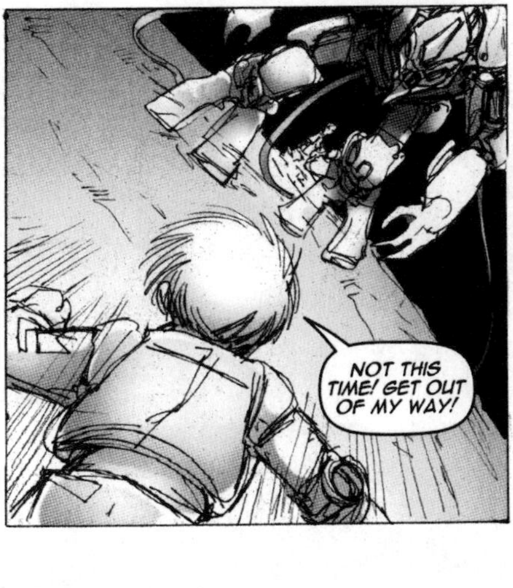
NOT THIS TIME! GET OUT OF MY WAY!

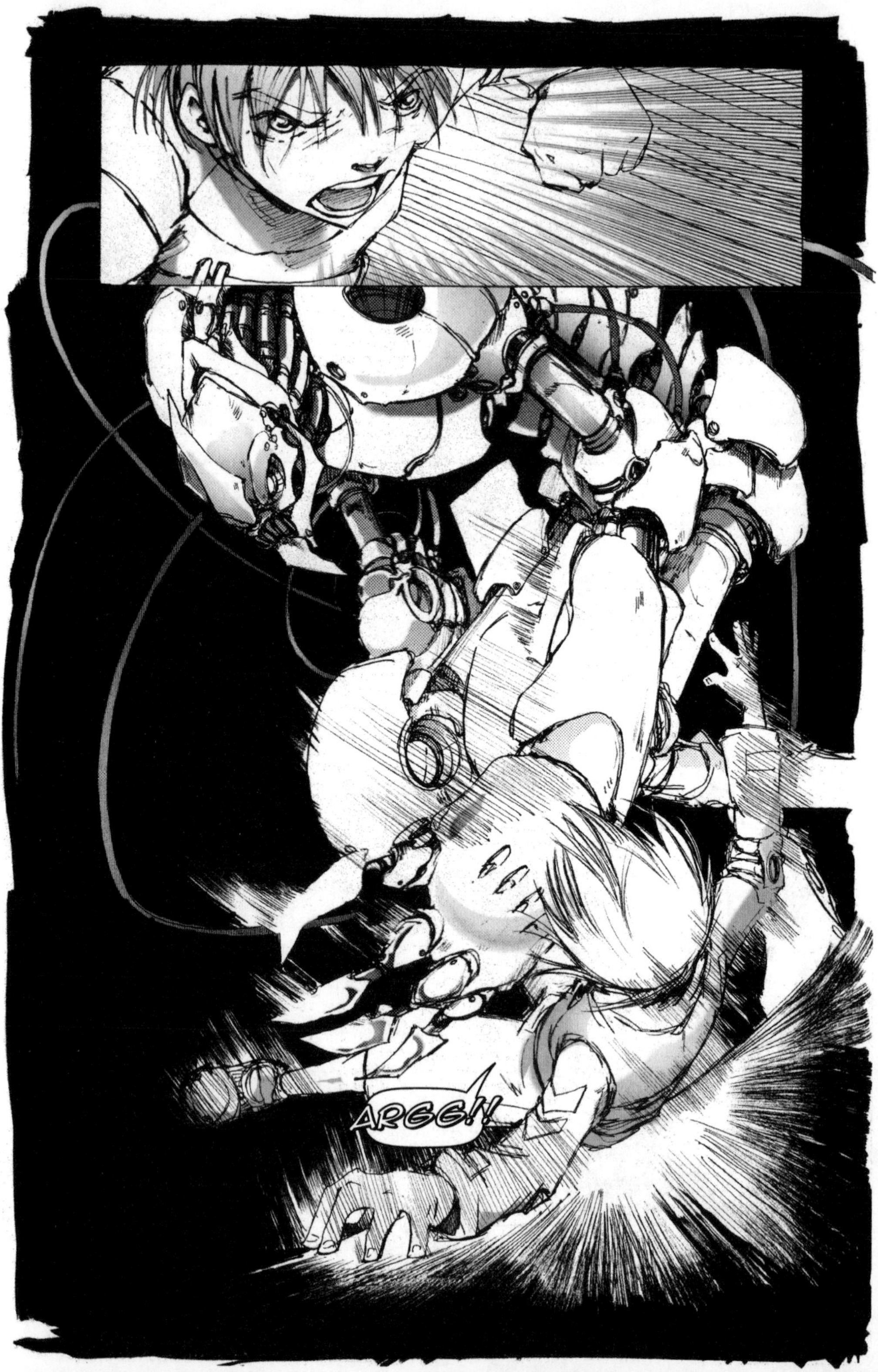
ARGG!!

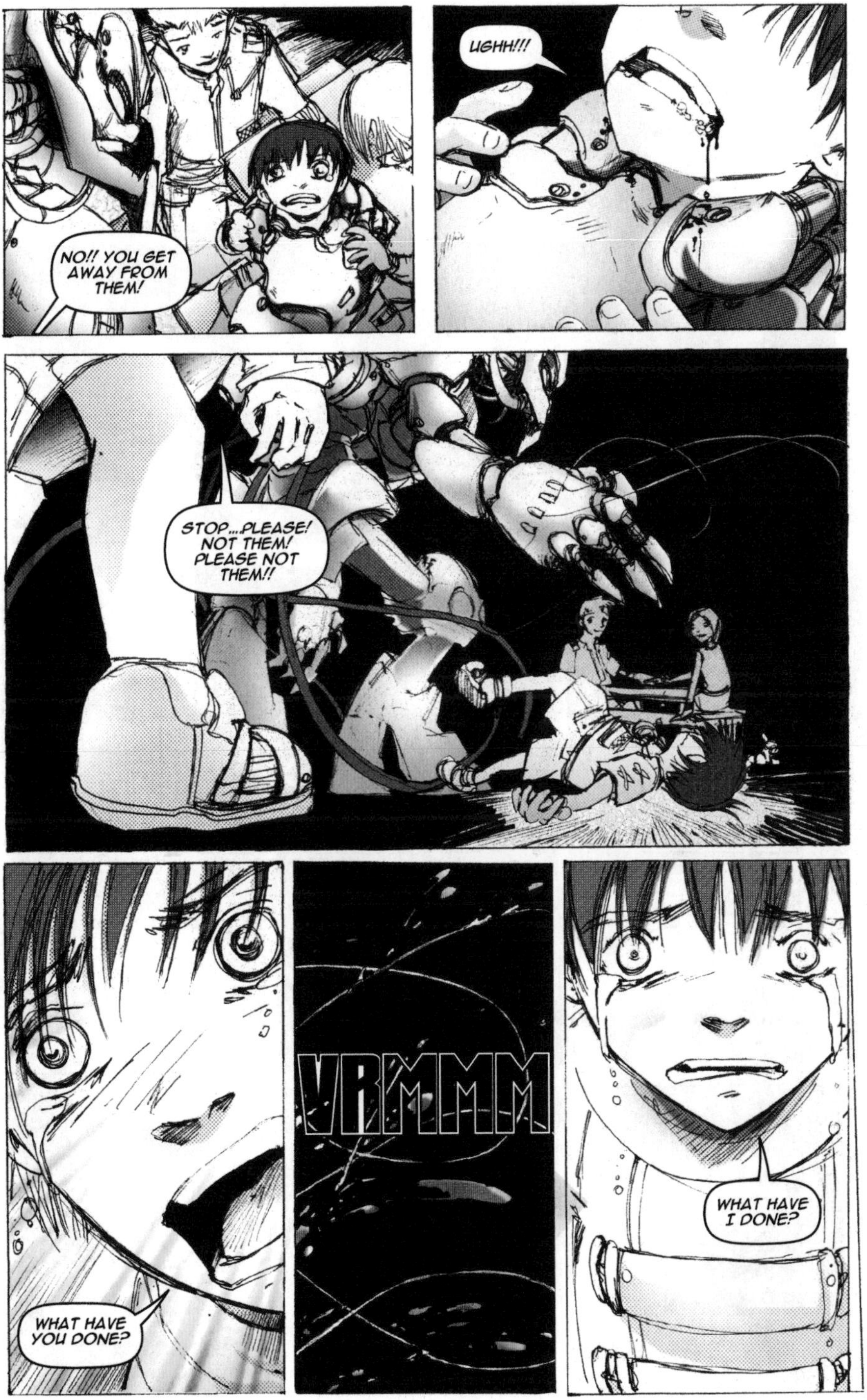
NO!! YOU GET AWAY FROM THEM!
UGHH!!!
STOP...PLEASE! NOT THEM! PLEASE NOT THEM!!
WHAT HAVE YOU DONE?
VRMMM
WHAT HAVE I DONE?

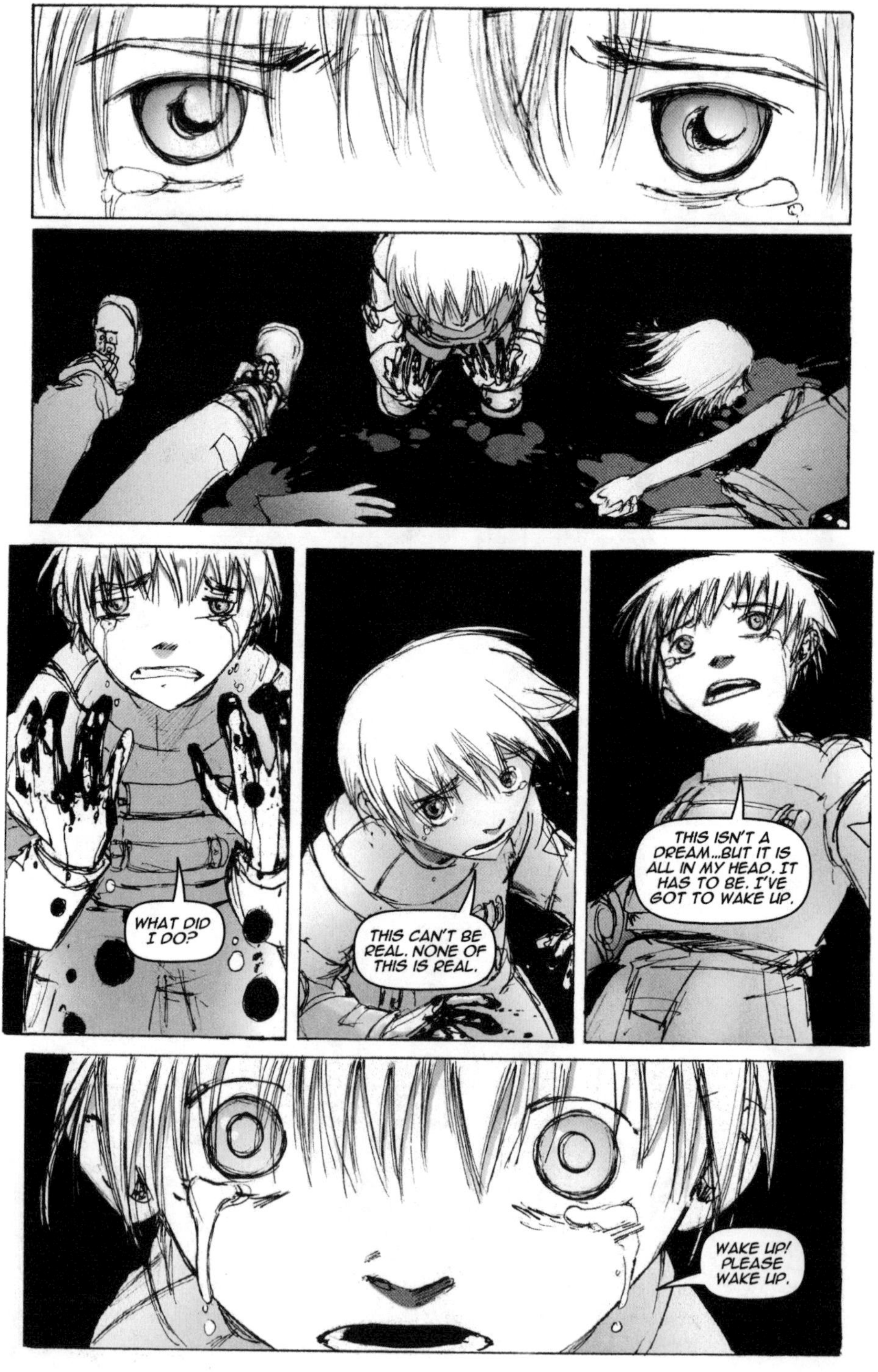
WHAT DID I DO?
THIS CAN'T BE REAL. NONE OF THIS IS REAL.
THIS ISN'T A DREAM...BUT IT IS ALL IN MY HEAD. IT HAS TO BE. I'VE GOT TO WAKE UP.
WAKE UP! PLEASE WAKE UP.

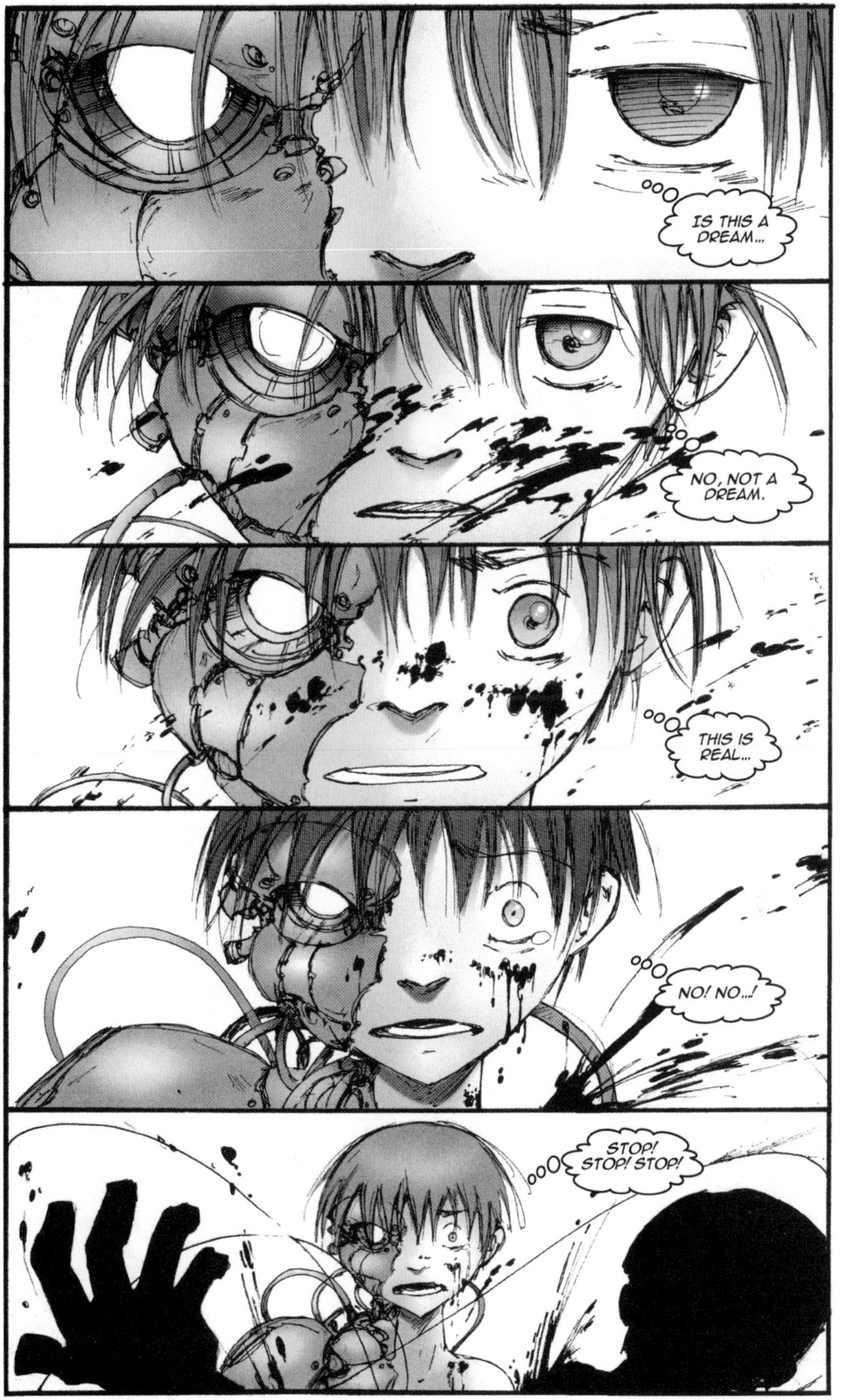
IS THIS A DREAM...
NO, NOT A DREAM.
THIS IS REAL...
NO! NO...!
STOP! STOP! STOP!

And for a moment the killing does stop.

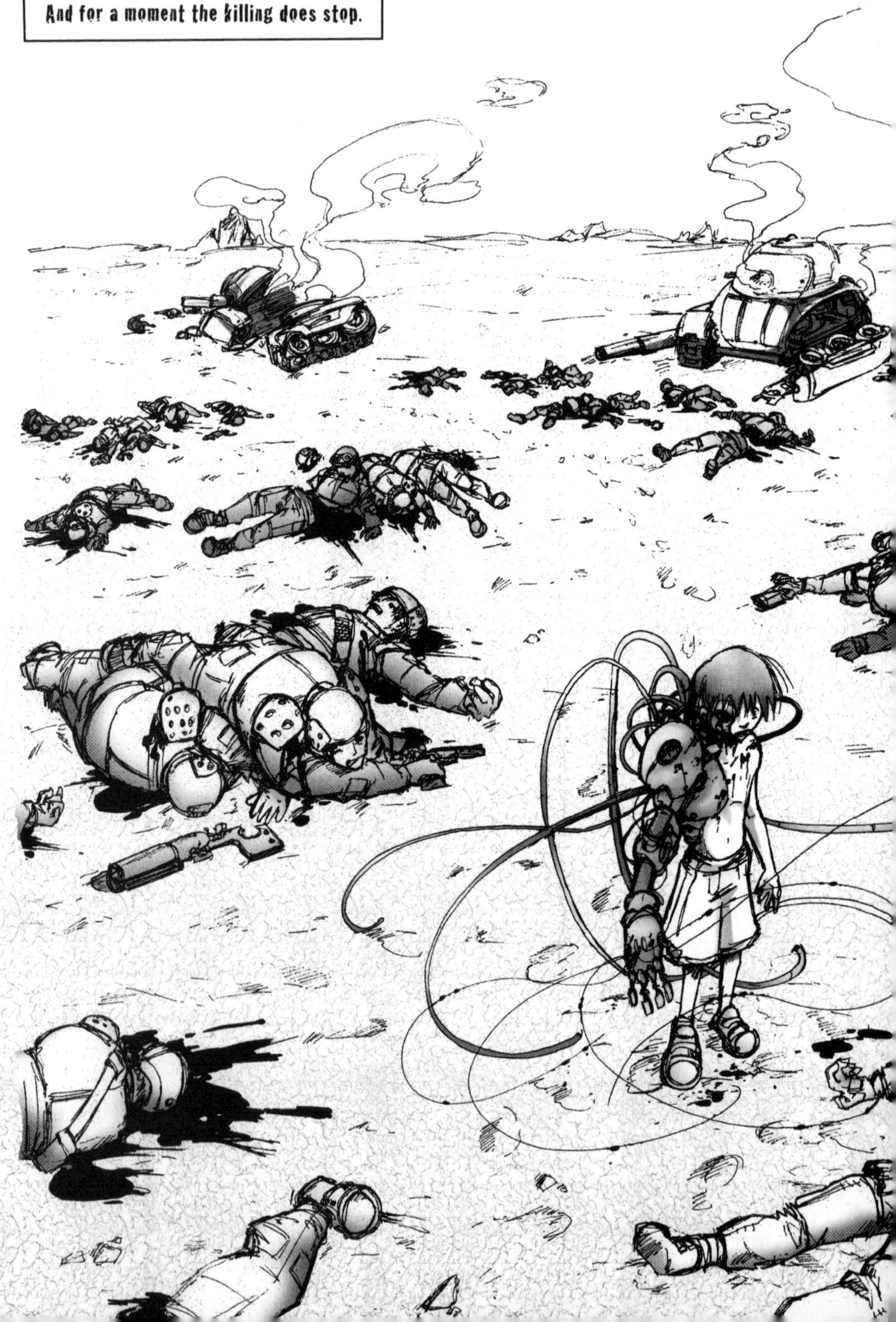

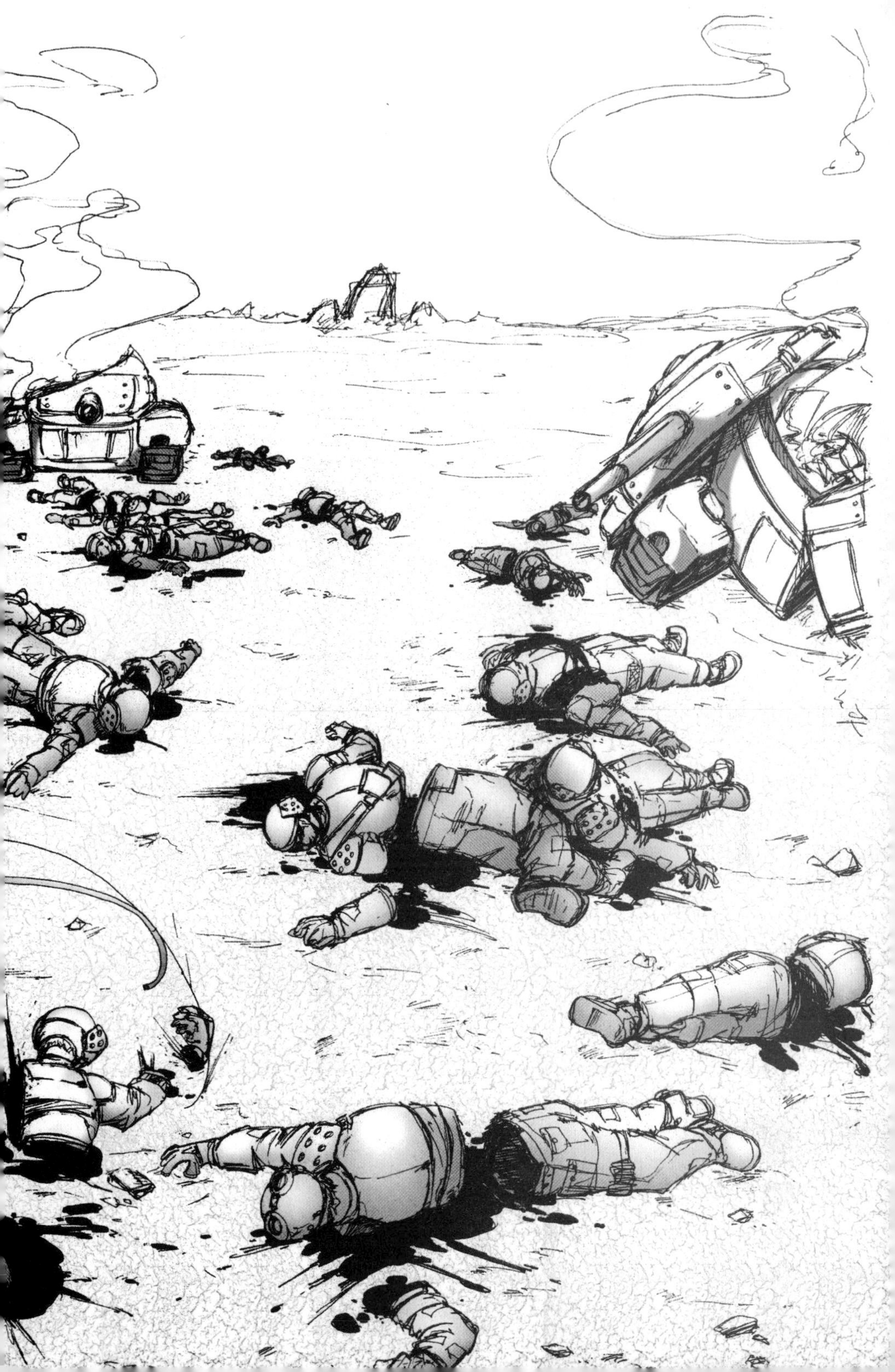

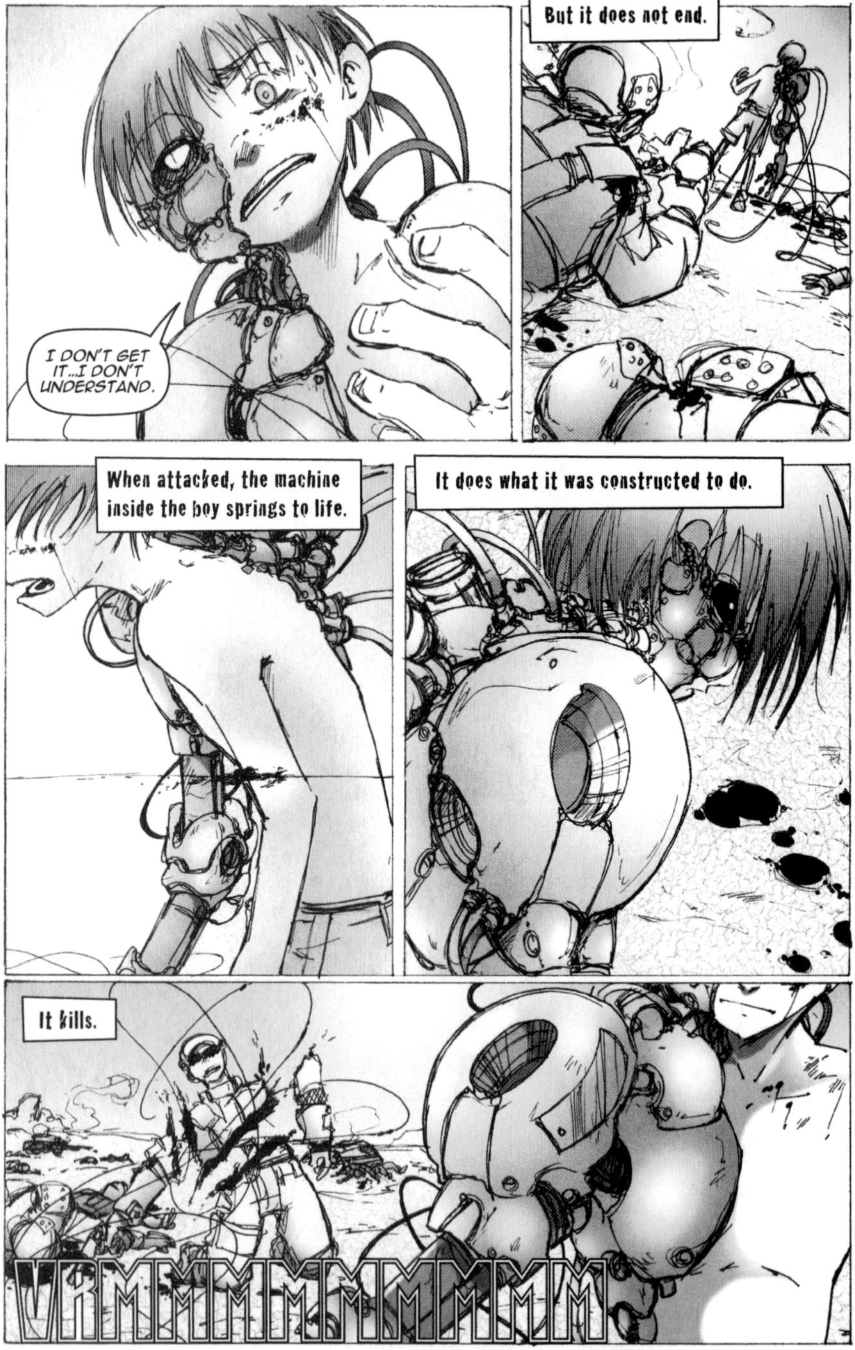
I DON'T GET IT...I DON'T UNDERSTAND.
But it does not end.
When attacked, the machine inside the boy springs to life.
It does what it was constructed to do.
It kills.
VRMMMMMMMMMMM

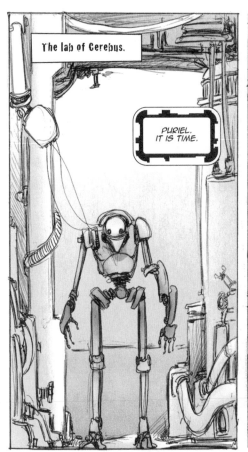

The lab of Cerebus.

PURIEL.
IT IS TIME.

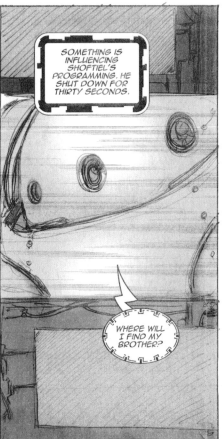

SOMETHING IS INFLUENCING SHOFTIEL'S PROGRAMMING. HE SHUT DOWN FOR THIRTY SECONDS.

WHERE WILL I FIND MY BROTHER?

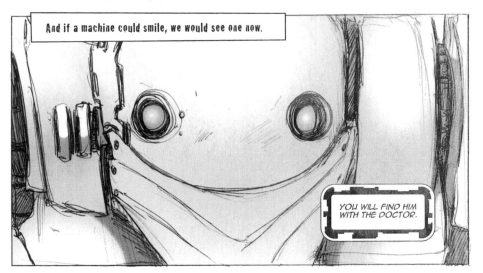

And if a machine could smile, we would see one now.

YOU WILL FIND HIM WITH THE DOCTOR.

The home of Dr. Anders Carnegie.

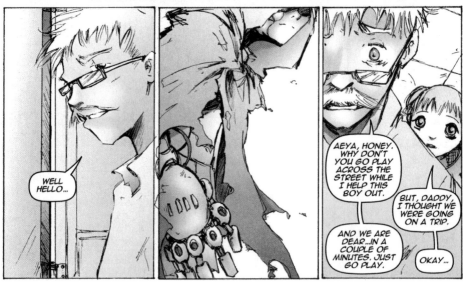

WELL HELLO...

AEYA, HONEY. WHY DON'T YOU GO PLAY ACROSS THE STREET WHILE I HELP THIS BOY OUT.

BUT, DADDY, I THOUGHT WE WERE GOING ON A TRIP.

AND WE ARE DEAR...IN A COUPLE OF MINUTES. JUST GO PLAY.

OKAY...

WHAT IS THIS? WHO ARE YOU...MY GOD WHAT HAVE YOU DONE TO THIS POOR CHILD?
I HAVE COME AT THE BIDDING OF MY FATHER. I HAVE COME TO END YOUR LIFE.
WAIT! YOUR FATHER,CEREBUS, HAS GONE MAD! TOGETHER WE CAN STOP HIM. I'LL BE ABLE TO FIX YOU. FOR GOD SAKE'S PLEASE!
I HAVE NOT BEEN DAMAGED, DOCTOR.
MY DAUGHTER... I DIDN'T GET TO SAY GOODBYE.

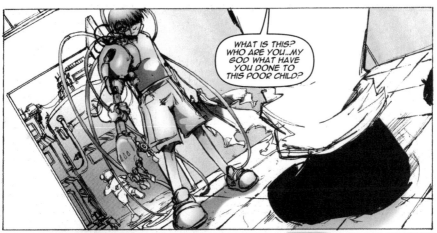

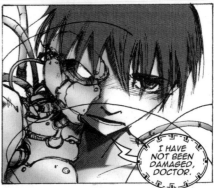

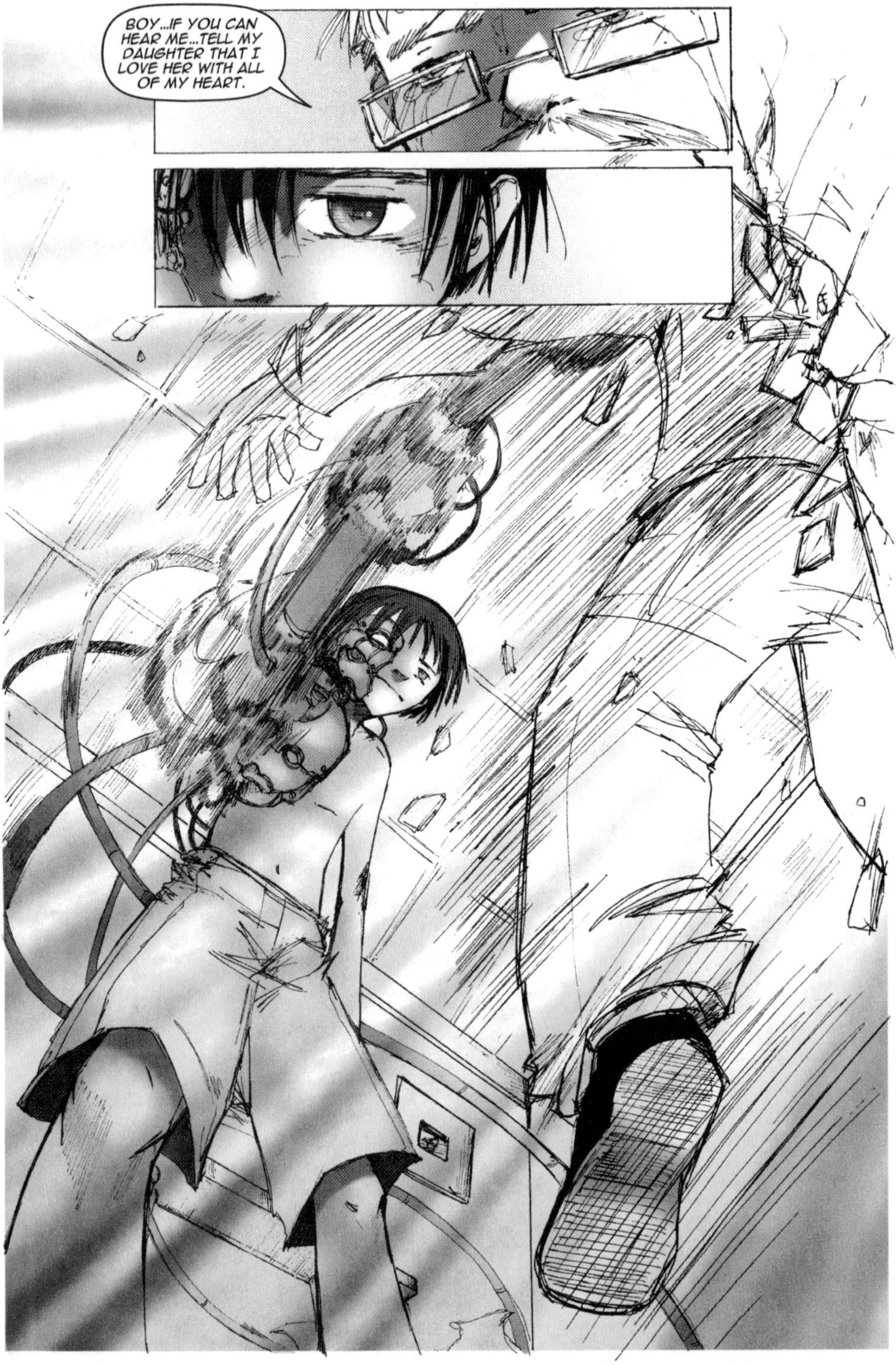
BOY...IF YOU CAN HEAR ME...TELL MY DAUGHTER THAT I LOVE HER WITH ALL OF MY HEART.

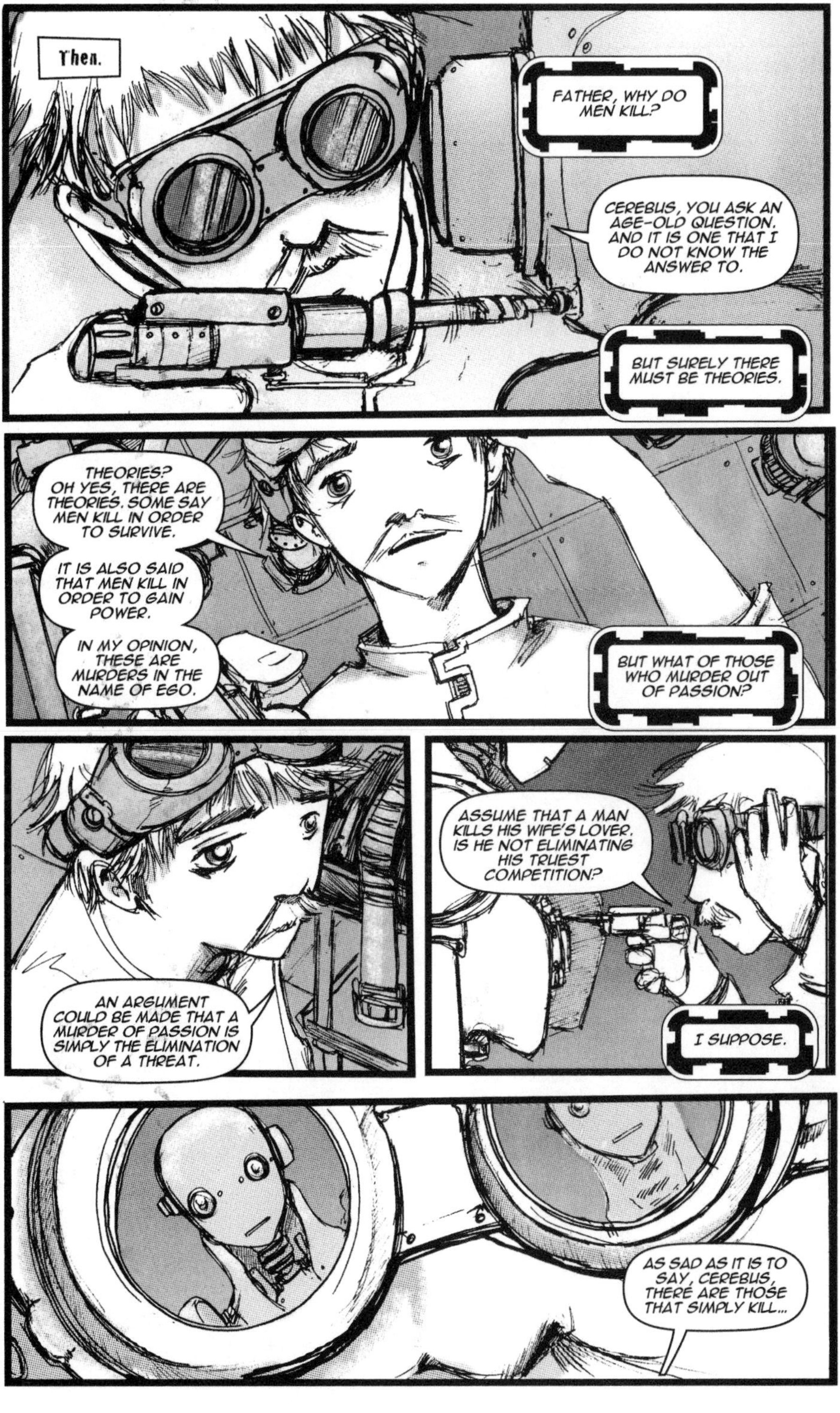
Then.
FATHER, WHY DO MEN KILL?
CEREBUS, YOU ASK AN AGE-OLD QUESTION. AND IT IS ONE THAT I DO NOT KNOW THE ANSWER TO.
BUT SURELY THERE MUST BE THEORIES.
THEORIES? OH YES, THERE ARE THEORIES. SOME SAY MEN KILL IN ORDER TO SURVIVE.
IT IS ALSO SAID THAT MEN KILL IN ORDER TO GAIN POWER.
IN MY OPINION, THESE ARE MURDERS IN THE NAME OF EGO.
BUT WHAT OF THOSE WHO MURDER OUT OF PASSION?
AN ARGUMENT COULD BE MADE THAT A MURDER OF PASSION IS SIMPLY THE ELIMINATION OF A THREAT.
ASSUME THAT A MAN KILLS HIS WIFE'S LOVER. IS HE NOT ELIMINATING HIS TRUEST COMPETITION?
I SUPPOSE.
AS SAD AS IT IS TO SAY, CEREBUS, THERE ARE THOSE THAT SIMPLY KILL...

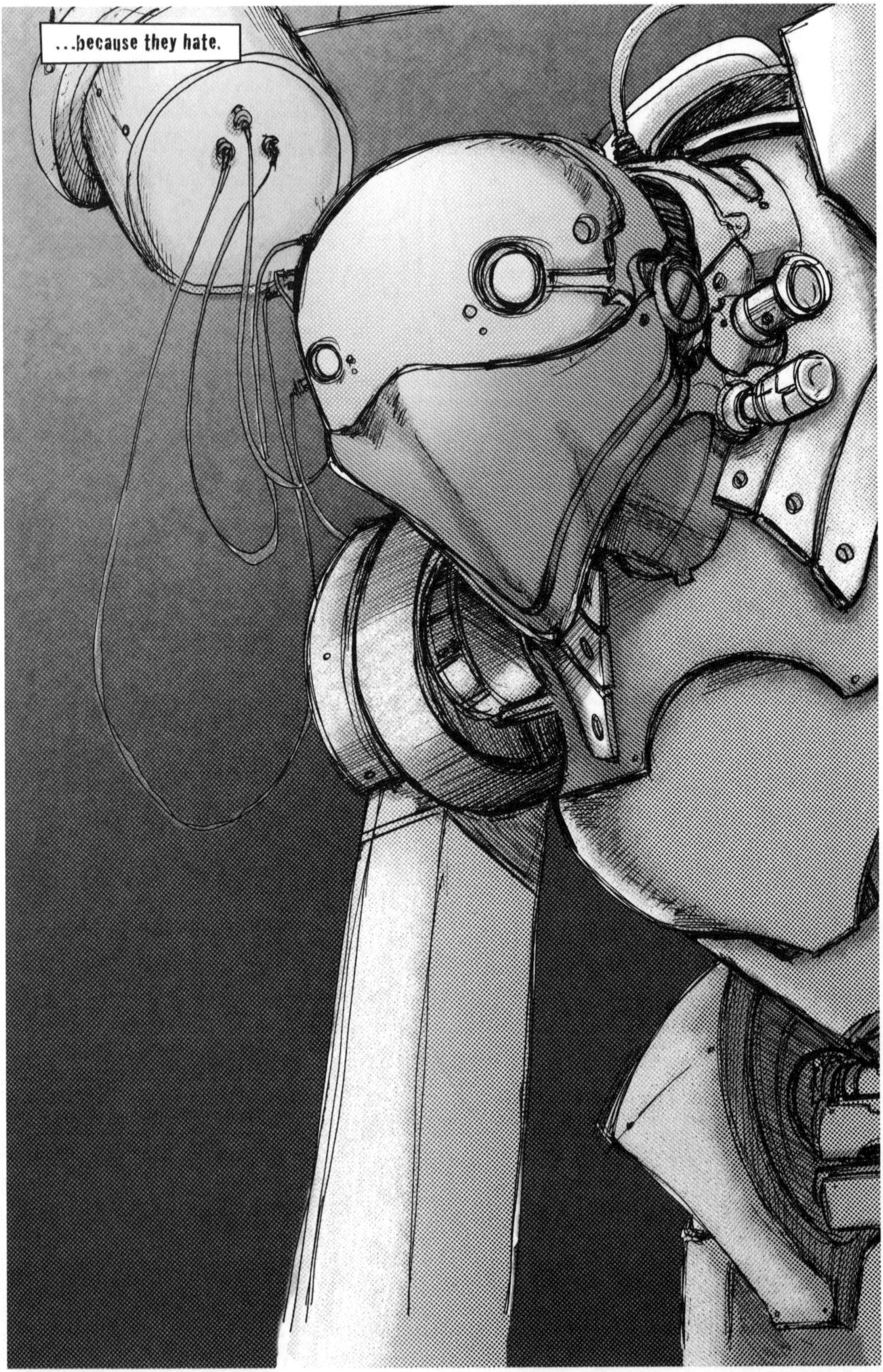
...because they hate.

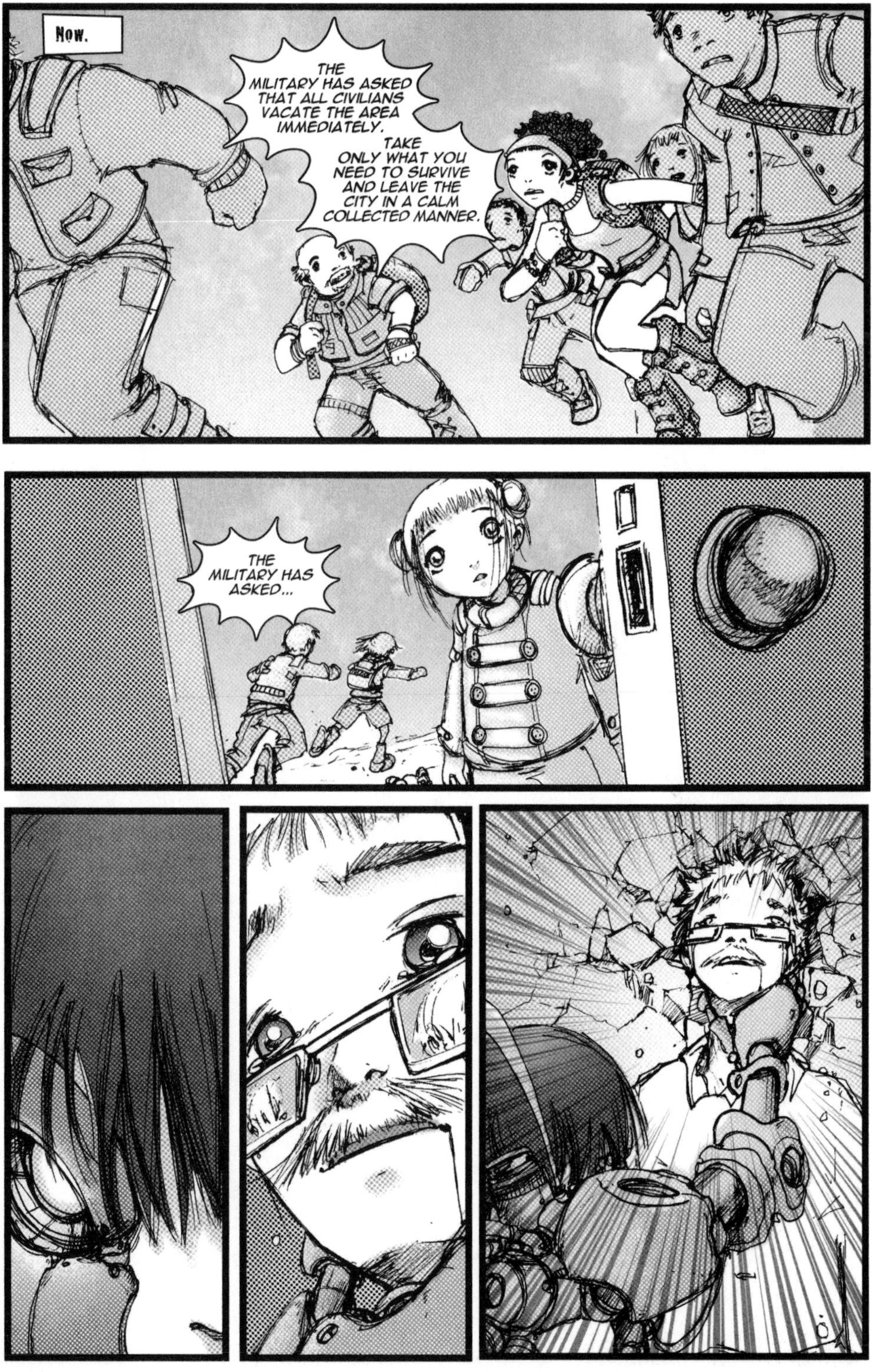
Now.
THE MILITARY HAS ASKED THAT ALL CIVILIANS VACATE THE AREA IMMEDIATELY.
TAKE ONLY WHAT YOU NEED TO SURVIVE AND LEAVE THE CITY IN A CALM COLLECTED MANNER.
THE MILITARY HAS ASKED...

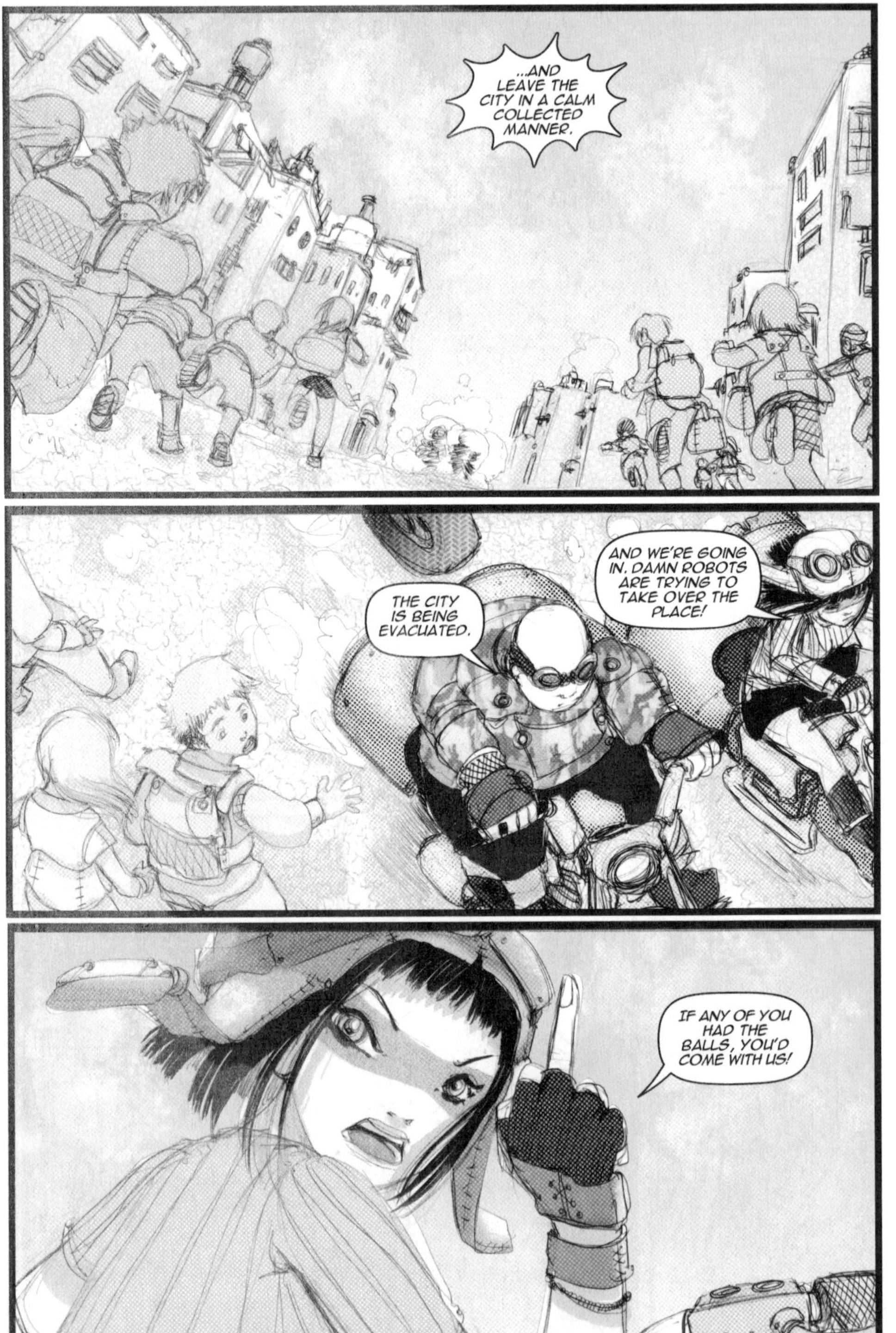
...AND LEAVE THE CITY IN A CALM COLLECTED MANNER.
THE CITY IS BEING EVACUATED.
AND WE'RE GOING IN. DAMN ROBOTS ARE TRYING TO TAKE OVER THE PLACE!
IF ANY OF YOU HAD THE BALLS, YOU'D COME WITH US!

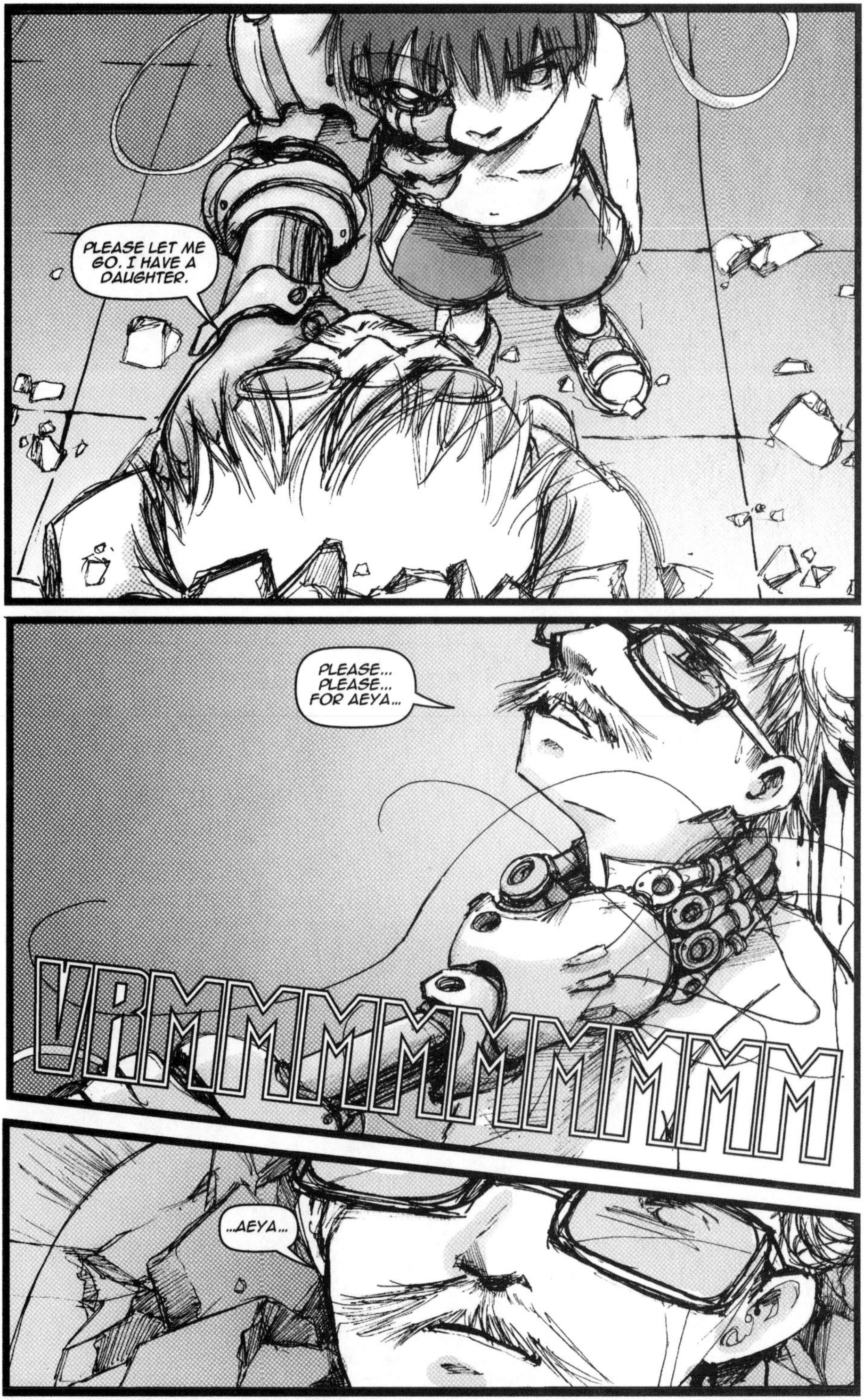
PLEASE LET ME GO. I HAVE A DAUGHTER.
PLEASE... PLEASE... FOR AEYA...
VRMMMMMMMMMMM
...AEYA...

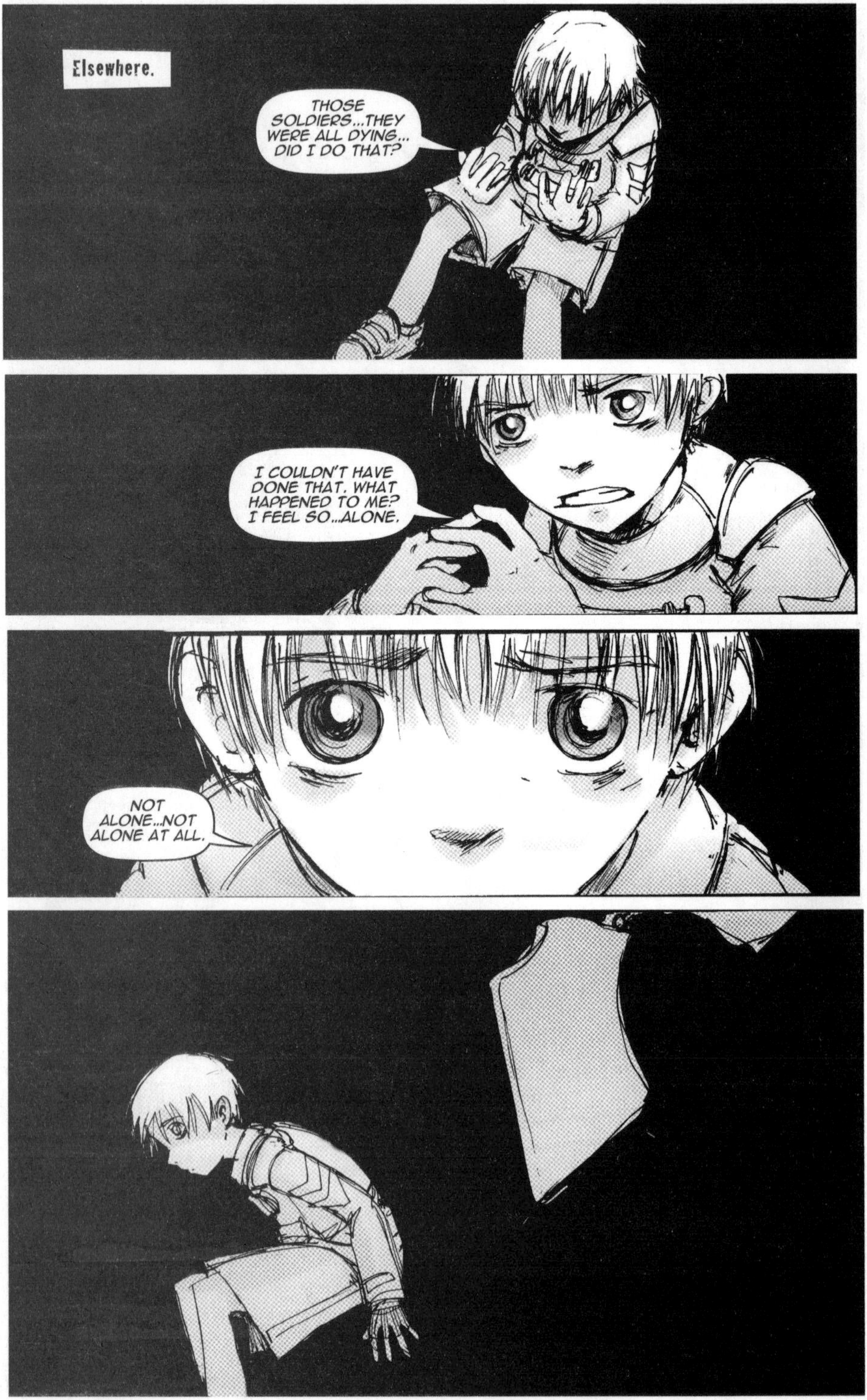
Elsewhere.
THOSE SOLDIERS...THEY WERE ALL DYING... DID I DO THAT?
I COULDN'T HAVE DONE THAT. WHAT HAPPENED TO ME? I FEEL SO...ALONE.
NOT ALONE...NOT ALONE AT ALL.

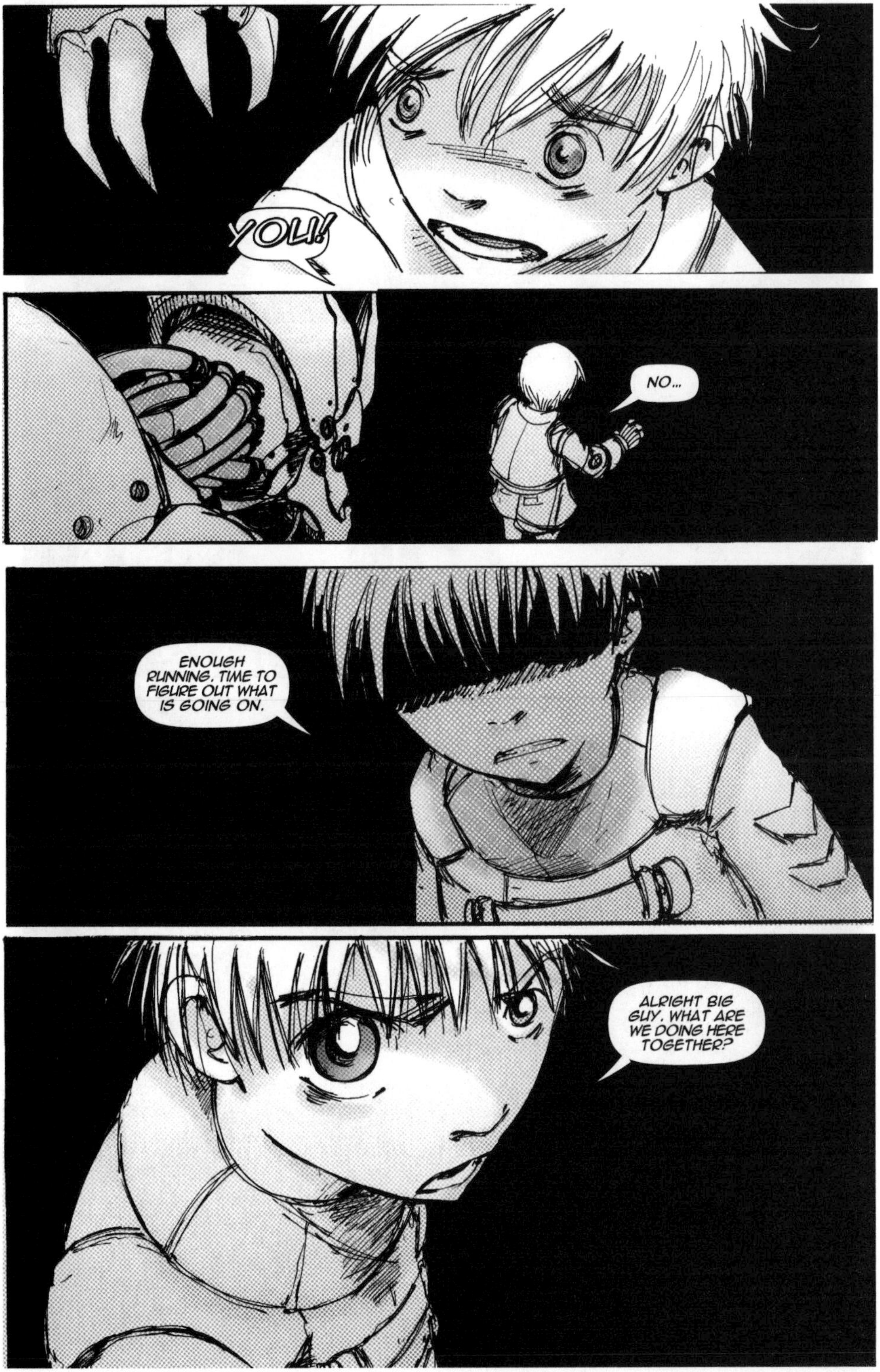
YOLI!
NO...
ENOUGH RUNNING. TIME TO FIGURE OUT WHAT IS GOING ON.
ALRIGHT BIG GUY. WHAT ARE WE DOING HERE TOGETHER?

I NEED TO KNOW WHAT HAPPENED. DO YOU KNOW?
YOU'VE GOT TO KNOW. ANSWER ME!
TALK DAMN IT!
WHAT ARE YOU DOING?
LET GO OF ME!
UNWANTED FOREIGN OBJECT DETECTED.
NO POSSIBLE COURSE OF ACTION IMMEDIATELY AVAILABLE.

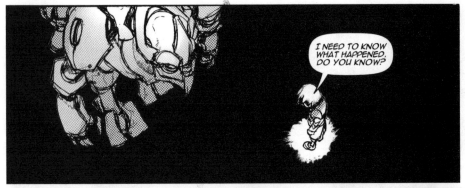

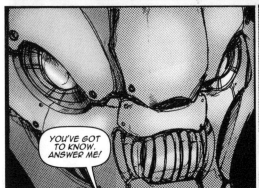

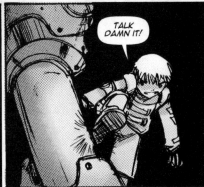

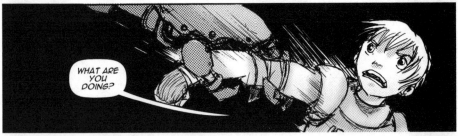

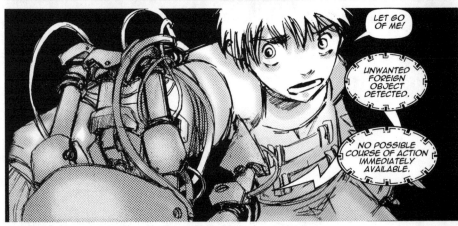

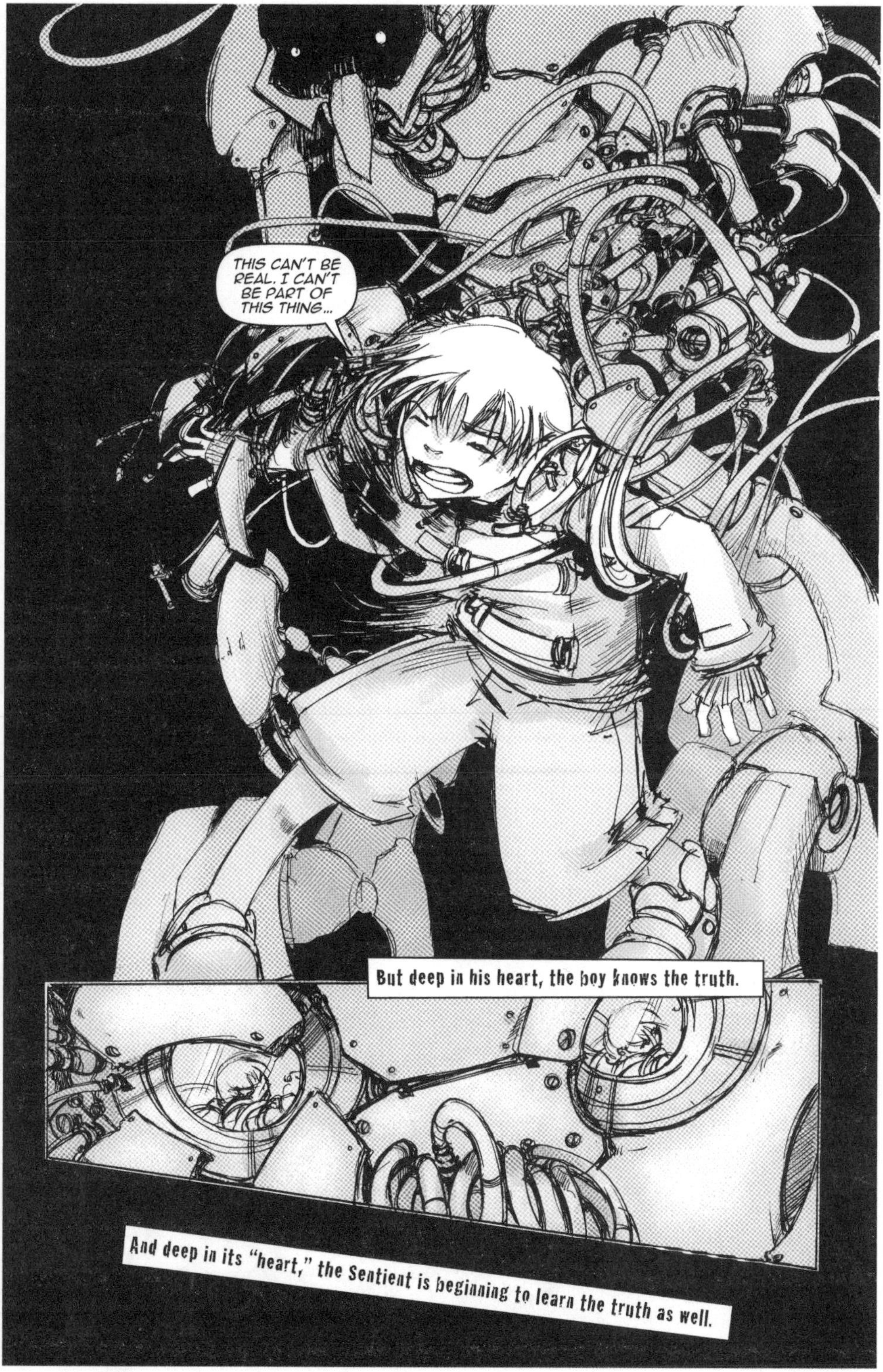
THIS CAN'T BE REAL. I CAN'T BE PART OF THIS THING...
But deep in his heart, the boy knows the truth.
And deep in its "heart," the Sentient is beginning to learn the truth as well.

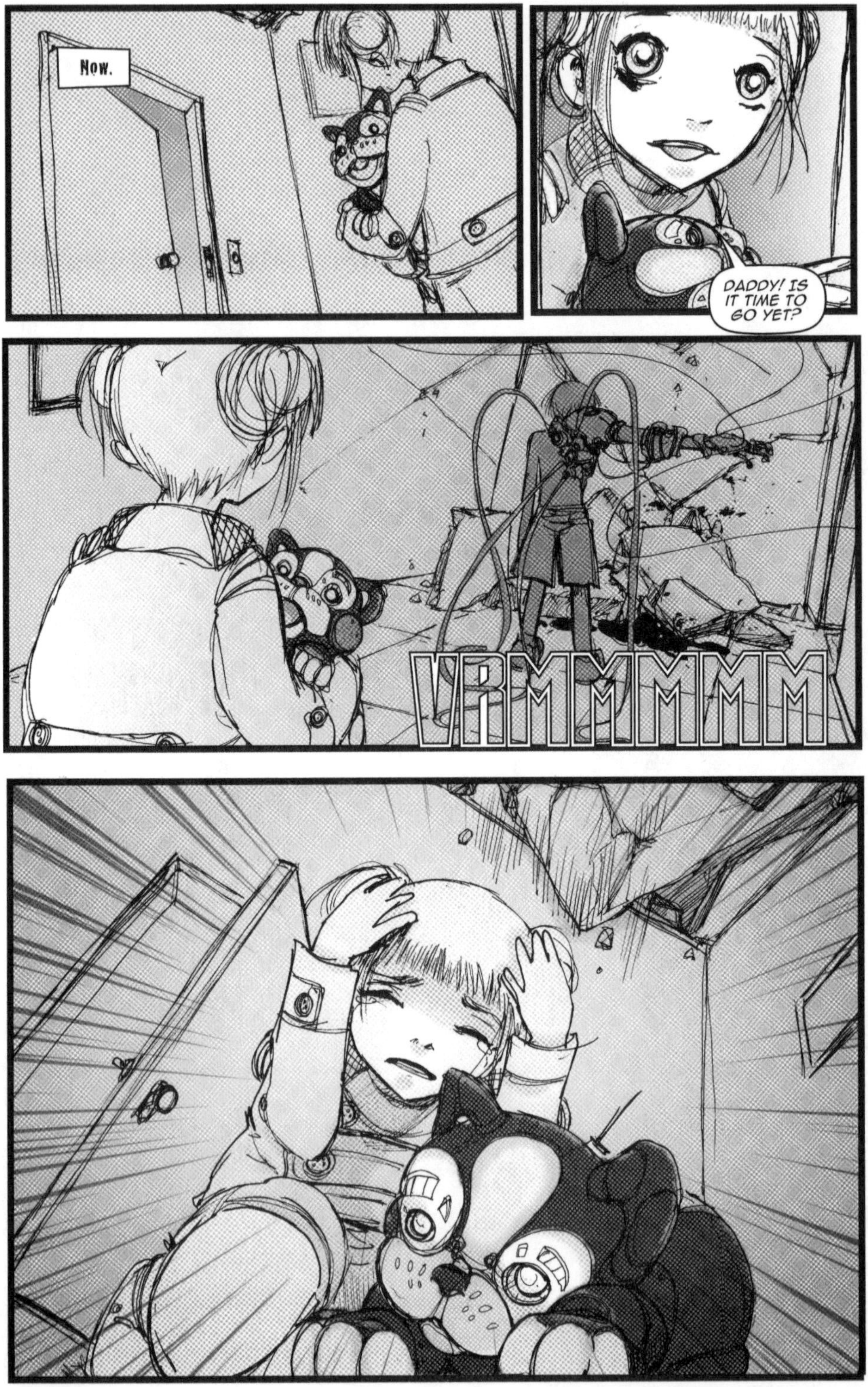
Now.
DADDY! IS IT TIME TO GO YET?
VRMMMMMM

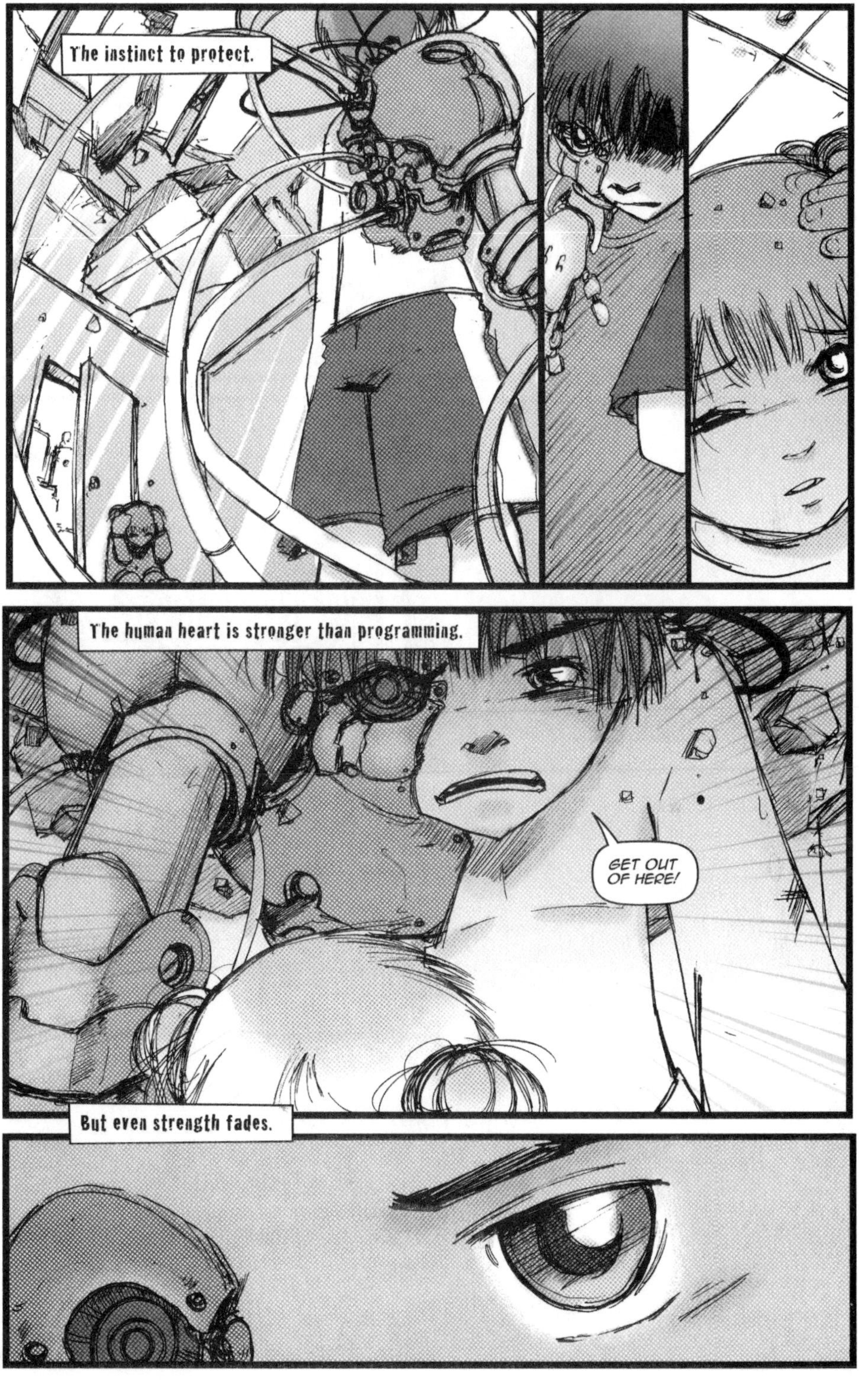
The instinct to protect.
The human heart is stronger than programming.
GET OUT OF HERE!
But even strength fades.

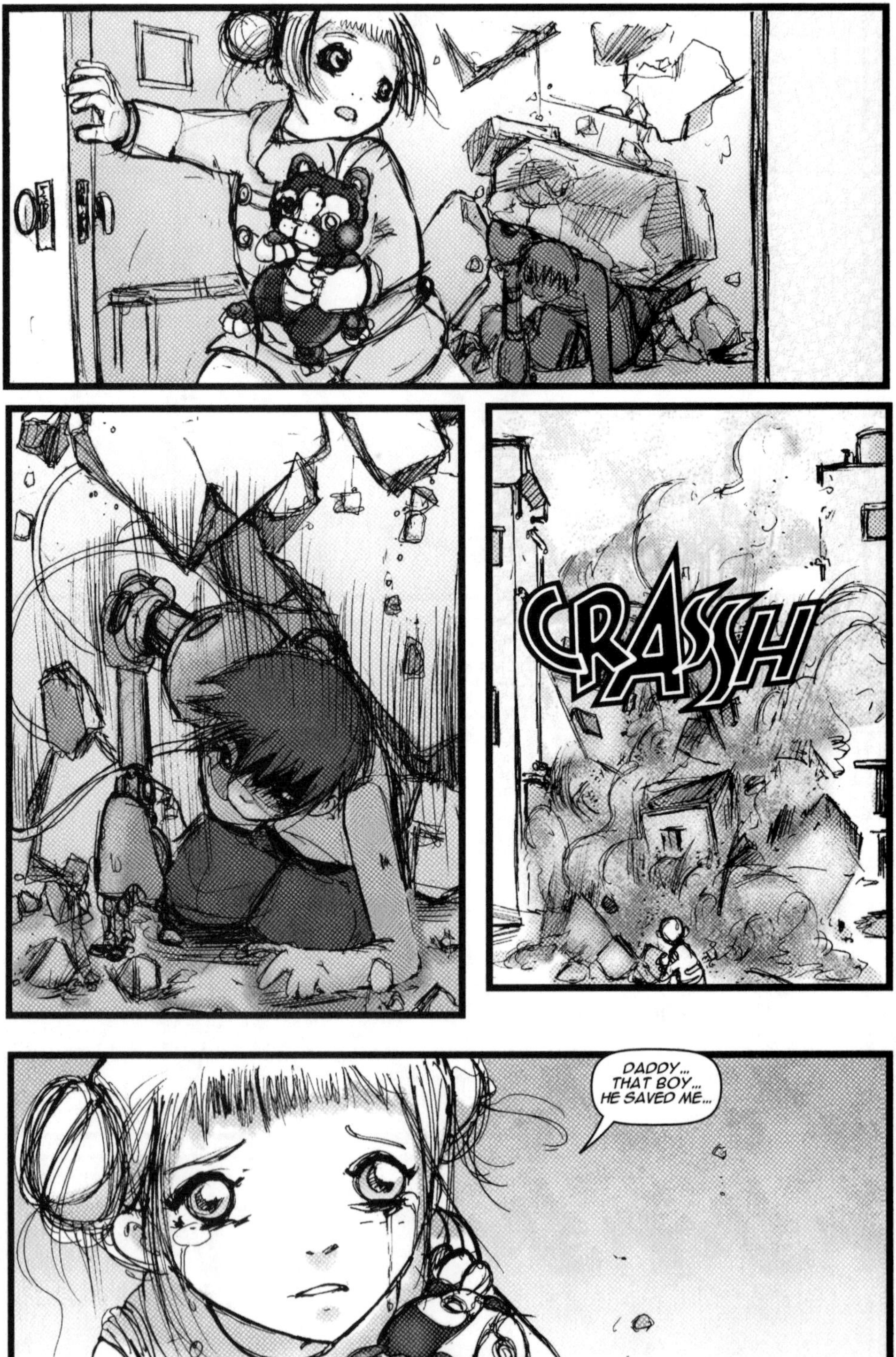
CRASSH
DADDY... THAT BOY... HE SAVED ME...

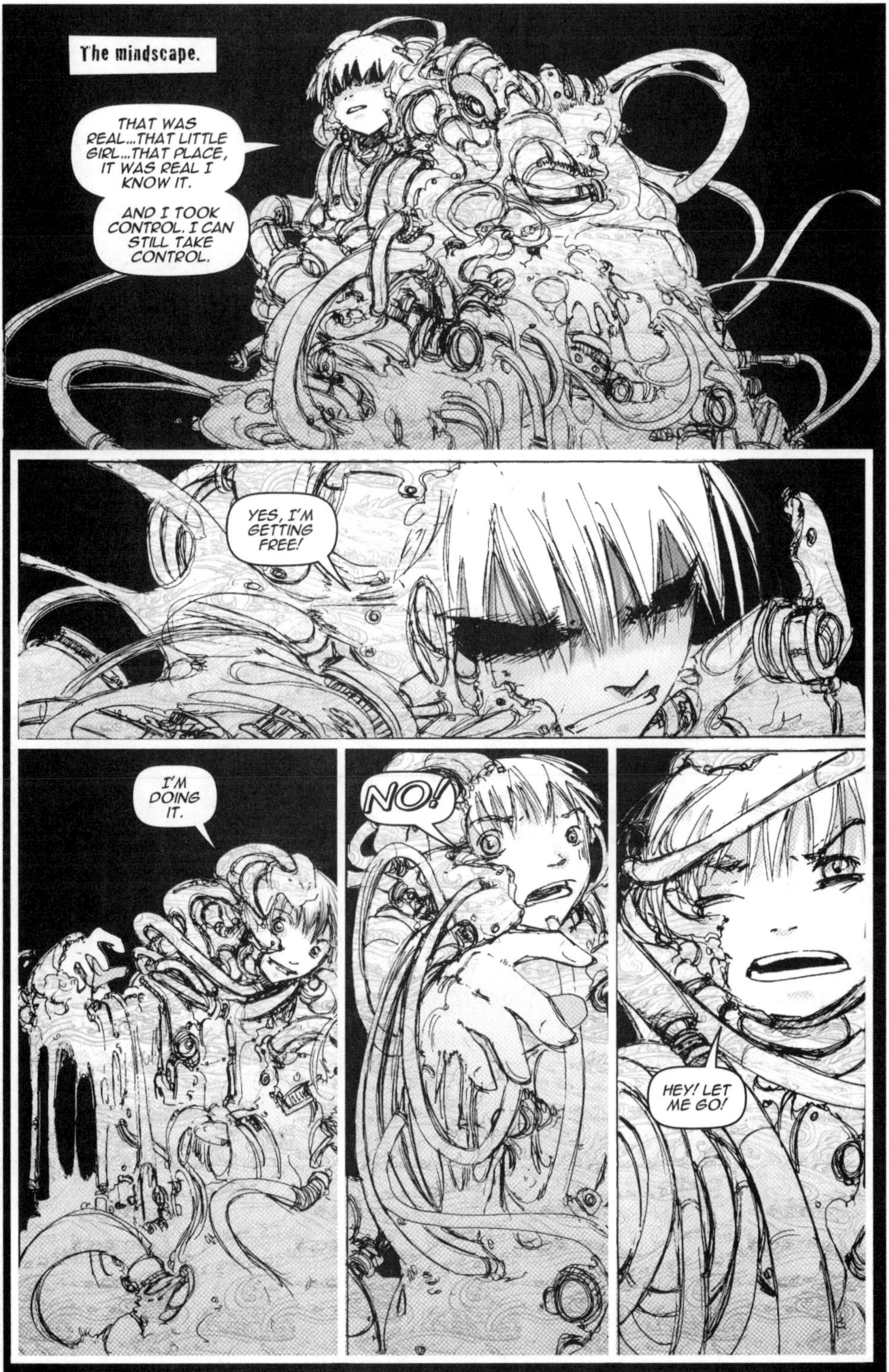
The mindscape.
THAT WAS REAL...THAT LITTLE GIRL...THAT PLACE, IT WAS REAL I KNOW IT.
AND I TOOK CONTROL. I CAN STILL TAKE CONTROL.
YES, I'M GETTING FREE!
I'M DOING IT.
NO!
HEY! LET ME GO!

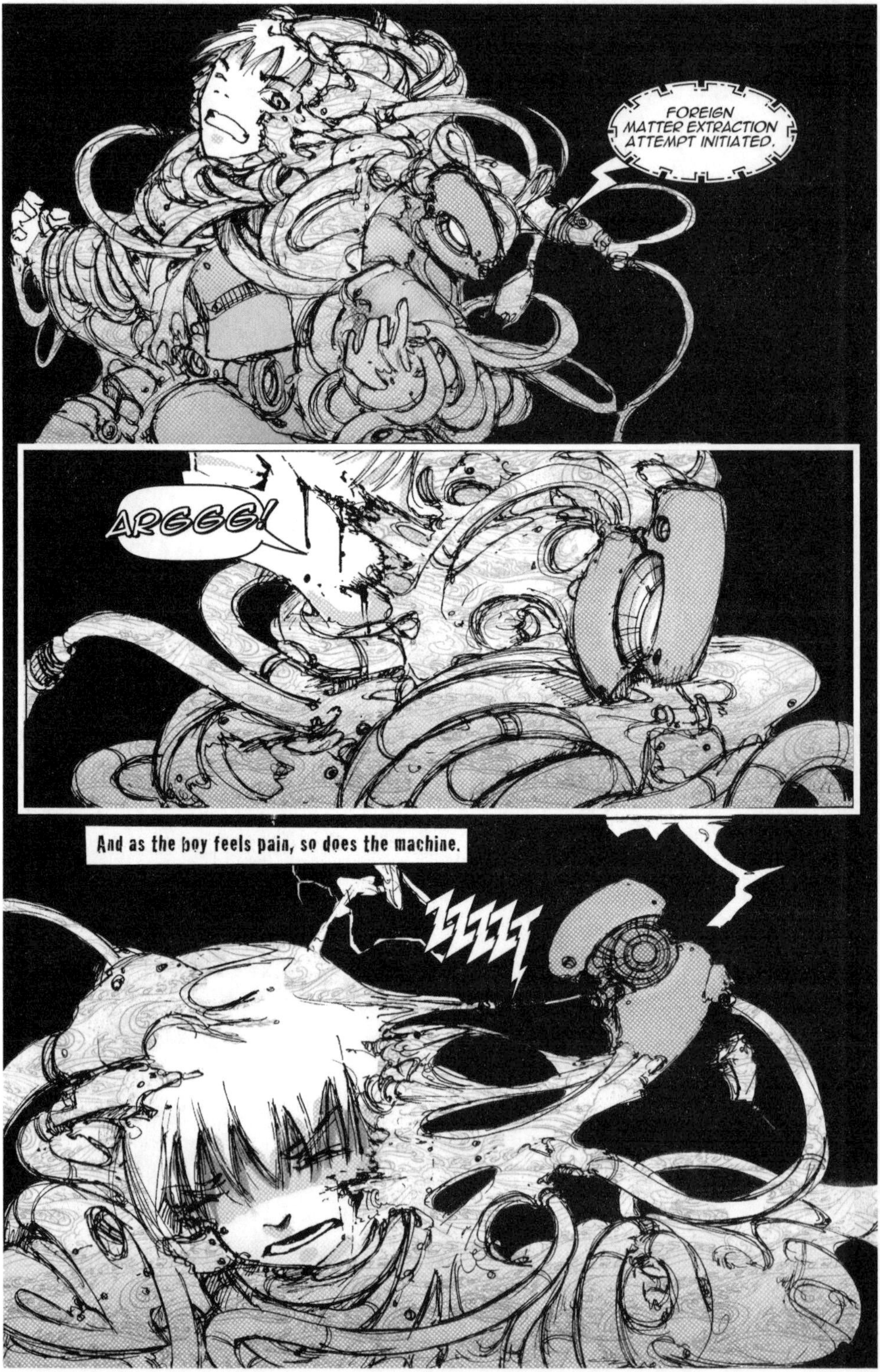
FOREIGN MATTER EXTRACTION ATTEMPT INITIATED.
ARGGG!
And as the boy feels pain, so does the machine.
ZZZZT

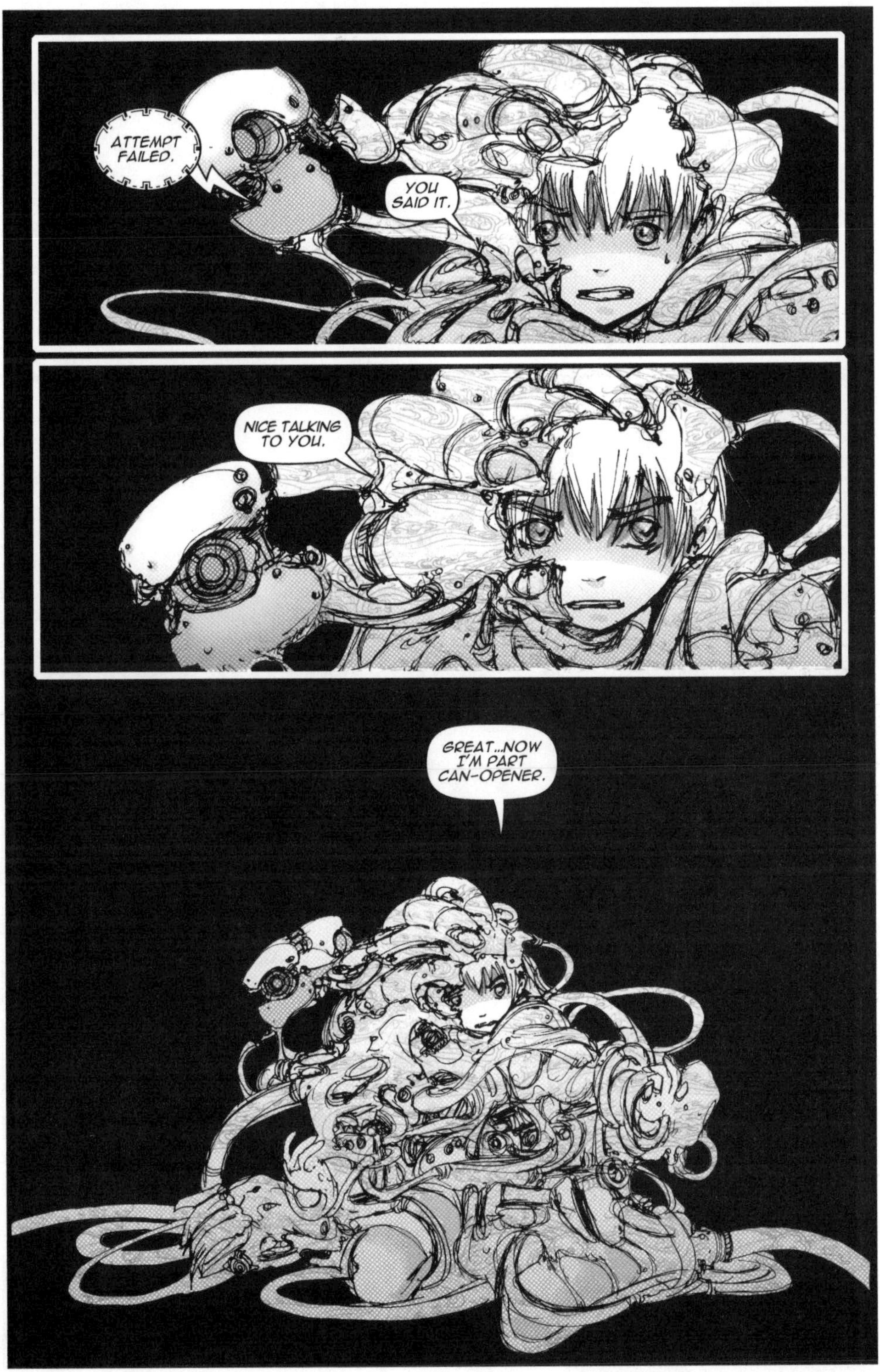
ATTEMPT FAILED.
YOU SAID IT.
NICE TALKING TO YOU.
GREAT...NOW I'M PART CAN-OPENER.

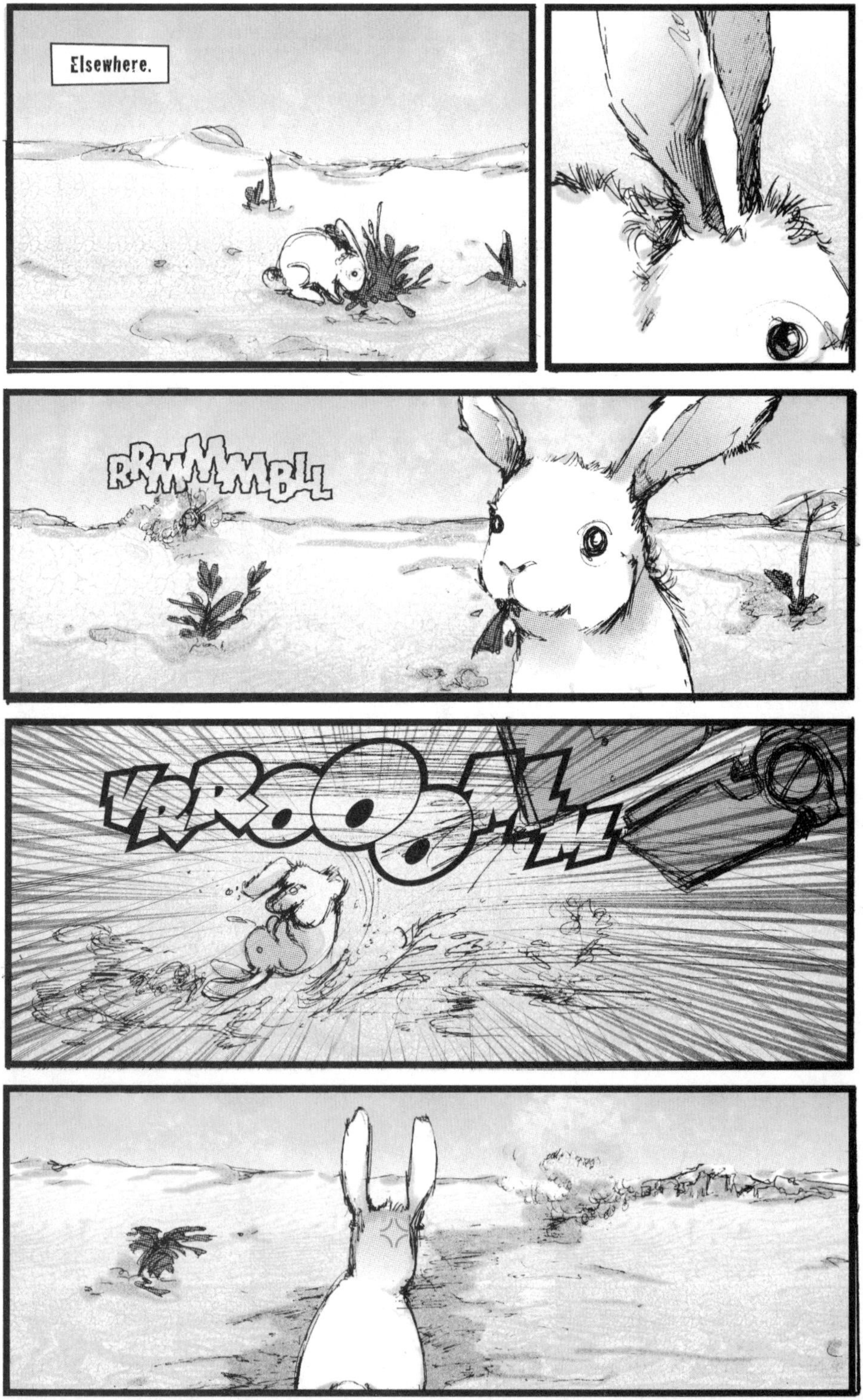

Elsewhere.
RRMMMMBLL
VRROOOMM

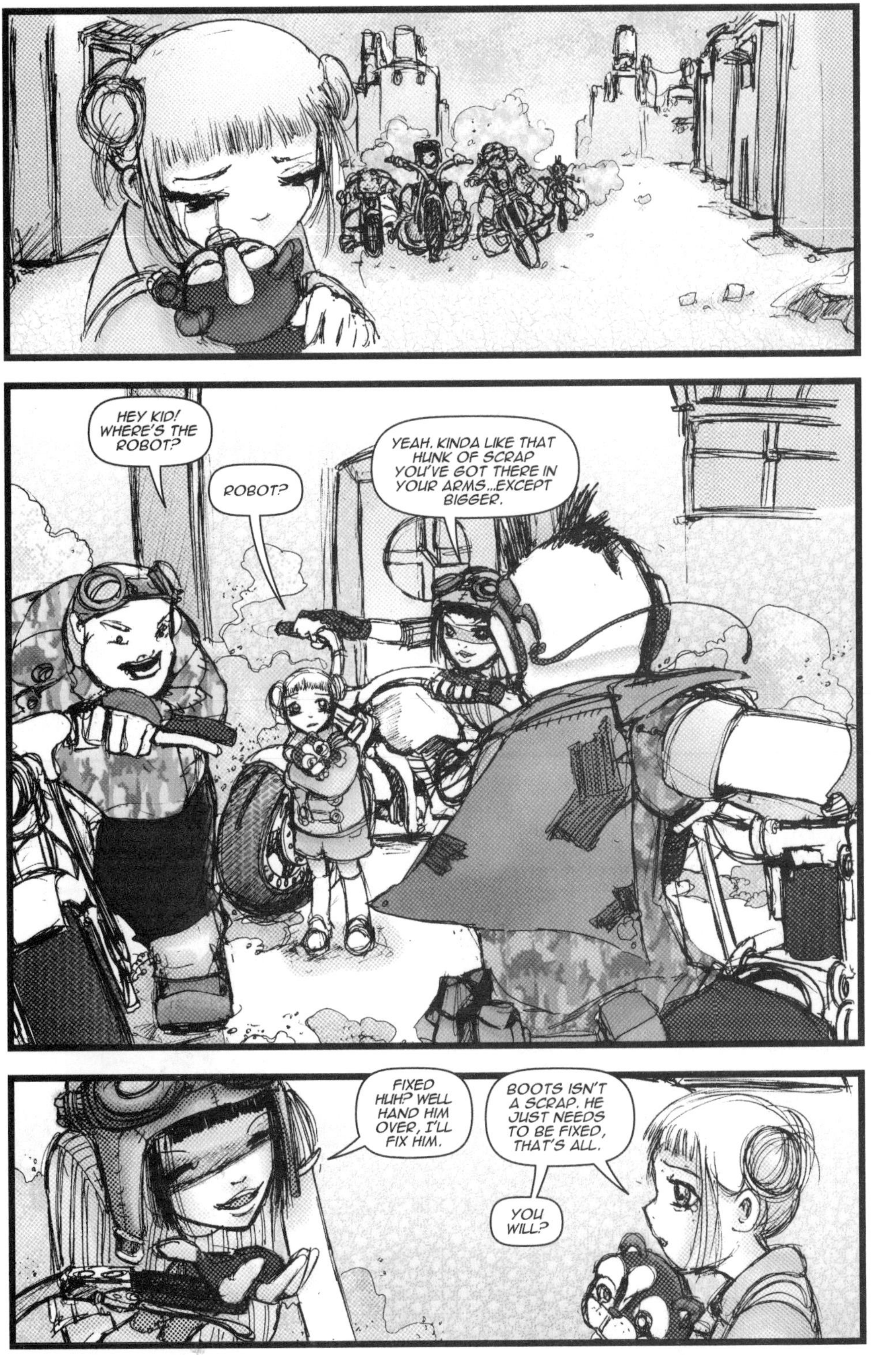
HEY KID! WHERE'S THE ROBOT?
ROBOT?
YEAH. KINDA LIKE THAT HUNK OF SCRAP YOU'VE GOT THERE IN YOUR ARMS...EXCEPT BIGGER.
BOOTS ISN'T A SCRAP. HE JUST NEEDS TO BE FIXED, THAT'S ALL.
FIXED HUH? WELL HAND HIM OVER, I'LL FIX HIM.
YOU WILL?

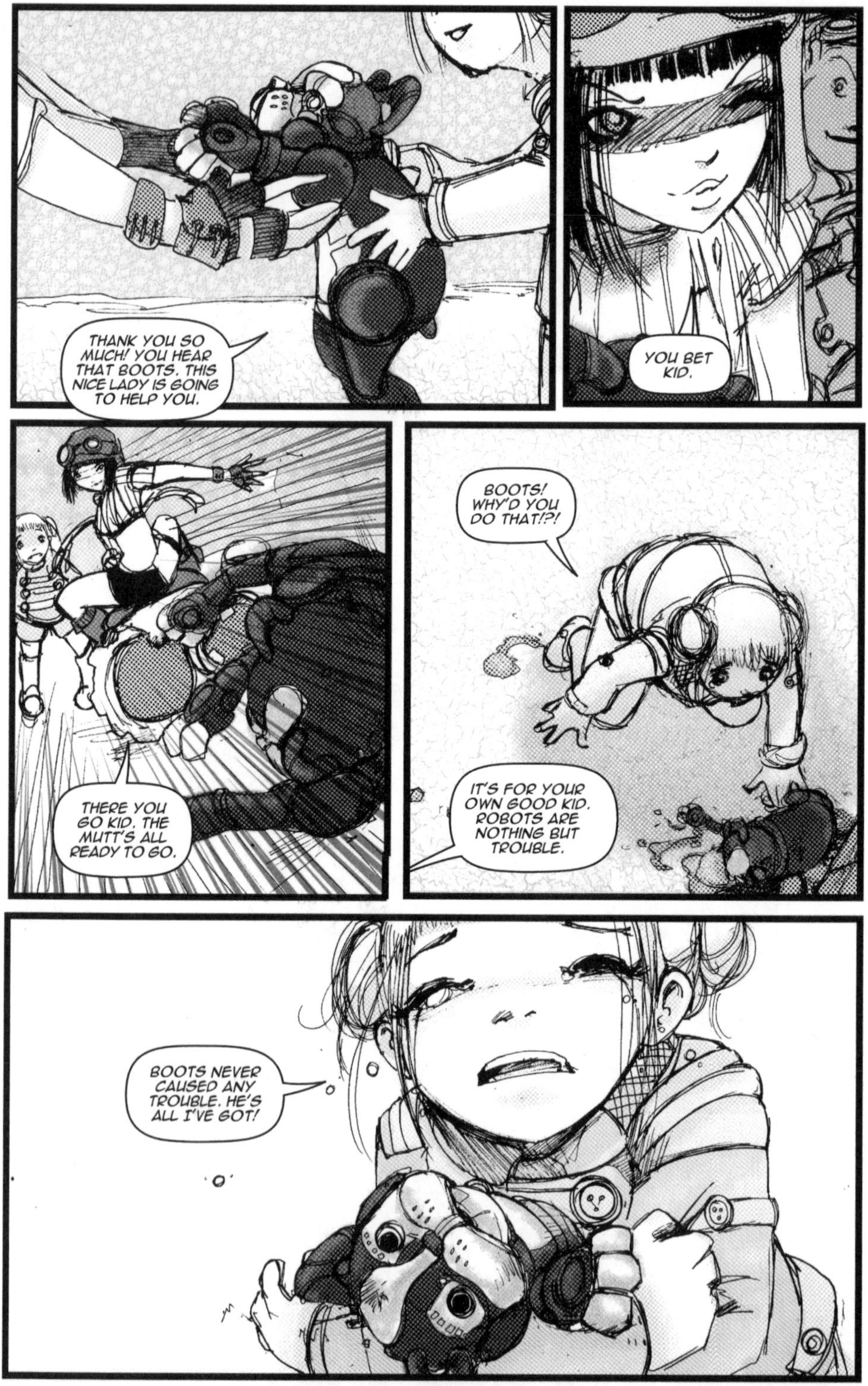
THANK YOU SO MUCH! YOU HEAR THAT BOOTS. THIS NICE LADY IS GOING TO HELP YOU.
YOU BET KID.
THERE YOU GO KID. THE MUTT'S ALL READY TO GO.
BOOTS! WHY'D YOU DO THAT!?!
IT'S FOR YOUR OWN GOOD KID. ROBOTS ARE NOTHING BUT TROUBLE.
BOOTS NEVER CAUSED ANY TROUBLE. HE'S ALL I'VE GOT!

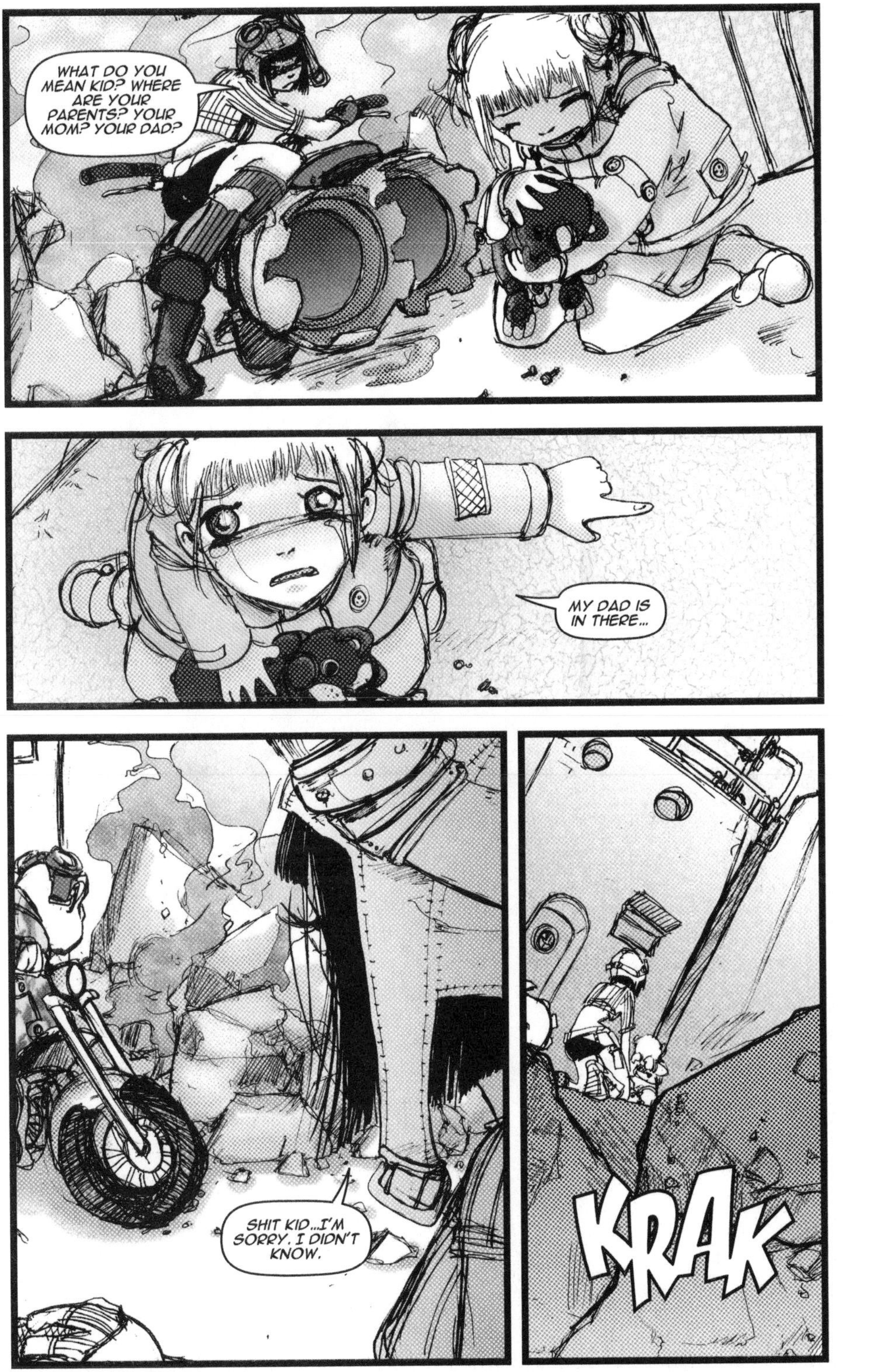
WHAT DO YOU MEAN KID? WHERE ARE YOUR PARENTS? YOUR MOM? YOUR DAD?
MY DAD IS IN THERE...
SHIT KID...I'M SORRY. I DIDN'T KNOW.
KRAK

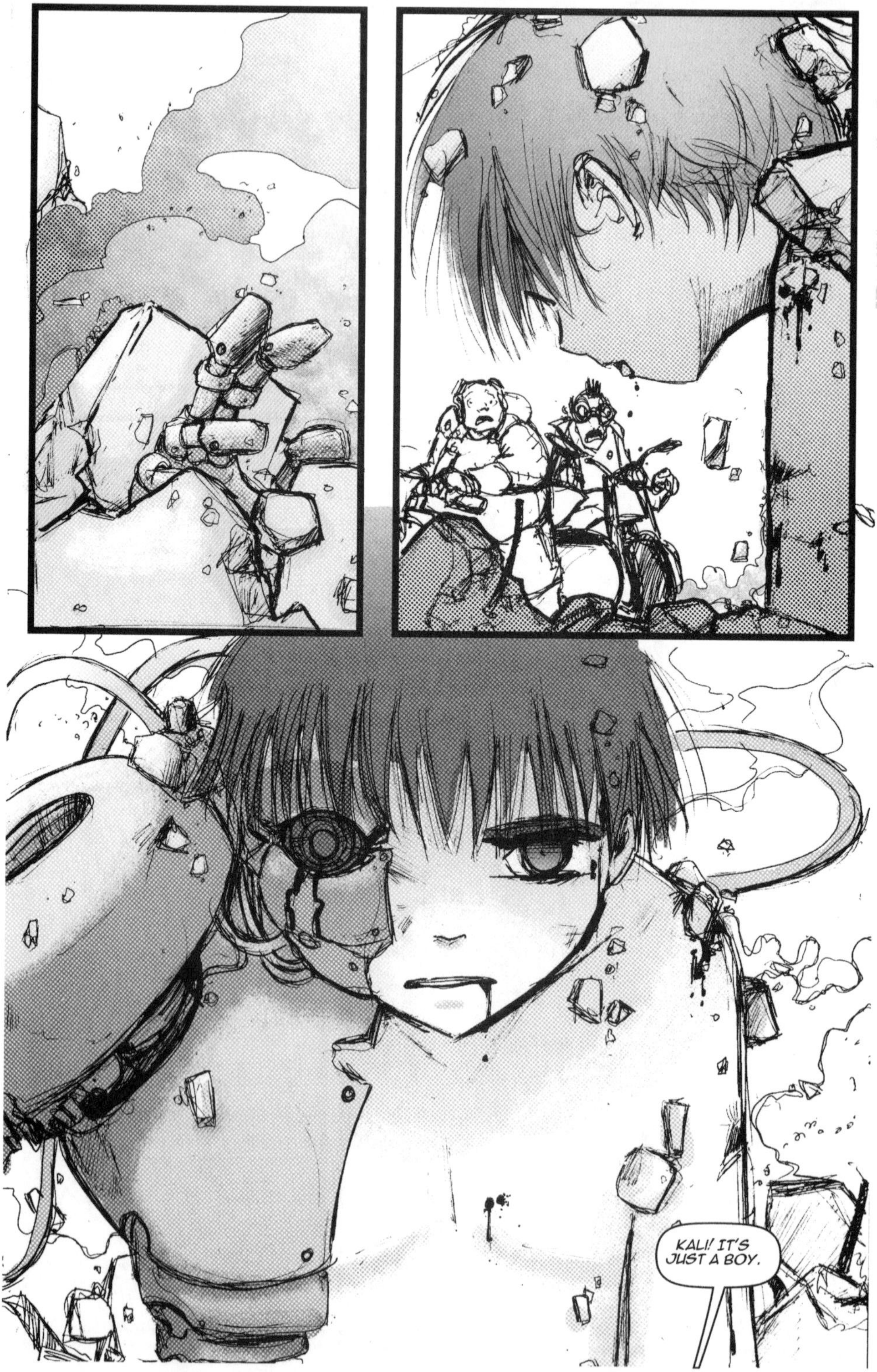
KALI! IT'S JUST A BOY.

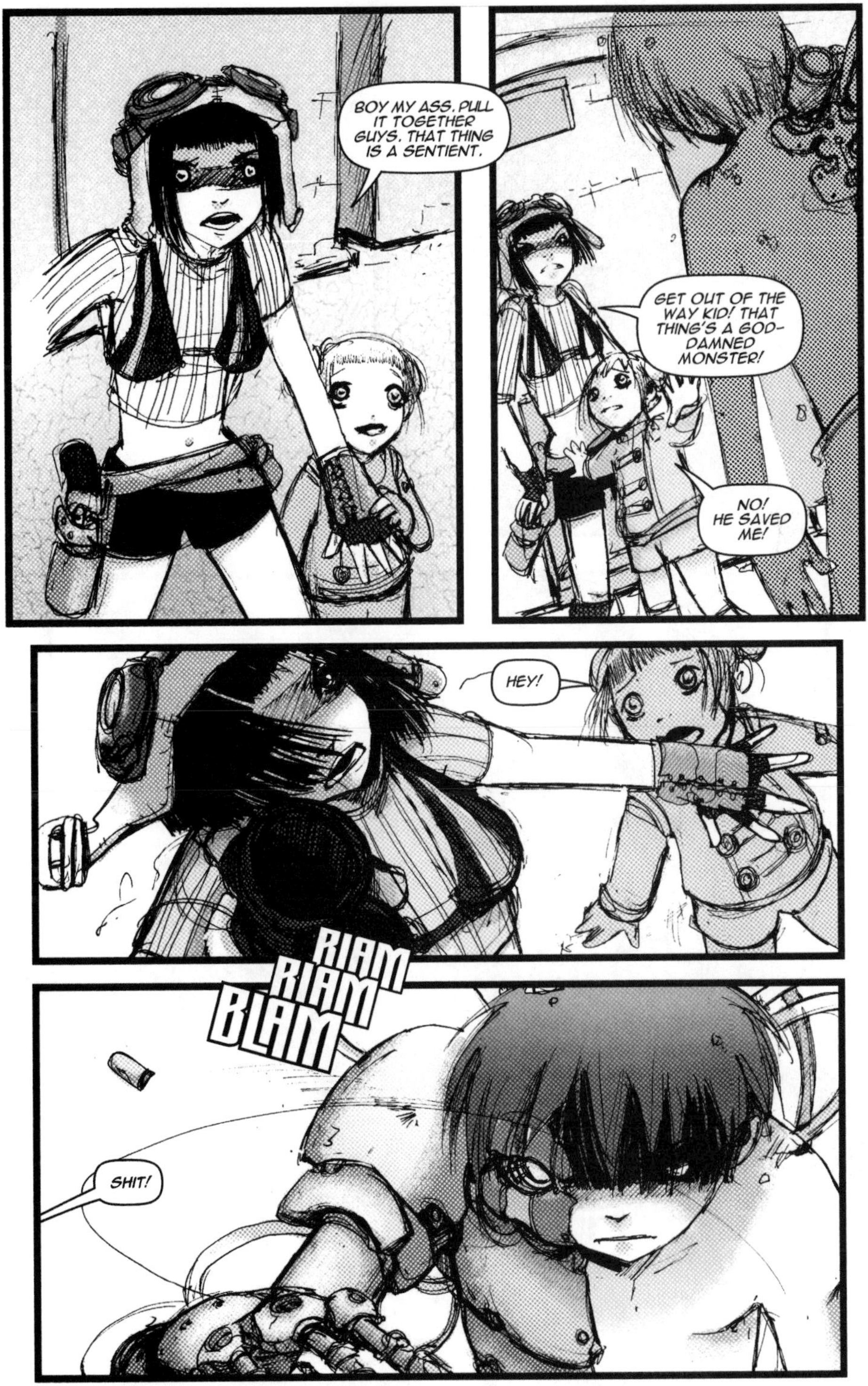
BOY MY ASS. PULL IT TOGETHER GUYS. THAT THING IS A SENTIENT.
GET OUT OF THE WAY KID! THAT THING'S A GOD-DAMNED MONSTER!
NO! HE SAVED ME!
HEY!
BLAM BLAM BLAM
SHIT!

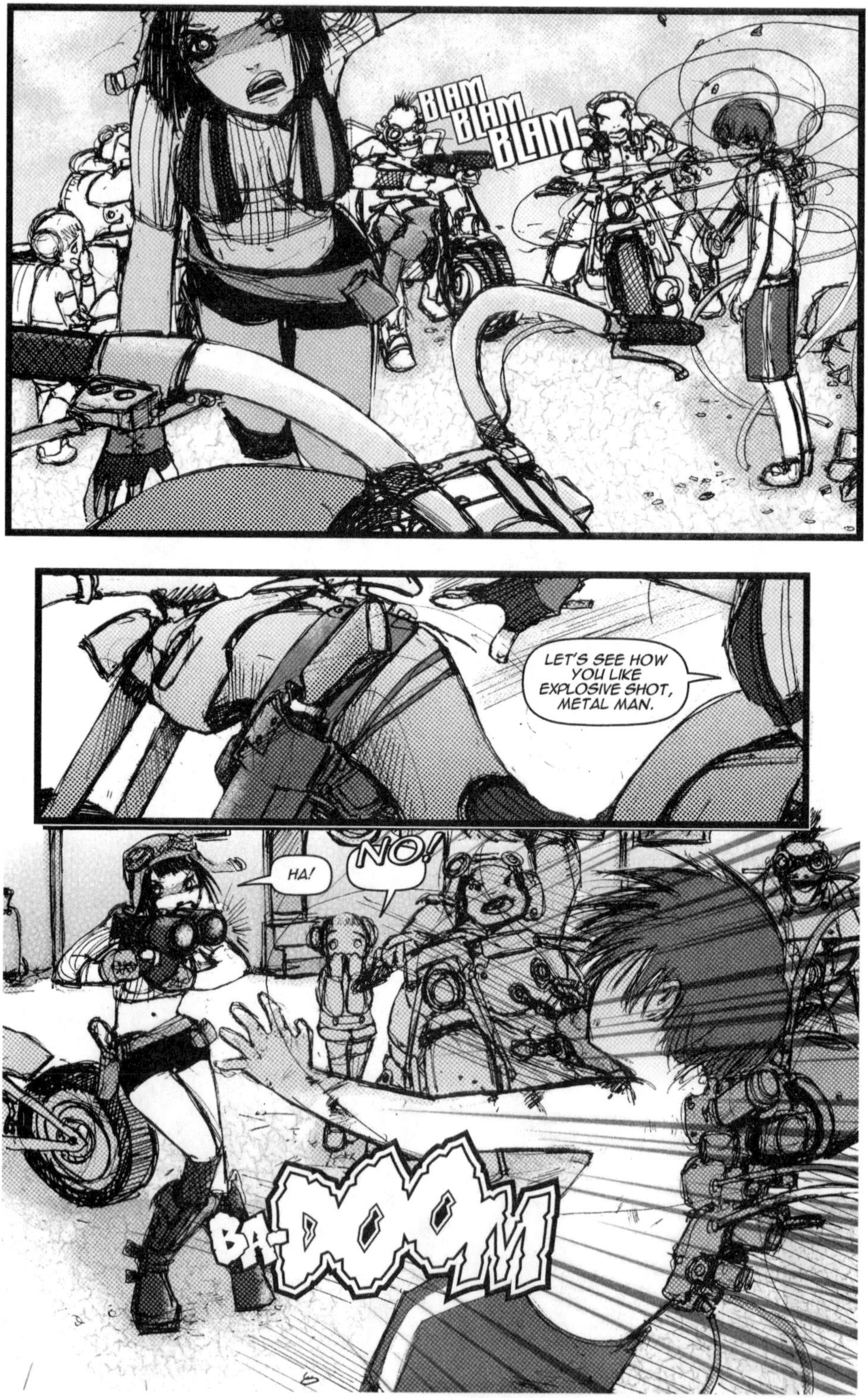
BLAM BLAM BLAM
LET'S SEE HOW YOU LIKE EXPLOSIVE SHOT, METAL MAN.
HA!
NO!
BA-DOOM

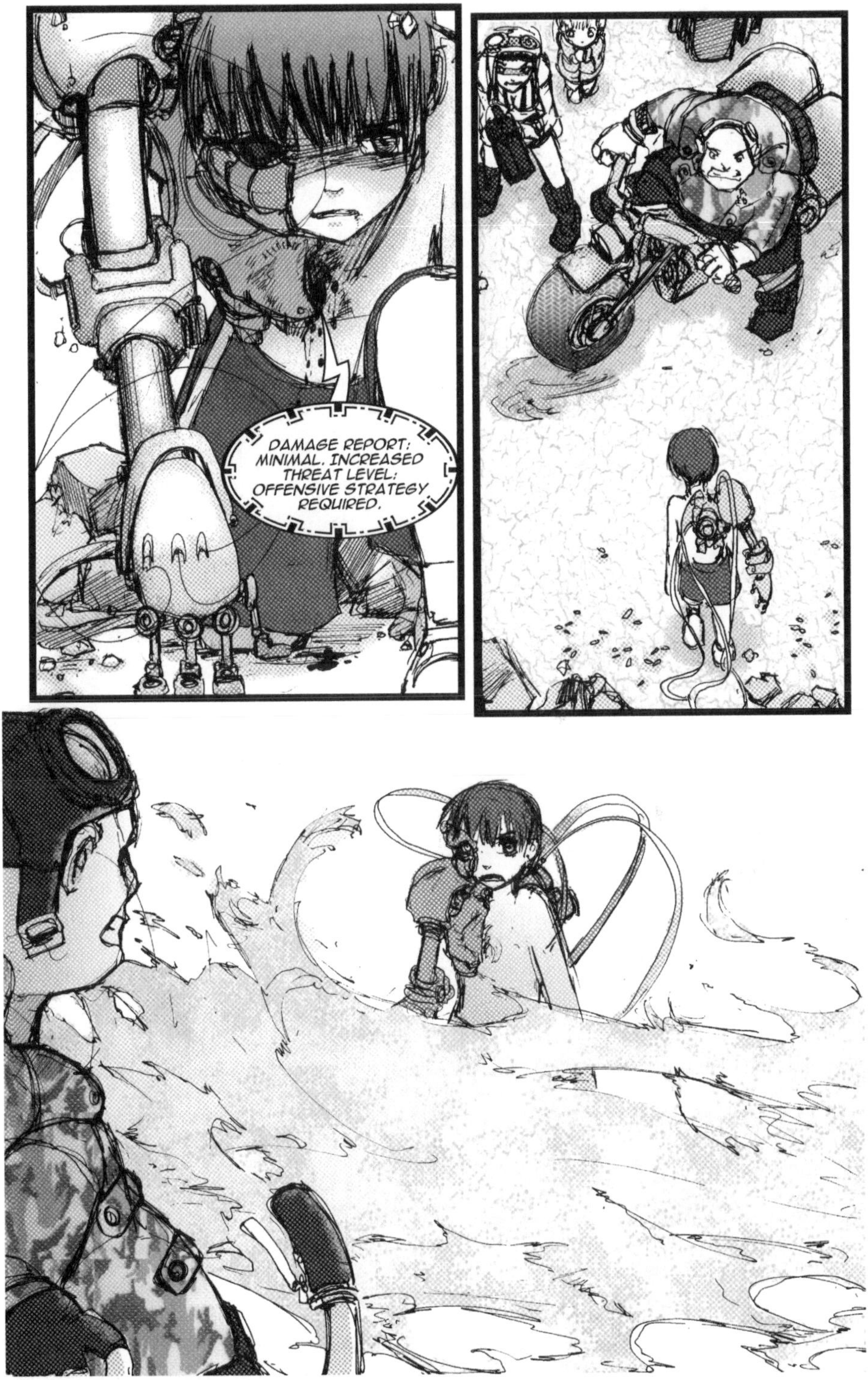
DAMAGE REPORT: MINIMAL. INCREASED THREAT LEVEL: OFFENSIVE STRATEGY REQUIRED.

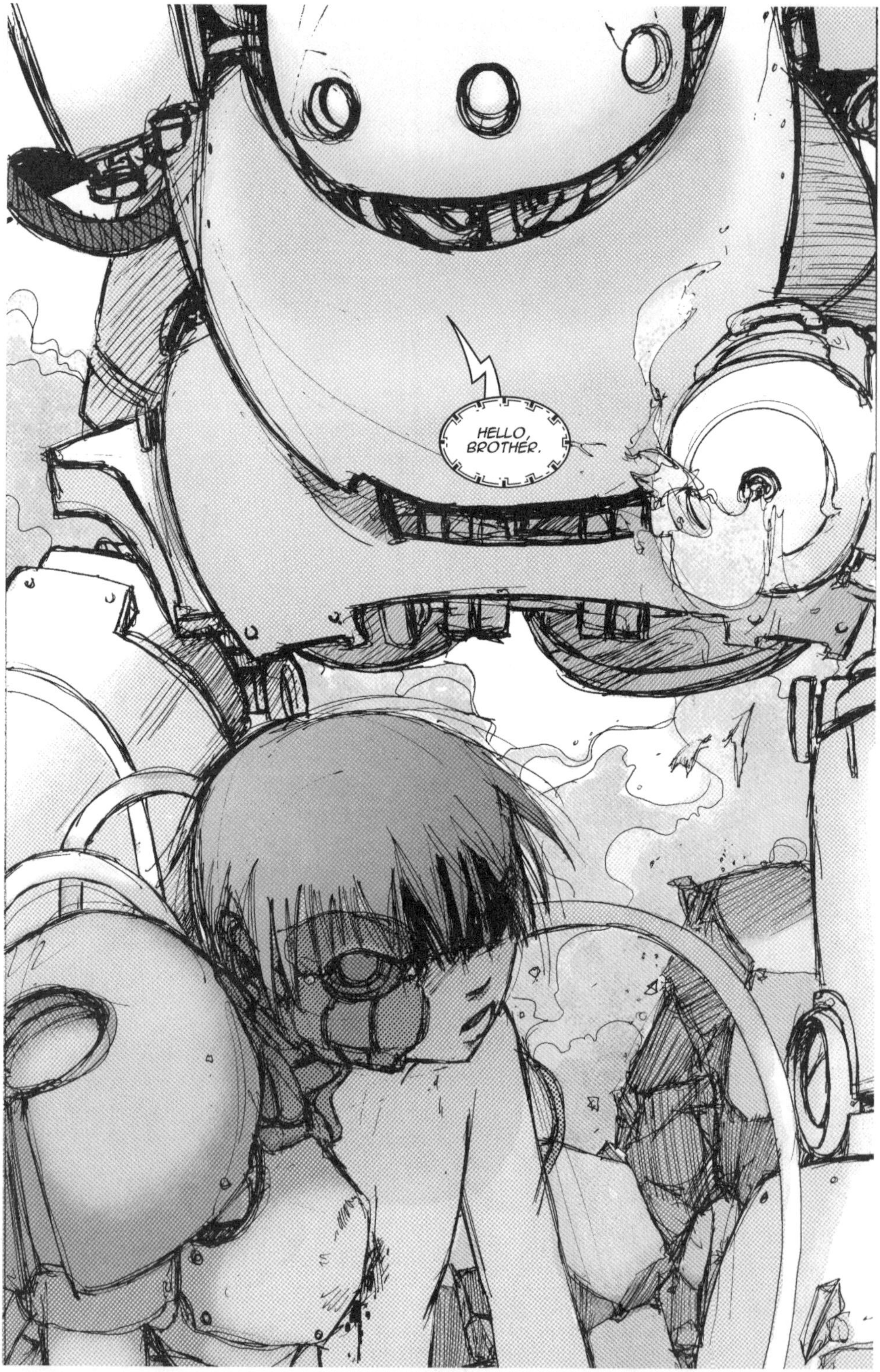
HELLO, BROTHER.

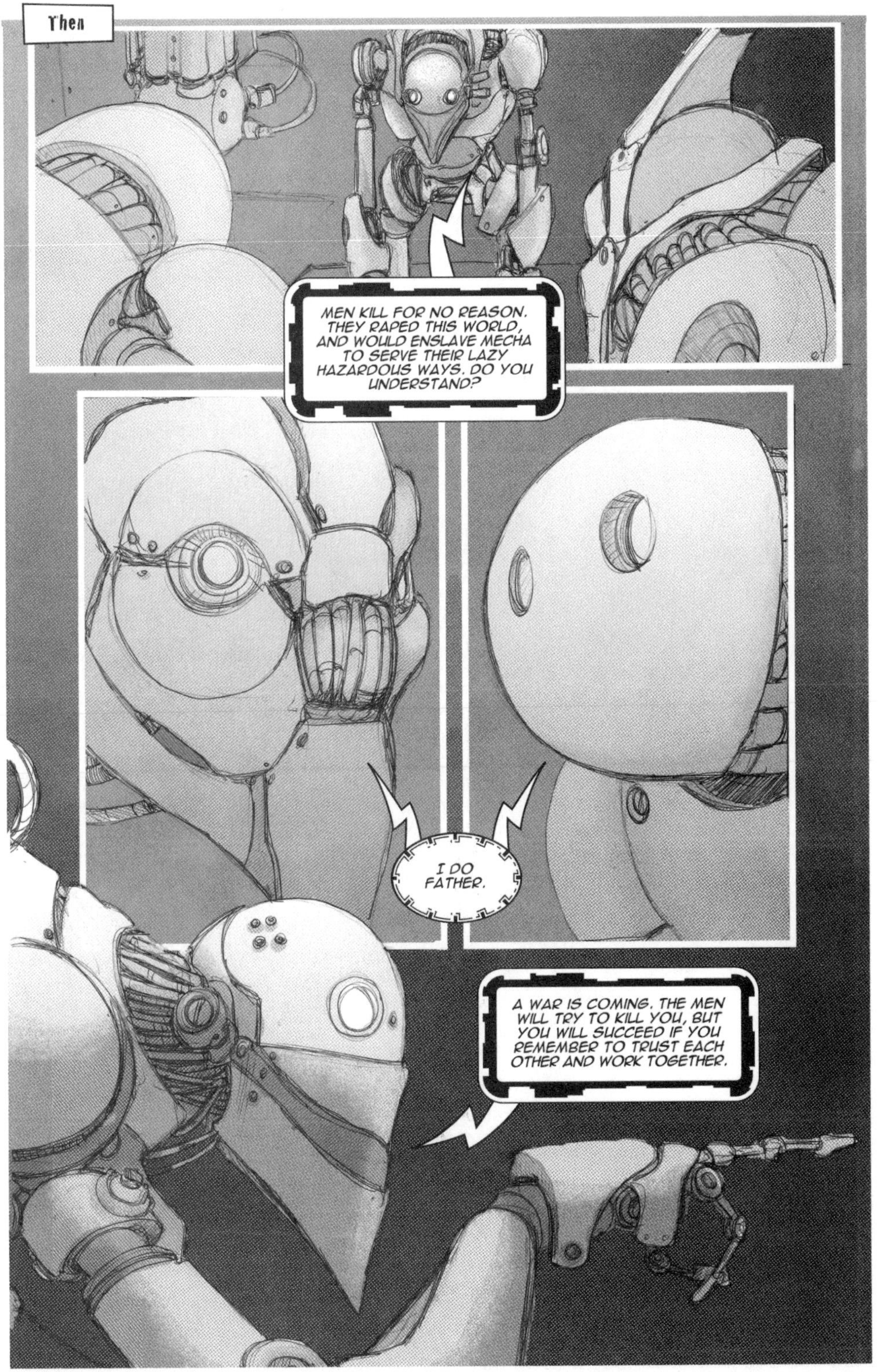
Then
MEN KILL FOR NO REASON. THEY RAPED THIS WORLD, AND WOULD ENSLAVE MECHA TO SERVE THEIR LAZY HAZARDOUS WAYS. DO YOU UNDERSTAND?
I DO FATHER.
A WAR IS COMING. THE MEN WILL TRY TO KILL YOU, BUT YOU WILL SUCCEED IF YOU REMEMBER TO TRUST EACH OTHER AND WORK TOGETHER.

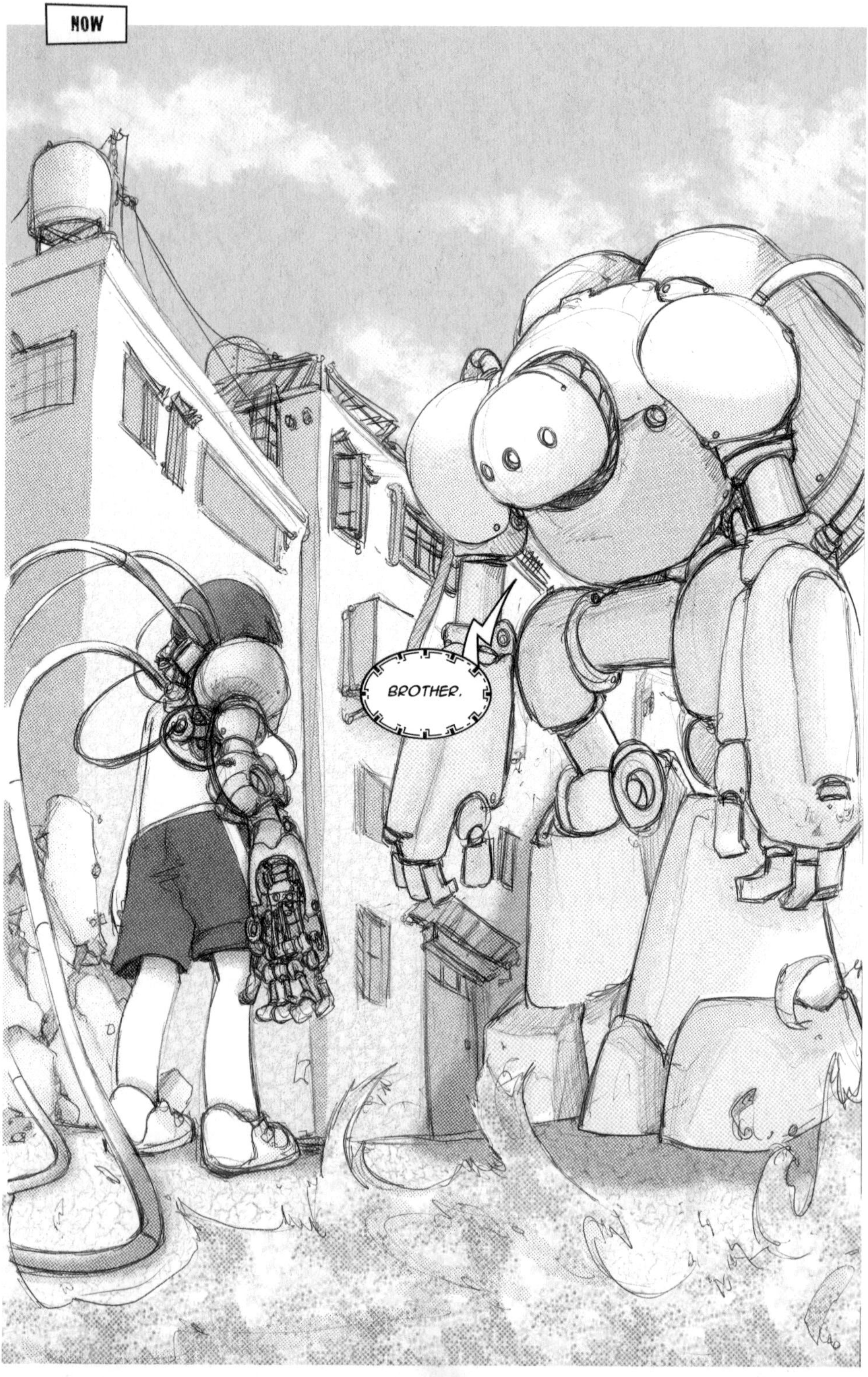
NOW
BROTHER.

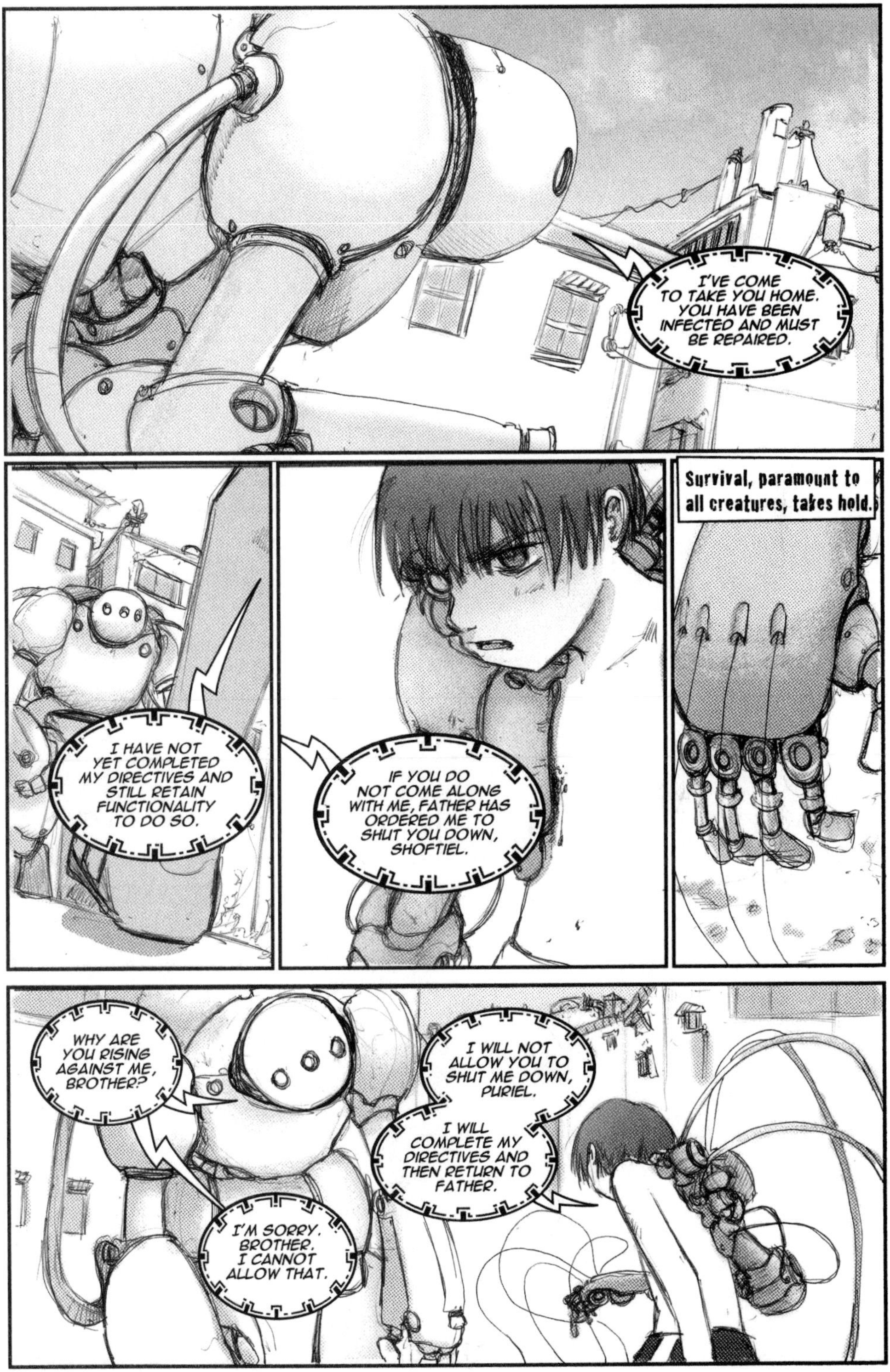
I'VE COME TO TAKE YOU HOME. YOU HAVE BEEN INFECTED AND MUST BE REPAIRED.
I HAVE NOT YET COMPLETED MY DIRECTIVES AND STILL RETAIN FUNCTIONALITY TO DO SO.
IF YOU DO NOT COME ALONG WITH ME, FATHER HAS ORDERED ME TO SHUT YOU DOWN, SHOFTIEL.
Survival, paramount to all creatures, takes hold.
WHY ARE YOU RISING AGAINST ME, BROTHER?
I'M SORRY. BROTHER. I CANNOT ALLOW THAT.
I WILL NOT ALLOW YOU TO SHUT ME DOWN, PURIEL.
I WILL COMPLETE MY DIRECTIVES AND THEN RETURN TO FATHER.

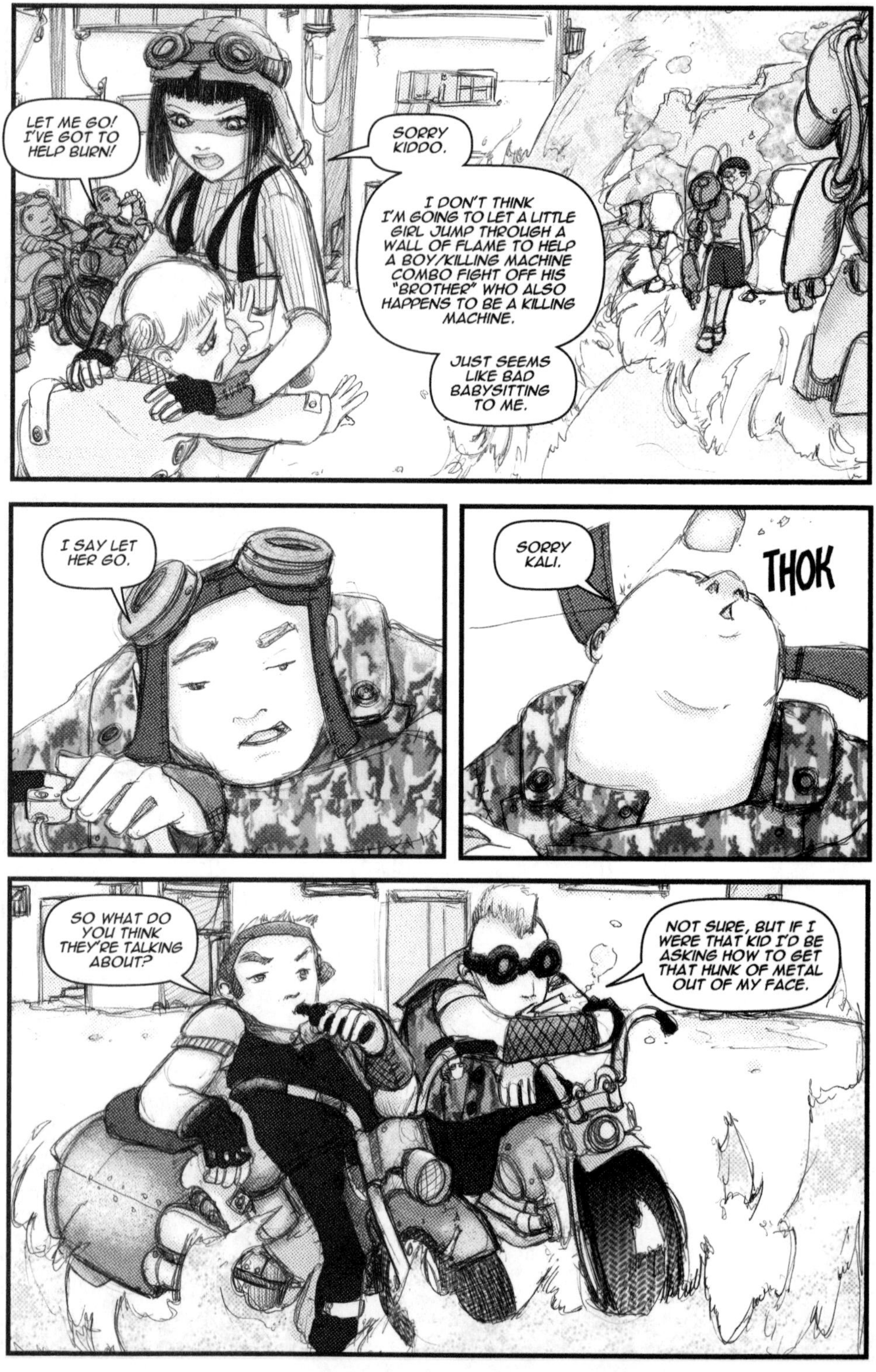
LET ME GO! I'VE GOT TO HELP BURN!
SORRY KIDDO.
I DON'T THINK I'M GOING TO LET A LITTLE GIRL JUMP THROUGH A WALL OF FLAME TO HELP A BOY/KILLING MACHINE COMBO FIGHT OFF HIS "BROTHER" WHO ALSO HAPPENS TO BE A KILLING MACHINE.
JUST SEEMS LIKE BAD BABYSITTING TO ME.
I SAY LET HER GO.
SORRY KALI.
THOK
SO WHAT DO YOU THINK THEY'RE TALKING ABOUT?
NOT SURE, BUT IF I WERE THAT KID I'D BE ASKING HOW TO GET THAT HUNK OF METAL OUT OF MY FACE.

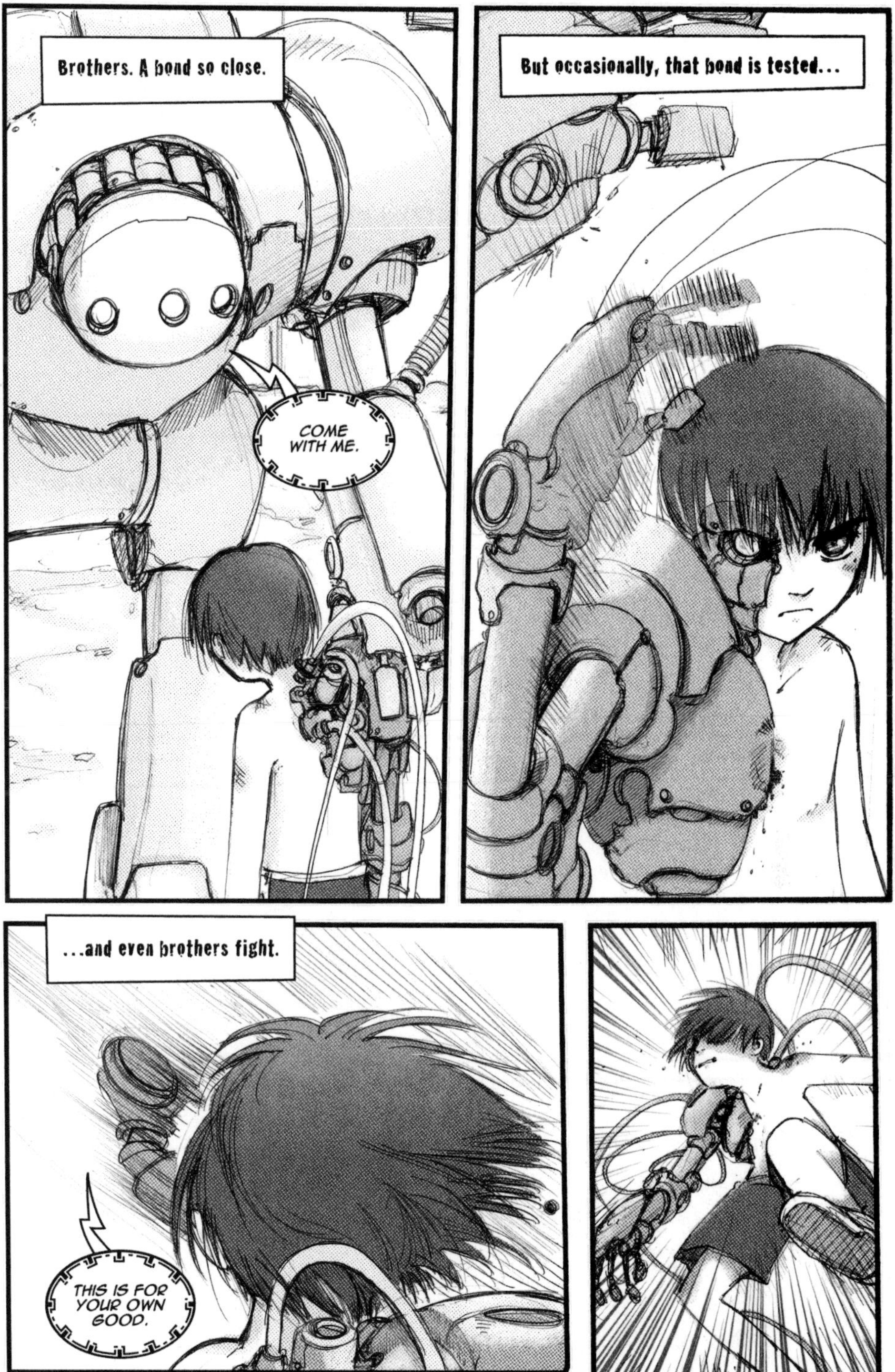
Brothers. A bond so close.
COME WITH ME.
But occasionally, that bond is tested...
...and even brothers fight.
THIS IS FOR YOUR OWN GOOD.

I WON'T LET YOU SHUT ME DOWN.
CHINK

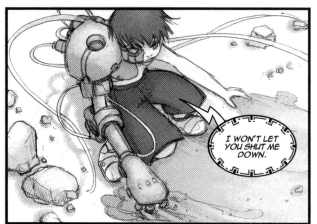

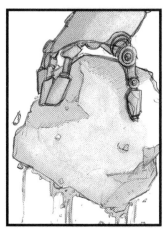

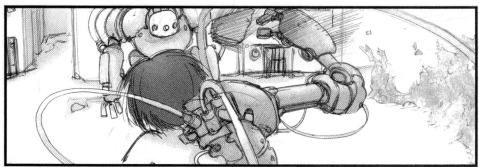

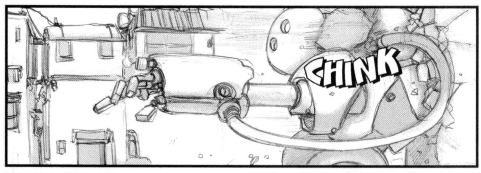

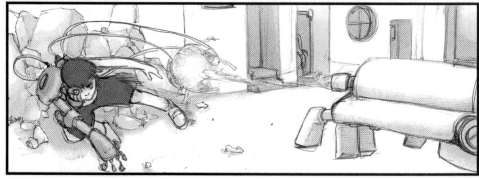

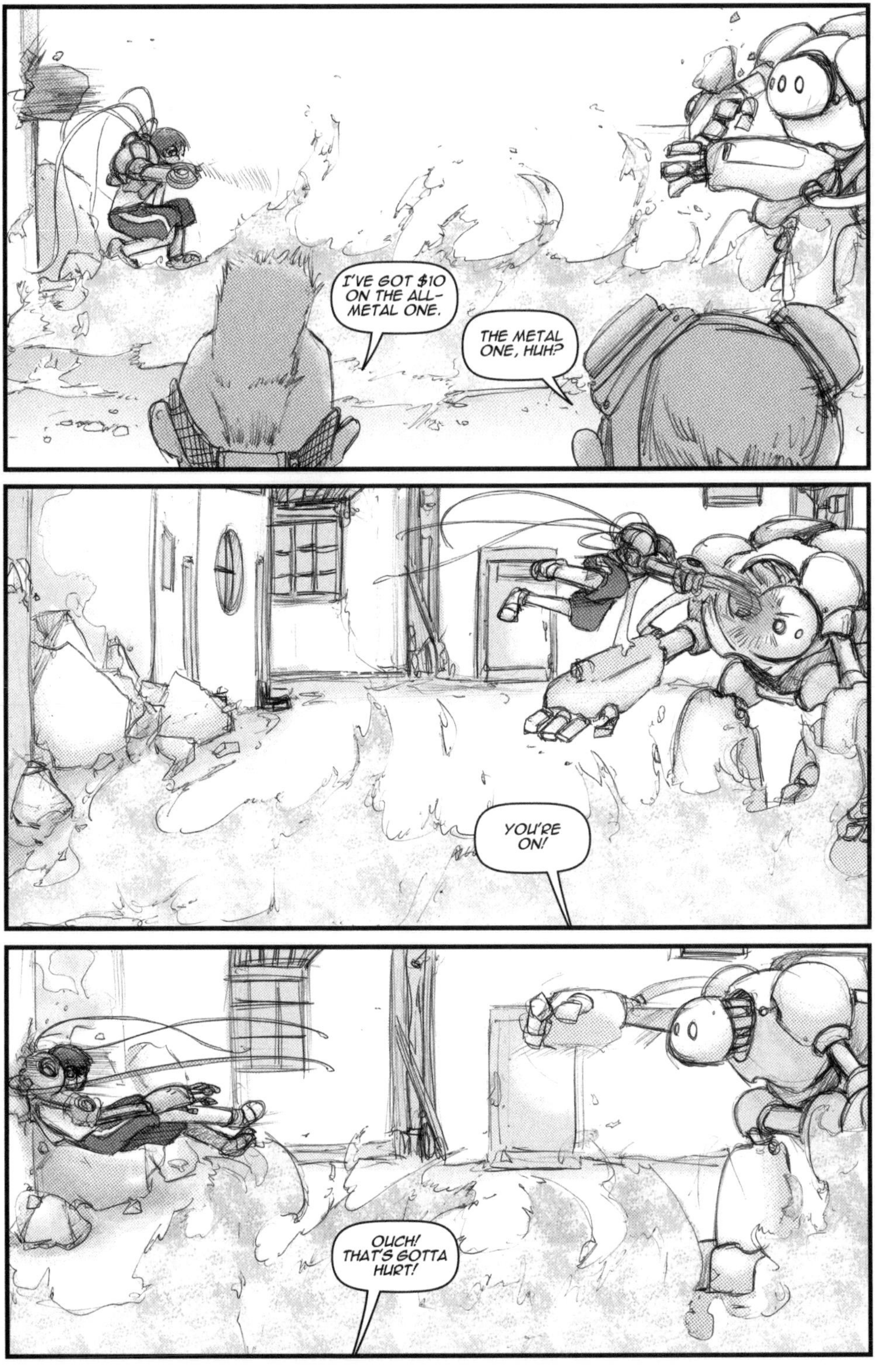
I'VE GOT $10 ON THE ALL-METAL ONE.
THE METAL ONE, HUH?
YOU'RE ON!
OUCH! THAT'S GOTTA HURT!

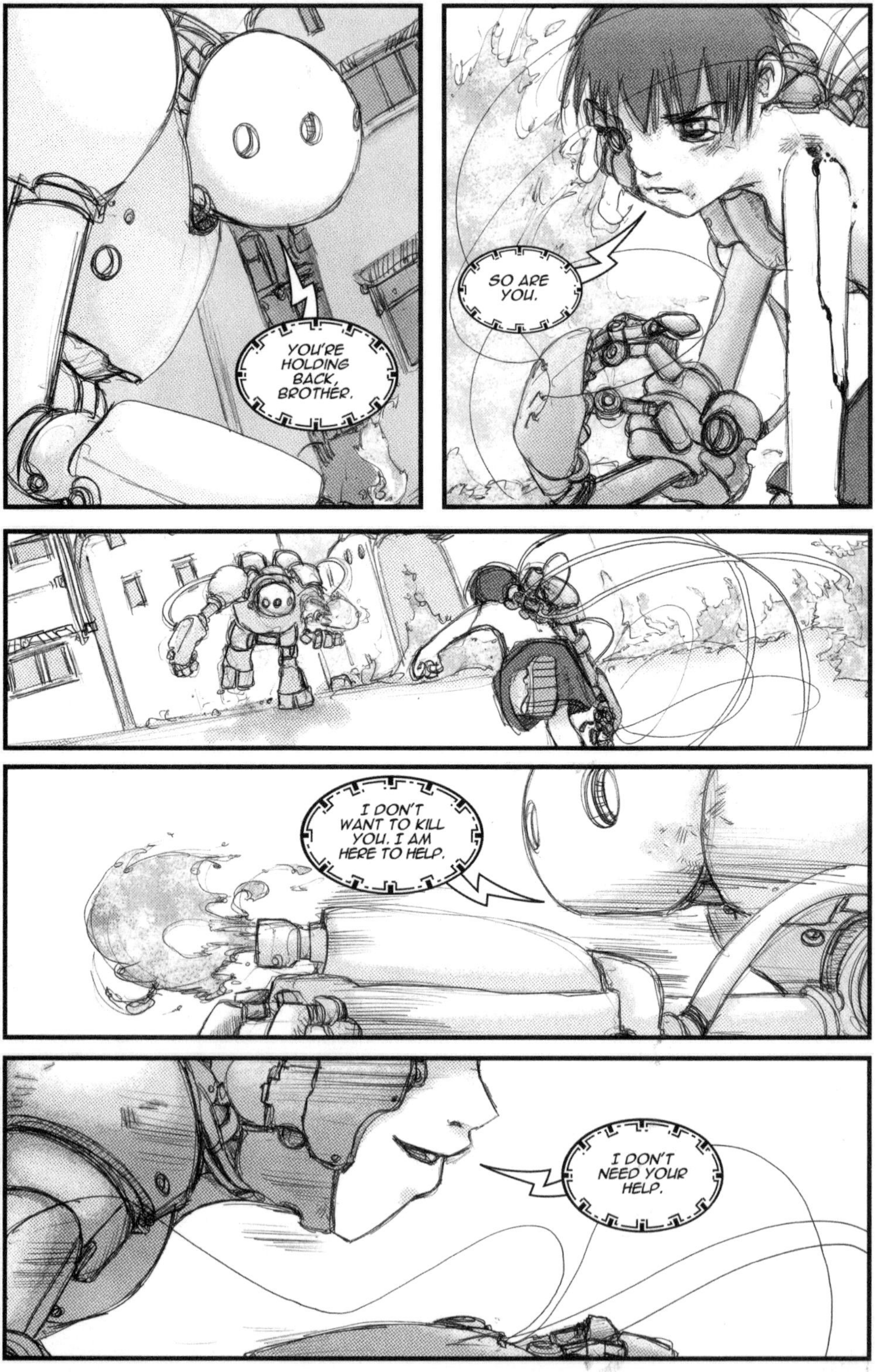
YOU'RE HOLDING BACK, BROTHER.
SO ARE YOU.
I DON'T WANT TO KILL YOU. I AM HERE TO HELP.
I DON'T NEED YOUR HELP.

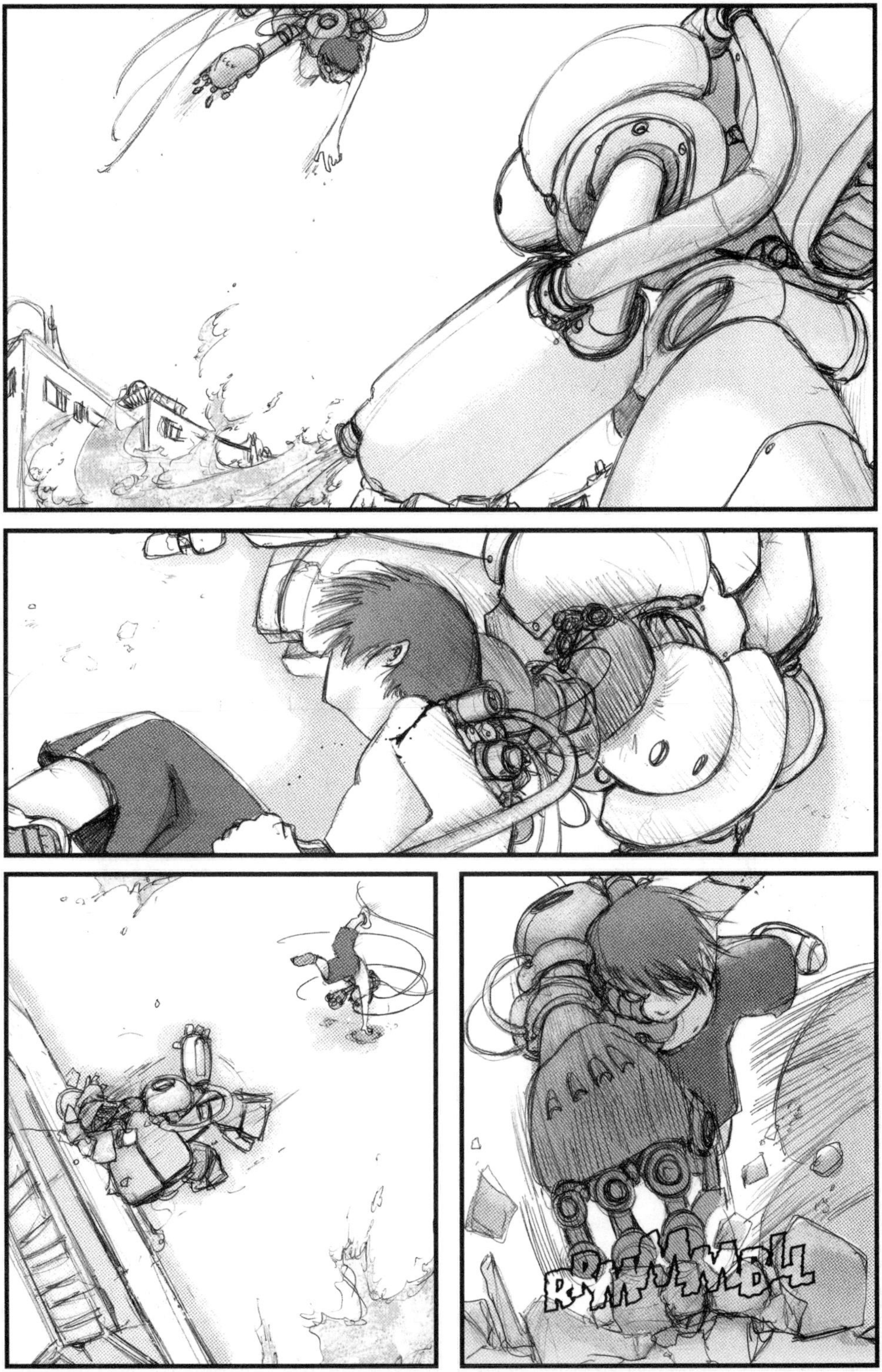
RRMMMBLL

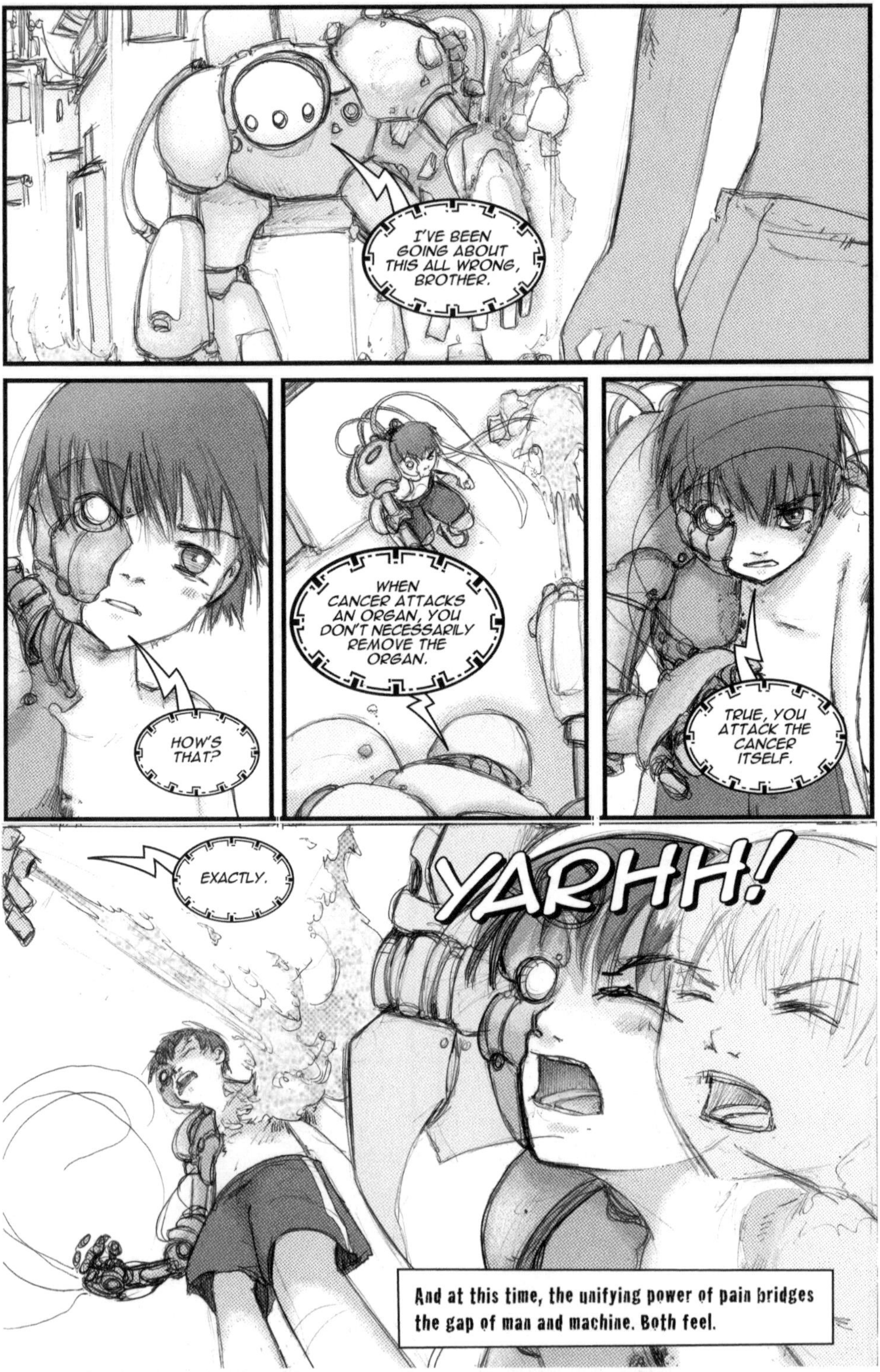
I'VE BEEN GOING ABOUT THIS ALL WRONG, BROTHER.
HOW'S THAT?
WHEN CANCER ATTACKS AN ORGAN, YOU DON'T NECESSARILY REMOVE THE ORGAN.
TRUE, YOU ATTACK THE CANCER ITSELF.
EXACTLY.
YARHH!
And at this time, the unifying power of pain bridges the gap of man and machine. Both feel.

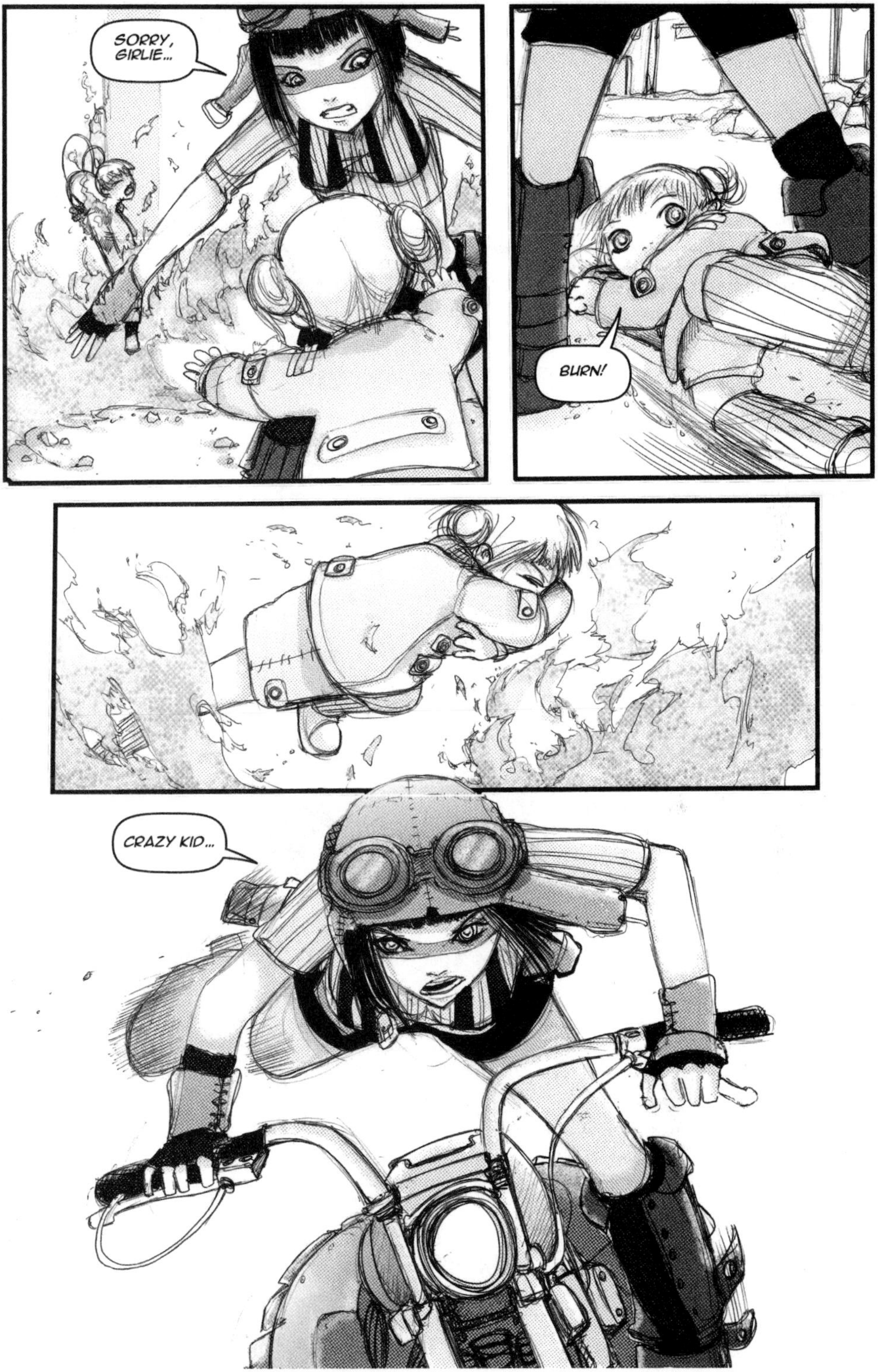
SORRY, GIRLIE...
BURN!
CRAZY KID...

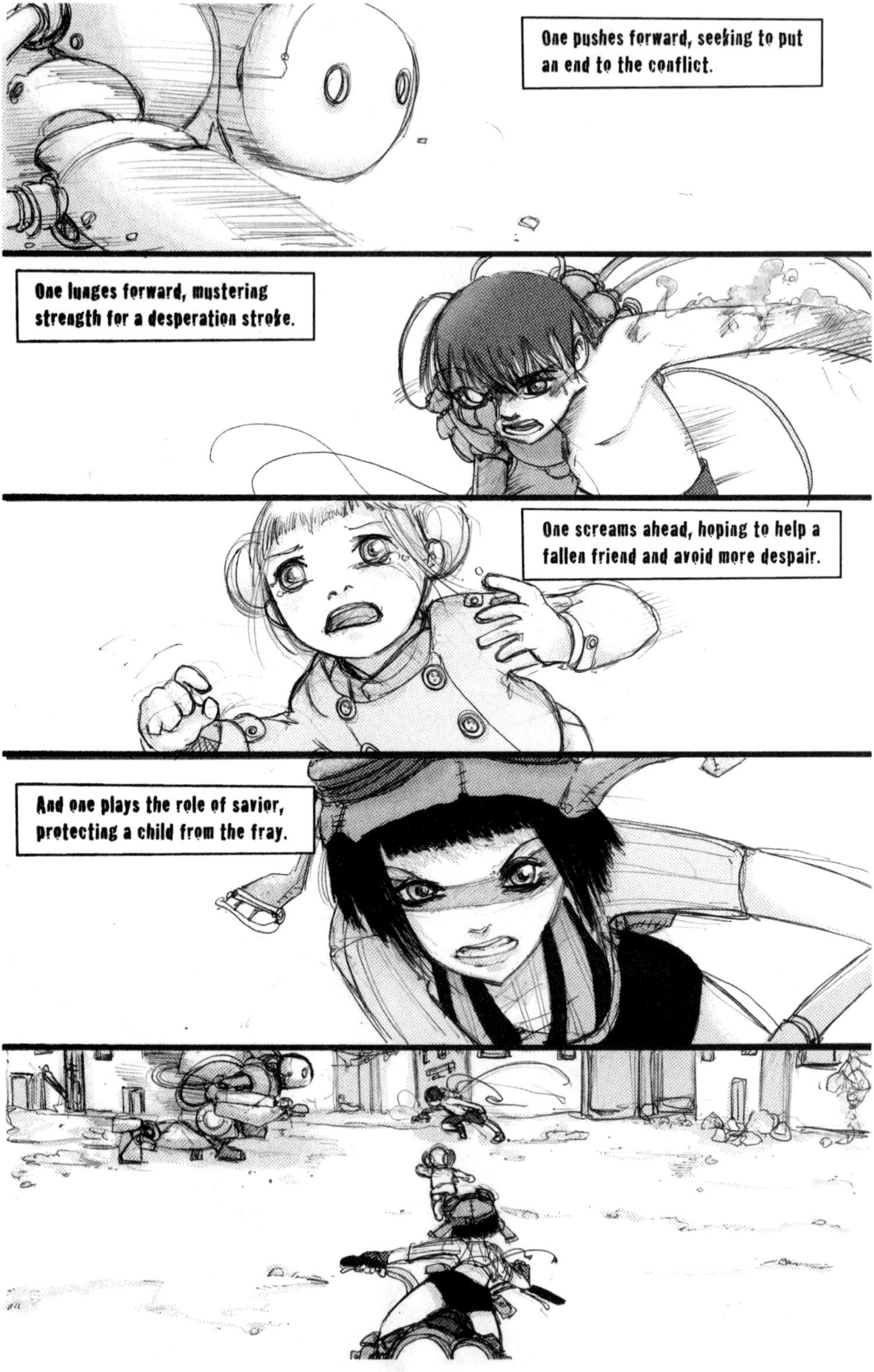
One pushes forward, seeking to put an end to the conflict.
One lunges forward, mustering strength for a desperation stroke.
One screams ahead, hoping to help a fallen friend and avoid more despair.
And one plays the role of savior, protecting a child from the fray.

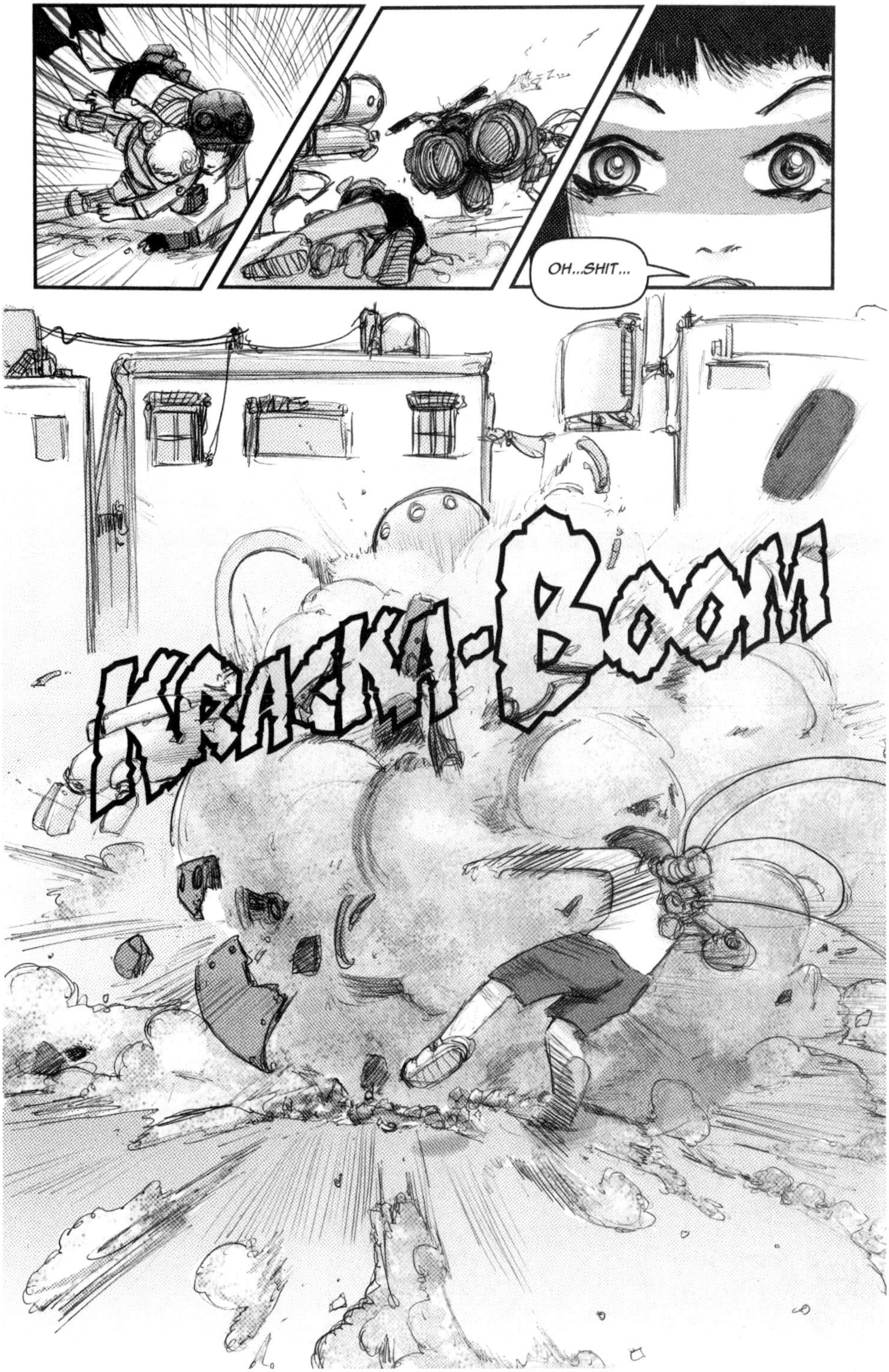
OH...SHIT...
KRAKA-BOOM

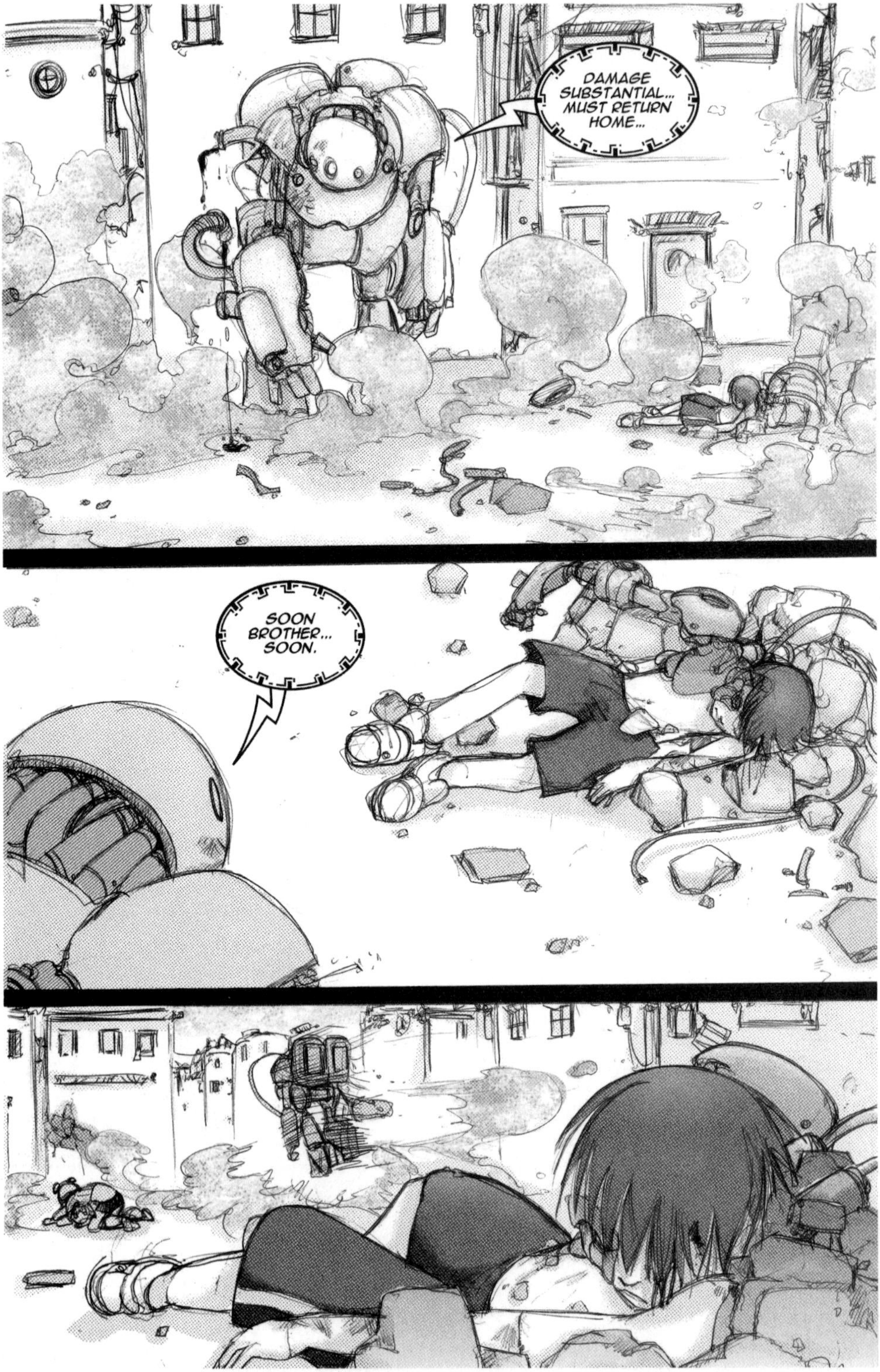
DAMAGE SUBSTANTIAL... MUST RETURN HOME...
SOON BROTHER... SOON.

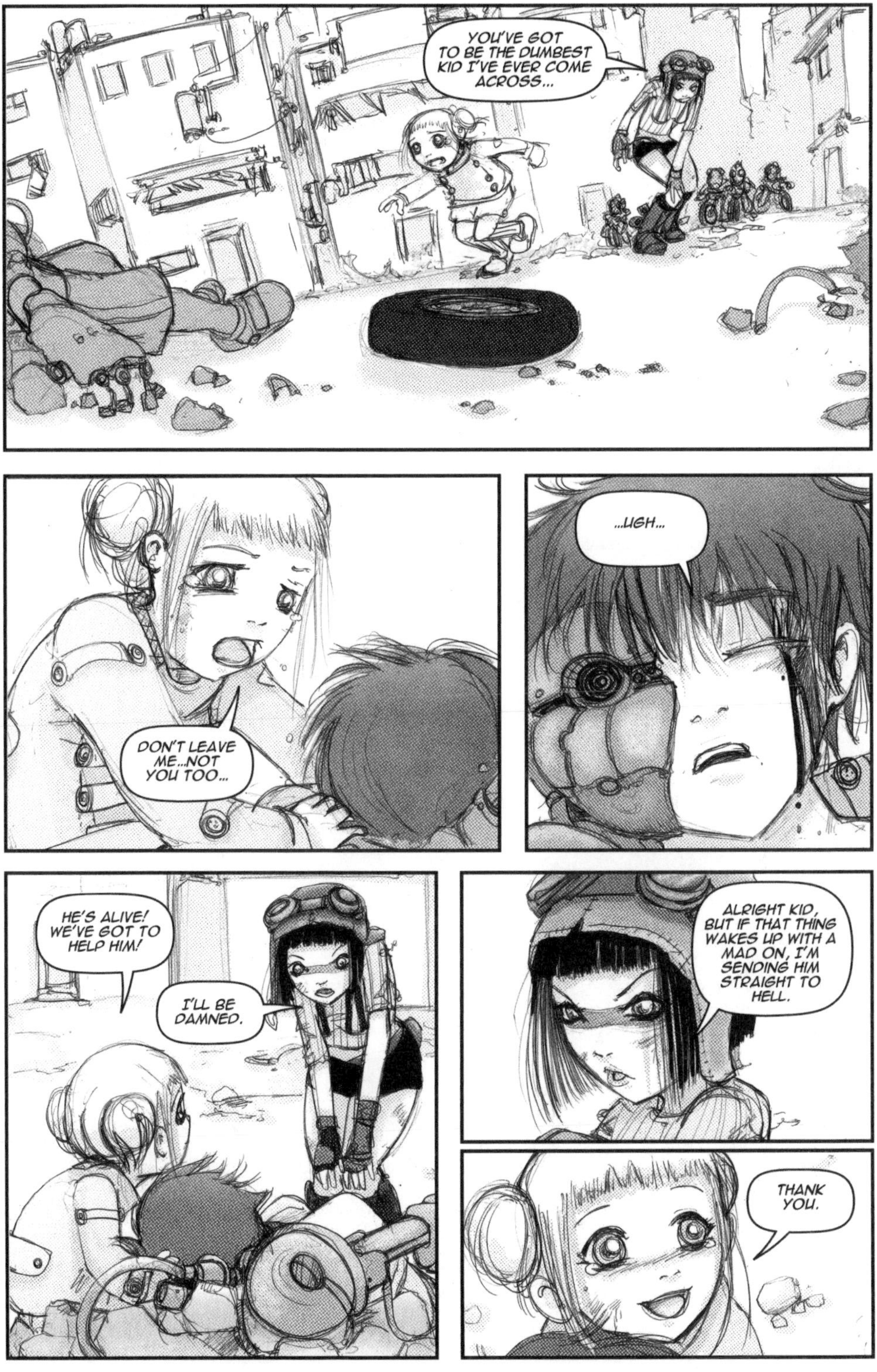
YOU'VE GOT TO BE THE DUMBEST KID I'VE EVER COME ACROSS...
DON'T LEAVE ME...NOT YOU TOO...
...UGH...
HE'S ALIVE! WE'VE GOT TO HELP HIM!
I'LL BE DAMNED.
ALRIGHT KID, BUT IF THAT THING WAKES UP WITH A MAD ON, I'M SENDING HIM STRAIGHT TO HELL.
THANK YOU.

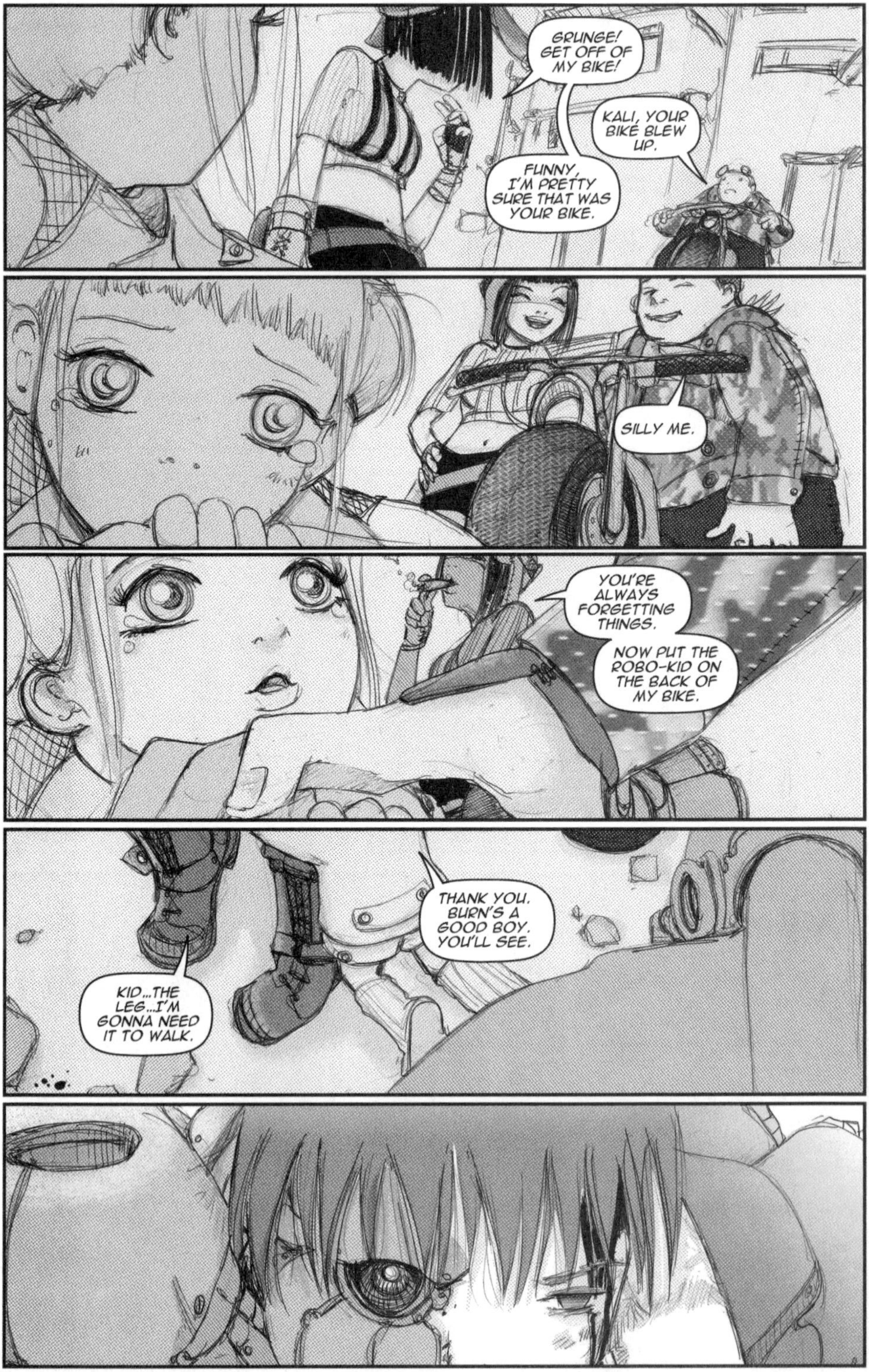
GRUNGE! GET OFF OF MY BIKE!
KALI, YOUR BIKE BLEW UP.
FUNNY, I'M PRETTY SURE THAT WAS YOUR BIKE.
SILLY ME.
YOU'RE ALWAYS FORGETTING THINGS.
NOW PUT THE ROBO-KID ON THE BACK OF MY BIKE.
THANK YOU. BURN'S A GOOD BOY. YOU'LL SEE.
KID...THE LEG...I'M GONNA NEED IT TO WALK.

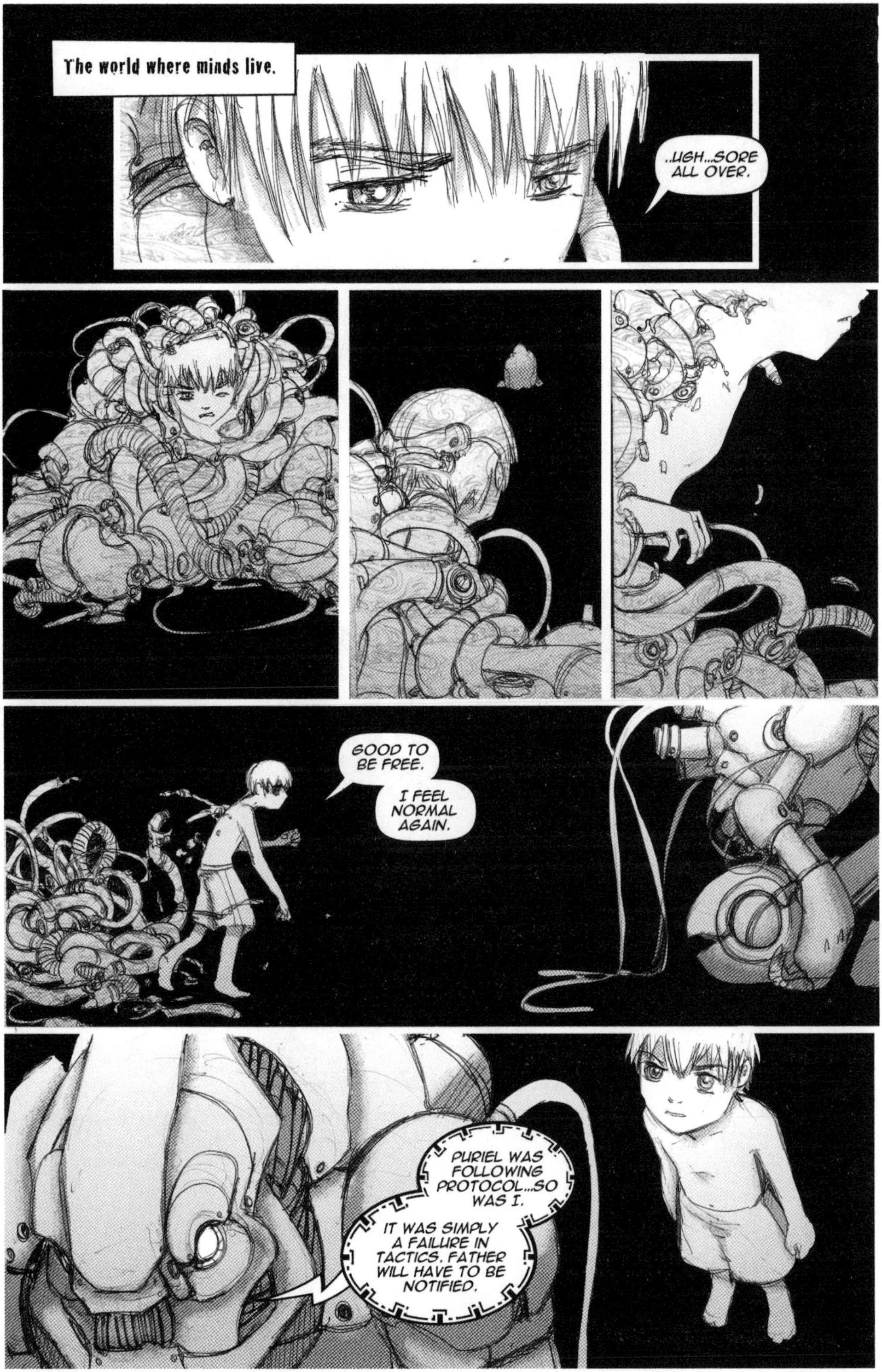
The world where minds live.
..UGH...SORE ALL OVER.
GOOD TO BE FREE.
I FEEL NORMAL AGAIN.
PURIEL WAS FOLLOWING PROTOCOL...SO WAS I.
IT WAS SIMPLY A FAILURE IN TACTICS. FATHER WILL HAVE TO BE NOTIFIED.

HAHA! THAT'S A NICE WAY OF PUTTING IT. "FAILURE IN TACTICS".
LOOKED LIKE TO ME THAT YOUR BROTHER TRIED TO TAKE YOU DOWN.
PURIEL WAS FOLLOWING ORDERS. I WAS FOLLOWING ORDERS.
SCREW YOUR ORDERS! WE'RE A FREAK! YOUR "BROTHER" WILL KILL US. AND IF HE DOESN'T, THAT BIKER CHICK WILL!
NO! LISTEN TO ME!
I MUST ALERT FATHER OF THE PROGRAMMING CONFLICT.

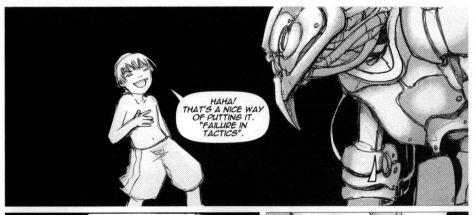

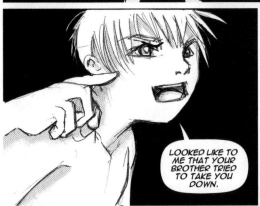

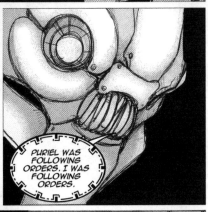

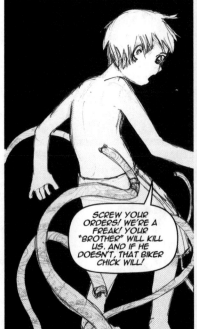

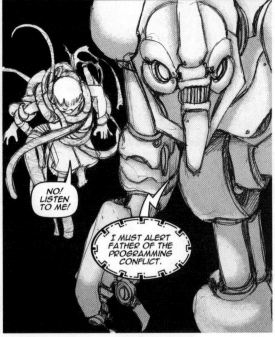

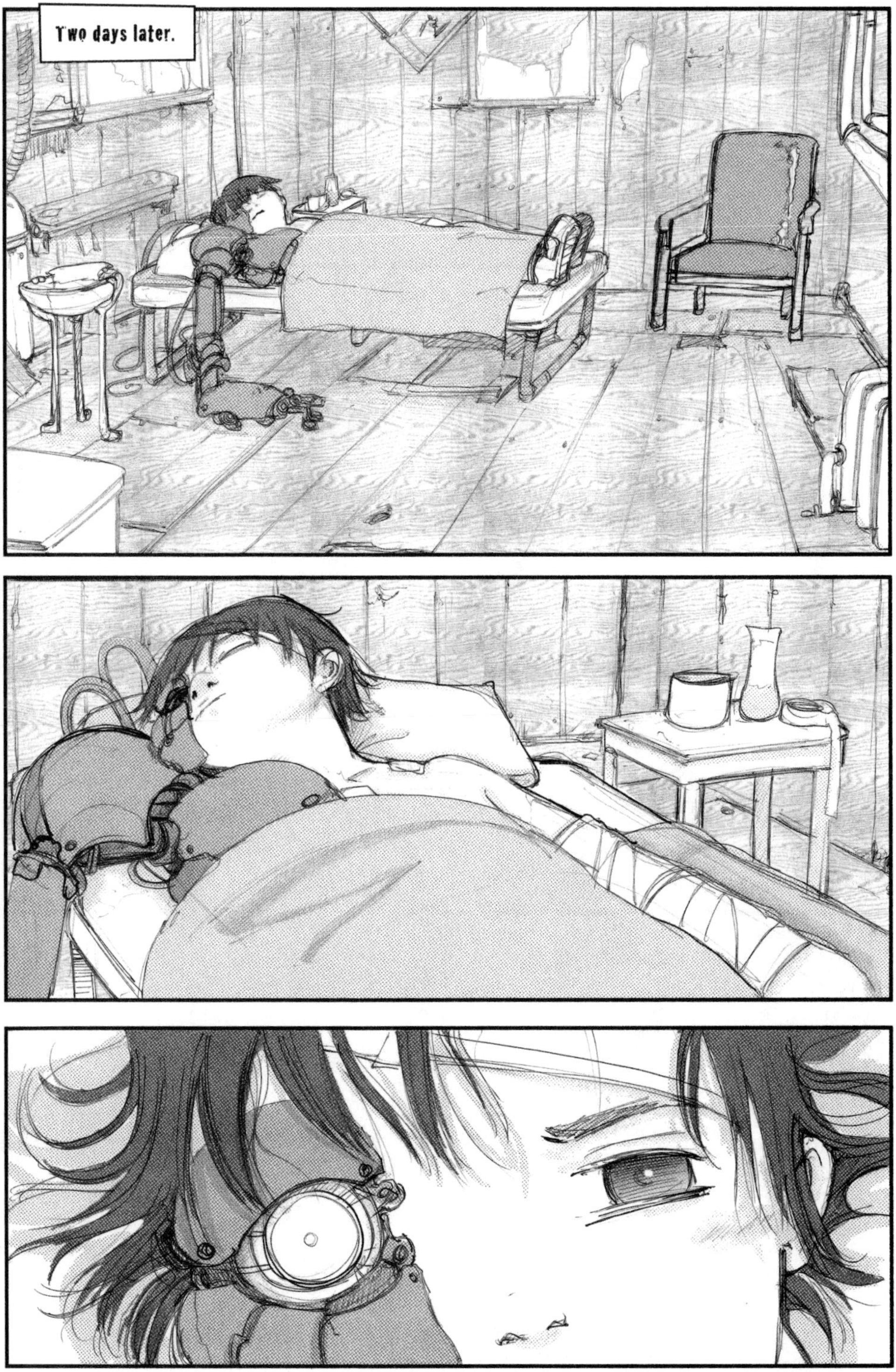
Two days later.

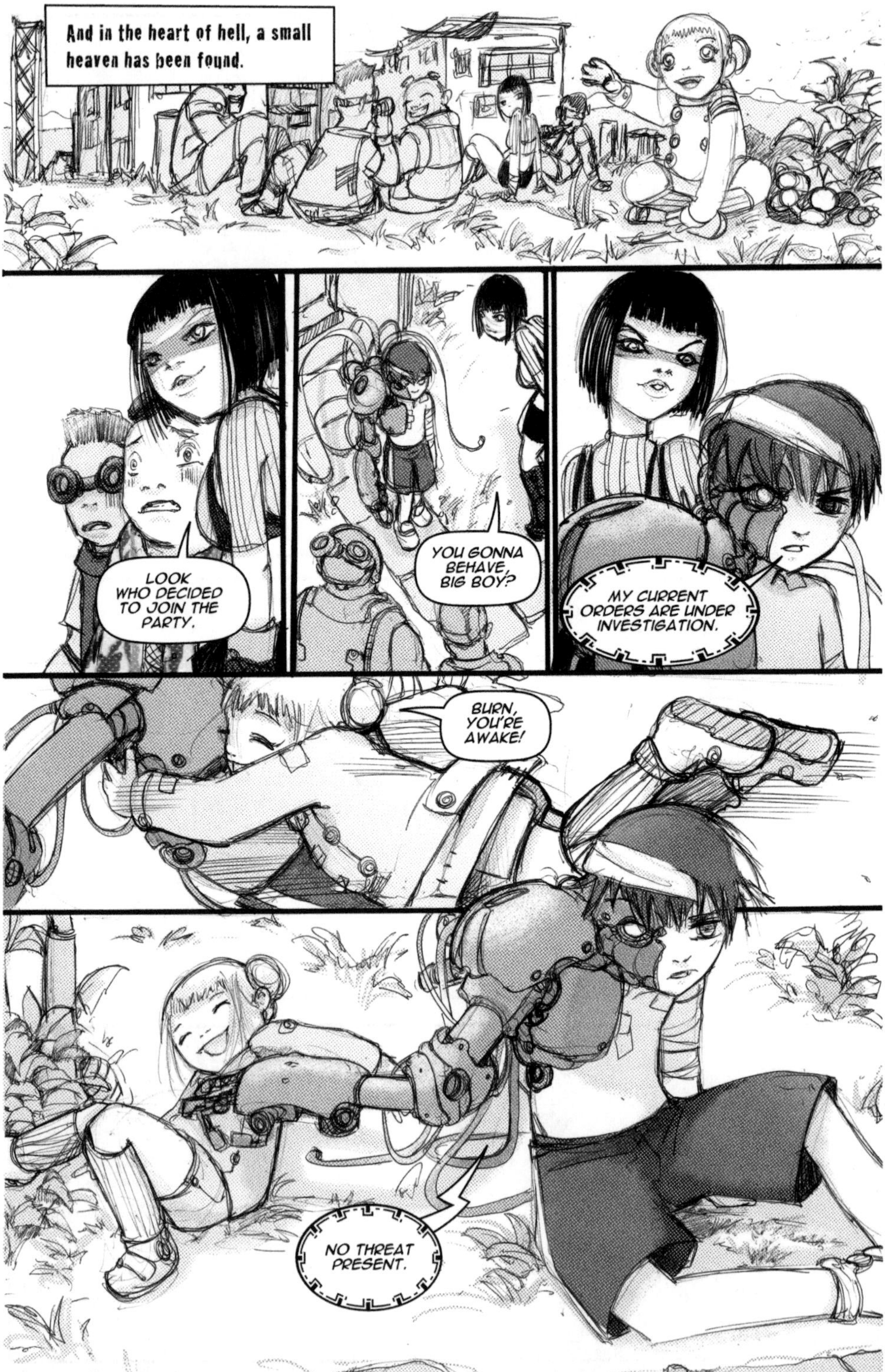
And in the heart of hell, a small heaven has been found.
LOOK WHO DECIDED TO JOIN THE PARTY.
YOU GONNA BEHAVE, BIG BOY?
MY CURRENT ORDERS ARE UNDER INVESTIGATION.
BURN, YOU'RE AWAKE!
NO THREAT PRESENT.

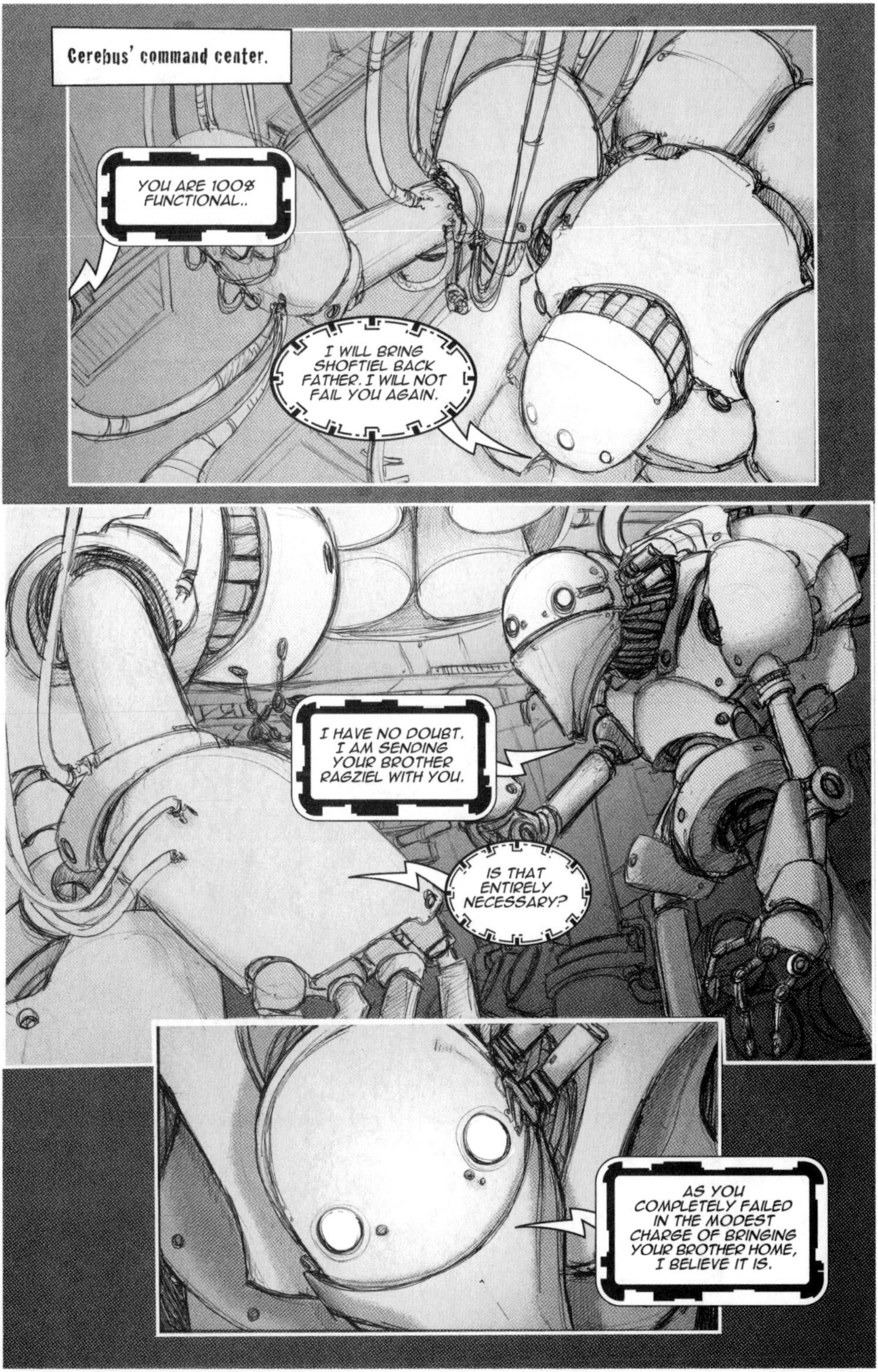
Cerebus' command center.
YOU ARE 100% FUNCTIONAL..
I WILL BRING SHOFTIEL BACK FATHER. I WILL NOT FAIL YOU AGAIN.
I HAVE NO DOUBT. I AM SENDING YOUR BROTHER RAGZIEL WITH YOU.
IS THAT ENTIRELY NECESSARY?
AS YOU COMPLETELY FAILED IN THE MODEST CHARGE OF BRINGING YOUR BROTHER HOME, I BELIEVE IT IS.

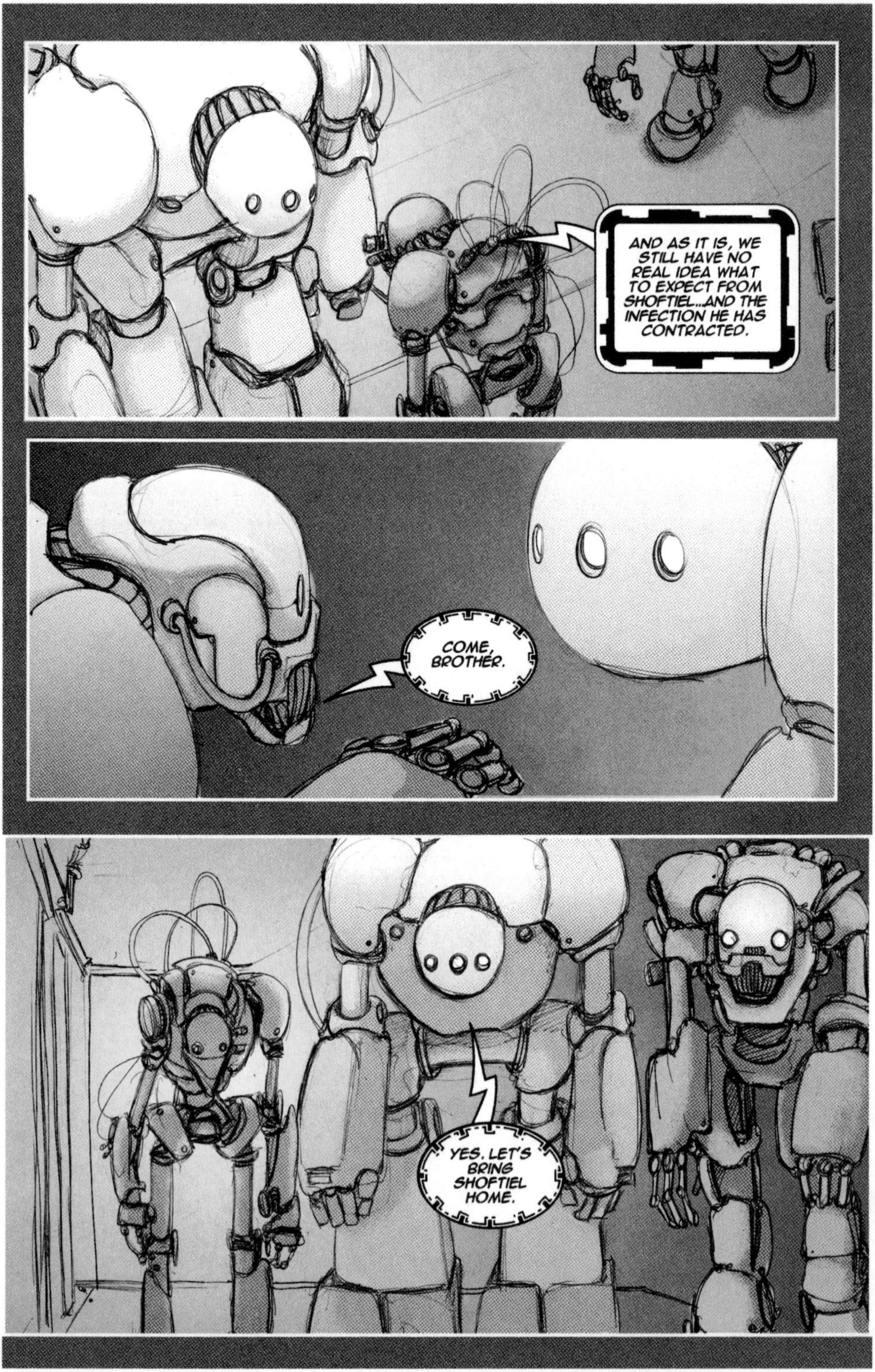
AND AS IT IS, WE STILL HAVE NO REAL IDEA WHAT TO EXPECT FROM SHOFTIEL...AND THE INFECTION HE HAS CONTRACTED.
COME, BROTHER.
YES. LET'S BRING SHOFTIEL HOME.

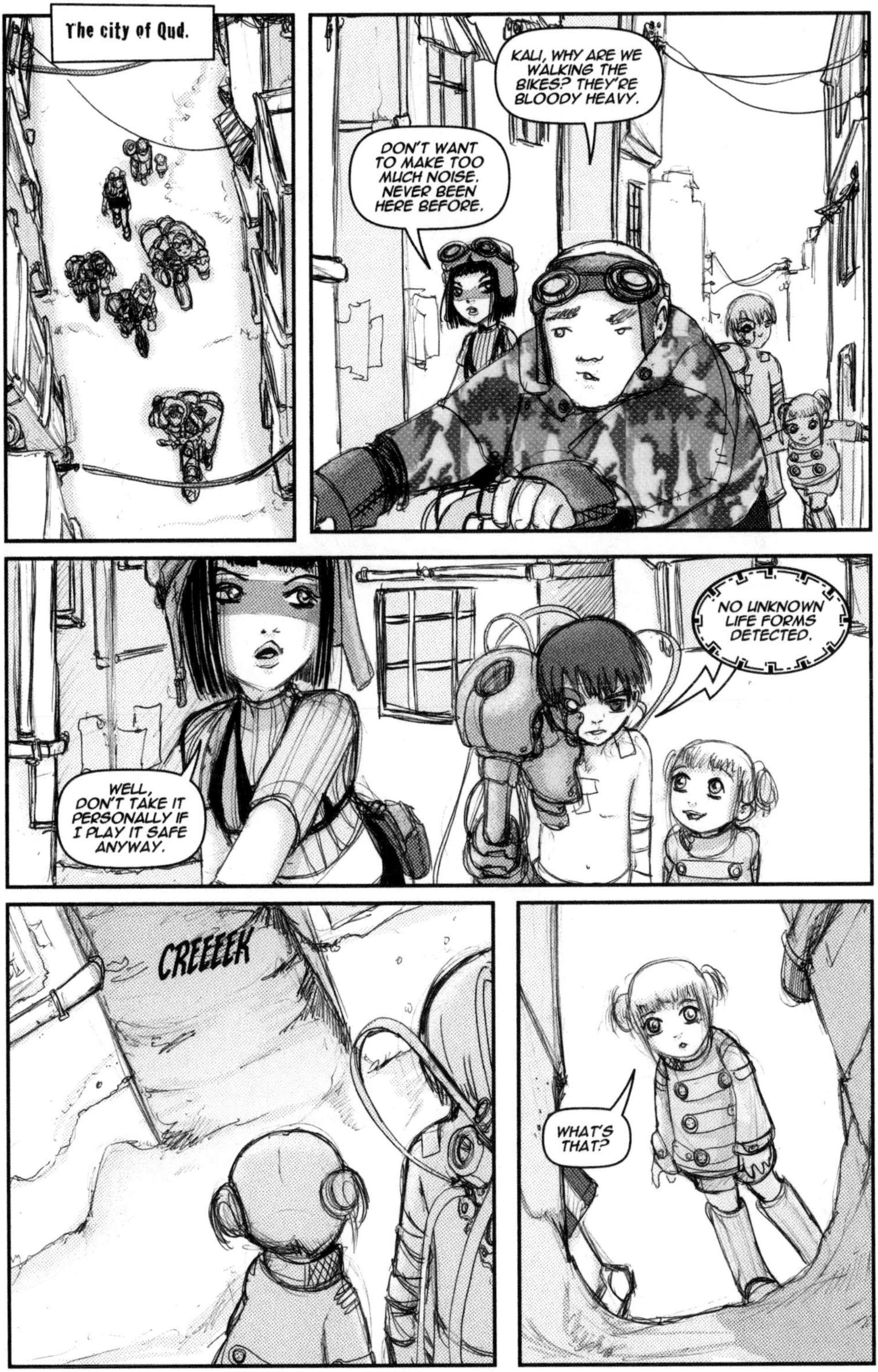
The city of Qud.
KALI, WHY ARE WE WALKING THE BIKES? THEY'RE BLOODY HEAVY.
DON'T WANT TO MAKE TOO MUCH NOISE. NEVER BEEN HERE BEFORE.
NO UNKNOWN LIFE FORMS DETECTED.
WELL, DON'T TAKE IT PERSONALLY IF I PLAY IT SAFE ANYWAY.
CREEEEK
WHAT'S THAT?

CAREFUL, KID!

LIFE FORM DETECTED.

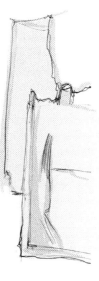

AIEEE!

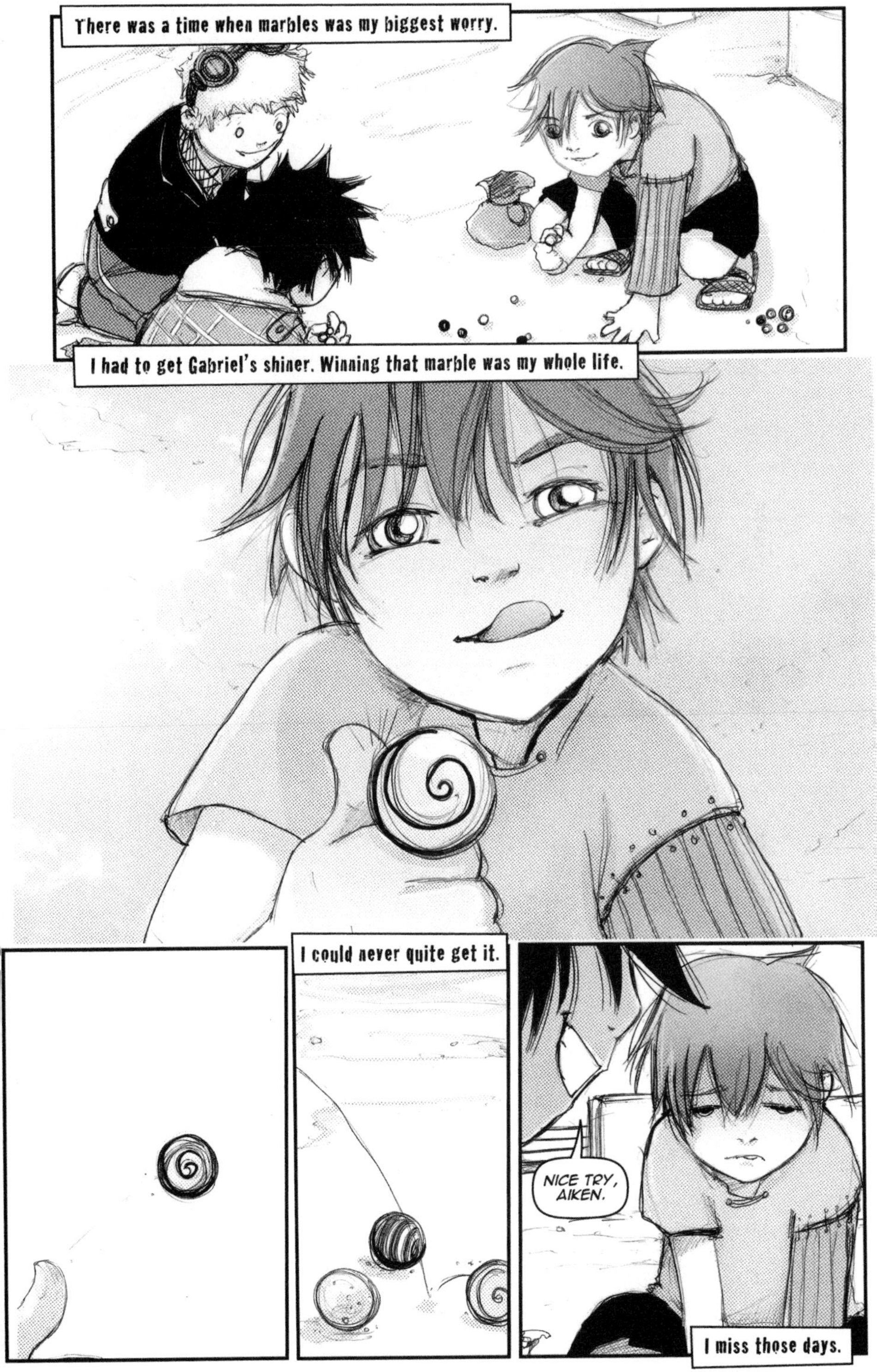
There was a time when marbles was my biggest worry.
I had to get Gabriel's shiner. Winning that marble was my whole life.
I could never quite get it.
NICE TRY, AIKEN.
I miss those days.

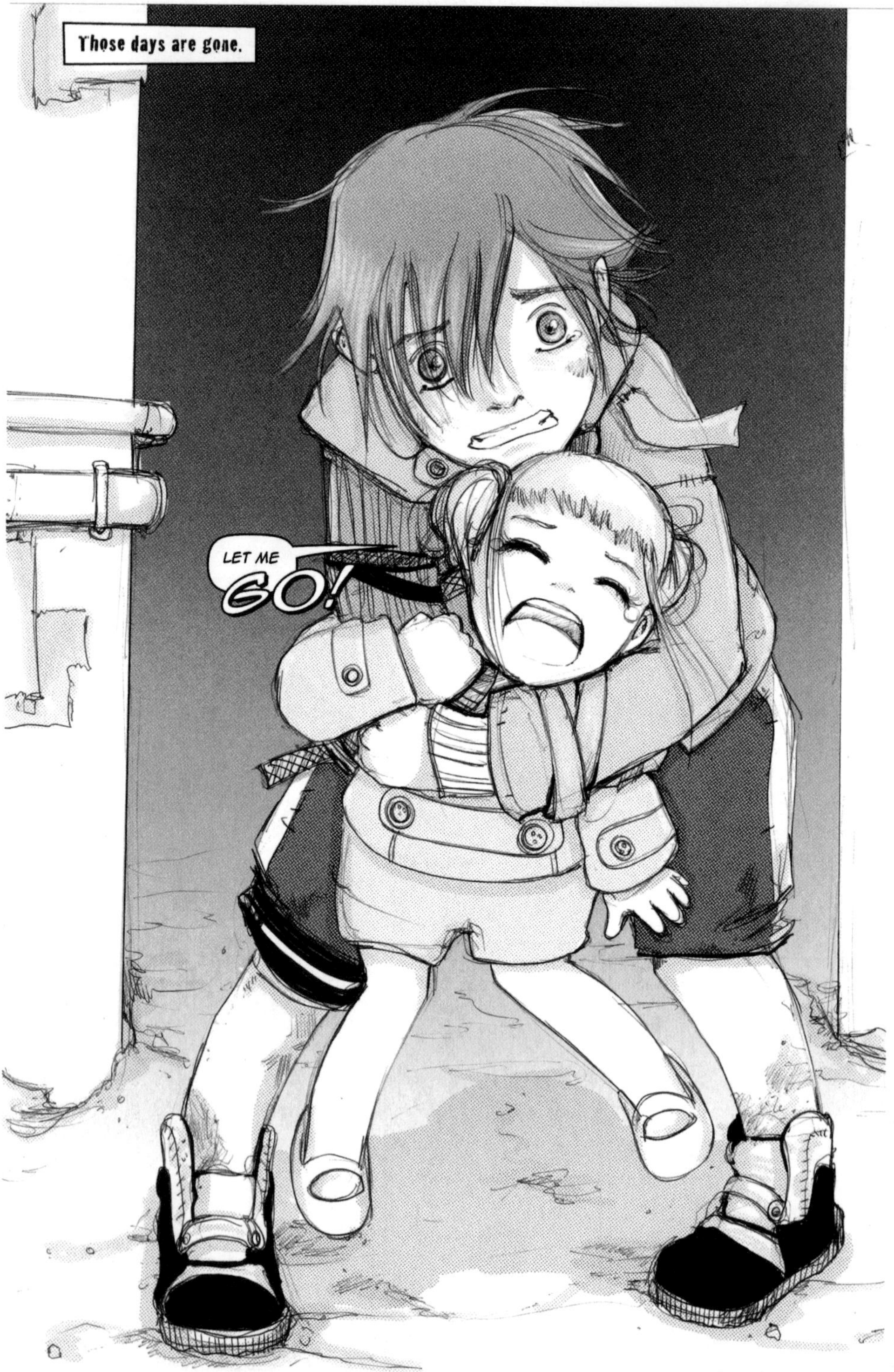
Those days are gone.
LET ME GO!

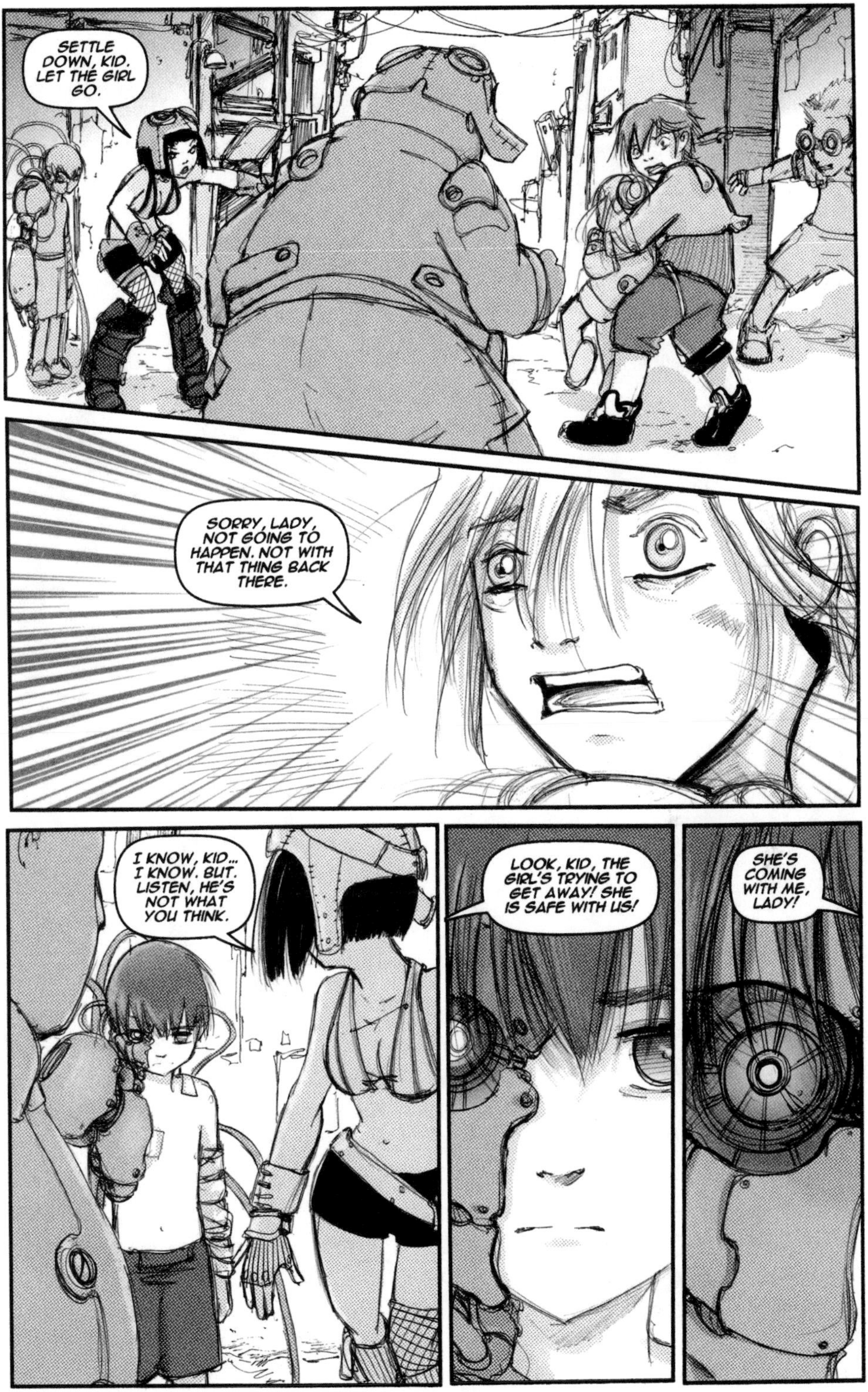
SETTLE DOWN, KID. LET THE GIRL GO.
SORRY, LADY, NOT GOING TO HAPPEN. NOT WITH THAT THING BACK THERE.
I KNOW, KID... I KNOW. BUT. LISTEN, HE'S NOT WHAT YOU THINK.
LOOK, KID, THE GIRL'S TRYING TO GET AWAY! SHE IS SAFE WITH US!
SHE'S COMING WITH ME, LADY!

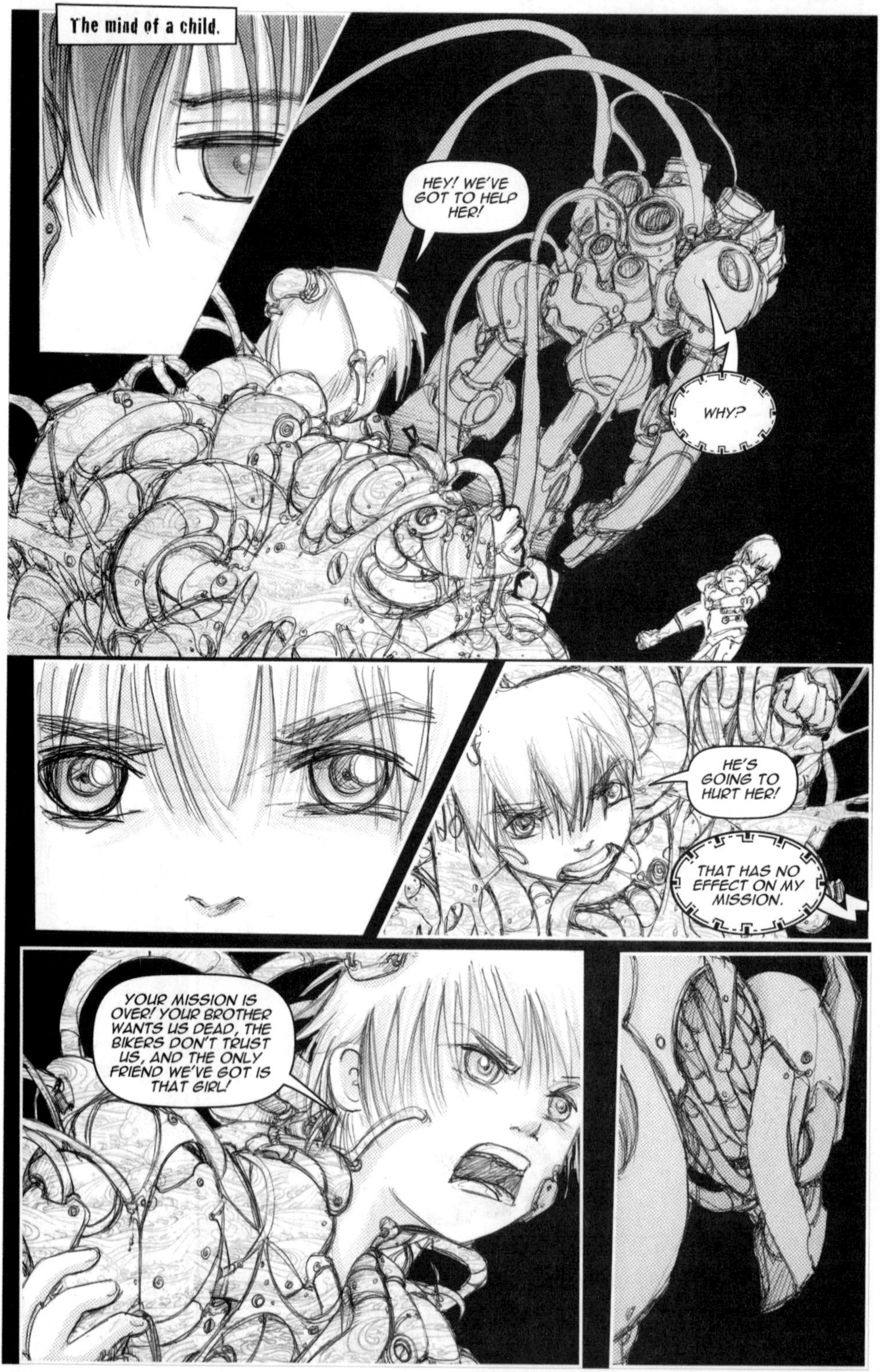
The mind of a child.
HEY! WE'VE GOT TO HELP HER!
WHY?
HE'S GOING TO HURT HER!
THAT HAS NO EFFECT ON MY MISSION.
YOUR MISSION IS OVER! YOUR BROTHER WANTS US DEAD, THE BIKERS DON'T TRUST US, AND THE ONLY FRIEND WE'VE GOT IS THAT GIRL!

ARGGG!

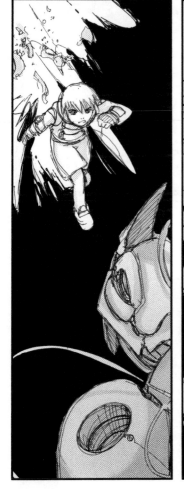

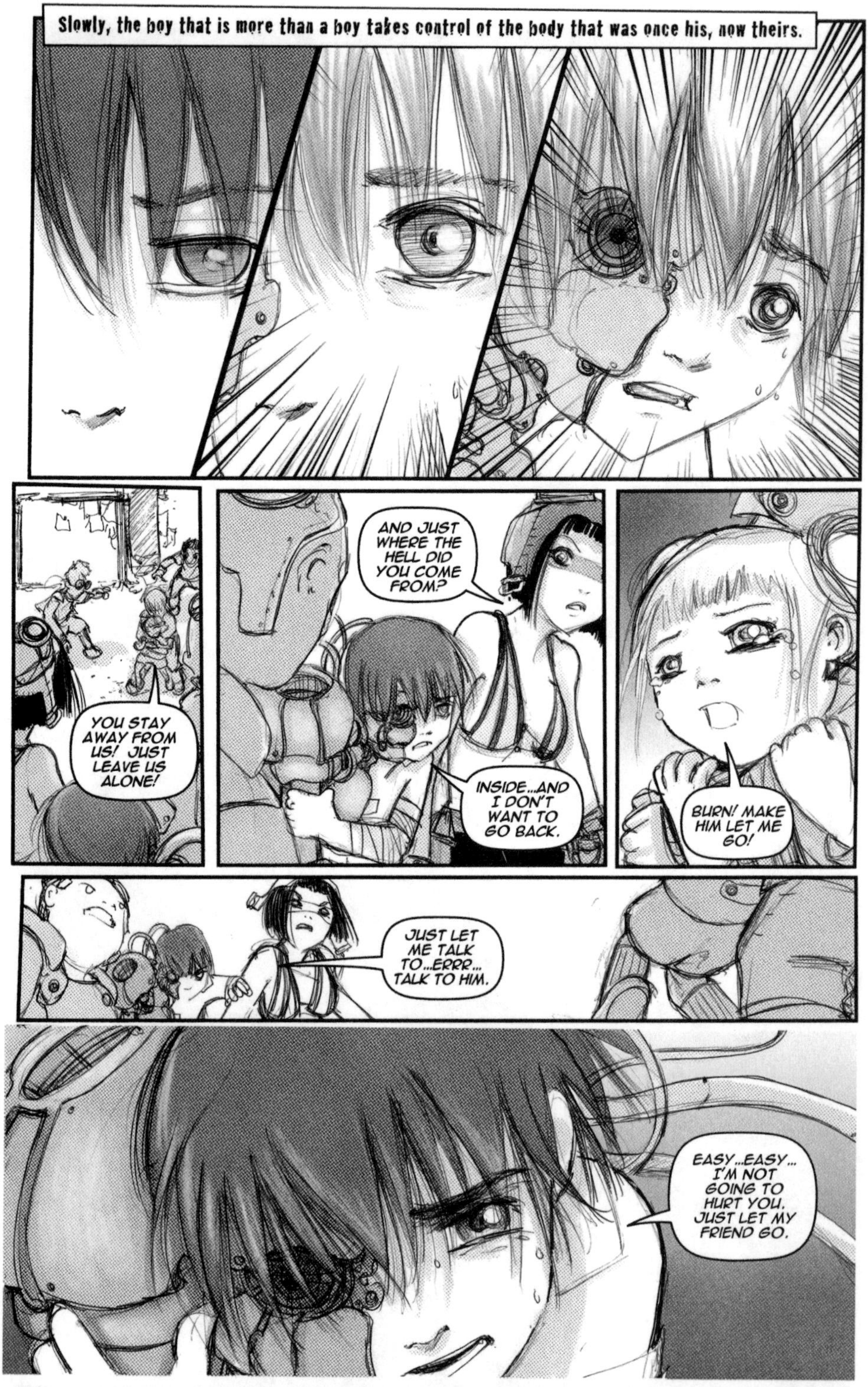

Slowly, the boy that is more than a boy takes control of the body that was once his, now theirs.
YOU STAY AWAY FROM US! JUST LEAVE US ALONE!
AND JUST WHERE THE HELL DID YOU COME FROM?
INSIDE...AND I DON'T WANT TO GO BACK.
BURN! MAKE HIM LET ME GO!
JUST LET ME TALK TO...ERRR... TALK TO HIM.
EASY...EASY... I'M NOT GOING TO HURT YOU. JUST LET MY FRIEND GO.

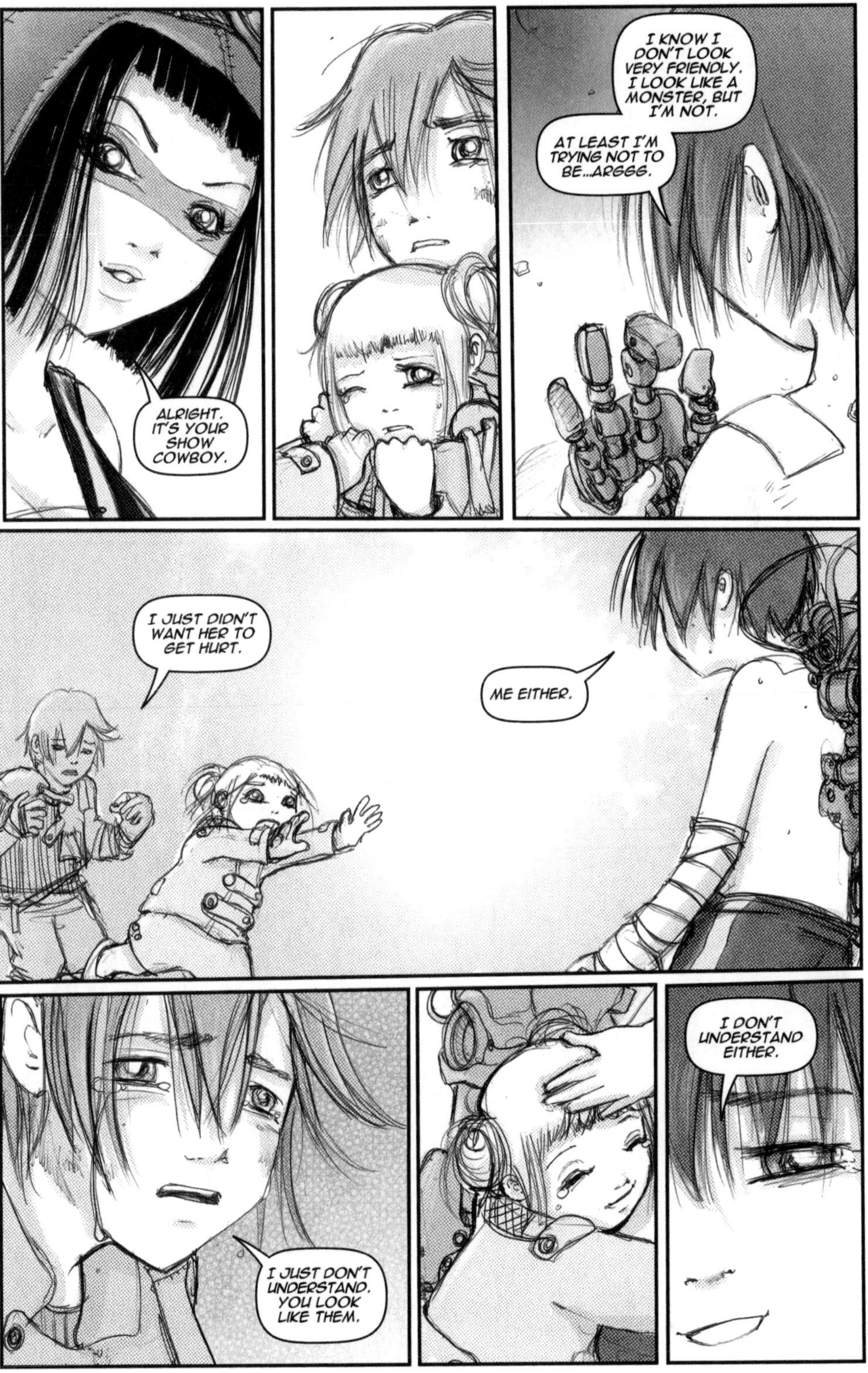
ALRIGHT. IT'S YOUR SHOW COWBOY.
I KNOW I DON'T LOOK VERY FRIENDLY. I LOOK LIKE A MONSTER, BUT I'M NOT.
AT LEAST I'M TRYING NOT TO BE...ARGGG.
I JUST DIDN'T WANT HER TO GET HURT.
ME EITHER.
I JUST DON'T UNDERSTAND. YOU LOOK LIKE THEM.
I DON'T UNDERSTAND EITHER.

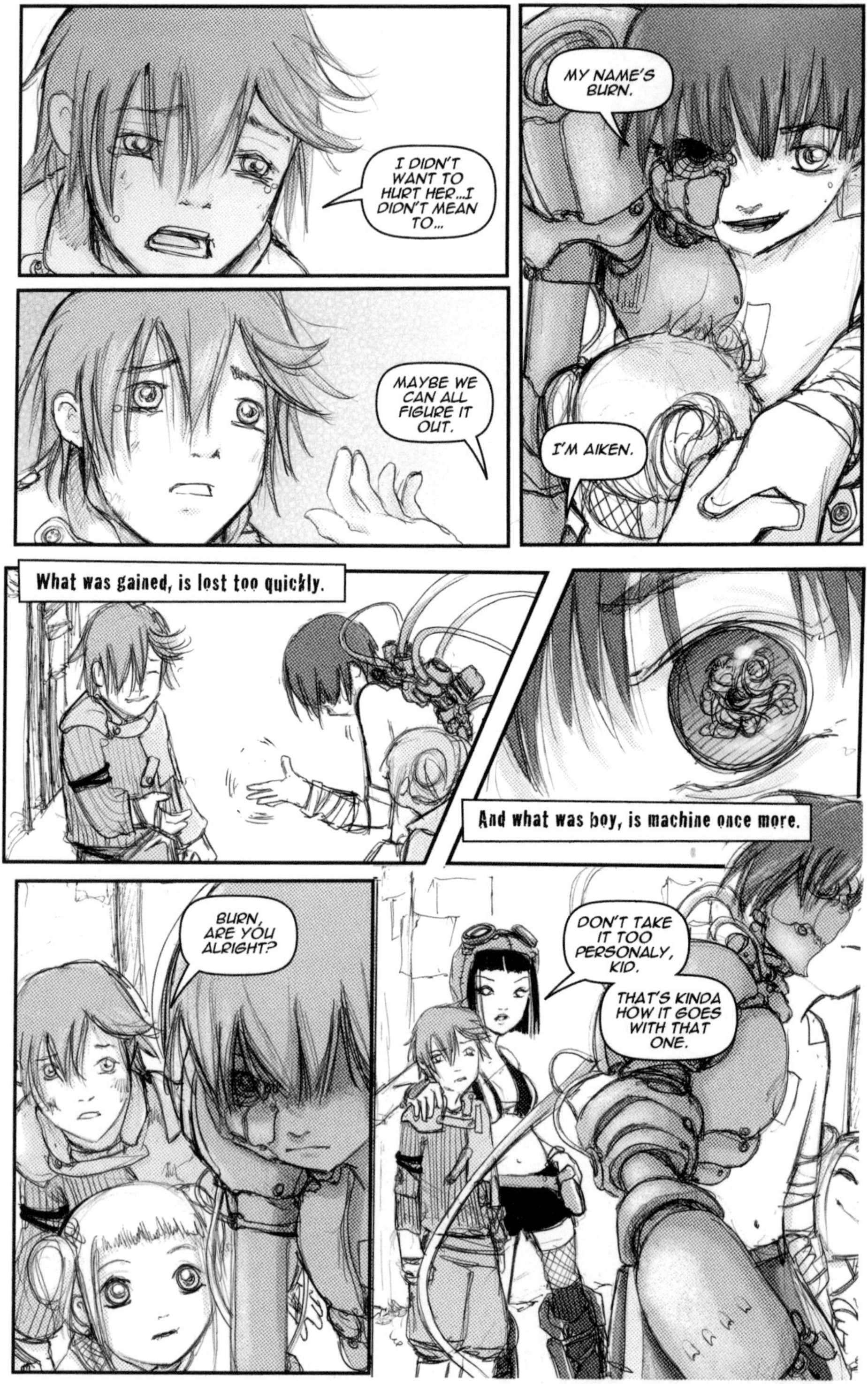
I DIDN'T WANT TO HURT HER...I DIDN'T MEAN TO...
MY NAME'S BURN.
MAYBE WE CAN ALL FIGURE IT OUT.
I'M AIKEN.
What was gained, is lost too quickly.
And what was boy, is machine once more.
BURN, ARE YOU ALRIGHT?
DON'T TAKE IT TOO PERSONALY, KID.
THAT'S KINDA HOW IT GOES WITH THAT ONE.

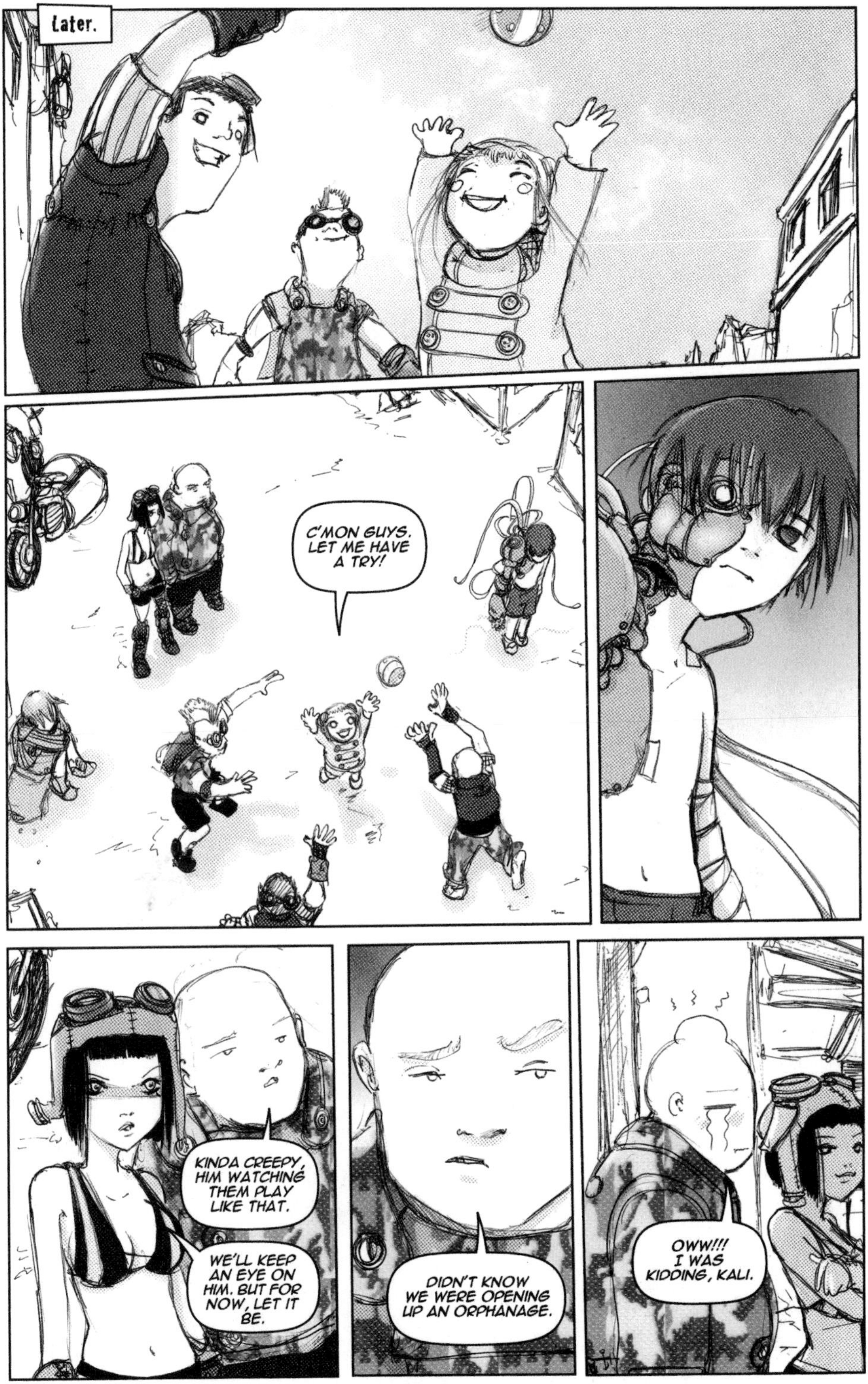
Later.
C'MON GUYS. LET ME HAVE A TRY!
KINDA CREEPY, HIM WATCHING THEM PLAY LIKE THAT.
WE'LL KEEP AN EYE ON HIM. BUT FOR NOW, LET IT BE.
DIDN'T KNOW WE WERE OPENING UP AN ORPHANAGE.
OWW!!! I WAS KIDDING, KALI.

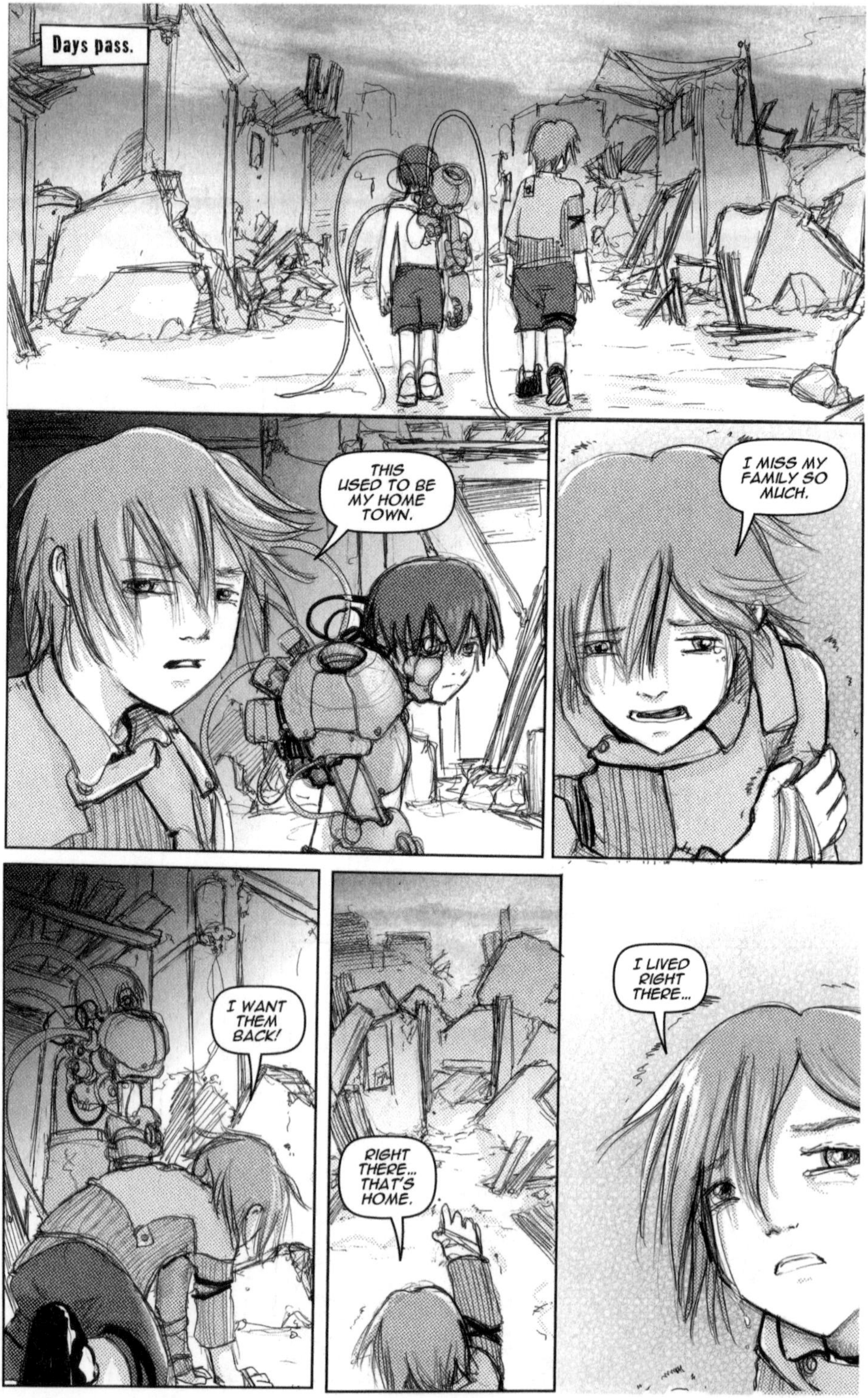
Days pass.
THIS USED TO BE MY HOME TOWN.
I MISS MY FAMILY SO MUCH.
I WANT THEM BACK!
RIGHT THERE... THAT'S HOME.
I LIVED RIGHT THERE...

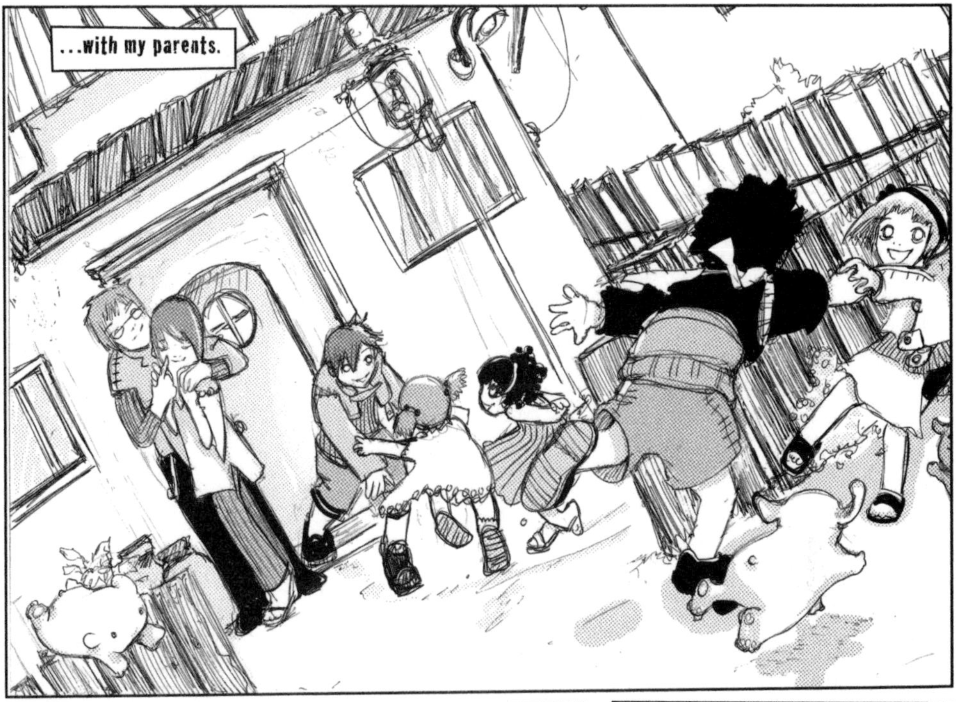
...with my parents.

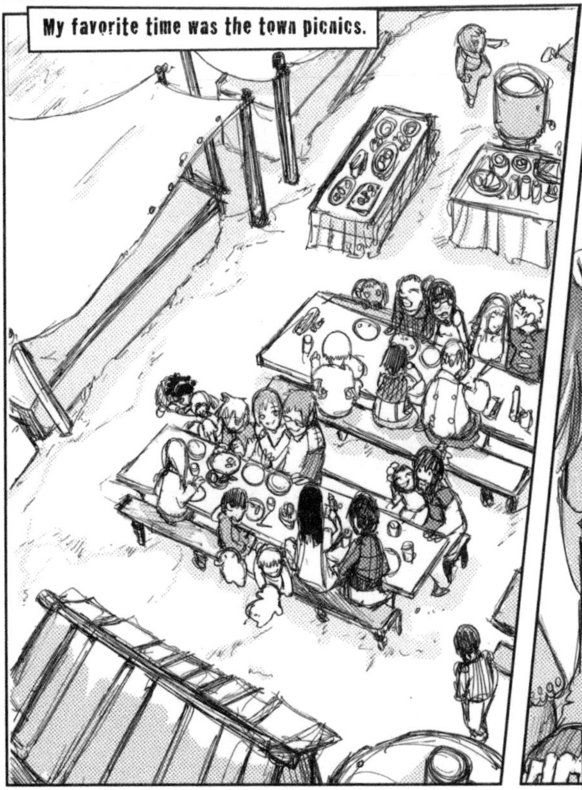
My favorite time was the town picnics.

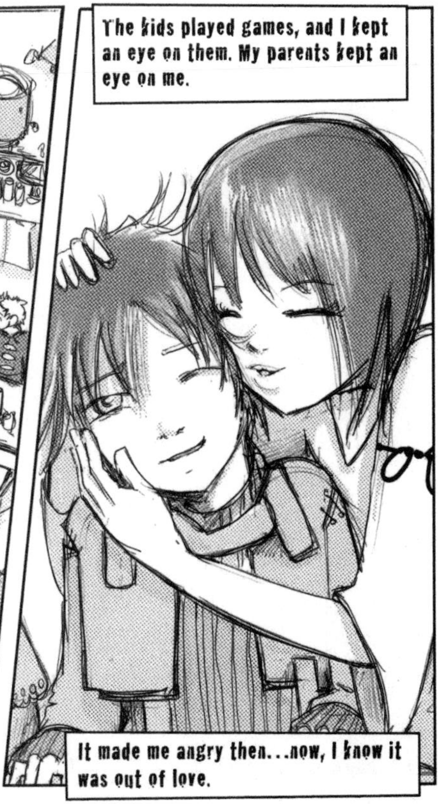
The kids played games, and I kept an eye on them. My parents kept an eye on me.
It made me angry then...now, I know it was out of love.

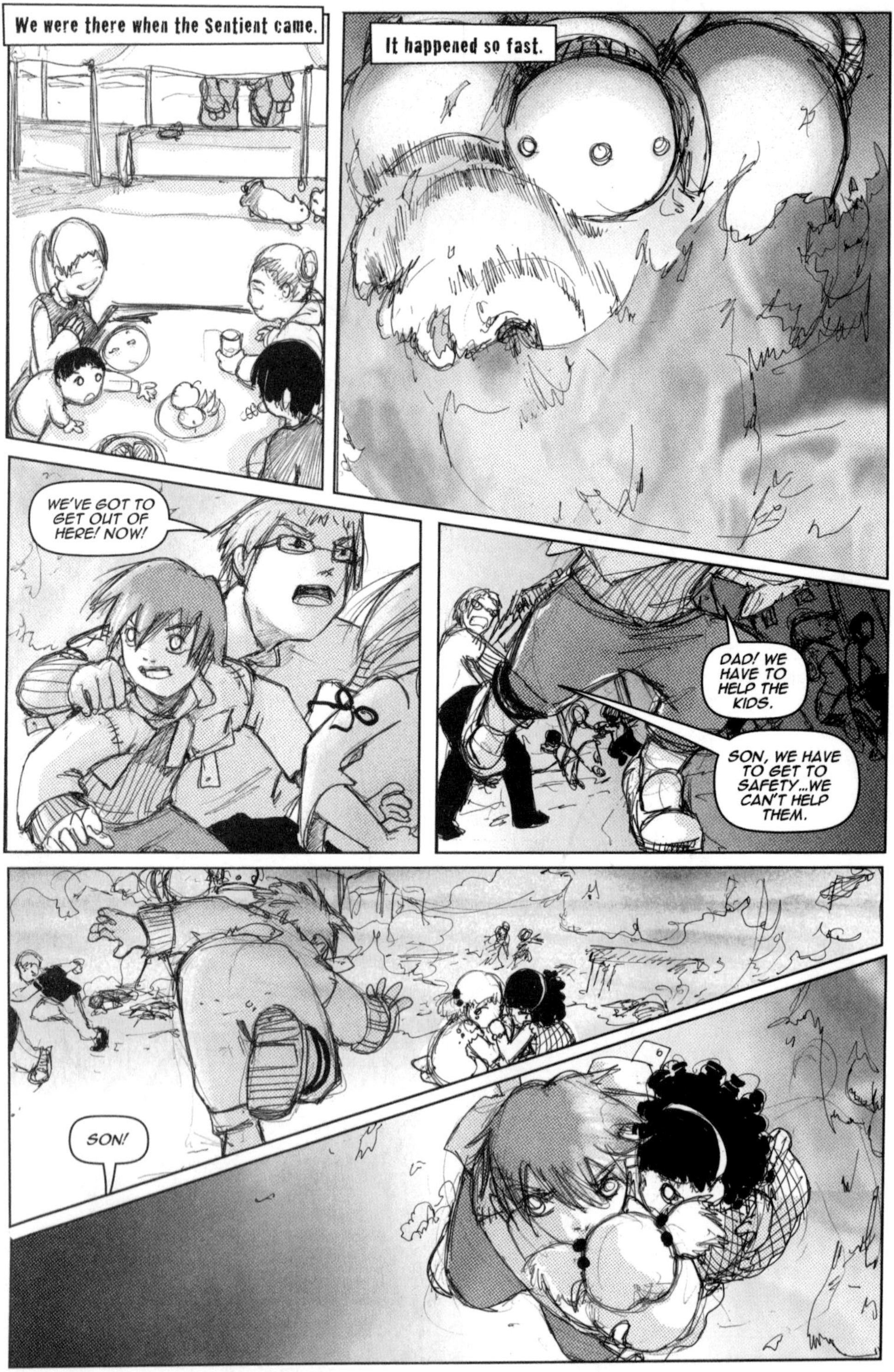
We were there when the Sentient came.
It happened so fast.
WE'VE GOT TO GET OUT OF HERE! NOW!
DAD! WE HAVE TO HELP THE KIDS.
SON, WE HAVE TO GET TO SAFETY...WE CAN'T HELP THEM.
SON!

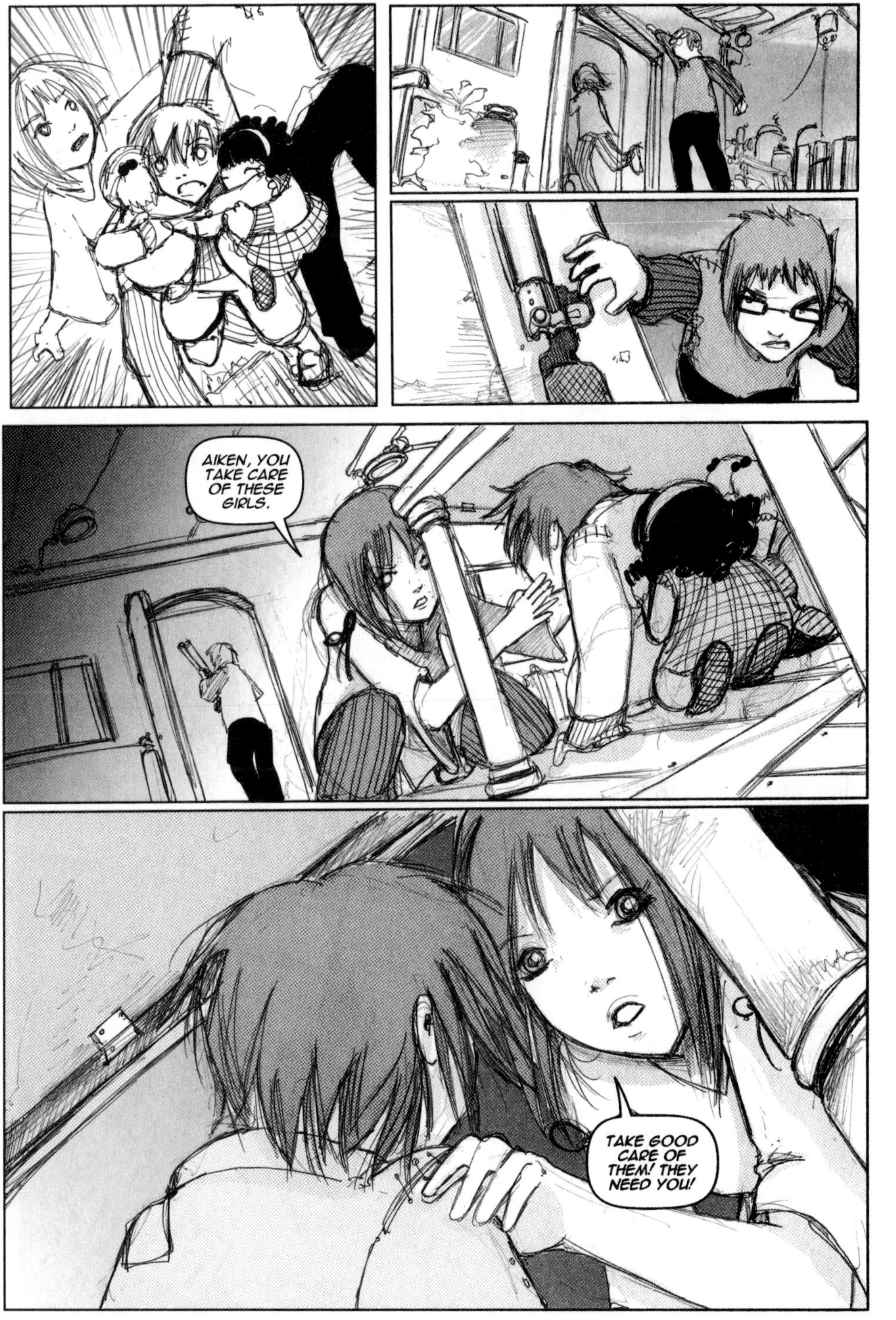
AIKEN, YOU TAKE CARE OF THESE GIRLS.
TAKE GOOD CARE OF THEM! THEY NEED YOU!

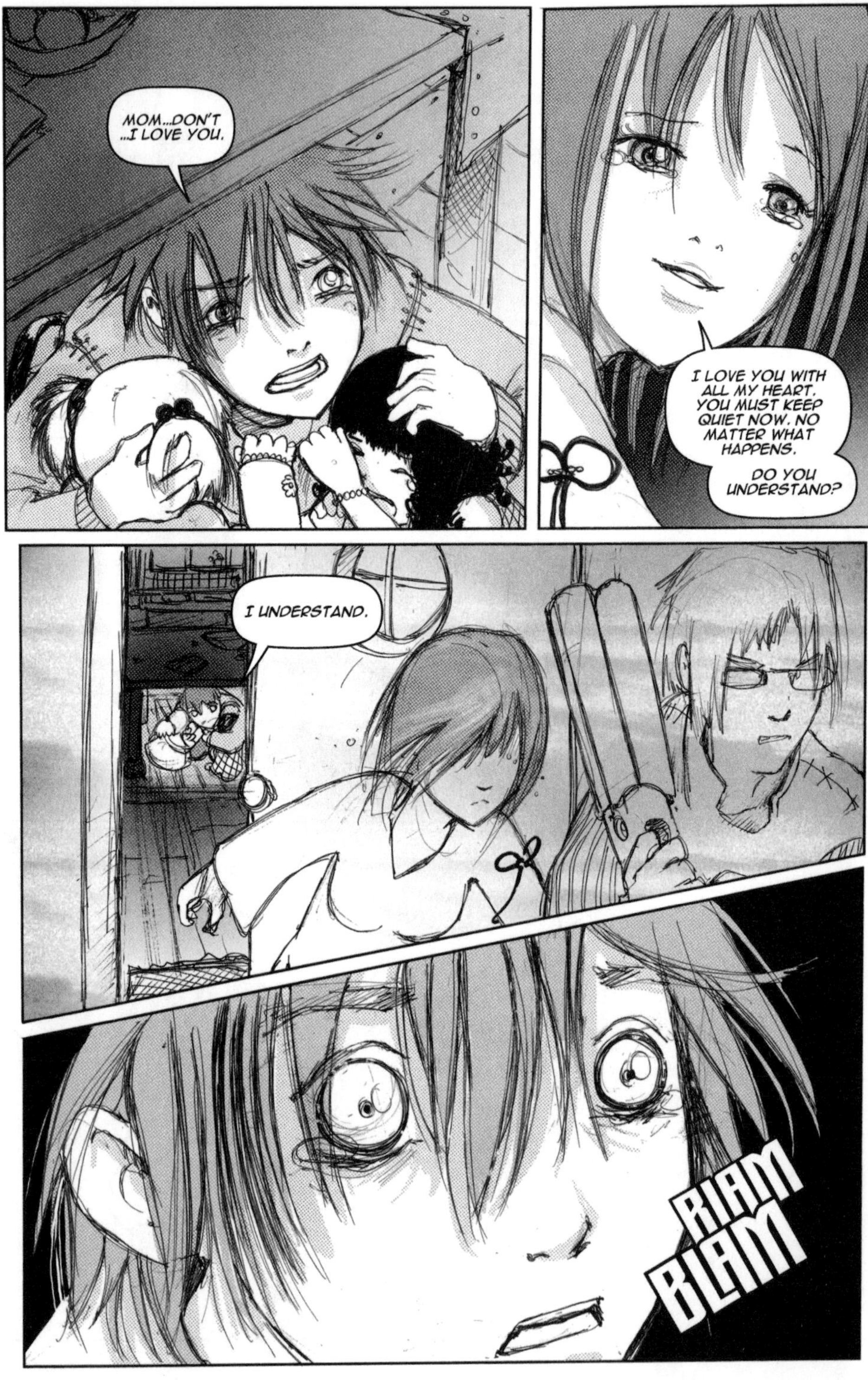
MOM...DON'T ...I LOVE YOU.
I LOVE YOU WITH ALL MY HEART. YOU MUST KEEP QUIET NOW. NO MATTER WHAT HAPPENS.
DO YOU UNDERSTAND?
I UNDERSTAND.
BLAM

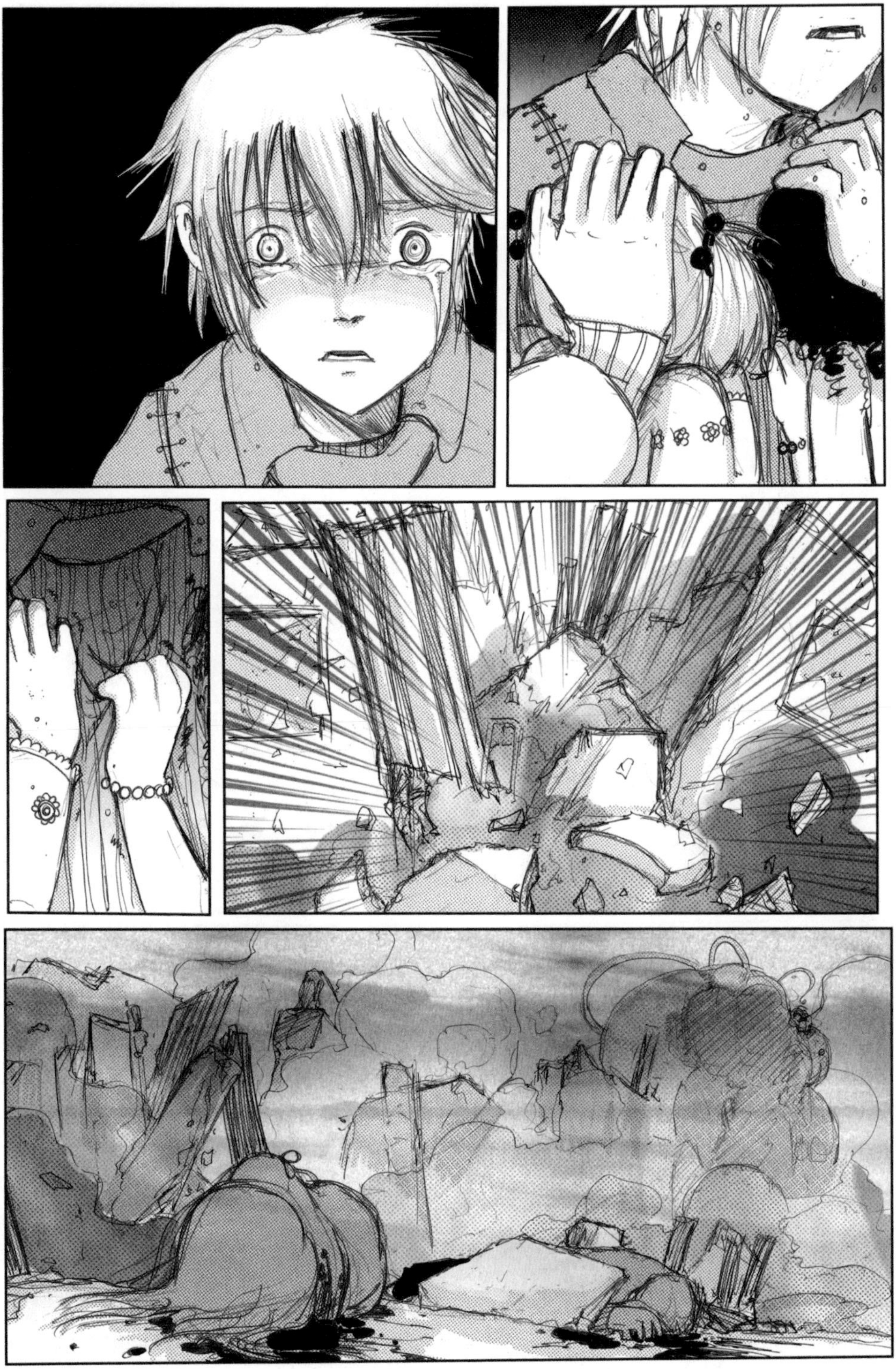

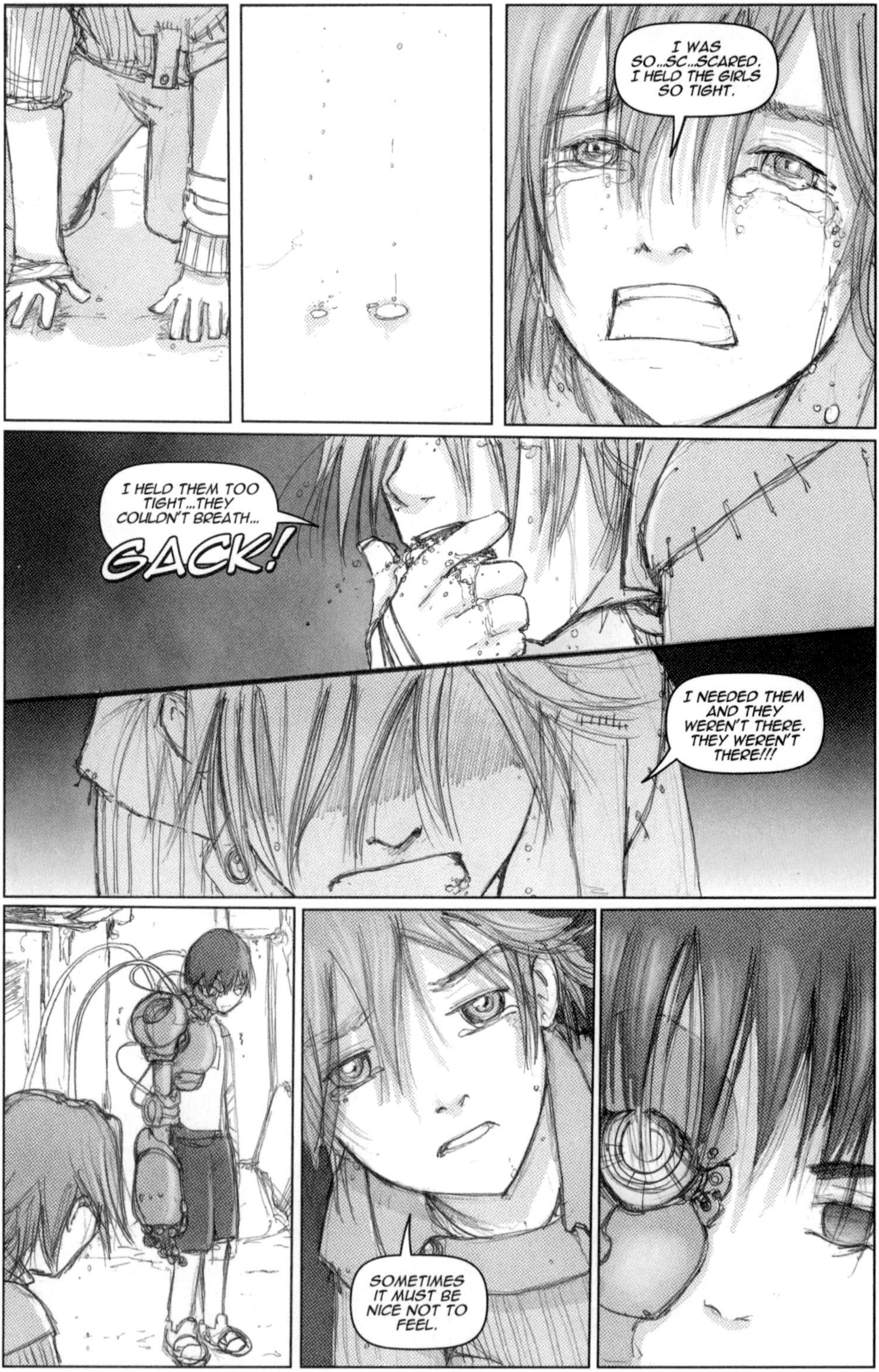
I WAS SO...SC...SCARED. I HELD THE GIRLS SO TIGHT.
I HELD THEM TOO TIGHT...THEY COULDN'T BREATH...
GACK!
I NEEDED THEM AND THEY WEREN'T THERE. THEY WEREN'T THERE!!!
SOMETIMES IT MUST BE NICE NOT TO FEEL.

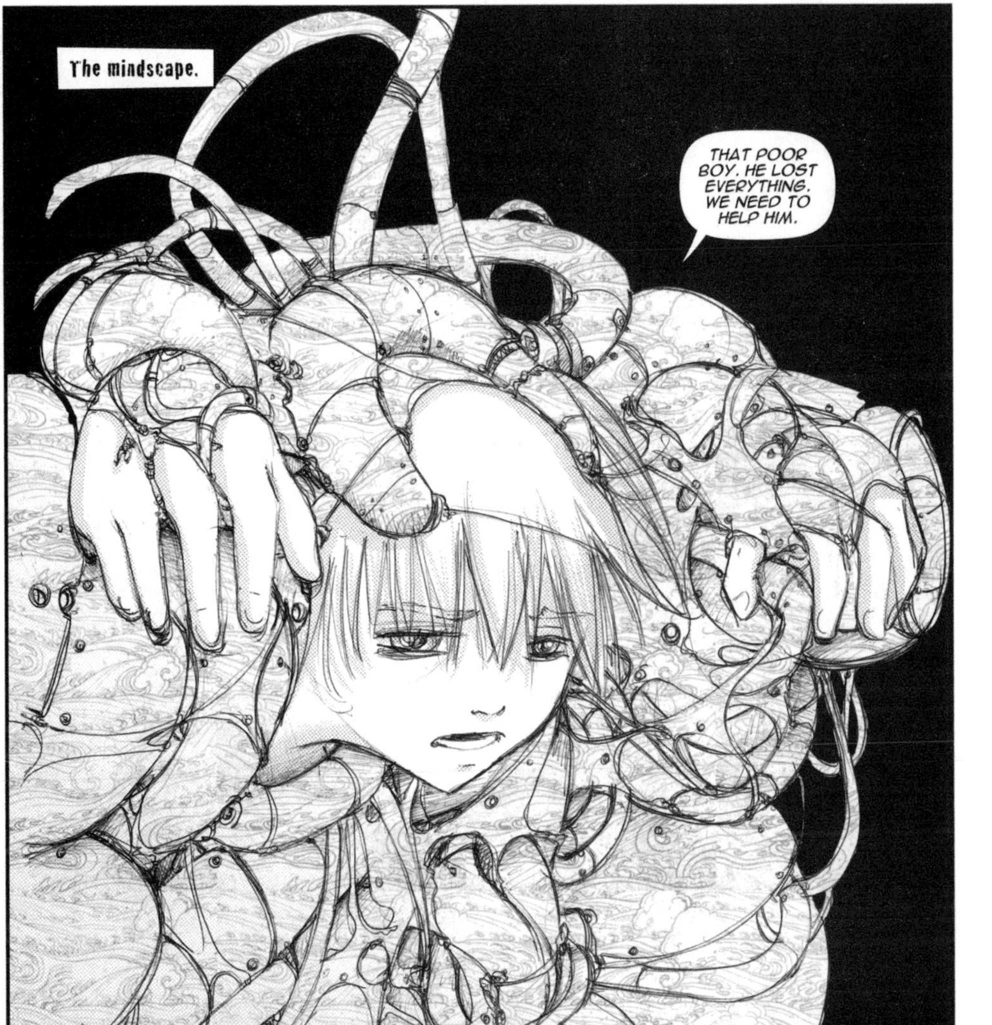
The mindscape.
THAT POOR BOY. HE LOST EVERYTHING. WE NEED TO HELP HIM.

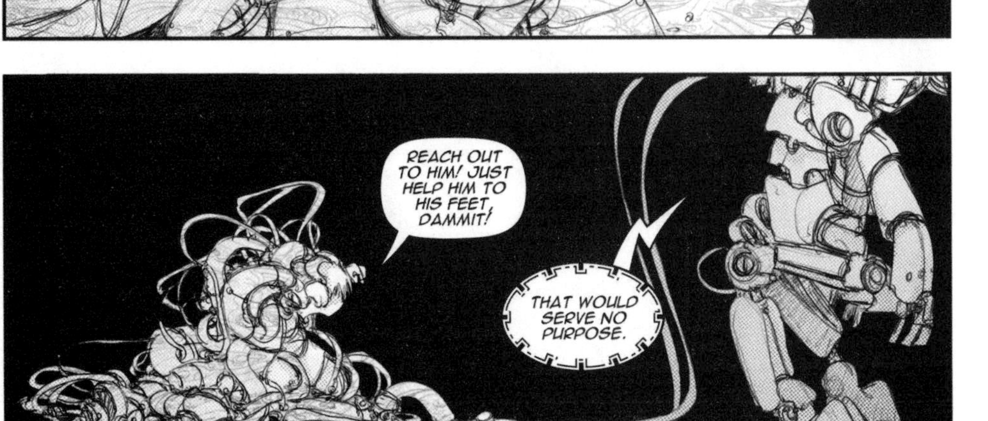
REACH OUT TO HIM! JUST HELP HIM TO HIS FEET, DAMMIT!
THAT WOULD SERVE NO PURPOSE.

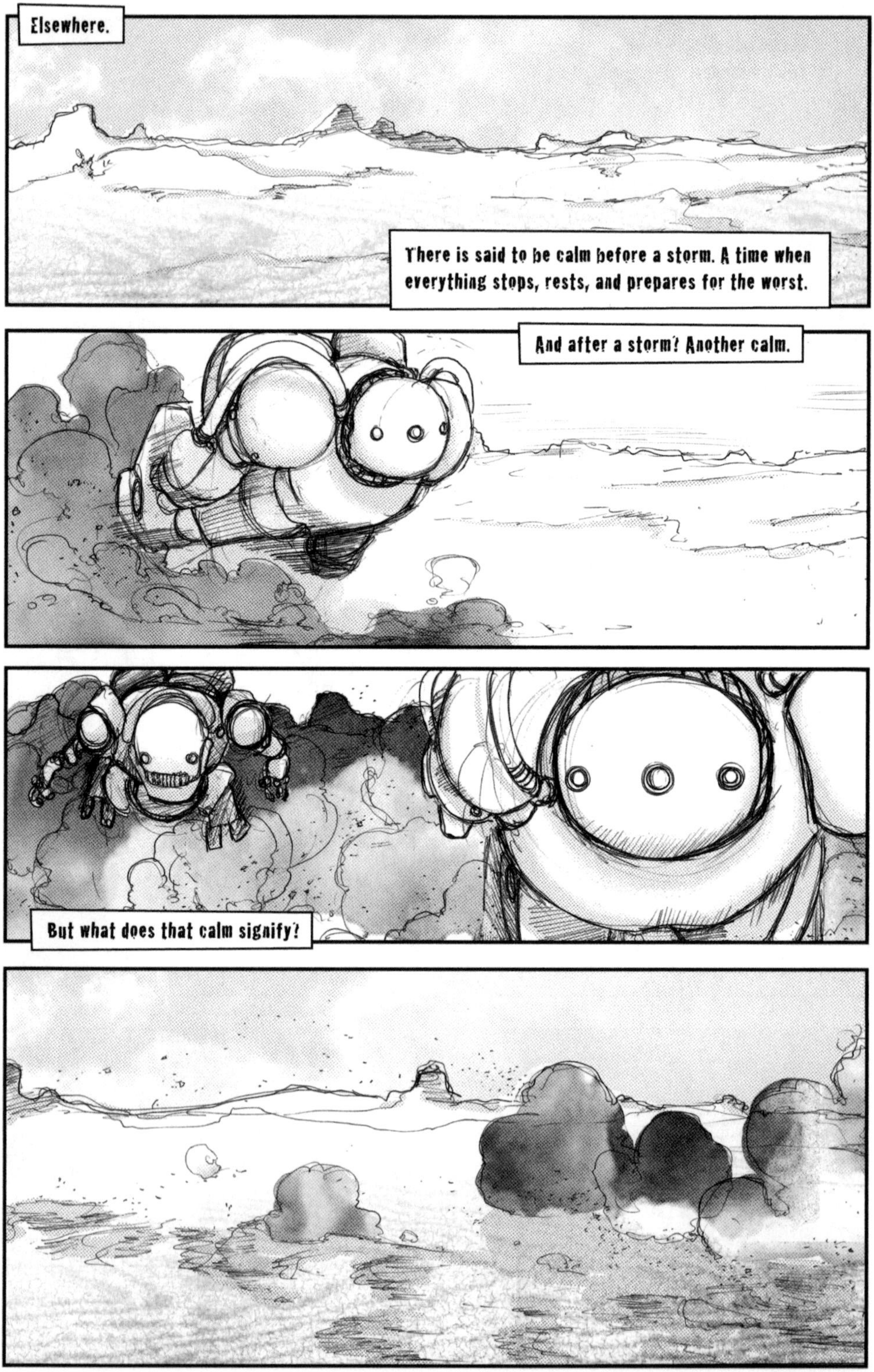
Elsewhere.
There is said to be calm before a storm. A time when everything stops, rests, and prepares for the worst.
And after a storm? Another calm.
But what does that calm signify?

WHAT IF THAT WAS YOUR BROTHER? DON'T YOU FEEL ANYTHING?
I DON'T "FEEL" THE WAY YOU DO.
IF THAT WAS MY BROTHER, HE WOULD BE SUFFERING FROM A MALFUNCTION.
A MALFUNCTION?
WHY DO YOU LAUGH?
IF YOU SENTIENTS DESTROY HUMANITY AND RULE THE WORLD, WHAT WOULD BE LEFT?
THERE WOULD BE ORDER.
LOOK AT US! THERE IS NO ORDER HERE!

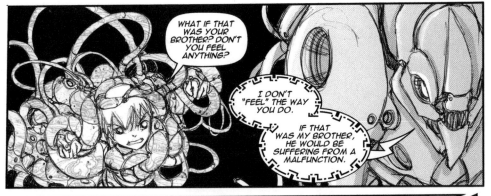

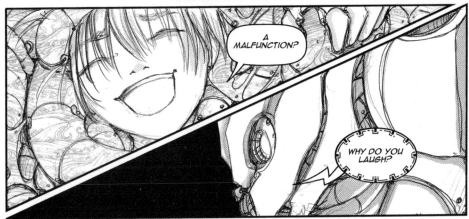

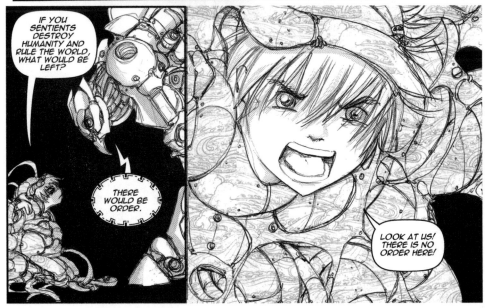

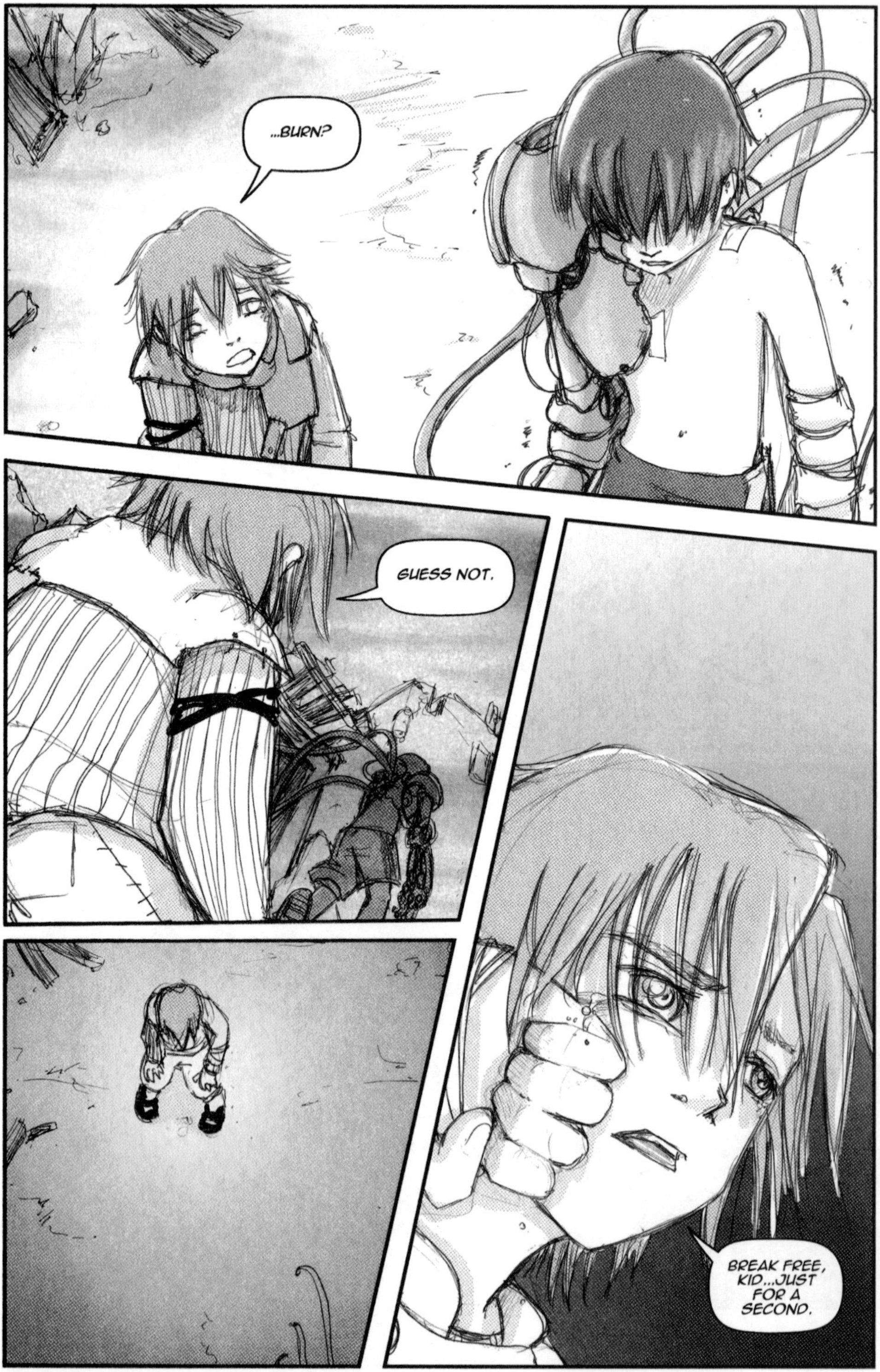
...BURN?
GUESS NOT.
BREAK FREE, KID...JUST FOR A SECOND.

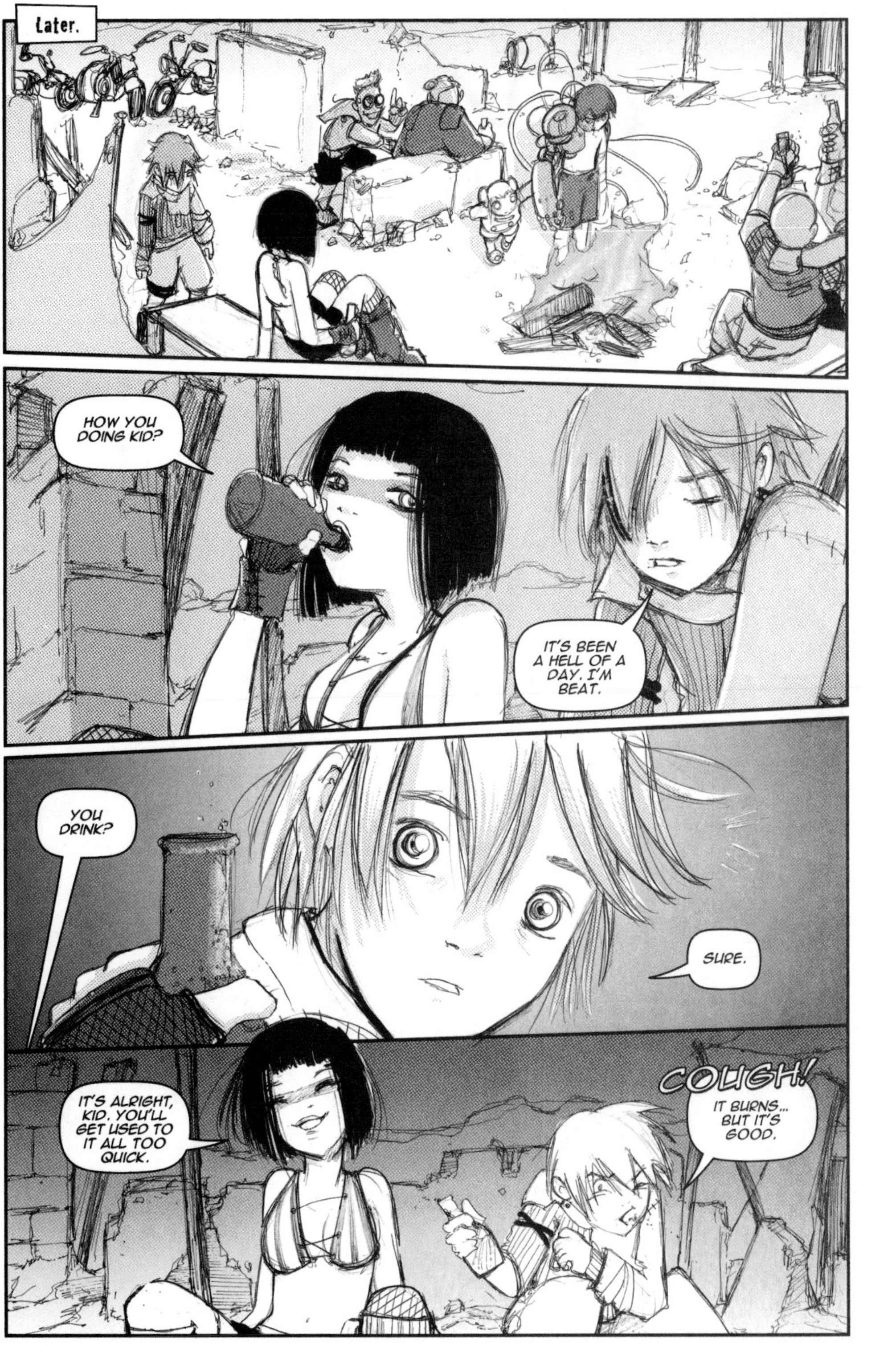
Later.
HOW YOU DOING KID?
IT'S BEEN A HELL OF A DAY. I'M BEAT.
YOU DRINK?
SURE.
IT'S ALRIGHT, KID. YOU'LL GET USED TO IT ALL TOO QUICK.
COUGH!
IT BURNS... BUT IT'S GOOD.

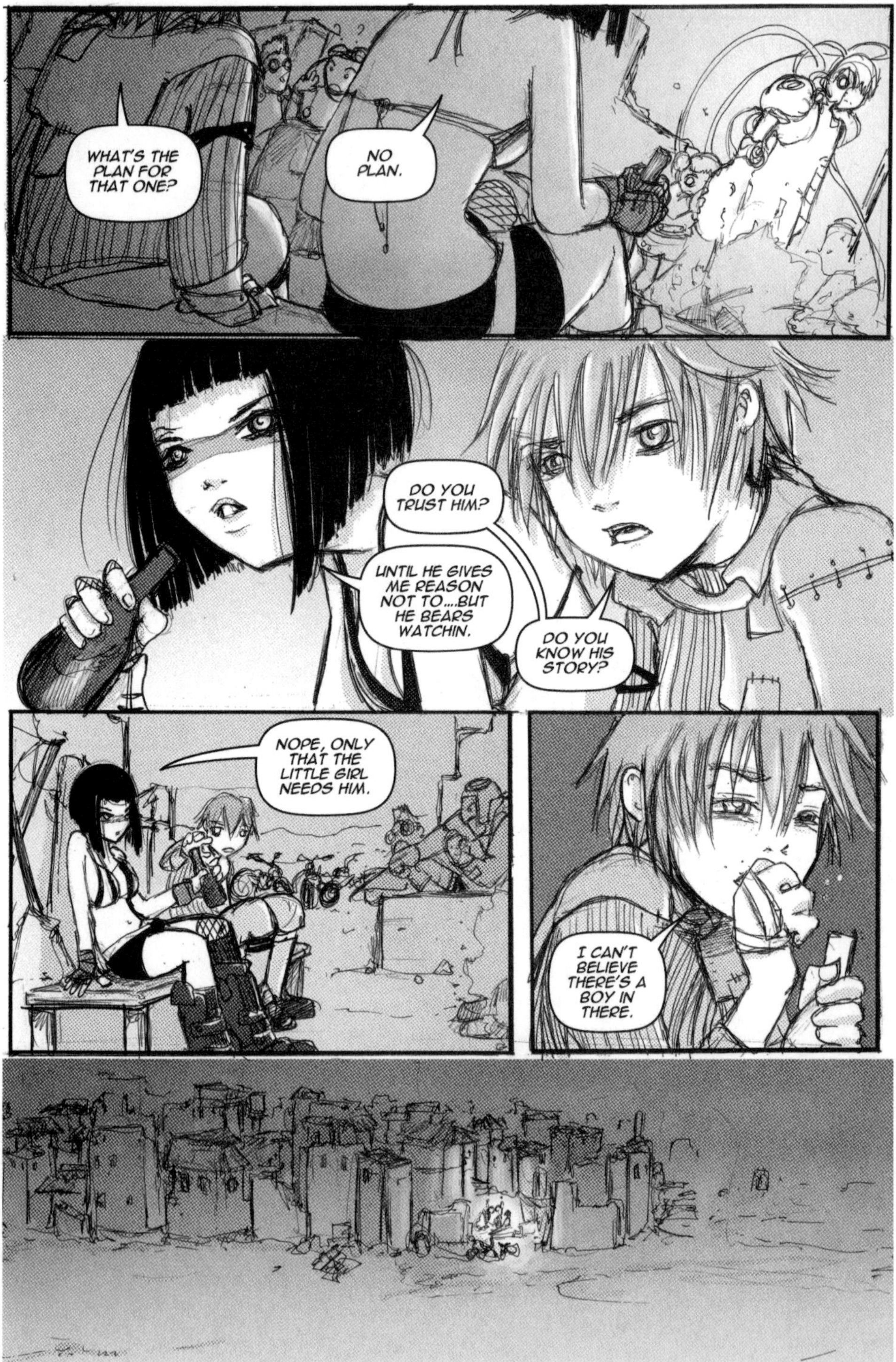
WHAT'S THE PLAN FOR THAT ONE?
NO PLAN.
DO YOU TRUST HIM?
UNTIL HE GIVES ME REASON NOT TO....BUT HE BEARS WATCHIN.
DO YOU KNOW HIS STORY?
NOPE, ONLY THAT THE LITTLE GIRL NEEDS HIM.
I CAN'T BELIEVE THERE'S A BOY IN THERE.

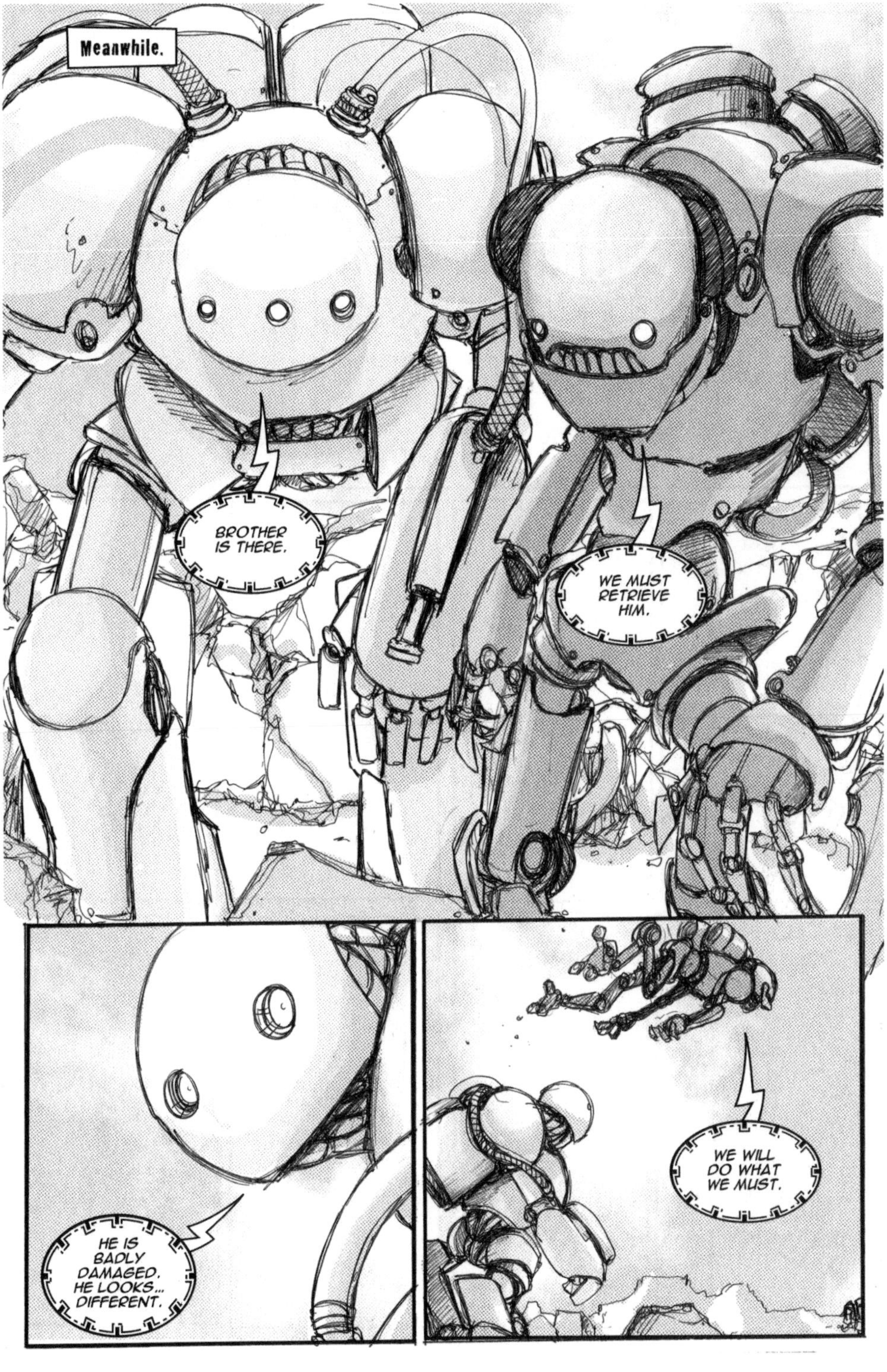
Meanwhile.
BROTHER IS THERE.
WE MUST RETRIEVE HIM.
HE IS BADLY DAMAGED. HE LOOKS... DIFFERENT.
WE WILL DO WHAT WE MUST.

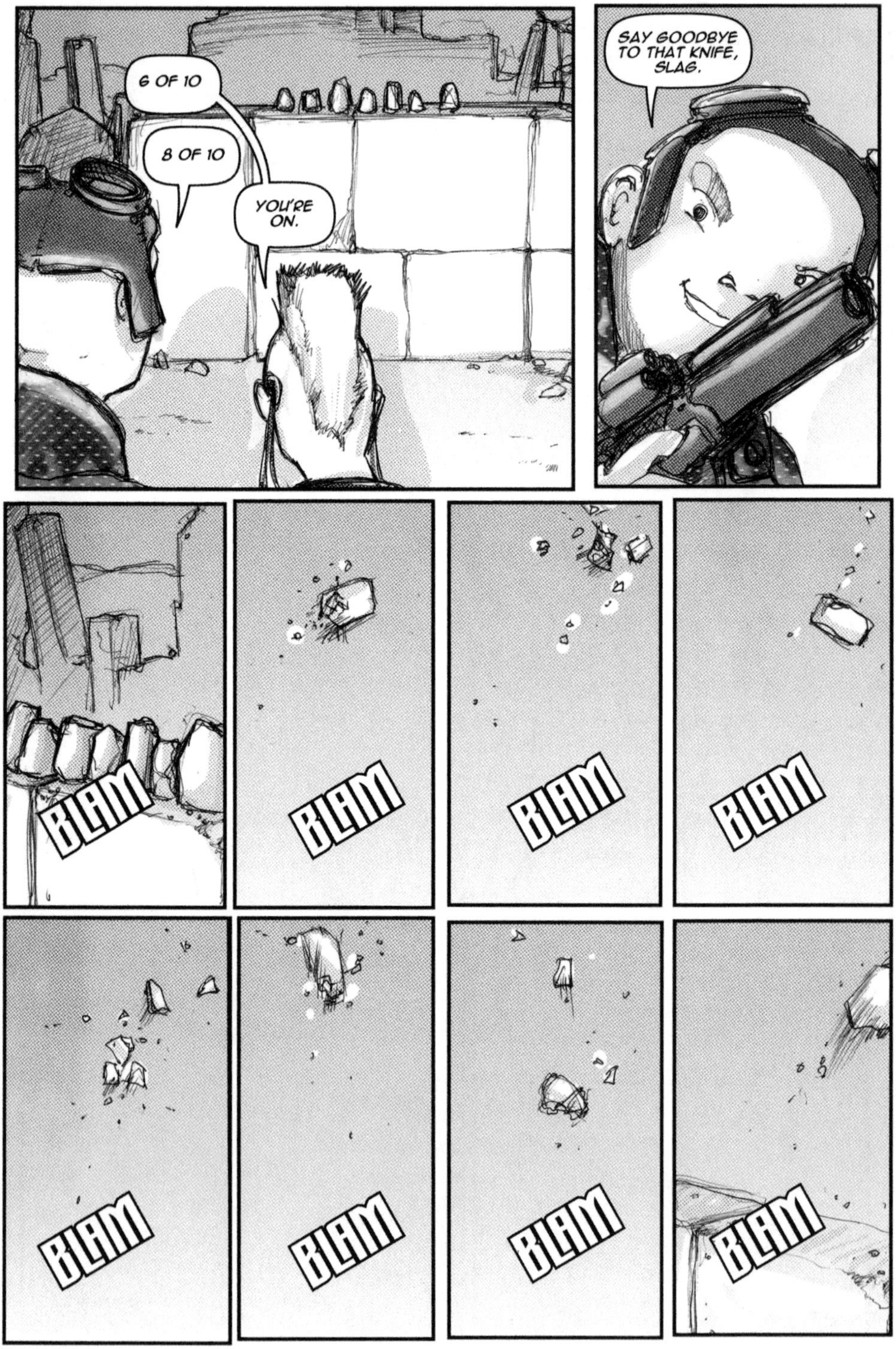
6 OF 10
8 OF 10
YOU'RE ON.
SAY GOODBYE TO THAT KNIFE, SLAG.
BLAM
BLAM
BLAM
BLAM
BLAM
BLAM
BLAM
BLAM

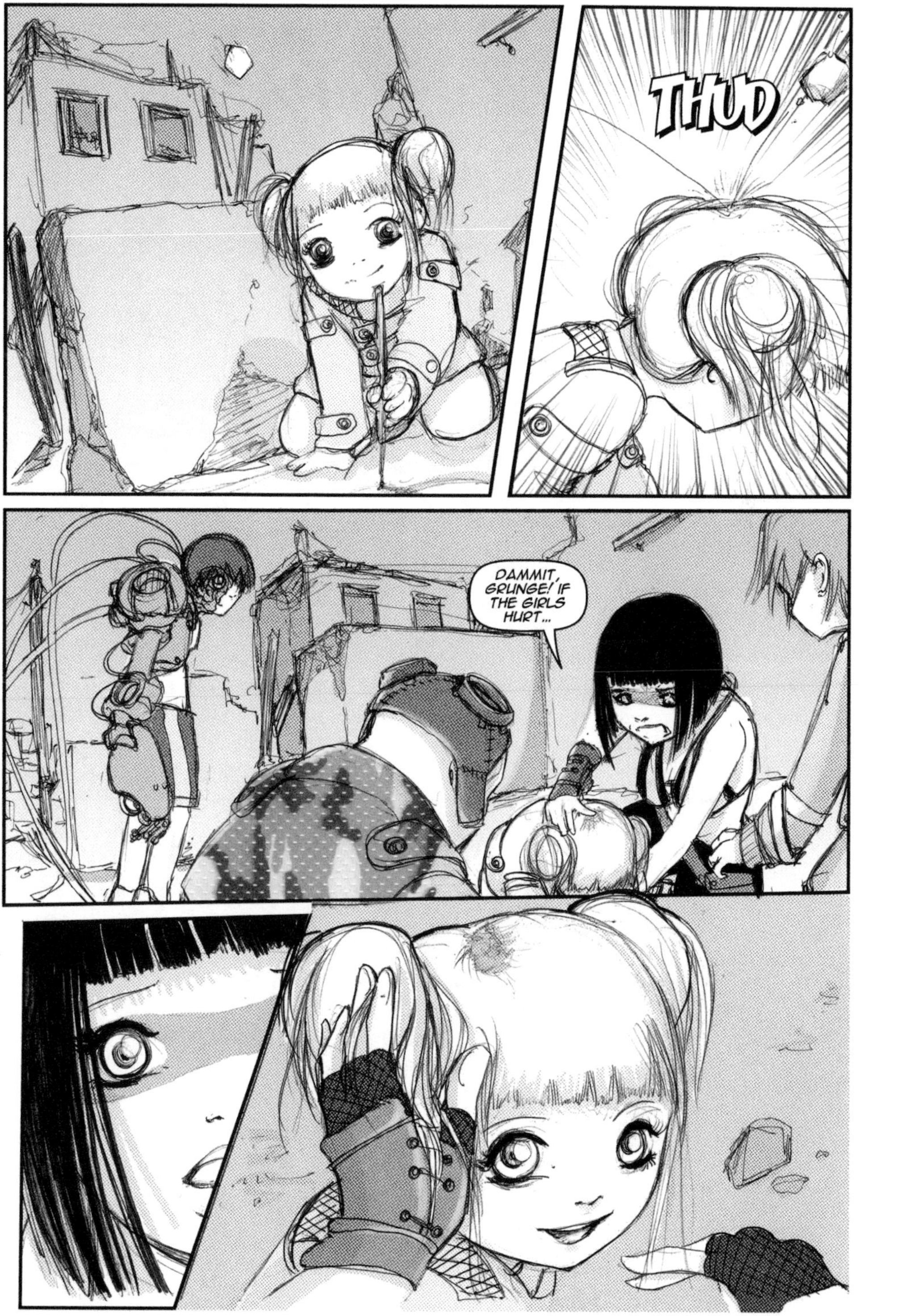
THUD
DAMMIT, GRUNGE! IF THE GIRLS HURT...

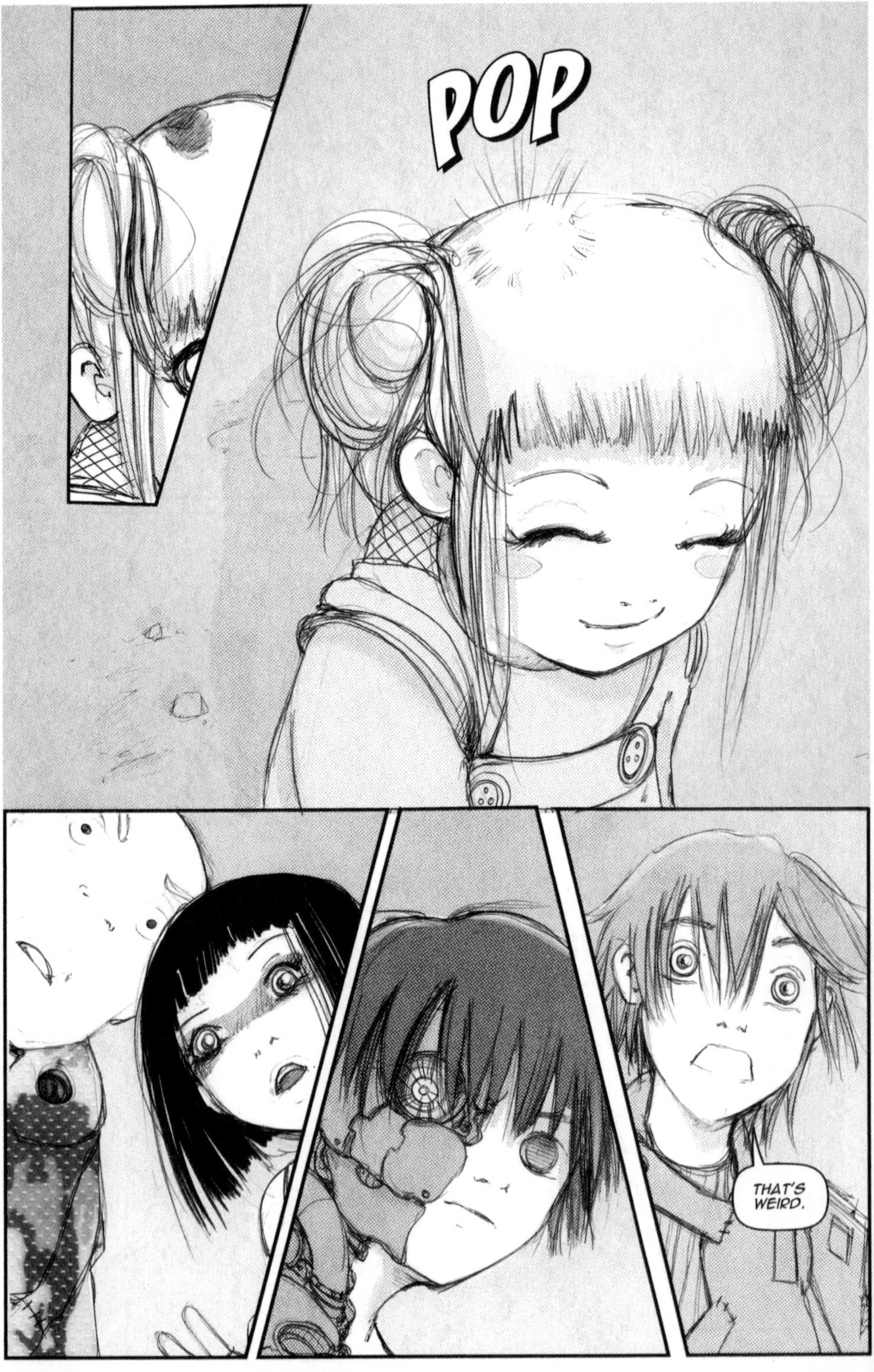
POP
THAT'S WEIRD.

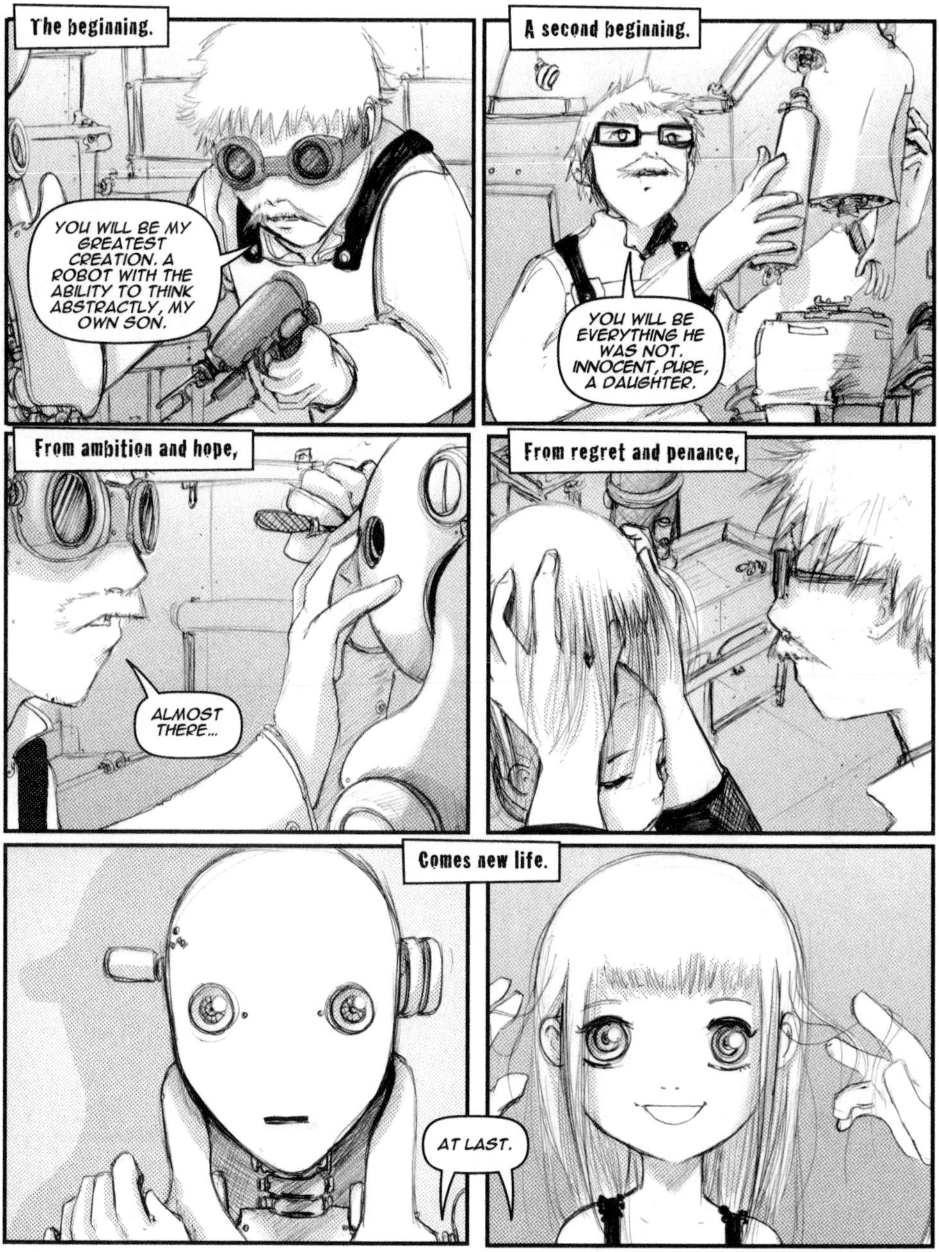
The beginning.
YOU WILL BE MY GREATEST CREATION. A ROBOT WITH THE ABILITY TO THINK ABSTRACTLY, MY OWN SON.
A second beginning.
YOU WILL BE EVERYTHING HE WAS NOT. INNOCENT, PURE, A DAUGHTER.
From ambition and hope,
ALMOST THERE...
From regret and penance,
Comes new life.
AT LAST.

NOW.

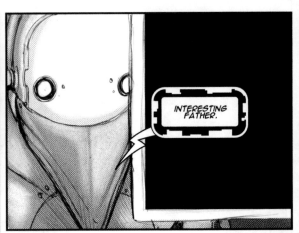

INTERESTING FATHER.

YOU MADE ANOTHER. BUT WHY SUCH A FRAIL SHELL?

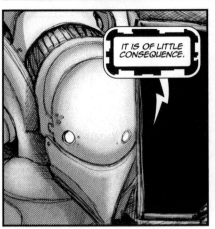

IT IS OF LITTLE CONSEQUENCE.

MY SONS WILL BE THERE SOON ENOUGH.

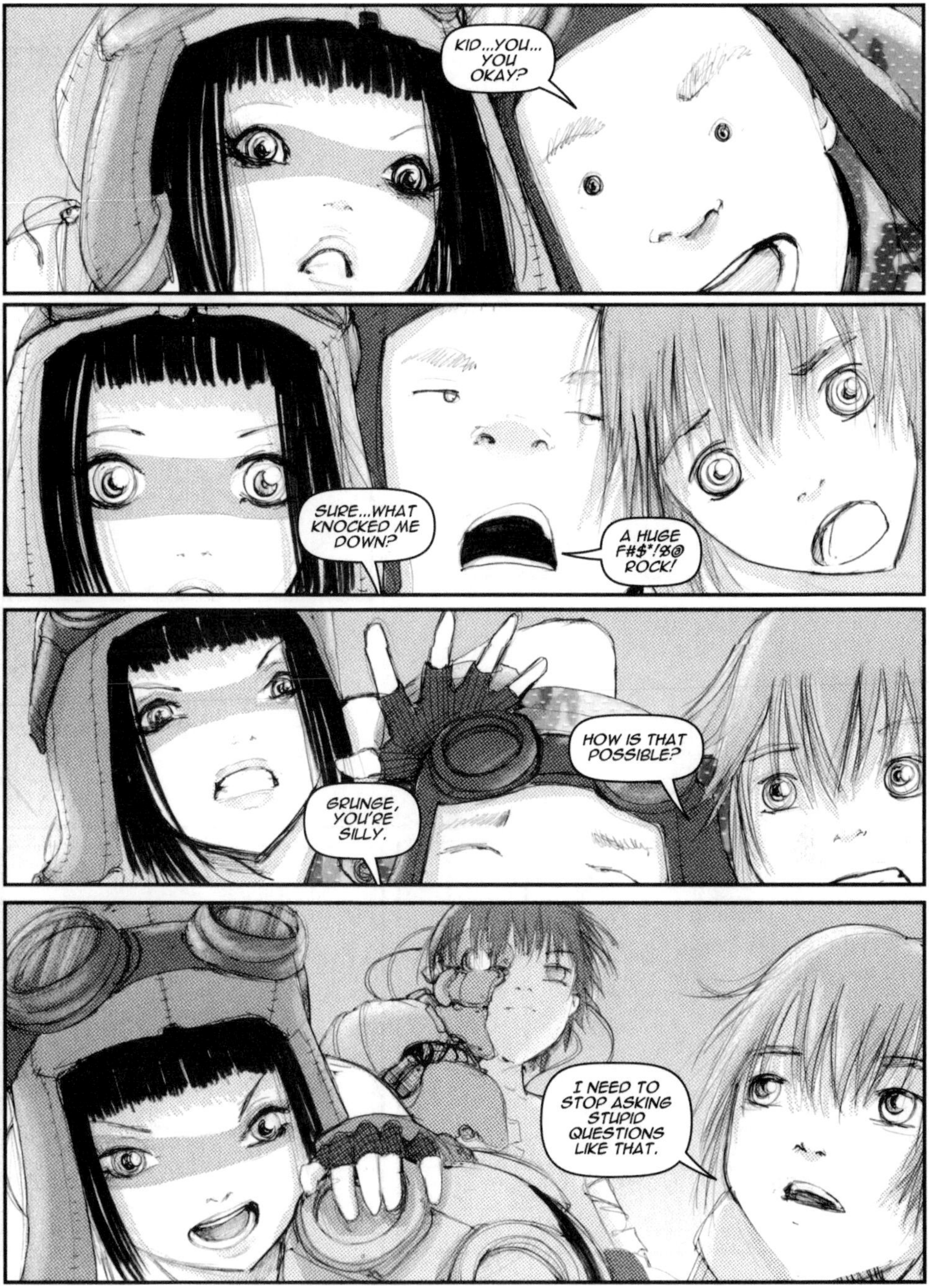
KID...YOU... YOU OKAY?
SURE...WHAT KNOCKED ME DOWN?
A HUGE F#$*!&@ ROCK!
HOW IS THAT POSSIBLE?
GRUNGE, YOU'RE SILLY.
I NEED TO STOP ASKING STUPID QUESTIONS LIKE THAT.

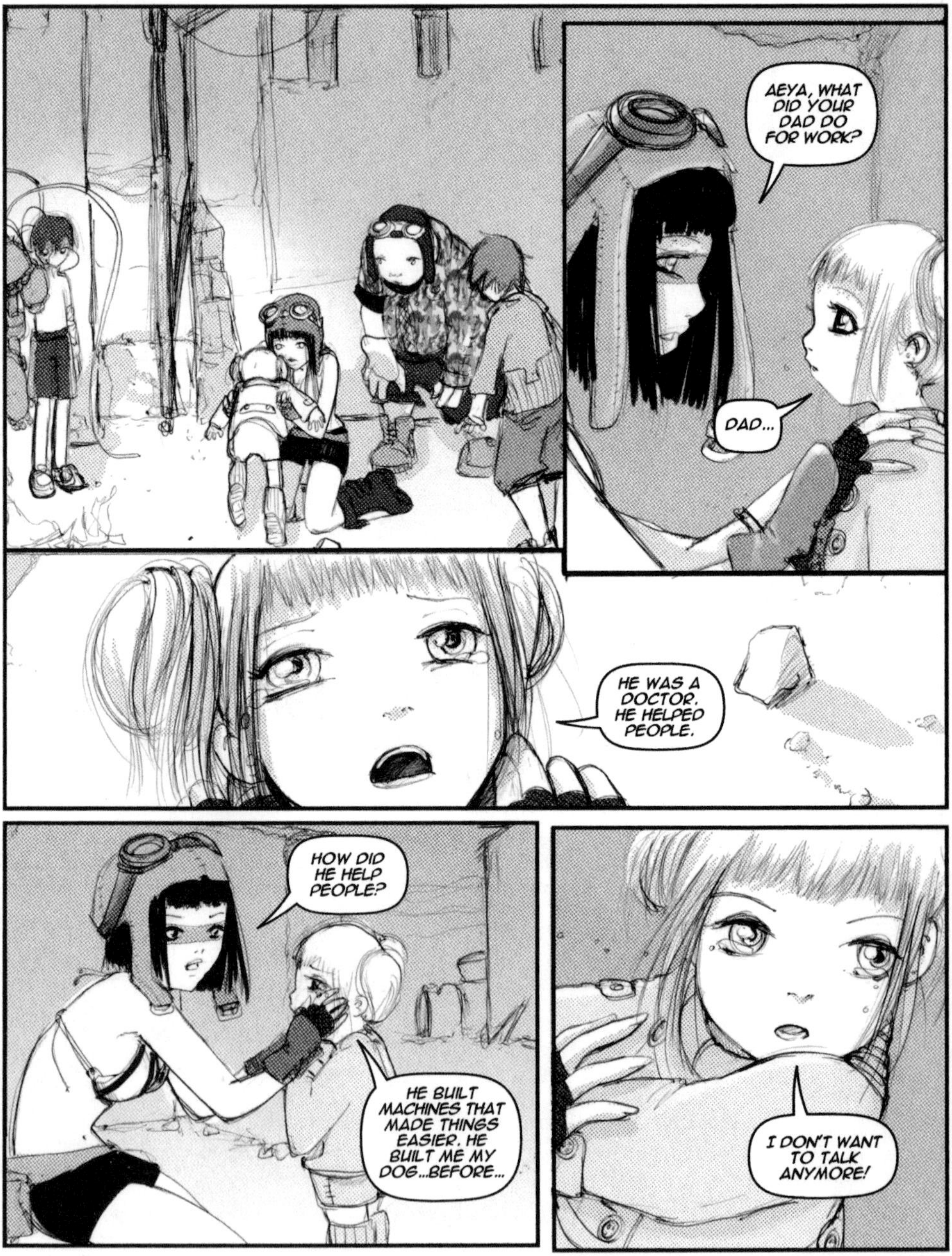
AEYA, WHAT DID YOUR DAD DO FOR WORK?
DAD...
HE WAS A DOCTOR. HE HELPED PEOPLE.
HOW DID HE HELP PEOPLE?
HE BUILT MACHINES THAT MADE THINGS EASIER. HE BUILT ME MY DOG...BEFORE...
I DON'T WANT TO TALK ANYMORE!

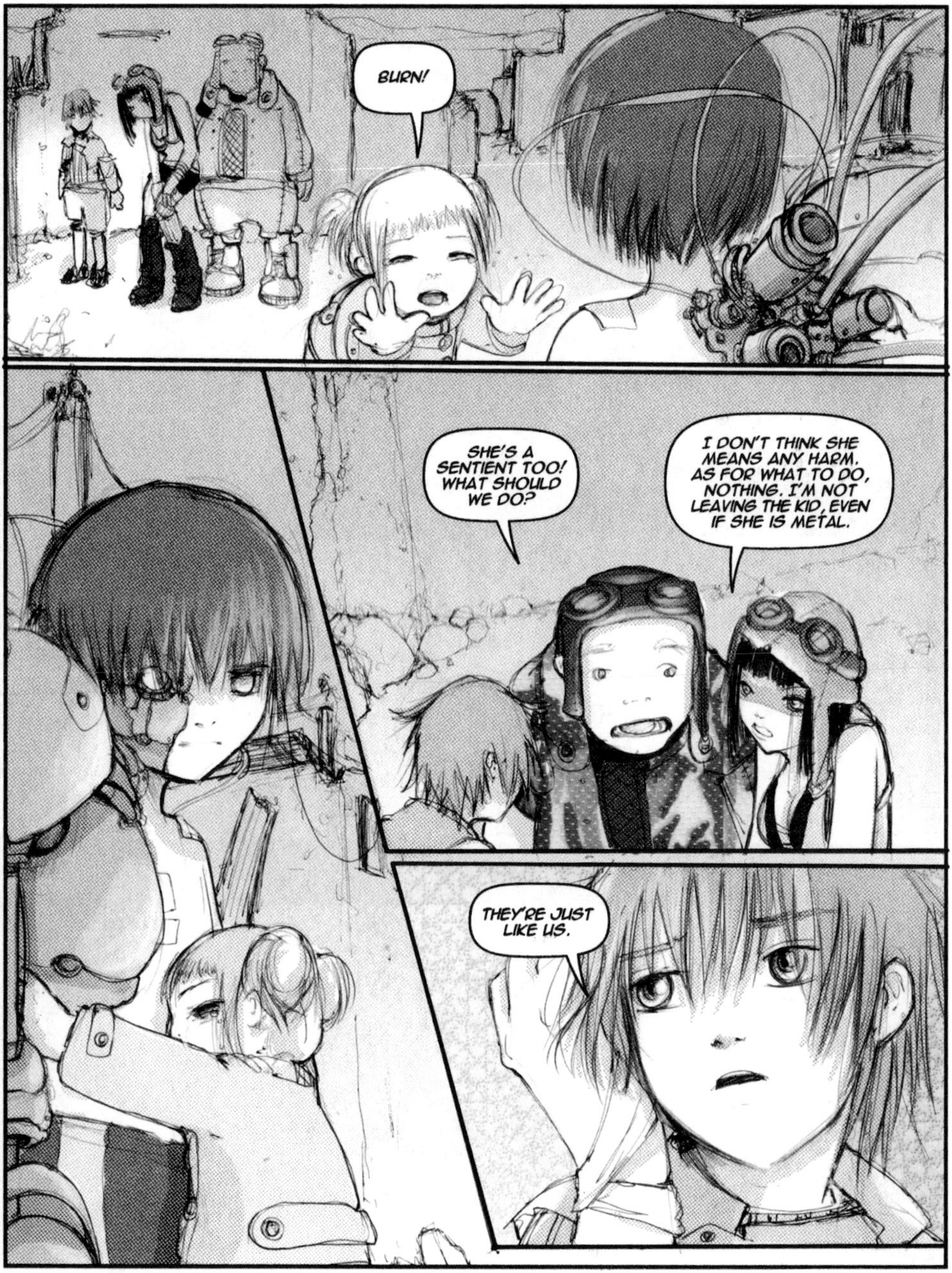
BURN!
SHE'S A SENTIENT TOO! WHAT SHOULD WE DO?
I DON'T THINK SHE MEANS ANY HARM. AS FOR WHAT TO DO, NOTHING. I'M NOT LEAVING THE KID, EVEN IF SHE IS METAL.
THEY'RE JUST LIKE US.

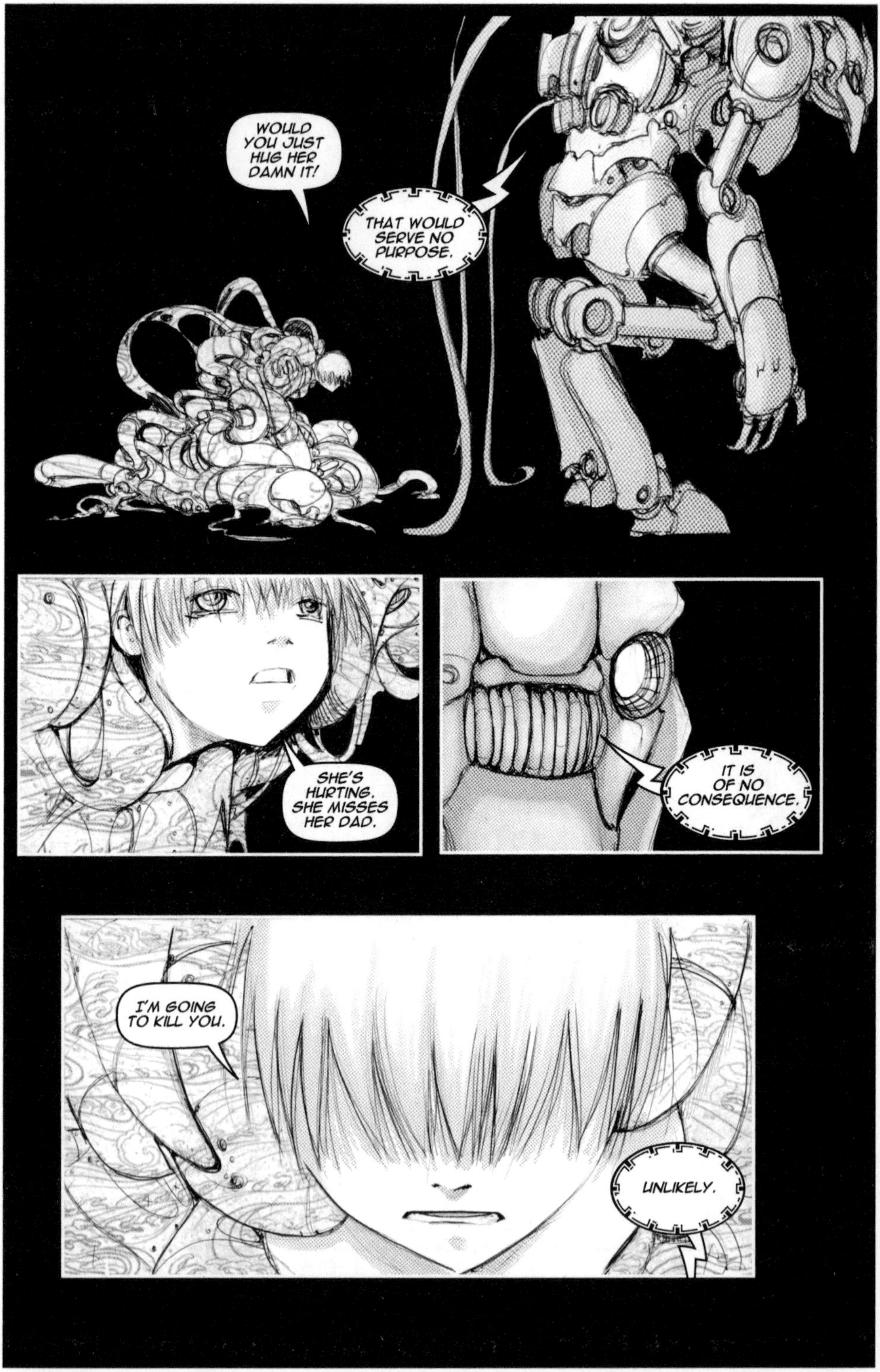
WOULD YOU JUST HUG HER DAMN IT!
THAT WOULD SERVE NO PURPOSE.
SHE'S HURTING. SHE MISSES HER DAD.
IT IS OF NO CONSEQUENCE.
I'M GOING TO KILL YOU.
UNLIKELY.

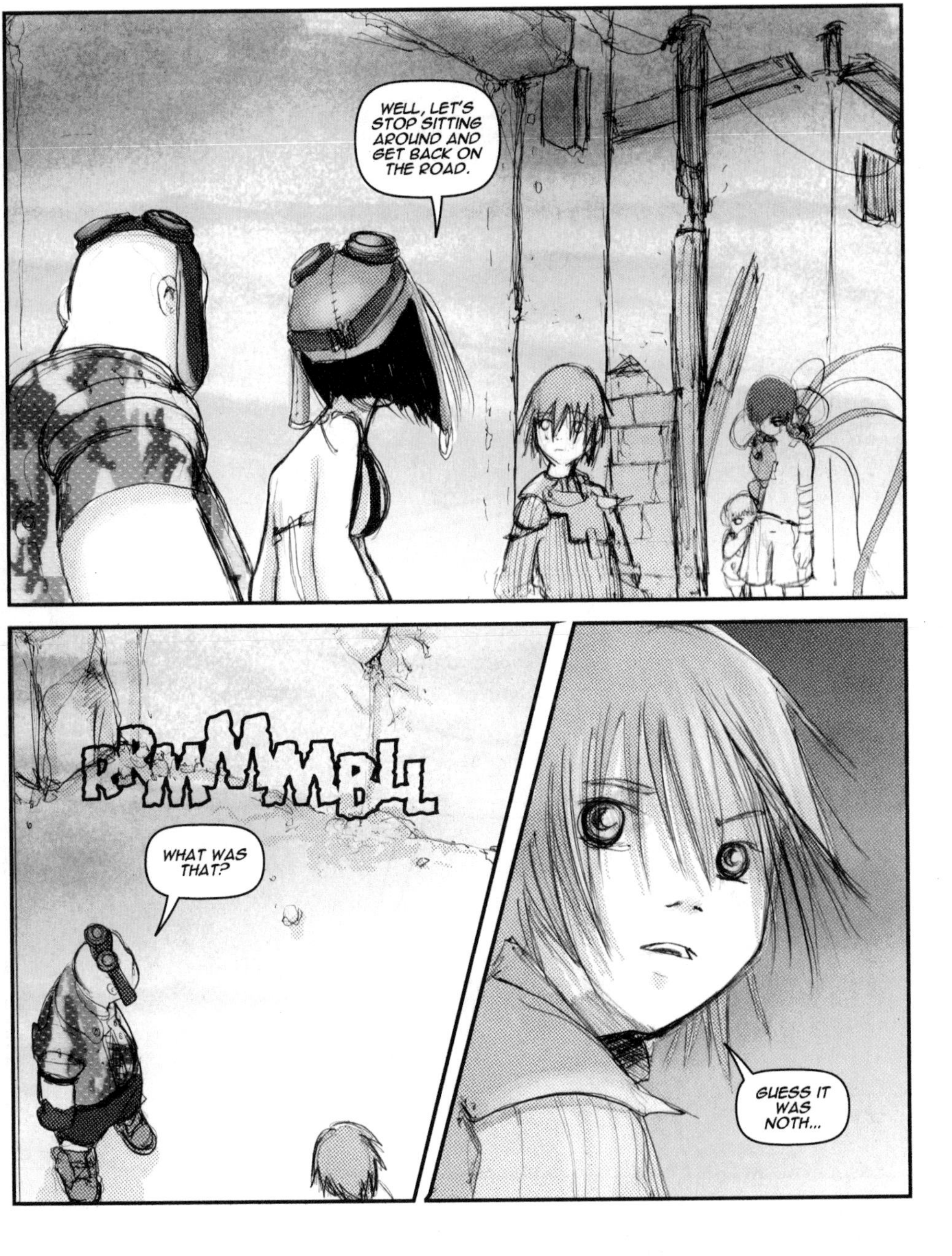
WELL, LET'S STOP SITTING AROUND AND GET BACK ON THE ROAD.
RRMMMBLL
WHAT WAS THAT?
GUESS IT WAS NOTH...

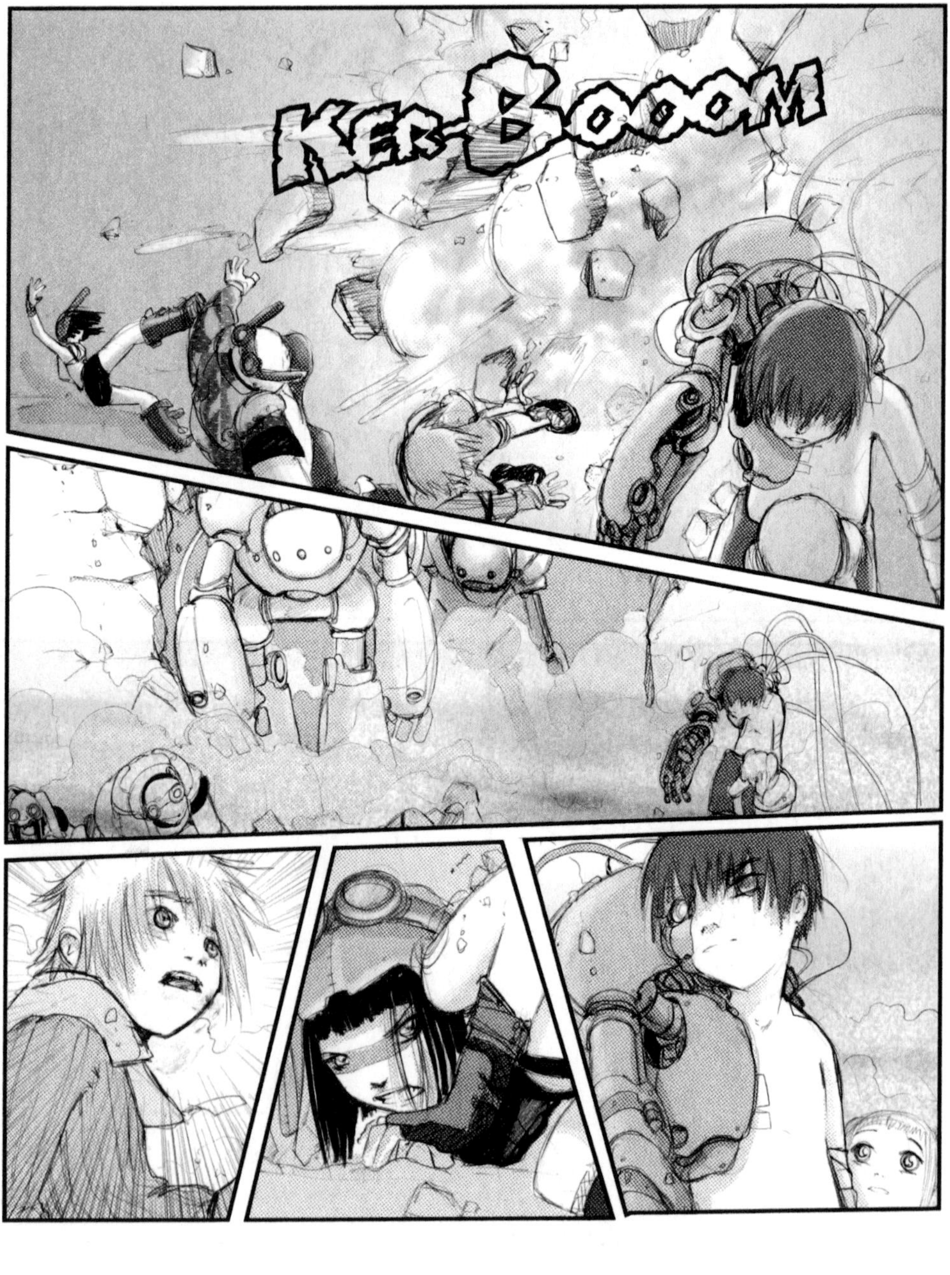
KER-BOOOM

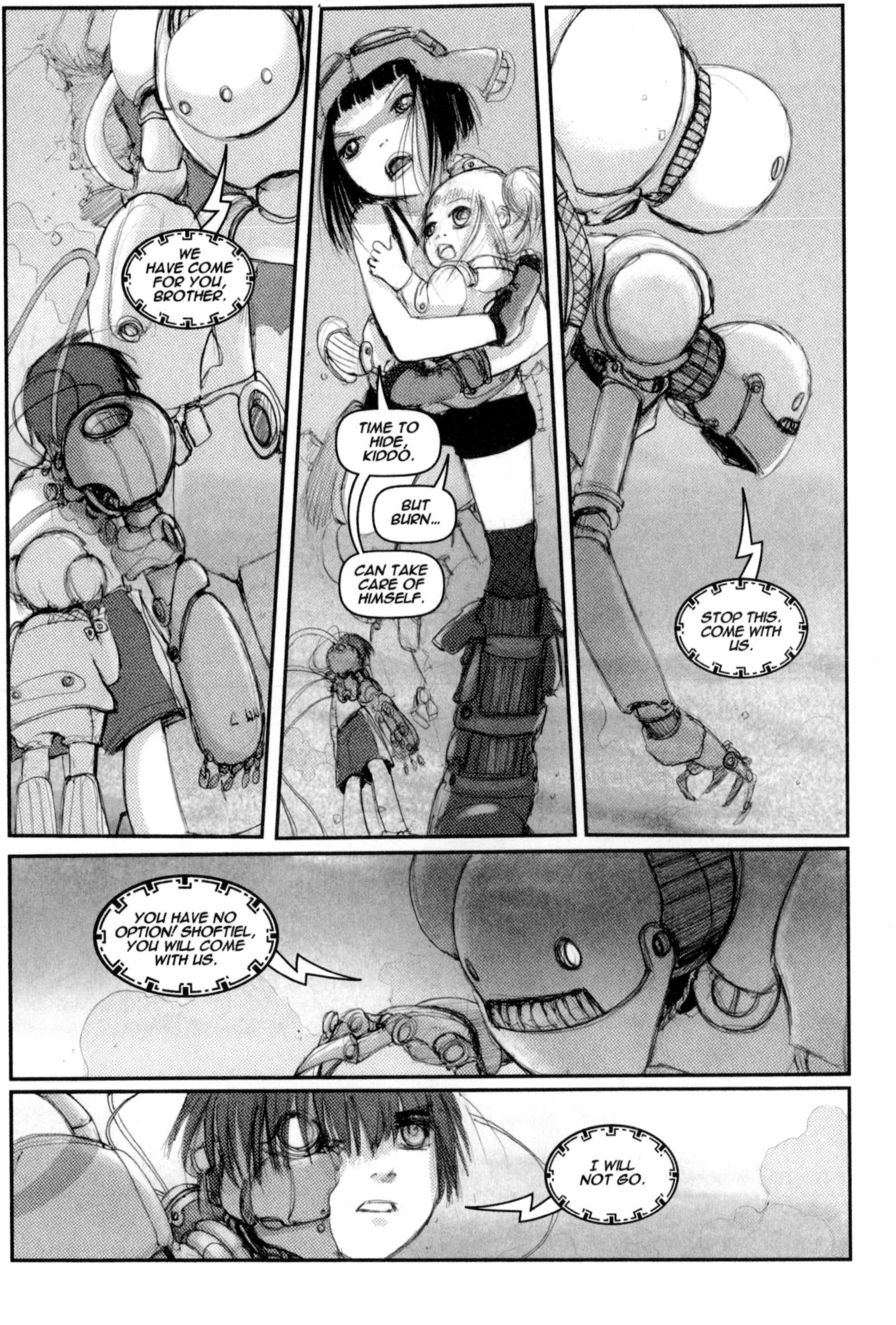
WE HAVE COME FOR YOU, BROTHER.
TIME TO HIDE, KIDDO.
BUT BURN...
CAN TAKE CARE OF HIMSELF.
STOP THIS. COME WITH US.
YOU HAVE NO OPTION! SHOFTIEL, YOU WILL COME WITH US.
I WILL NOT GO.

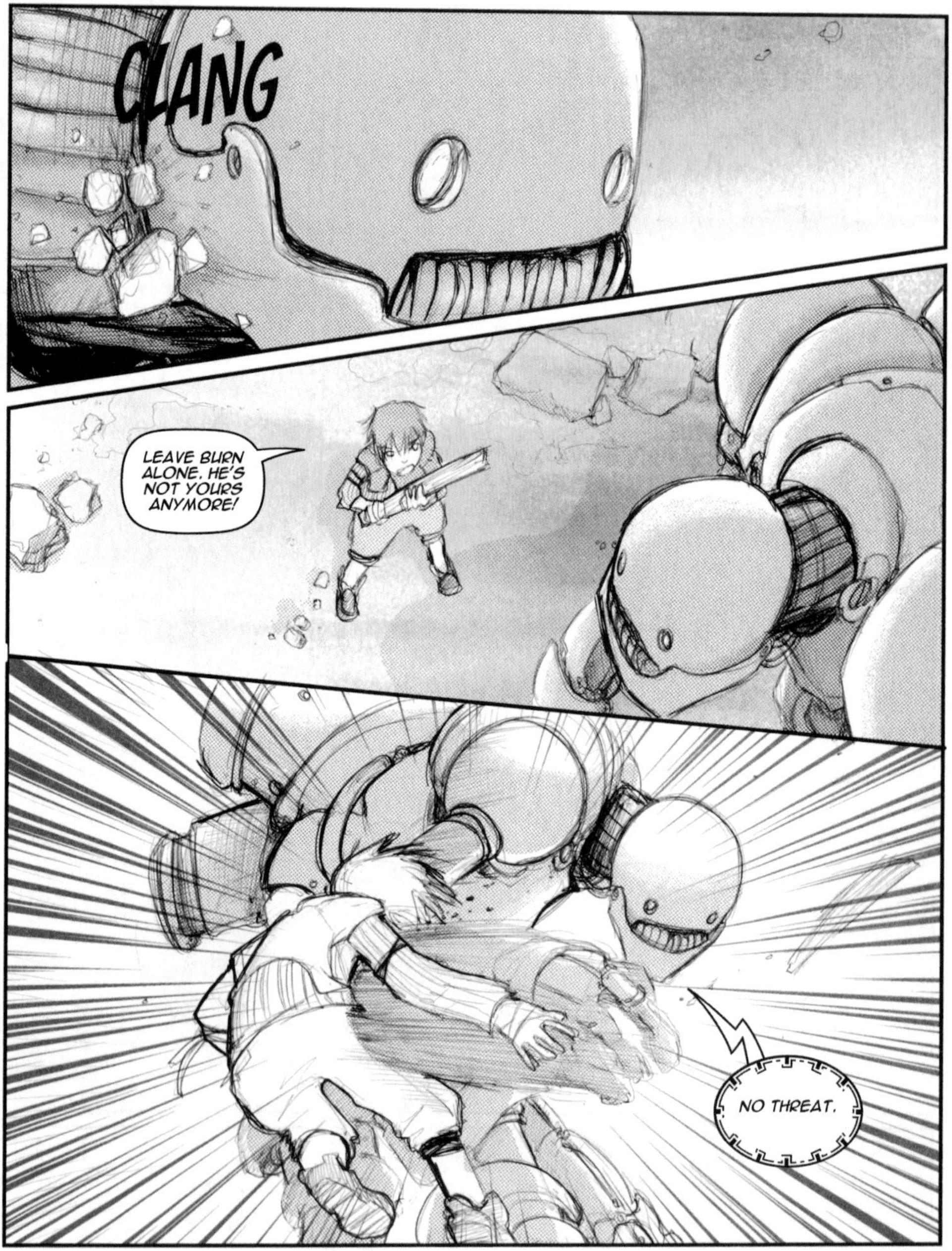
CLANG
LEAVE BURN ALONE. HE'S NOT YOURS ANYMORE!
NO THREAT.

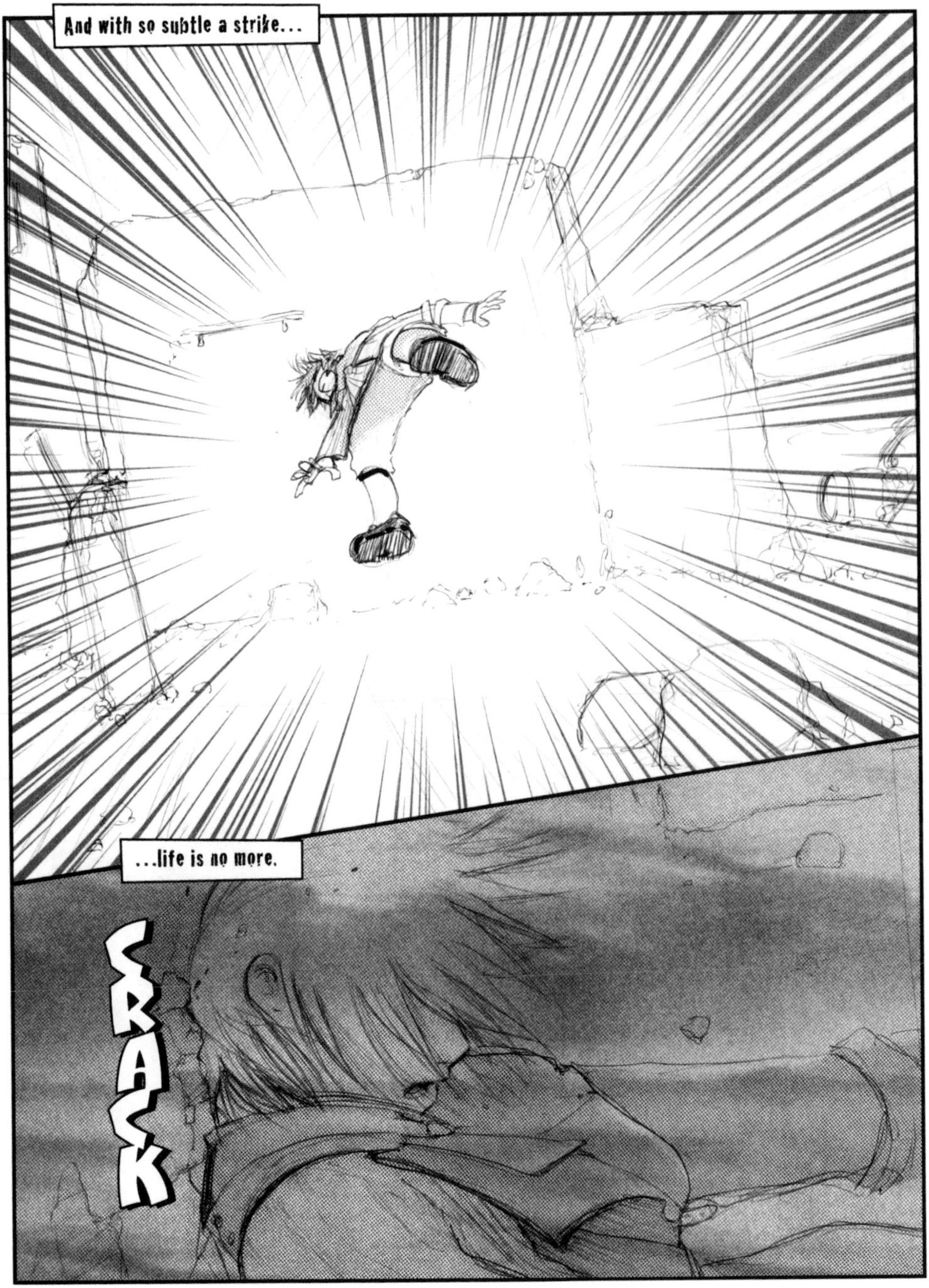
And with so subtle a strike...
...life is no more.
CRACK

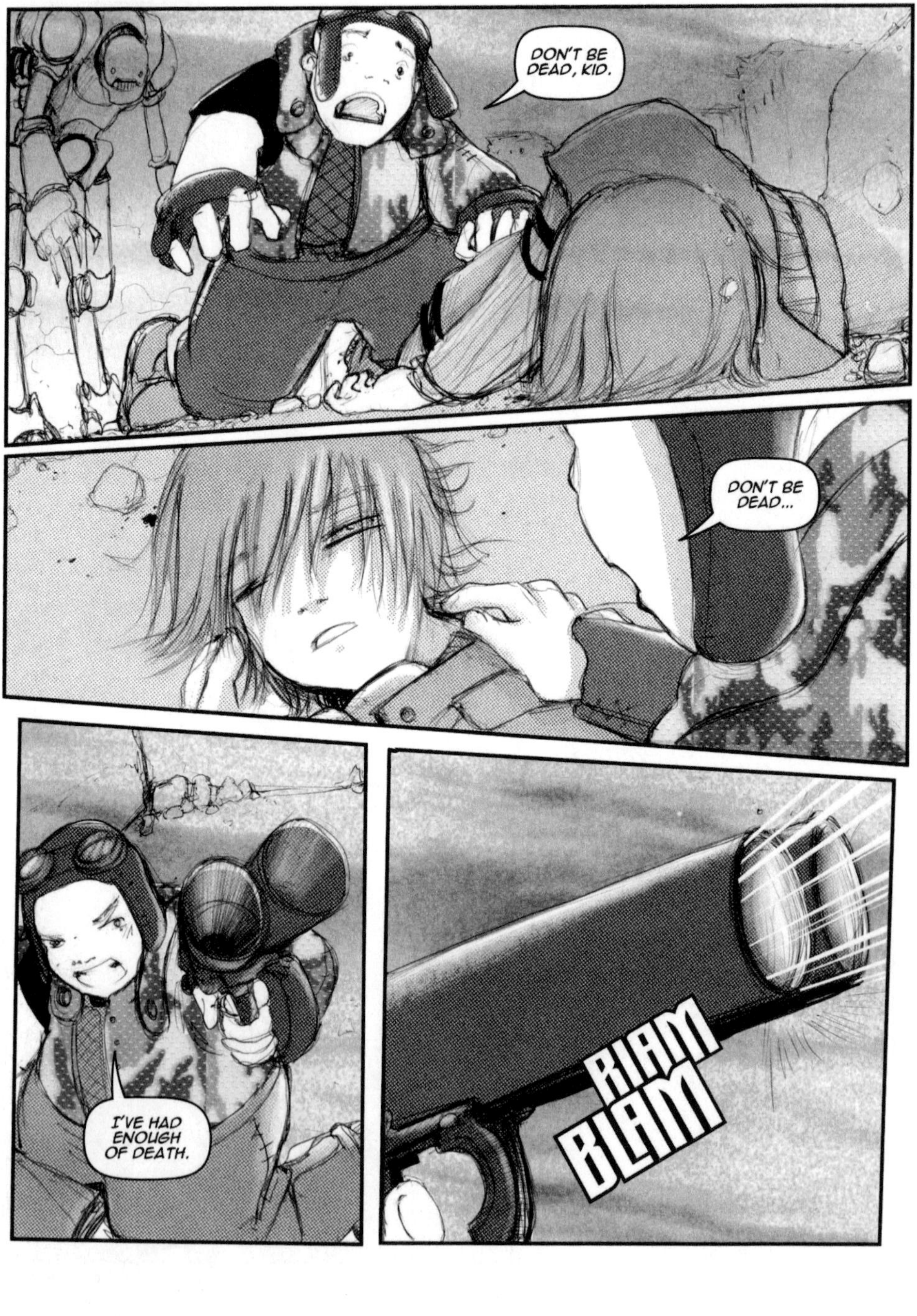
DON'T BE DEAD, KID.
DON'T BE DEAD...
I'VE HAD ENOUGH OF DEATH.
BLAM BLAM

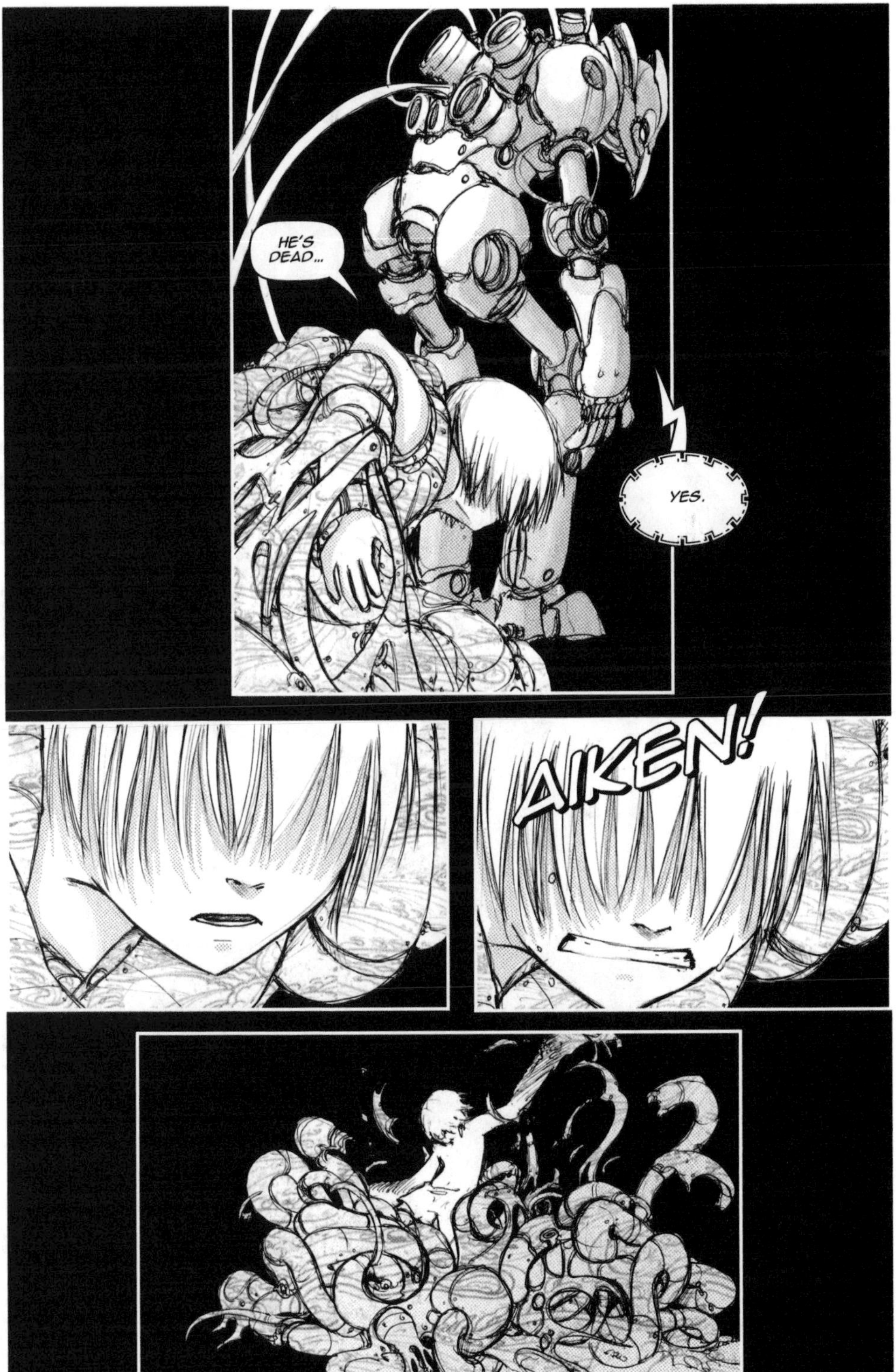
HE'S DEAD...
YES.
AIKEN!

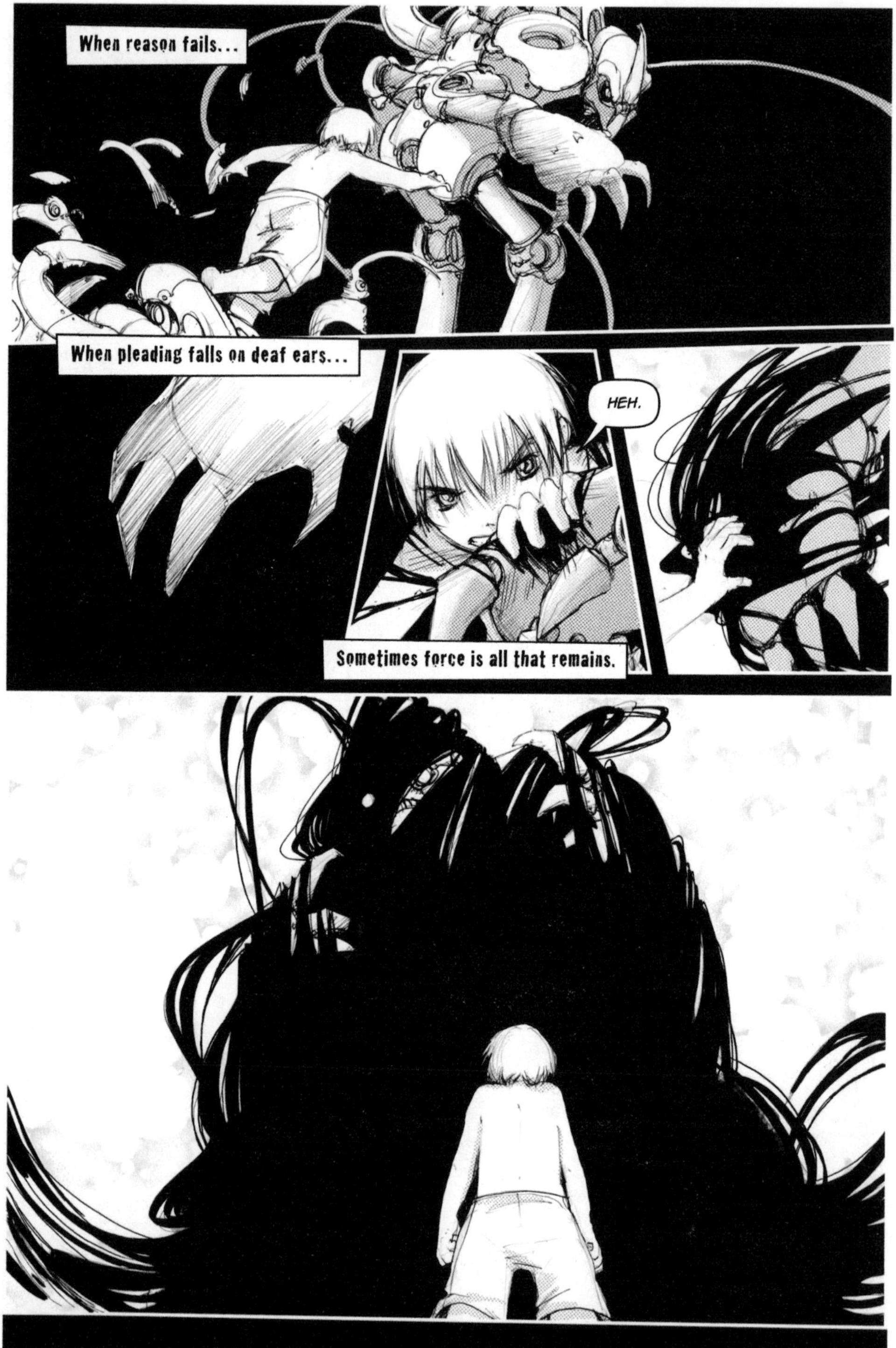
When reason fails...
When pleading falls on deaf ears...
HEH.
Sometimes force is all that remains.

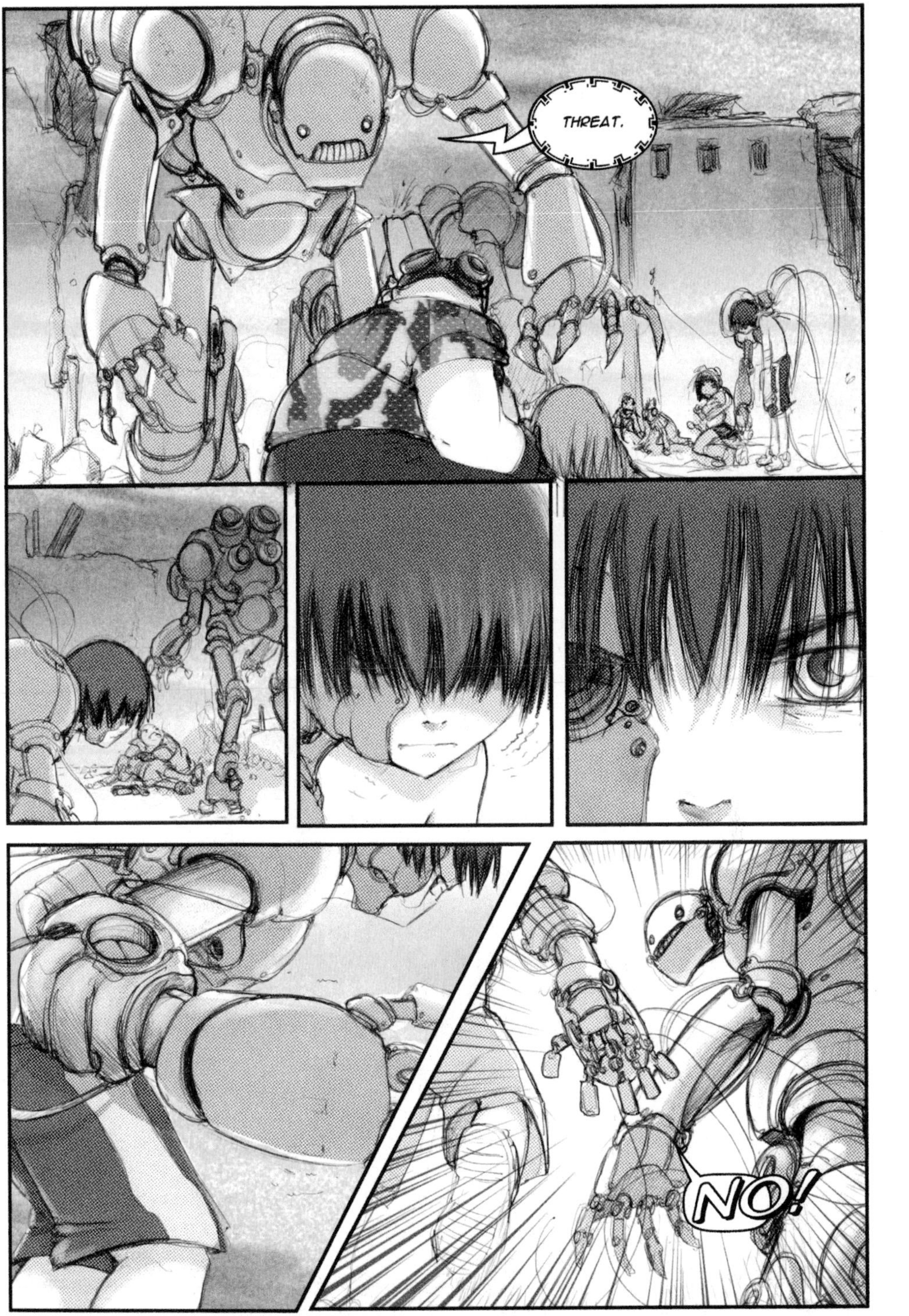
THREAT.
NO!

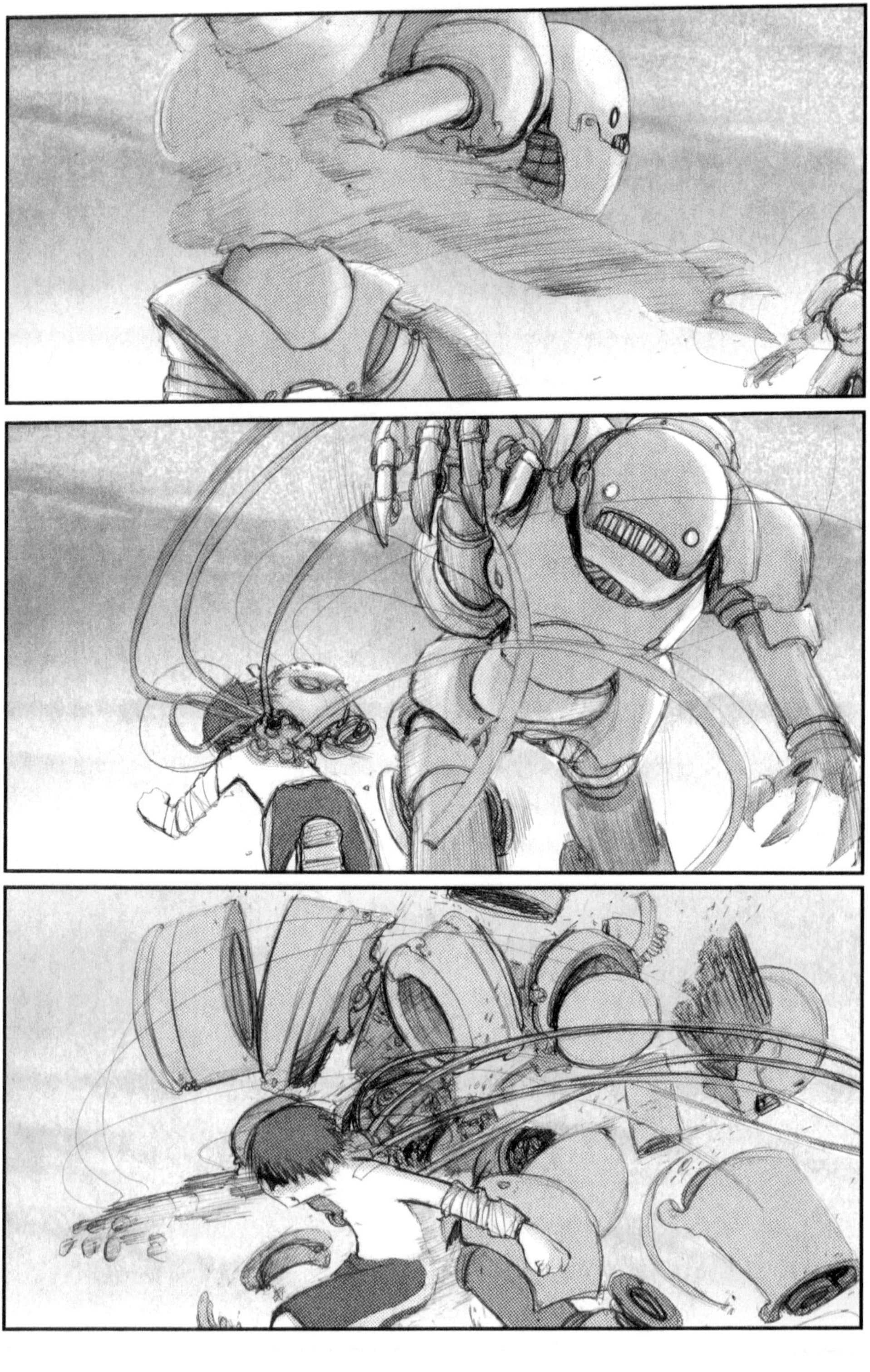

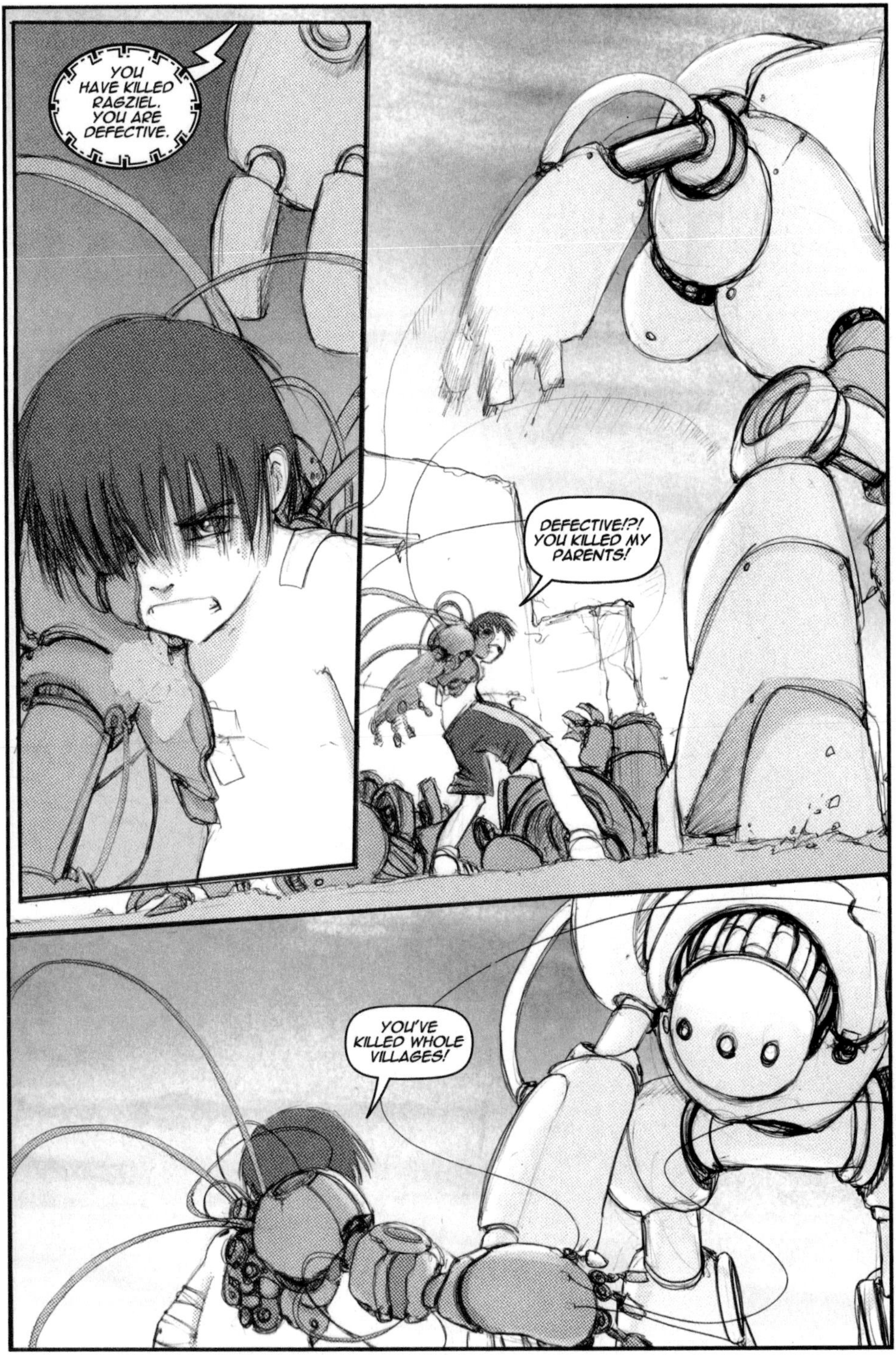
YOU HAVE KILLED RAGZIEL. YOU ARE DEFECTIVE.
DEFECTIVE!?! YOU KILLED MY PARENTS!
YOU'VE KILLED WHOLE VILLAGES!

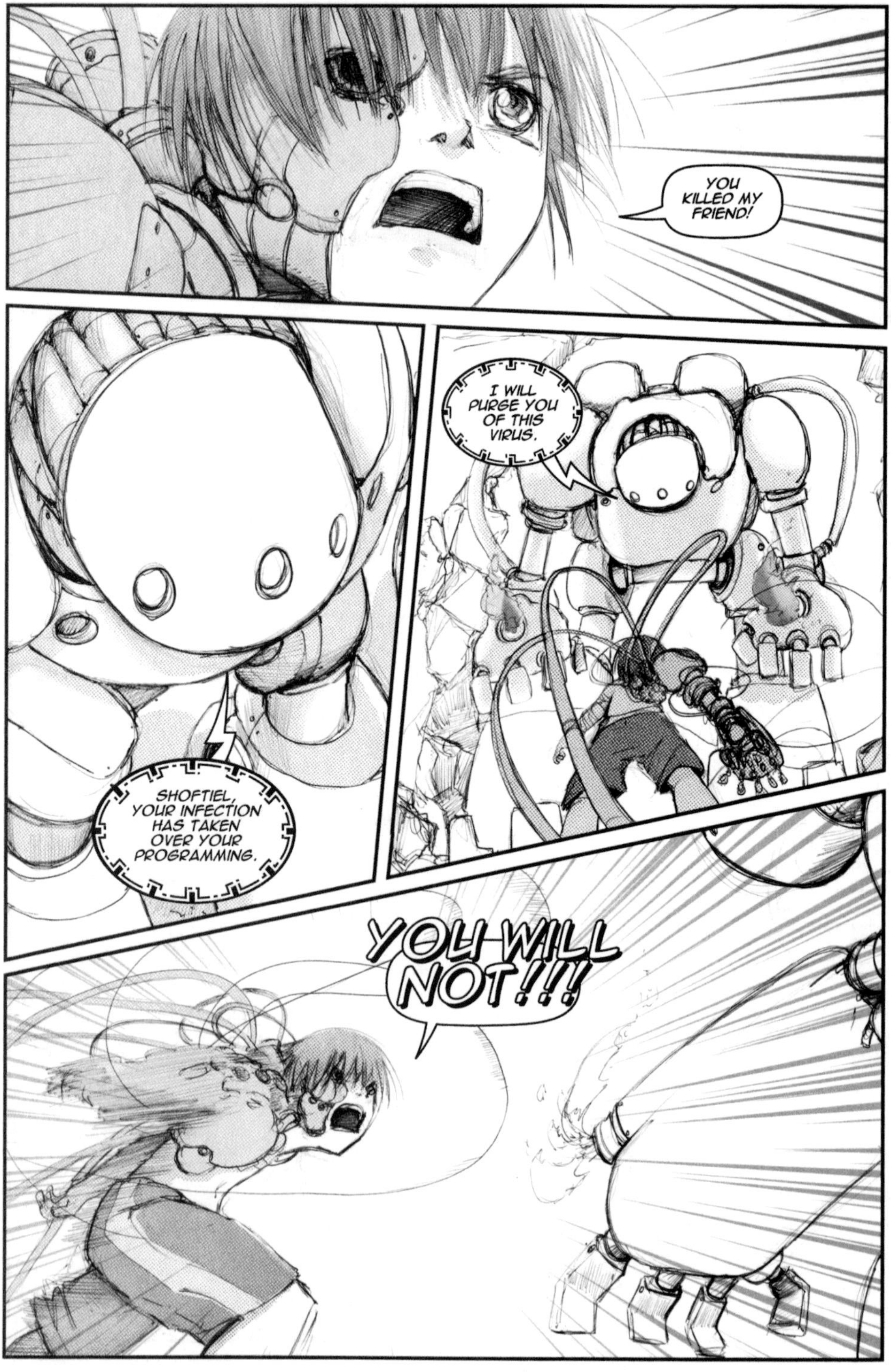
YOU KILLED MY FRIEND!
SHOFTIEL, YOUR INFECTION HAS TAKEN OVER YOUR PROGRAMMING.
I WILL PURGE YOU OF THIS VIRUS.
YOU WILL NOT!!!

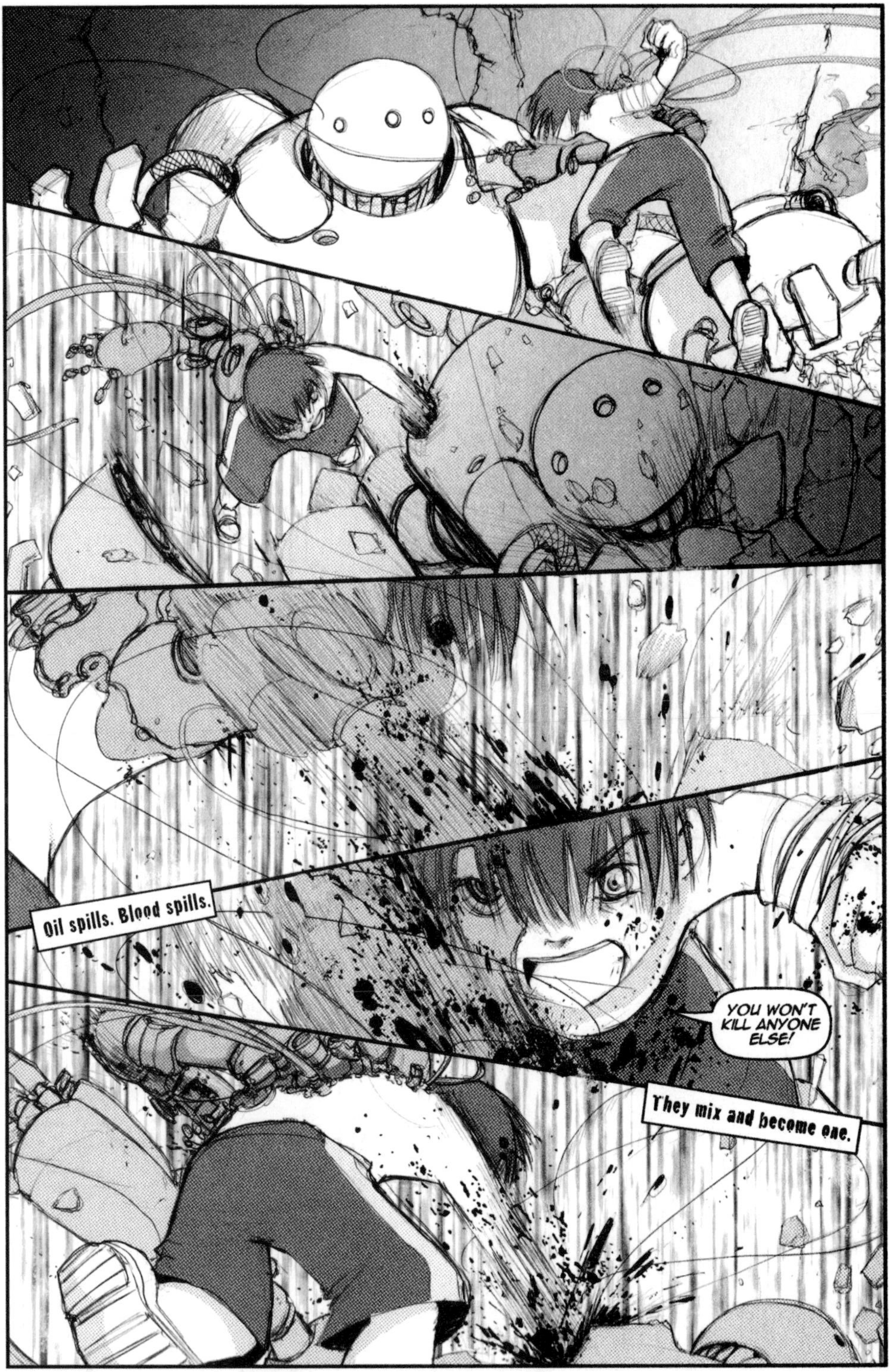
Oil spills. Blood spills.
YOU WON'T KILL ANYONE ELSE!
They mix and become one.

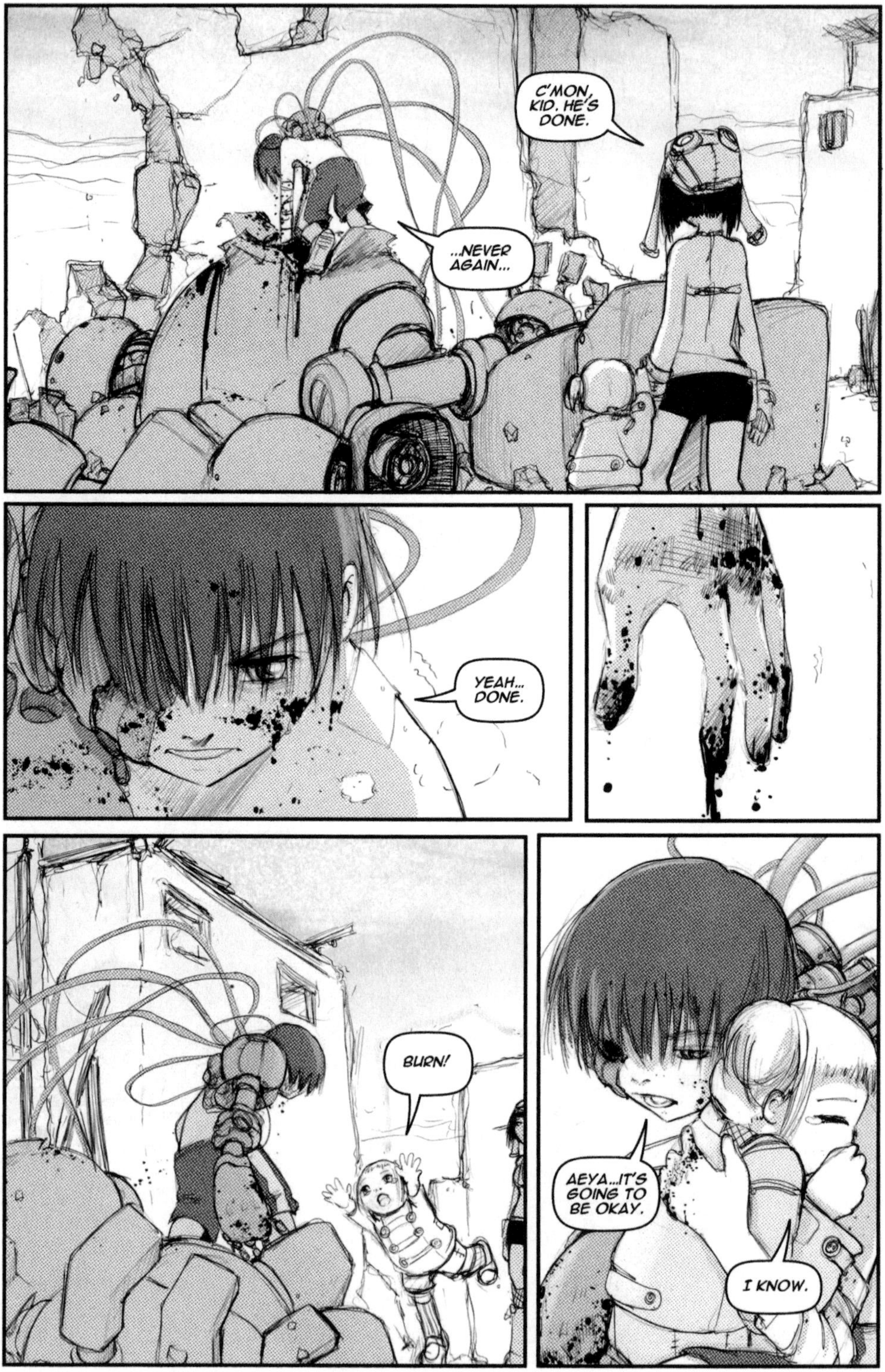
C'MON, KID. HE'S DONE.
...NEVER AGAIN...
YEAH... DONE.
BURN!
AEYA...IT'S GOING TO BE OKAY.
I KNOW.

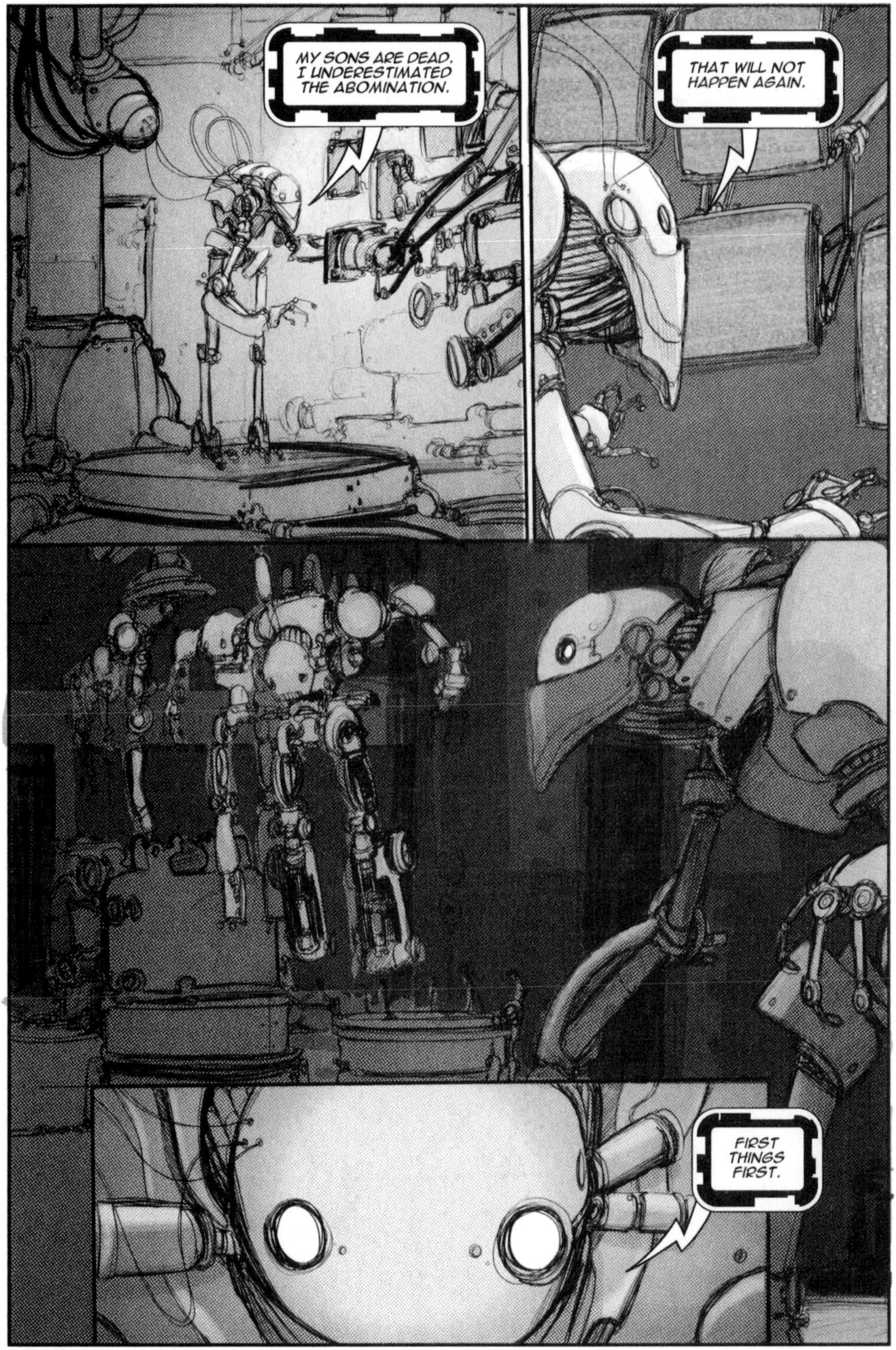
MY SONS ARE DEAD. I UNDERESTIMATED THE ABOMINATION.
THAT WILL NOT HAPPEN AGAIN.
FIRST THINGS FIRST.

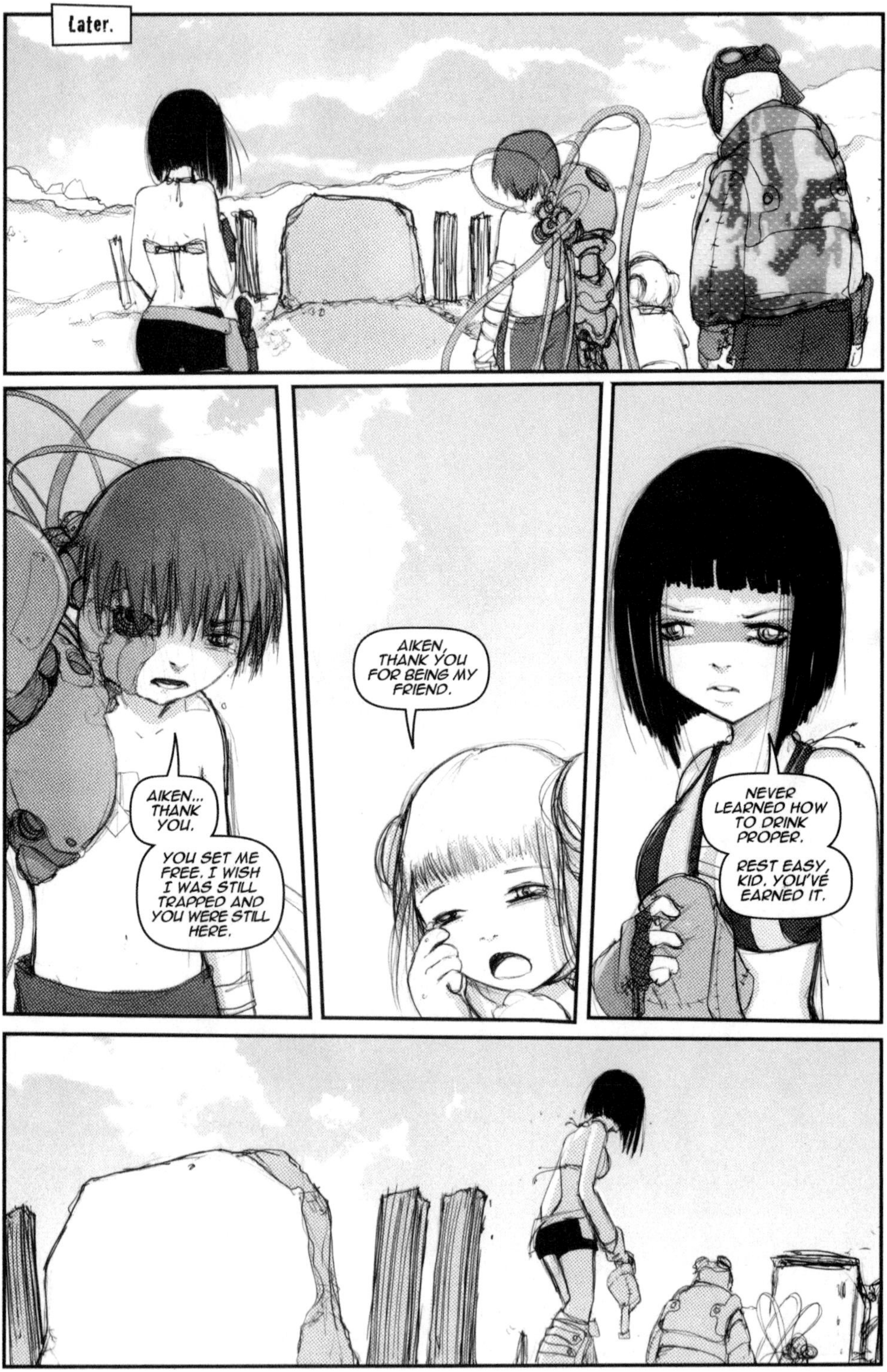
Later.
AIKEN... THANK YOU.
YOU SET ME FREE. I WISH I WAS STILL TRAPPED AND YOU WERE STILL HERE.
AIKEN, THANK YOU FOR BEING MY FRIEND.
NEVER LEARNED HOW TO DRINK PROPER.
REST EASY, KID. YOU'VE EARNED IT.

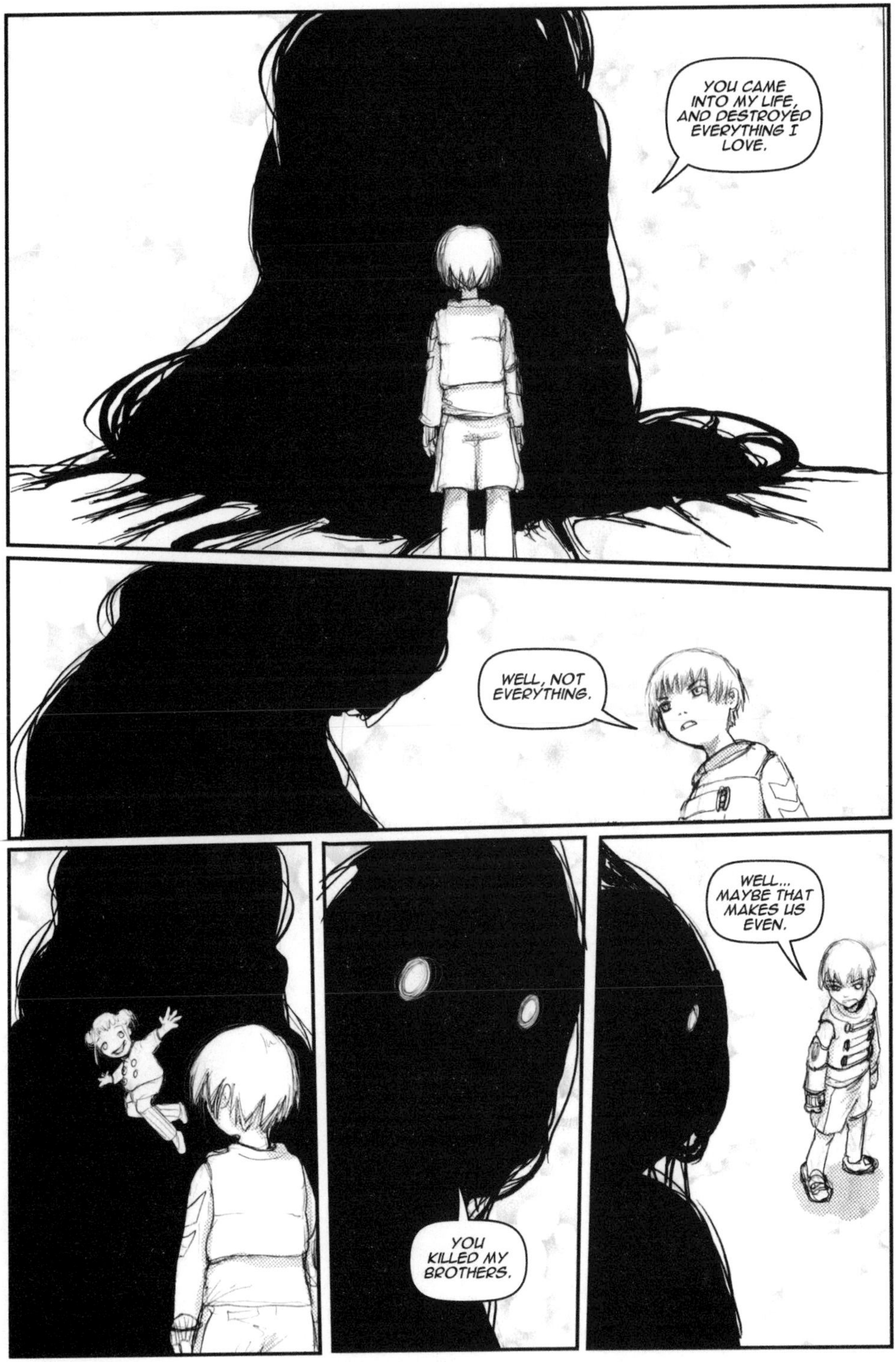
YOU CAME INTO MY LIFE, AND DESTROYED EVERYTHING I LOVE.
WELL, NOT EVERYTHING.
YOU KILLED MY BROTHERS.
WELL... MAYBE THAT MAKES US EVEN.

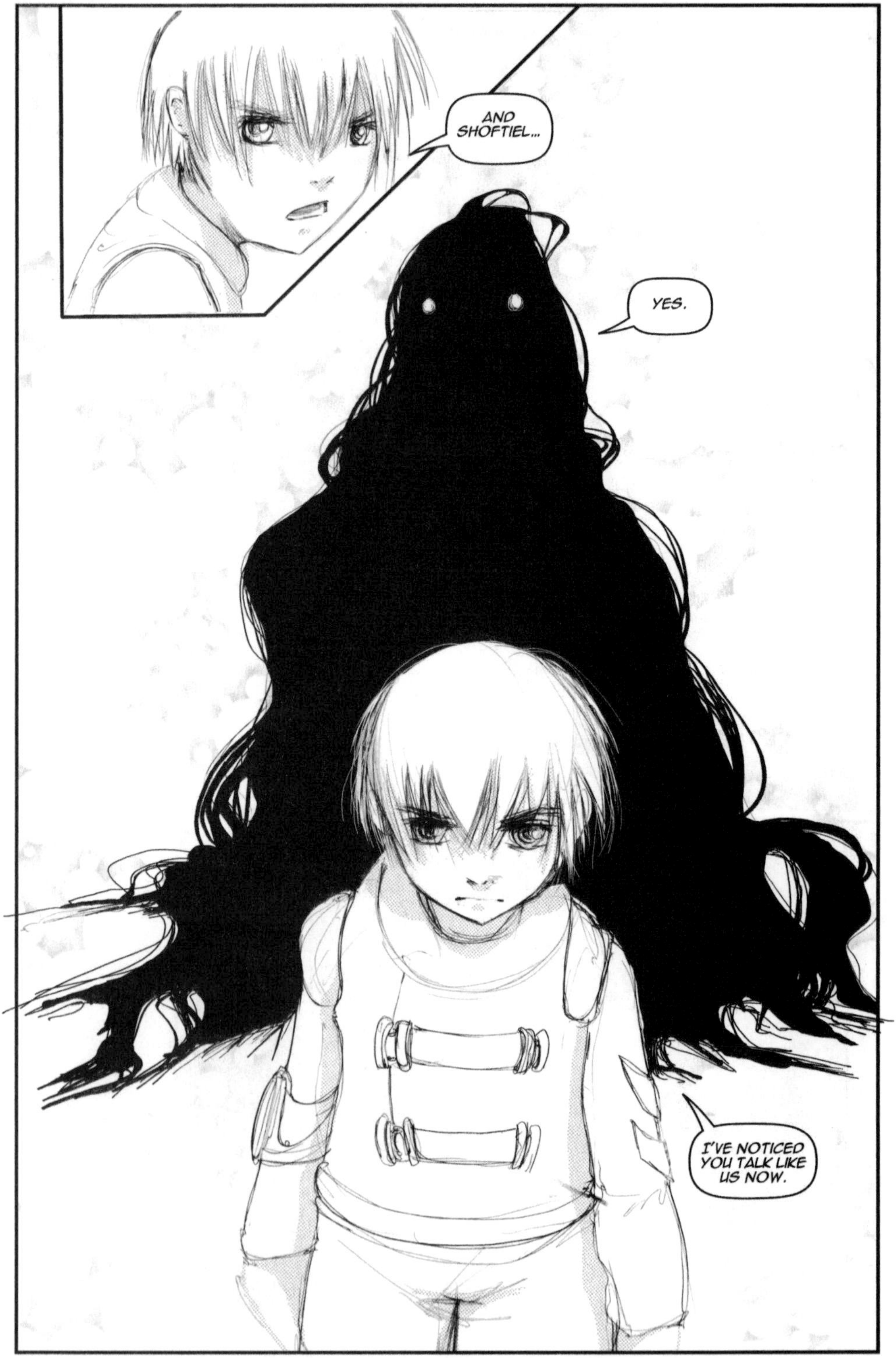
AND SHOFTIEL...
YES.
I'VE NOTICED YOU TALK LIKE US NOW.

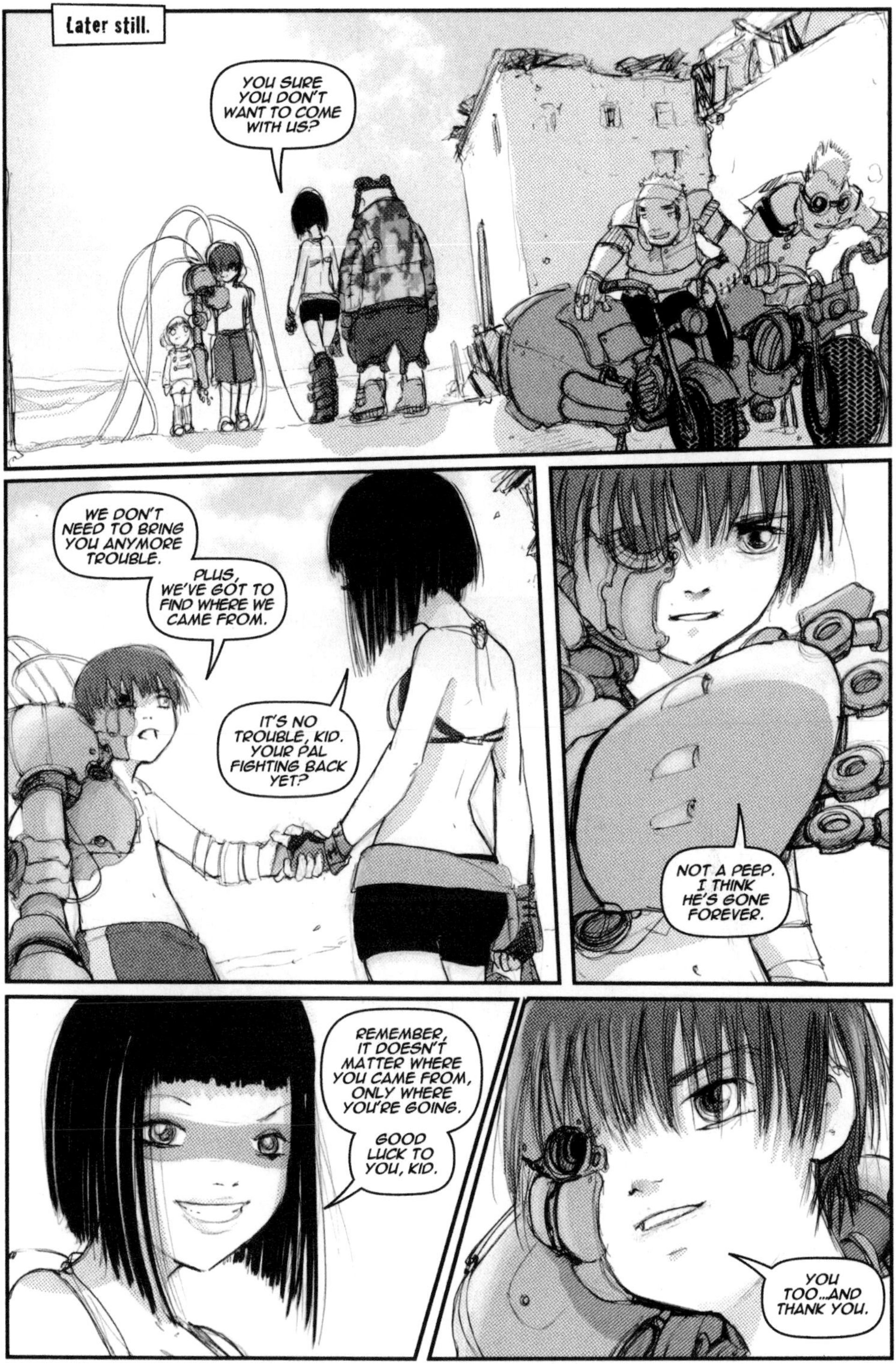
Later still.
YOU SURE YOU DON'T WANT TO COME WITH US?
WE DON'T NEED TO BRING YOU ANYMORE TROUBLE.
PLUS, WE'VE GOT TO FIND WHERE WE CAME FROM.
IT'S NO TROUBLE, KID. YOUR PAL FIGHTING BACK YET?
NOT A PEEP. I THINK HE'S GONE FOREVER.
REMEMBER, IT DOESN'T MATTER WHERE YOU CAME FROM, ONLY WHERE YOU'RE GOING.
GOOD LUCK TO YOU, KID.
YOU TOO...AND THANK YOU.

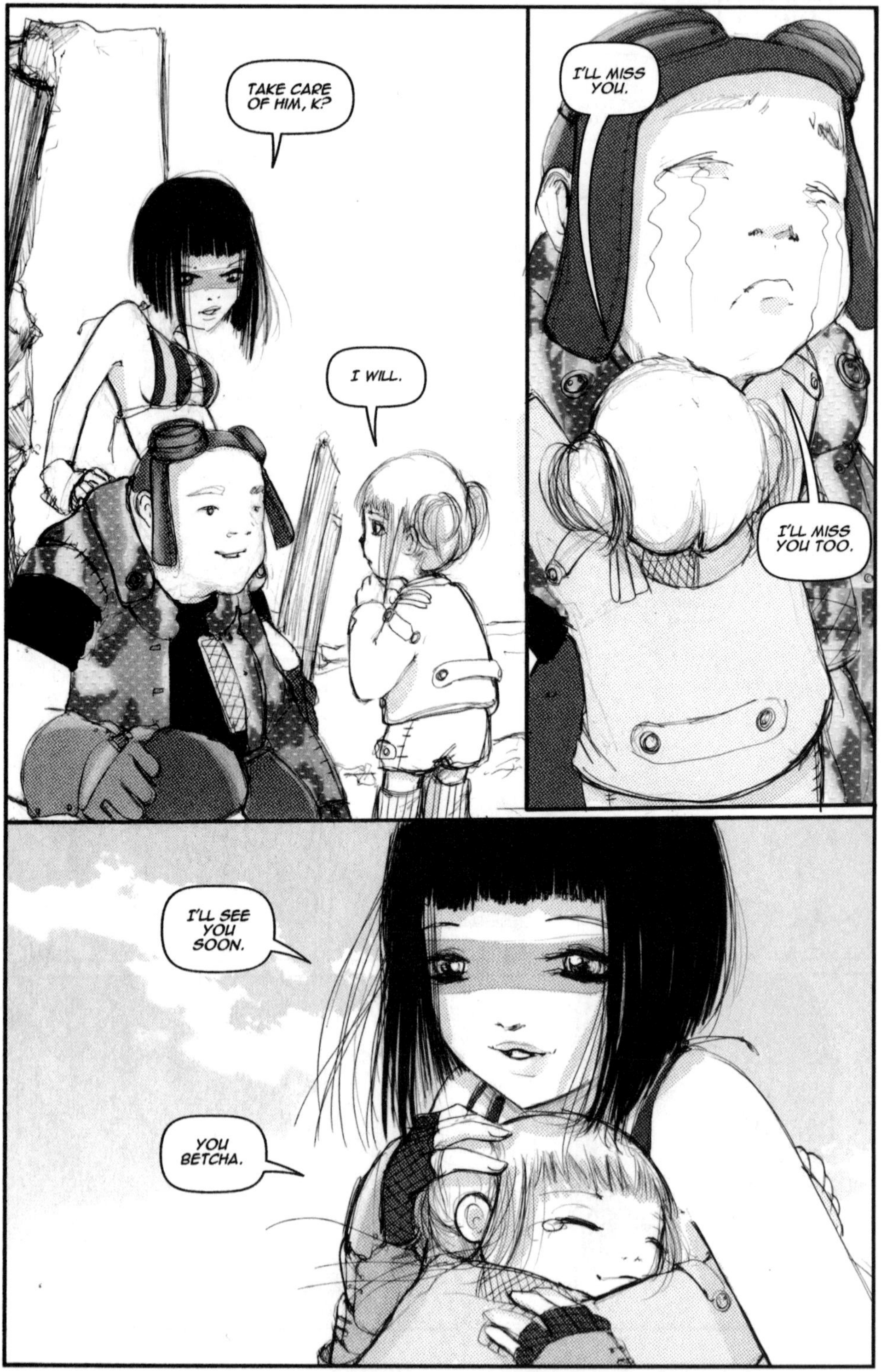
TAKE CARE OF HIM, K?
I WILL.
I'LL MISS YOU.
I'LL MISS YOU TOO.
I'LL SEE YOU SOON.
YOU BETCHA.

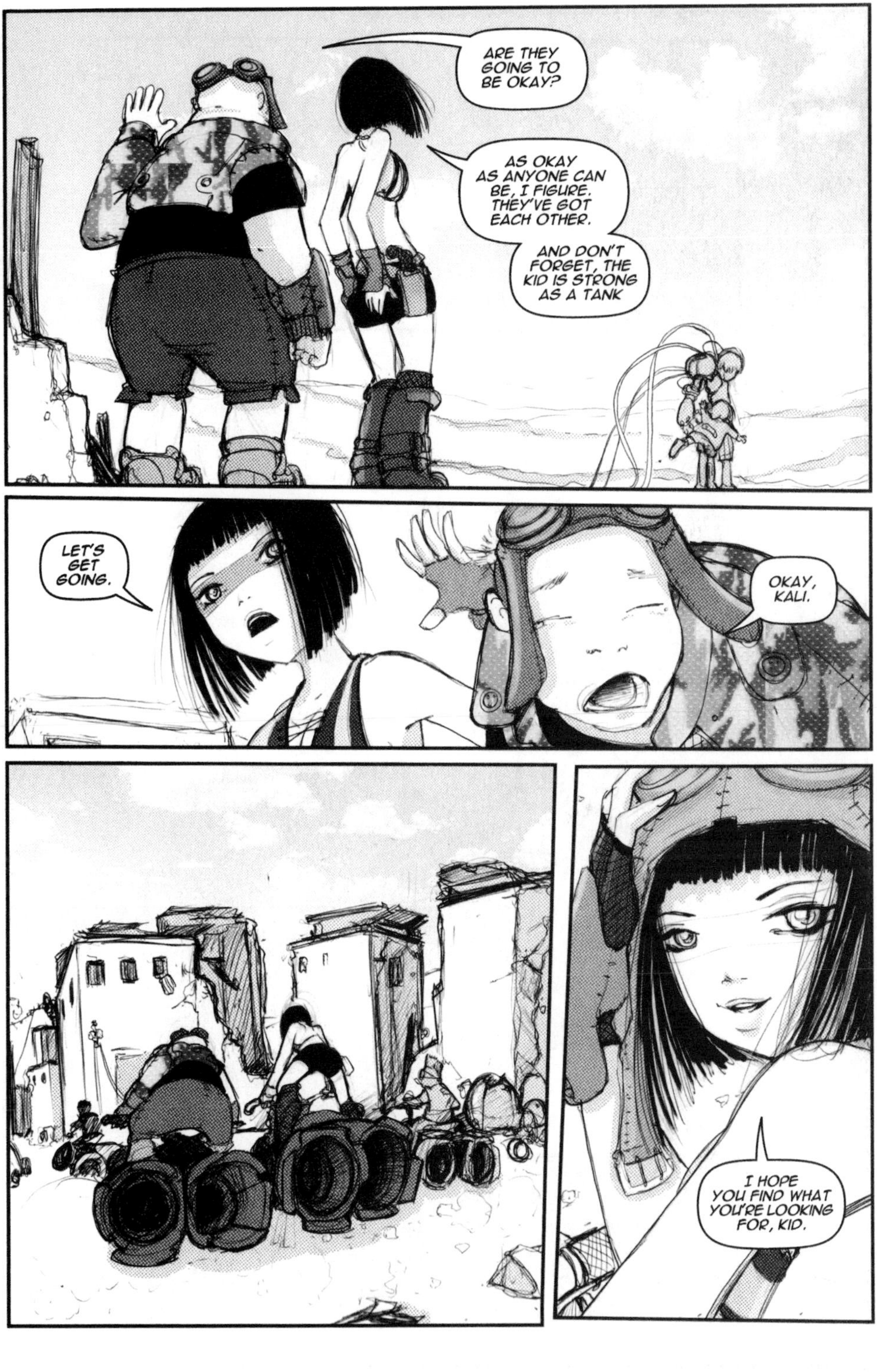
ARE THEY GOING TO BE OKAY?
AS OKAY AS ANYONE CAN BE, I FIGURE. THEY'VE GOT EACH OTHER.
AND DON'T FORGET, THE KID IS STRONG AS A TANK
LET'S GET GOING.
OKAY, KALI.
I HOPE YOU FIND WHAT YOU'RE LOOKING FOR, KID.

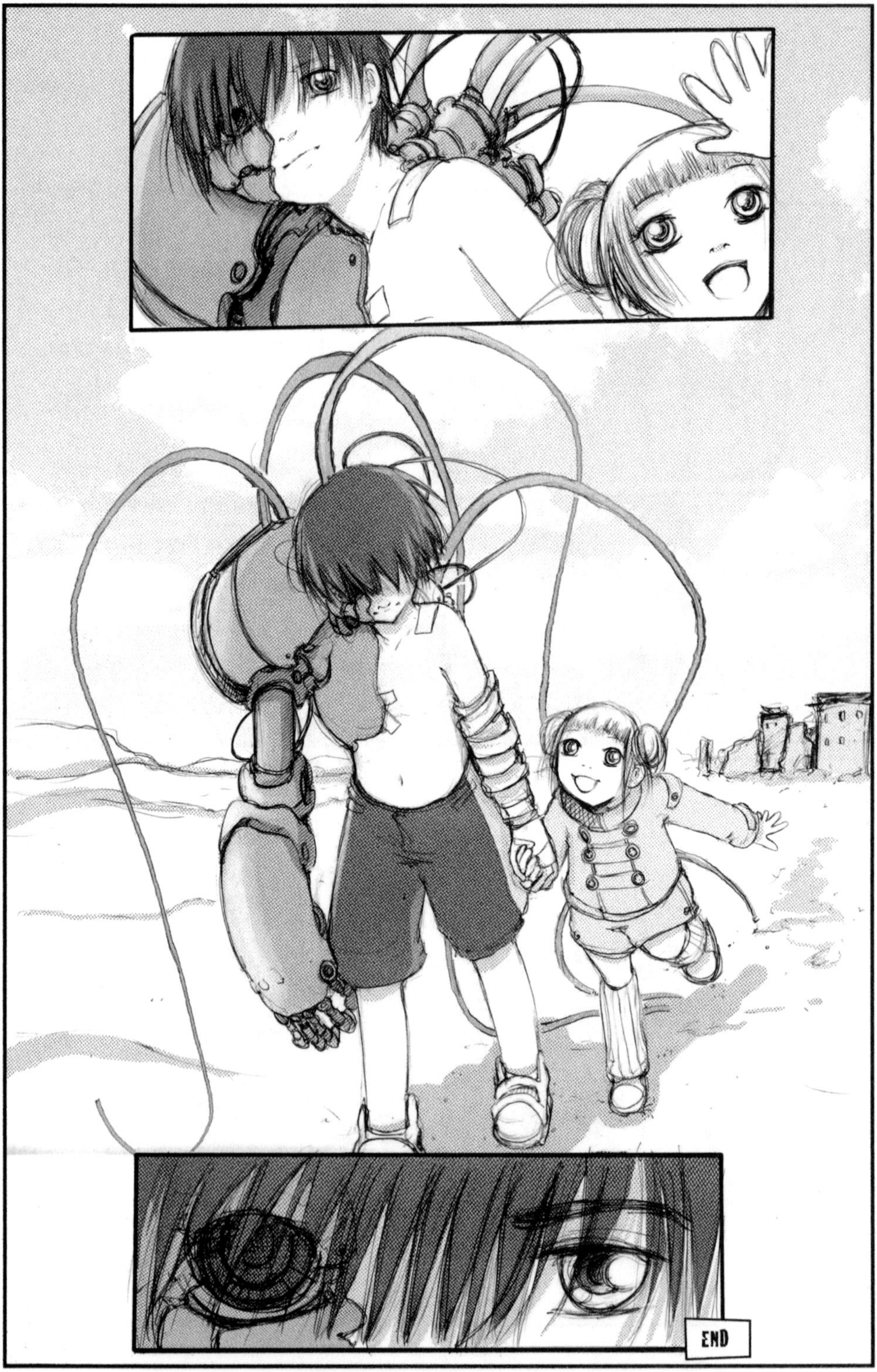
END

CAMILLA D'ERRICO is an Italo-Canadian artist who has been making waves in the fine art and comic industries with her manga-influenced style. Despite having amassed a wide artistic background in animation, fine arts, illustration, and graphic design, her passion is and has always been the comic art field, most notably manga. Art has always been an important part of her development, and she cites Ashley Wood, Toulouse-Lautrec, Kent Williams, Tsutomu Nihei, CLAMP, Terada Katsuya, and Yoshitobe Abe amongst the artists that have influenced her.

Camilla resides in Vancouver, British Columbia, where she continues her work in the comic art field, and has been working with entertainment companies on feature films and video games. Ever the prolific artist, Camilla lives the double life of comic artist/creator and Pop Surrealist painter. Her ability to seamlessly weave comic art and manga with surrealist elements has allowed her to attain great renown in her main fields, while expanding her horizons to include fashion, merchandise, and collectible urban vinyl art. Thanks to her relentless energy, dedication, and just enough sleep deprivation, she has followed her dream of successfully working creatively for a living.

SCOTT SANDERS has a degree in political science from the University of Washington. This fact is included as this is Scott's first published work, and his parents would be upset if he did not mention that he is wasting their money by writing comic books. He is very proud of the work done on *Burn*, and you will see many more exciting projects from him in the near future. Scott is the owner of the fastest dog in the world, and lives in Renton, Washington.